THE FIRST B‹  1
and well-paced. I
introduced, I fee. it in
two days, you know you have a good book when you can't wait
to get back to it. My husband is reading it now and enjoying it
very much. You always hate to see a good book end, but we have
the whole series to look forward to. The suspense is building!

OBSESSED STRAIGHT AWAY! Such an easy read and
couldn't put the book down. Found the story gripping and so
excited for the second! Never wanted it to end, truly talented
authors!

THIS IS A UNIQUE TALE and I enjoyed how strong of a
character Gia Delgado was…I don't know that I've ever read
another book with this sort of arrangement…

THE KILLINGS BEGIN **IS A CAPTIVATING READ.** I
couldn't wait to get back to reading it. Now, I look so forward to
reading the next book in the series. It couldn't come too soon.

I BOUGHT THE BOOK IMMEDIATELY, and once I
received it, I was hooked. I give books the first chapter to hook
me before abandoning [them]. This book hooked me before the
first page was over… I bought the physical book so that [my
husband] can read it to me out loud, but then I had to get the
kindle edition to keep reading throughout my day no matter
where I was.

MY WIFE BOUGHT THIS BOOK. Because of the
lockdown, I decided to read it. I was skeptical because it is called
a romance, but I really enjoyed the story. It is very well written, a
quick and easy read. The romance is not too heavy or sappy and
is more than offset by the suspense, making it a great read, even
for someone who would not typically read a romance story. I
also enjoyed the focus on the geography and culture of the
various cities visited in the novel. When book two debuts, I will
be one of the first to read it.

The Killings Begin

Bradley Pay

This is a work of fiction. Names, characters, places and incidents either are the product of the authors' imaginations or are used fictitiously. Any resemblance to actual persons, living or dead, events or locales is entirely coincidental.

Copyright © 2022 by Bradley Pay

First paperback edition June 2022
Previously published as *Murder in Zaporozhye*, February 2020

ISBN 978-1-7345212-4-5 (paperback)
ISBN 978-1-7345212-5-2 (e-book)

https://BradleyPay.com
https://Facebook.com/BradleyPayBooks
https://Instagram.com/BradleyPayBooks

For Gavin Pay and Bis Bradley

Dear Reader,

In this book, we have taken certain liberties with businesses, individuals and locales. The Spectrum River Cruise Line was invented as one of the unifying elements of the Spectrum Series and is not intended to represent any existing river cruise line.

We created the characters, and then they took on a life of their own. While we like them all and would love to include some of them in our circle of friends, we take no responsibility for any of their behavior.

Interestingly, the Toilet History Museum in Kyiv does exist—although we have added a few details to the description. We plan to visit if we ever make it to Ukraine.

There is no Bowe's Funeral Home, Longleaf Cemetery, or Lauch Art Museum in Raleigh, North Carolina and no Bagley Farm Golf Club with its Cigar Bar. Nor is there a paper known as the Raleigh Weekly News. The single shop in Fregenal de la Sierra that sold everything from underwear and toasters to lawnmowers, Jaime's Taberna in Madrid, the Oliver family's casita and vineyard in Seville, Sasha's and Kisho's estate in Slovenia and Lilla's Coffee & Cream in Zaporizhzhya were all invented for this book.

Both of us would love to visit these places if we could, and of course, we want to live in Gia's apartment at The Peacock in Madrid—if only it had three bedrooms.

Enjoy!

Robin and Jody

Table of Contents

Chapter One

April 1998

The Funeral

Raleigh, North Carolina

Tracey watched the family gathered under the canopy of new leaves and flowers on the red maple trees. Some bowed their heads as they placed roses on the coffin, while others simply reached out and gently brushed the top with their fingertips.

"For as much as it has pleased Almighty God to take out of this world the soul of Maggie Wilson, we, therefore, commit her body to the ground, earth to earth, ashes to ashes, dust to dust," As family members cried quietly, the minister continued, "wherefore comfort ye one another with these words—"

Michael gave a choked sob as his wife's body was lowered into the grave, and then he stepped forward, reached down for a handful of earth and scattered it lovingly onto the coffin. Mikey wrapped his arms around his father's legs, buried his face against him and cried out, "I want my mommy. I want my mommy. I miss her!" The woman standing next to them put her hands over her mouth, and her shoulders shook as tears ran down her face.

Michael reached down and picked up his son and hugged him tightly. "I know, son. I know. So do I." Then he turned and put his wailing child into the arms of the woman beside him. "Here,

Mikey, take care of Aunty Elizabeth while I talk with these people." He briefly ruffled Mikey's hair and wiped the tears from his cheek with gentle fingers before turning to the people filing past.

The mourners departed slowly, pausing to give the family their condolences. Among the last to leave, Tracey approached Michael and shook his hand. "On behalf of the Lauch Art Museum Board, I want to tell you how sorry we are for your loss. Your wife was a talented artist, and her work was extraordinary. We were very proud to include her art in our collection of new artists' work. She will be missed."

Michael nodded and said quietly, "Her art was so important to her. Thank you for coming to pay your respects."

As Tracey turned away, he heard a small voice cry out, "When is she coming back?"

Michael reached over and took his son from Elizabeth's arms and buried his face in Mikey's neck. He took a deep breath and said, "Mommy's not coming back. She's gone to heaven. She's with Jesus now."

"But I want her here. Where will I live? Who will take care of me? I miss her," Mikey wailed again.

As he walked away, Tracey looked up at the clear spring sky and thought, *I miss her, too.* He climbed into his vintage Mercedes and opened the sunroof and the back windows. With the sun warm on his head, he drew in a deep breath and slowly drove away, thinking about his mother.

We were only Mikey's age, and she forgot about us. She forgot about us—she didn't even recognize me when I ran into her at that museum event last year. We were standing next to each other, both looking at a piece of modern art. I said, "I admire this artist's work."

She said, "Thank you, I'm Maggie Wilson, the artist."

As we shook hands, I recognized her as my mother. She still had that same beautiful red hair she'd had when I was small. It looked just as soft as back then. I longed to reach out and touch it, to bury my face in it like I'd done as a child. But even though I was shocked, I didn't let on that I knew who she was. Instead, I just introduced myself. "I'm Tracey Lauch. I'm on the museum board. It's always a pleasure to meet one of our artists."

I asked her about her other pieces of work, and she took me around to show them to me. We had a great conversation about her choice of media and the meanings behind her pieces of abstract art. I thought we really connected.

Tracey realized he had parked out in front of her art gallery, MJW Expressions. He had been so lost in his memories that he had no recollection of driving there. He put his elbows on the steering wheel and leaned his face in his hands.

During that year after I met her, I followed her. Her art was becoming well known, and then she set up her own gallery. I attended the opening. And I found out where she lived. I saw her with her new family. She'd had another son. She'd named him Mikey.

I'd built a relationship with her, but all that time, she didn't realize I was her son. All I could think was, "What about me—did you just forget about me?"

So many times, I wanted to confront her and tell her how much I loved her, that we needed to be a family again.

Tracey turned to look at the gallery and said to himself in a raw voice, "So, one evening, I decided it was time. I didn't know it then, but she would die that night."

Chapter Two

April 2004

Jaime's Taberna

Madrid, Spain

The sound of jackhammers drilling across the street preceded the two young men as they burst through the tall door of Jaime's Taberna. The door swung shut, and their laughter filled the bar as they loudly and vigorously debated the last Real Madrid football match.

It was Wednesday, mid-afternoon, and Jaime's was nearly empty. They waved hello to the old man reading his newspaper and sipping his beer at his usual table tucked away in the corner between the bar and the fireplace. He looked up with a smile and nodded to them before going back to his paper.

This was *their* local, *their* bar, *their* establishment, with its burnished brass and copper fixtures and Jaime serving drinks behind the long, polished bar. For other long-time residents of the neighborhood, this was their local, too. This was a second home, a place of warmth and comfort where family and friends came to escape the confines of their cramped apartments, to exchange local gossip or play a game of chess. Jaime's Taberna had been this way when his grandfather had opened it, and it had changed very little in the past sixty years.

Joseph and Sal greeted Jaime as they took off their jackets and threw them on a nearby chair. Joseph's beer had already been poured, and Jaime opened a bottle of Sal's favorite Garnacha Tintorera. They leaned against the old hand-carved bar where the mellow light from well-polished, antique pendants reflected off the gleaming surface, and they placed a foot on the polished brass footrest below. Joseph and Sal picked up their drinks and tipped them in thanks to Jaime as they continued complaining about a referee's questionable call during the game the weekend before. Jaime chimed in, defending the ref, and a debate among them began.

Across the bar, at a table in front of the old, mullioned windows, a slender young brunette sipped her sangria and impatiently tapped her fingers on the table. Between glances at her phone for messages, she gazed idly out the window, watching the few pedestrians meander past, stopping to look into the windows of the local shops. It was her first time here, and already, she loved this place and this quaint street with colorful doors set into deep arches that led to tiny apartments above. In this block alone, there were a traditional butcher with all the best meats arranged carefully in the window, a bakery with breads and rolls piled on display to appeal to the passers-by and a small grocery where you could purchase almost anything else on your shopping list, from wine and vegetables to fruit and spices. It was on the brink of gentrification, and modern clothing boutiques, shoe shops and even a real estate office had popped up. *This neighborhood has everything a person could need. How much better this is than the old, scary area where I live. How I wish*—she checked her phone again. Nothing.

Though he appeared to be completely engrossed in the conversation, Jaime noticed Raul wending his way through the tables and poured him a glass from the open bottle of wine. Raul, Joseph and Sal all greeted each other with slaps on the back.

Raul, who wasn't as interested in football, changed the conversation abruptly. "So, Sal, what's so important that I don't get to go home to sleep? I'm exhausted after my double shift at the hospital." Reaching for his wine, he said across the bar, "Gracias, Jaime."

Raul took a sip of wine. He saw his reflection in the mirror that ran the length of the bar behind Jaime. His face was pale under his disheveled black hair, dark circles under his eyes. He muttered to himself, "Dear God, I look like death warmed over."

Sal turned to look at him directly, slapped his hand on the bar and said, "Raul, you had to be here—Jaime, we're going to need a bottle of cava."

Raul glanced over at Joseph and raised his eyebrows. "This must be a celebration." They both shook their heads and shrugged.

Jaime pulled a bottle from the wine cooler under the bar. "What's the special occasion?"

"Beats me. It's a mystery. Sal ordered us here today, so here we are." Joseph turned to Sal and said, "You owe me, man!"

Jaime twisted the cork from the bottle with a quiet pop and

poured three glasses of crisp, bubbling wine. Sal handed each person a glass and looked over at Jaime. "You're going to need one as well."

As Jaime poured a little into his own glass, Sal stepped back to announce, "Today we finished the three-year renovation of The Peacock, and all nine condos are on the market! They're going to go like hotcakes!"

Raul slapped him on the back. "Congratulations, brother, I can't wait to see them."

"Not to mention, we'll finally stop hearing about your renovation woes!" said Joseph.

They all laughed, clinked glasses, and took large gulps of the sparkling wine. Jaime smiled, having heard all about this for years. He looked over at Sal and tilted his glass. "And here is to more business for my taberna."

Raul's enormous yawn almost swallowed his "Hear! Hear!" as he took another drink of wine.

"Sorry to bore you, old chap," drawled Sal, as he watched Jaime take another beer to the old man by the fireplace. Before returning to his place behind the bar, Jaime looked over at the young woman, raised his eyebrows and pointed to her drink. She shook her head.

Joseph ignored Sal's sarcasm. "It's certainly a good time to have those condos on the market."

Sal turned his attention back to his friends. "Mmmm-hmmm, and it's a very good time to be a realtor."

"I've been watching the real estate market closely. I think it has a few more years before the bubble bursts," continued Joseph.

"That's what I'm countin' on." Sal smiled broadly and tipped his glass toward his friends.

Joseph said, "You couldn't have finished your condos at a better time."

Sal nodded in agreement and looked at Joseph. "I know I pulled you away from your trading desk before the stock market closed, so thanks for coming to celebrate with me. I wanted you and Raul to know before anyone else, and I wanted to do it before Jaime's gets too busy."

Raul yawned again loudly. Sal laughed at him. "Do you yawn like that in front of all your little patients?"

"Ha, ha. Those kids are much nicer to me than you are."

"But they don't know you like we do."

Joseph interjected, "Honestly, the hospital is lucky to have you, Dr. Hernandez."

Raul smiled and gave another jaw-breaking yawn.

The three of them stood quietly for a moment, enjoying their drinks before Joseph broke the silence. "I spoke to my mom over the weekend, and she says they are building on our empty lot."

Sal turned his head quickly. "Nooo waaay!"

"They can't, that was ours," said Raul sadly. "It's the end of an era."

"Do you think they took down our forts or built around them like they do with historic ruins?" Joseph joked. They laughed loudly and raised their glasses. "The good old days."

"Remember how we started out with cardboard boxes? Last time I was home, I saw the new kids on the block had torn those down and brought in wood to build better forts."

Sal smiled, remembering, "The football matches we used to have there were epic."

"And the *policia* left us alone, even when we had campfires in the summer," Raul added. "Ha! Remember when we built that massive ramp? At least, it looked massive back then. Then you," he pointed at Sal, "came barreling down the hill like a madman, up the ramp—and it collapsed. Then we built it again, bigger and stronger, we thought, and it collapsed—again."

Joseph looked at Sal and grinned. "I'd totally forgotten about that. There was obviously no engineer in our group back then!"

Sal gently punched him on the shoulder. "Yeah, I like to think I'm better at that now. And you weren't the one who crashed and burned twice! I broke my collarbone that second time, and we had to explain to my parents how it happened. Mamá was not happy at all."

"But, you know, they never stopped us from playing there," Raul smiled.

Joseph said, "They knew we were just having good, old-fashioned fun. No technology, no helmets, no fears of being abducted."

Sal smirked. "Who would want to abduct a dirty, smelly, loud boy?"

They all threw back their heads in laughter, remembering.

After a pause, Raul solemnly said, "All things come to an end. So, Joseph, what did your mom say they are building there?"

"Condos." Joseph looked at Sal, clinking his glass.

Sal grinned. "I'll have to take a drive to the old neighborhood to check them out. Never want to miss an opportunity."

As Raul yawned again, Sal glanced back over toward the brunette to see her looking down at her phone.

"Sorry, can't come to Jaime's. Stayed at work too long. Need to pack for Seville. Talk later," she read to herself. She made a face at her phone, dropped it on the table and took a big swallow of her sangria.

Sal saw the woman's gaze drift toward the bar, a look of disappointment on her face. A second later, she finished her drink.

"I guess I need some food now—and another drink," she grumbled to herself and got up and walked to the bar.

Sal's eyes widened as he noticed her height. *She must be at least as tall as I am,* he thought, looking at her tall-heeled boots. *There's something so sexy about women who are taller than me. I definitely need to meet her.*

He gestured in her direction with his chin and said to the others, "Watch, I'm going to get a date with her before she leaves."

Jaime moved along the bar to where she stood, and Sal, trying to be inconspicuous, slid closer to listen. She ordered a few plates of light tapas and another sangria, and as she turned to go back to her seat, Sal winked at her.

She saw the wink and thought, *Boys!* But, flattered by his attention, she gave him a half-smile. As she returned to her table, she wondered, *What will I do with my afternoon and evening now?*

◆

"Jaime, we'll need another bottle of Garnacha and a beer for Joseph." Sal turned to the others. "Grab your glasses, and let's go sit at a table," and he sauntered off toward the windows, glass in hand. Joseph nudged Raul, and they both rolled their eyes and grinned at Jaime. They picked up their drinks and wandered over to join Sal at the table.

Sal smiled at the brunette as they sat down at the table next to hers. "Hi. I've never seen you here before."

"No."

Joseph whispered to Raul, "That's the lamest pickup line I've ever heard."

"But they always seem to work for Sal," Raul chuckled.

Sal turned his chair toward her and asked, "Do you come here often?"

"No."

"Whoa-ho, he's going to have to try harder with this one," whispered Joseph.

Sal paused and drank the last of the wine from his glass. "Would you like to join us? We don't bite."

Joseph spoke up, "We'll be on our best behavior."

Raul yawned, and Sal pointed with his thumb. "He's harmless. He'll just sleep."

"Hey, be nice to me. I'm just a tired doctor. You're lucky I'm out with you at all," he grinned.

Sal turned to face her. "So, will you join us—please?"

They seem like a group of fun guys. It's still daylight outside, and I'm close to the door in case I need to run—she thought and replied, "Why not?"

Sal stood up, pulled out the chair next to him and made sure she was comfortable before he sat back down.

Joseph joked, "Chivalry is not dead."

She smiled at Joseph. "I guess not," and then looked back at Sal. "*Gracias.*"

After they sat, Sal introduced them. "I'm Sal Medina, realtor. This is Dr. Raul Hernandez, pediatrician. And this is Joseph Espada, stockbroker," hoping their titles would reassure her that they were professionals and safe to be with.

"I'm Gia."

Jaime arrived at the table with the men's drinks and Gia's

sangria and tapas.

"Gia, this is Jaime, and he owns this dive," joked Joseph irreverently.

Raul said, "It's not a dive. Don't listen to Joseph."

Jaime smiled at Gia as he refilled the wine glasses. "These boys are harmless. I've known them for years, but if you need help, just yell for me." Gia returned his smile and nodded her head.

Jaime looked around at the three of them sternly, as if to say, *you behave*, and then smiled. "Those tapas aren't going to be enough for all of you. Do you want me to bring more?"

Raul said, "Yep, I'm starving. You know what we like, Jaime."

"Bring 'em on," Joseph added.

Jaime smiled and turned back to the bar. *She seems to be a nice young thing. I wonder if she's new to the area,* he thought as he placed their order.

Raul asked Gia, "What are you doing here alone?"

Gia wasn't fazed by the bluntness of his question, but Joseph jumped in before she could answer. "Raul, maybe she just wanted to be alone."

Gia laughed. "That's okay. My brothers are just like that. They all come right to the point when they say something, and they are all fiercely protective of me."

"Raul has three sisters, and he protects them, too," Sal added.

"With you hitting on them when we were teenagers, he had to," said Joseph.

Sal gently punched Joseph on the shoulder as he looked at Gia. "So, are you meeting someone here?"

Gia took a sip of her sangria, making him wait for her response. "I was just stood up by my best friend."

"I'd never stand you up."

Gia recognized his come-on immediately. She'd watched her brothers do the same as she was growing up, and she replied coolly, "Sal, you have all the pickup lines, don't you?"

Raul and Joseph roared with laughter as Sal, looking slightly abashed, took another drink.

Then he recovered. "Well it worked, didn't it? You're here."

The four of them laughed congenially as Jaime put small

plates of olives, thick slices of bola cheese and some assorted meats, sausages and bread down on the table and said, "Warm ones are coming out shortly."

Raul yawned as he dug in. With his mouth full, he turned to Joseph and asked, "When's your next gig?"

As they talked about Joseph's music, Sal looked at Gia. "Do you work around here?"

"I'm a maid at a hotel nearby."

"Why on earth would a beautiful girl like you be a maid?"

"Oh, another pickup line, huh?" Gia parried sarcastically.

Sal blushed—no woman had ever called him out like that twice in rapid succession.

"I don't mind housekeeping, and I'm good at it. I did all the housework back home. Not to mention, when I'm done, I put on my normal clothes, and I don't worry about work until my next shift."

"Do you live in Madrid? Did you grow up here?"

"Yes, I live here, but I haven't been here long."

"Why did you come to Madrid?"

She paused in the midst of his questioning and turned to look directly at him. "To get away from an arranged marriage." She wanted to sound like she was in control of her life, so she added in a matter-of-fact tone, "There are a lot of things I plan to do with my life before I get married."

As they continued to chat, Jaime set more tapas and another round of drinks on the table.

Raul noticed Gia looking at her new drink. "Jaime is a mind reader," he said, and they smiled at one another.

Everyone began to eat eagerly. Raul turned to Joseph. "So, how is your mom doing?" Then he said to Gia, "We are true *Madrilenians*. We all grew up together, here, in Madrid."

"And went to university together," Sal added.

Gia nodded and sat back and listened to them as they continued to chat amongst themselves.

Joseph replied, "Mamá is good. She's recovered from her gallbladder surgery and is back to working as hard as ever at the bakery. Dad's happy to have her back because he's no good at keeping the books. Mamá said he made a total mess of them, and she is happy to be back to get them straightened out."

Sal said, "Your mom's always been the one who has really run the business from behind the scenes."

Raul asked, "Did she say anything about my mom?"

"Can't you call your mom?" asked Joseph.

"I will, but I've had a whole series of double shifts, and all I have time or energy to do when I am off is sleep."

"My mom has been seeing yours a lot in the last six months since your dad died. And she was a huge help during my mom's recovery from surgery."

Gia was touched that they talked about their moms so freely, and she thought about how much she missed her mother. The last few months had been the longest they had gone without seeing each other or even talking. Gia listened and smiled contently as she noticed how relaxed their conversation was and how frequently they finished each other's sentences.

◆

"You don't have time to ask someone to go out with you?" Gia interrupted them, as they complained about not having had time to find dates for work events.

They were startled by Gia's interruption. She'd been sitting quietly, just listening to them, and they'd almost forgotten she was there. They all turned to look at her. She smiled and repeated, "Seriously—you don't have time to ask someone out? That's hard for me to believe. Seriously?"

Raul replied, "I haven't had time for years. I just completed my residency last year, and since then, I've been working non-stop. Now, as a doctor on staff, I'm expected to attend all the holiday parties, fundraisers, etcetera. I haven't dated anyone since my divorce, and I wouldn't even know where to begin."

"We're all really busy," said Joseph. "I work market hours and then entertain clients after work. And on top of that, my company frequently hosts dinners with clients and their significant others, where I'm expected to bring an appropriate date. Besides, I'd much rather be playing music here or with my group at clubs than dating women I don't care about."

"Yeah, my company frequently courts their clients over dinner, and what's more, I have to attend openings of new buildings, where I'm expected to have someone on my arm," said Sal. "It's complicated further by the fact that this is the year we all turn thirty, and all the women our age are expecting a real relationship. They're expecting it to get serious and eventually lead to marriage and kids—I'm so far from ready for that."

"I'm not ready to settle down. I want to make millions before I even start to think about that," said Joseph emphatically.

Gia hadn't realized a simple question would result in such an emotional response and was surprised at how serious they were.

After the group paused, Sal said slyly, "I do miss the sex, though."

The men all laughed. "Amen to that!" said Joseph and lifted his glass to them briefly before taking a long drink of his beer.

Raul glanced at Gia and saw that she was laughing, too. He thought, *Good for her! She isn't intimidated by us.*

While the men continued their discussion and the bar filled up, Gia's attention wandered to a couple stopped outside the window, yelling at one another. Gia listened to their argument through the glass and thought, *Ah, the same sounds I hear from my horrible apartment. People arguing at all hours of the day and night. I wish there were a way out of there.*

She turned her attention back to the men as they continued to carry on about how miserable their predicament was. *How can they make this little thing into such a big thing—why don't they just do something about it?*

She was only half-listening as her mind continued to wander and they continued to complain. Then, suddenly, Gia sat up abruptly, tapped a nail on the table, and the men went quiet. They had been so caught up in their own conversation, that once again, they'd forgotten she was there.

"The solution is simple—

"Sounds like you guys need a no-strings wife—

"You need to be accommodated in the way you deserve."

Gia's dad had a big ego, and she'd learned how to manipulate him, *mostly,* so she knew exactly how to butter them up. "You are all successful professionals—obviously, you are all extremely busy—you're not ready to settle down—what you really need is a no-strings wife—someone to accompany you to professional functions, parties and so on—someone you can trust to be there when you need her—someone for good sex but who has no expectations of a real relationship, marriage, family—simply put, you need me."

After Gia's proposal, the men were stunned, a look of *Did we really hear what we think we heard?* on their faces. They sat in silence.

Gia stood up and said, "Think about it," and walked off toward the toilet at the back of the bar.

Jaime approached the table with another round of drinks. The men remained silent as he placed the glasses on the table. They looked at each other sheepishly.

"You look like you're up to something."

The table burst out in laughter, and Jaime smiled at them.

After he walked away, Gia returned to the table and looked around. "Well—?"

She sat down and took a deep breath and said, "You guys have a problem, and I have a solution. I can be your no-strings wife."

They all jumped in:

"Why are you proposing this?"

"Are you serious?"

"What are you talking about?"

"What do you get out of this?"

Raul thought to himself, *We don't know this woman from Eve— we've just met her—in a bar—would this work for me—can I afford to take a risk like that—what the fuck just happened?*

"You just ran away from an arranged marriage, and now you are proposing *this?*" he said out loud.

"That was an arranged marriage—and 'this' would only be an *arrangement.*"

The men all looked at one another, still stunned, and Joseph asked, "You're joking, right?"

"Do I look like I'm joking?"

"How does it benefit you?" Raul asked.

"I live in a drafty, fourth-floor walk-up, and it's a dump, in a bad neighborhood. My mom would never approve if she knew, but it's all I can afford. It takes more than an hour to get to it from here. You can't visit your 'no-strings wife' there, so I'll need your help to find a better place closer to here, and I'm on a tight budget."

Raul said sympathetically, "It's really that bad, huh?"

Gia nodded, took a sip of her sangria, and looked at Sal. "You're a realtor. I bet you could help me find something."

After a lengthy pause, Sal finally broke his silence and said slowly, "Well, actually, I do have a place. I just finished furnishing the model in my condo building, and it's ready to occupy."

"She's on a tight budget," said Raul, "and your condos aren't cheap. Besides, don't you need the model to sell the other units?"

"We'll figure out the price." Sal winked at Gia and continued in response to Raul, "I'll just furnish another one. No big deal."

Gia smiled and added boldly, "And I'll need a stipend, so I can dress appropriately for your events."

Sal pressed Raul and Joseph, "You two cover that, I'll cover the apartment, and this could work!"

The men all looked at each other, questions on their faces. Raul sipped his wine. *Hmmm*, he thought. *Does she realize what she's just proposed?*

"Whoa, whoa, whoa. What do you mean, you'll cover the apartment?" Gia asked.

Joseph explained, "Sal is a successful real estate agent. He owns The Peacock, and he's just finished renovating all the condos. He's selling the other eight units in the building, and he'll make a bundle. Keeping one of those places for his own use is really no big deal to him."

Sal nodded, teasing, "And it's no 'dump' either."

After a silence, Gia said, "I couldn't—that would make me a—uhmmm—nervous—I would also need some kind of protection. Some kind of guarantee."

Raul said cautiously, "If we do this, it's imperative that none of this goes beyond this group because if it got out, it would ruin my professional reputation. And it wouldn't be good for you two, either."

Gia reached over and touched Raul's hand. She smiled at him and then around at all of them. "I would never want to affect your career or anyone's reputation."

Sal and Joseph exchanged a *This could work* look.

"Gia's right," Sal said. "She does need a guarantee. We all do. If we are going to do this, we should do it right, and for that, we need it all in writing and signed. I'll draft a contract."

Raul and Joseph nodded in agreement, Joseph enthusiastic, Raul still hesitant, and Joseph said, "Well, let's do it right, then."

Gia smiled, "Perfect."

Sal turned to Gia, "The condos are located in a fabulous art deco building that I got for a song, and I restored them to their original glory. It's actually quite close to here." He leaned in intimately to describe the area and the building to Gia.

"Oh my, that sounds like heaven."

Raul listened to them. *She is being very cool and rational about this extremely unconventional proposal.*

Sal went on, "We can probably wrap this up by the end of the week." The others were shocked at how quickly he wanted to move forward.

Impulsively, Gia pulled a paper placemat from under a plate, turned it over and took out a pen. "Let's write down the rules."

Sal and Joseph smiled at Gia's take-command attitude. Raul put his hand up to stop the conversation. "Hang on a sec. I have to ask a personal question before we go on."

They all stared at him as he looked at Gia. "I don't mean to be rude, but how old are you?"

"Raul, what are you doing?" Sal was annoyed.

Before Raul could answer, Gia replied, "It's okay. I could be underage, so it's good that he asked." She looked at Raul. "I'm eighteen years old," and she reached over for her purse, opened it, and handed him her identification.

Raul smiled at Gia. "Thank you," he said.

"Are you satisfied, Doc?" Sal snapped. Raul nodded his head.

Gia continued as though Raul had never asked the question,

"No group anything, okay? No group sex, no group dates, no guests at the apartment except the four of us without my permission."

They all nodded in agreement, and she wrote it down.

She continued, "One scheduled overnight per week for each of you, and anything more is at my discretion. Any additional nights, for events or other occasions, have to be scheduled in advance with me. And I'll keep the calendar."

Gia stopped and looked at each of them closely. "Before we go any further, are you guys actually serious about this?"

Raul said, "Well, hold on a minute. We should talk about this some more. Sharing one woman will change our lives and could change our friendship."

Sal said, "*Carpe diem.* When it's right, you have to seize the day—or the moment. I'm in."

Joseph shifted in his seat. "I'm in."

Raul looked at them and then at Gia. "No matter what you call it, a contract or not, this would be one of those life events," he insisted.

After he thought for a moment, Sal responded, "We're all adults here. Let's give it a try for four months. Then we can decide if we want to continue or not."

I'll take four months, thought Gia. *At least, in that amount of time, I could probably save up enough money to get a nicer place than I have now. The longer it lasts, the better for me financially.*

Raul, who had been quietly mulling it all over, said, "If we do this, no one can fall in love. It's all professional. And birth control is a must."

Gia wrote this down and said with a shy smile, "The birth control is already covered." She added, "And no rough sex."

"We each have to get HIV tests and share the results with Gia," Raul continued.

Sal looked at him with a frown, but Joseph nodded his head in agreement.

"If we do this, it is a must," Raul insisted, as he looked directly at Sal and then around the group.

"It's for everyone's protection. It'll be in the contract!" Gia agreed.

Embarrassed at the idea of having to ask for an HIV test, much less share the results with anyone, Sal changed the subject, "And no claiming that any sex under the terms of the contract is rape."

The others looked at him, nodding.

Raul added, "No one can talk about their relationship with Gia with anyone else, not even within this group."

Gia's head was down, scribbling quickly.

She looked up. "I'll add in my notes about the apartment and stipend. If this goes beyond the trial period, I'll also want four weeks of vacation a year."

Joseph nodded in agreement, "You'll need a break from us."

"We'll need some back-out clauses." Sal counted them off on his fingers. "If anyone breaks the rules, they're out. If anyone wants to opt out, the rest of us can continue without them, or the contract becomes null and void. Am I missing anything?"

No one replied.

"Oh, wait," Gia's eyes widened, "I also need some kind of insurance."

"What do you mean?" asked Raul, a note of skepticism in his voice. *Is she going to ask for more money?*

She smiled. "For my safety, my best friend has to meet you, and she is allowed to know about the contract for my protection. Other than her, no one is to know about this."

Relieved, Raul yawned and said, "That's a great idea. As a single woman, you absolutely need some sort of insurance policy, and your friend's knowledge of it'll help provide that protection for you."

He added, "One more thing—if we sign the contract, Jaime's is off-limits."

They all went silent and looked at him.

"What do you mean?" Gia asked. "I love this place."

"Off-limits for dates. We need to protect Gia's reputation, so we can only come here as a group of friends, or Gia can come here with her best friend."

Sal caught on to what Raul was saying. "What if going out

with Gia only applies to the events we go to?"

"On our dates, we stay in?" Gia asked.

"Yep, the 'dates'," Sal said, making air quotes with his fingers, "are about sex, not going out. That works for me. Good point. I'll add it to the contract." Joseph, not sure what he thought about this, stayed quiet. Sal grabbed the pen from Gia and jotted it down.

Then Sal, Joseph and Gia began to talk excitedly about upcoming events. Sal had the grand opening for The Peacock coming up in a few days, as well as openings for other buildings. Joseph had client dinners every week or so.

Raul sat watching and contemplating. Abruptly, he interrupted the group and looked at Gia. "No disrespect, but we don't even know you."

The group stared at Raul, and he continued, "And you don't know us."

"Man, just embrace the moment. Stop being a wet blanket. We have a great opportunity here!"

Joseph leaned forward and picked up where Sal had left off. "Raul, you always hold us back. Can't you let go and have fun for a change?"

Gia held up her hands, "Hey guys, stop beating up Raul. He's made a good point there. Let's hear him out."

Raul gently smiled his thanks at Gia. "The idea is intriguing. I'm not saying I won't do this. I'm just saying, let's walk before we run."

"Okay, so you're saying I'm trying to close the deal too quickly?" Sal said as he nodded in understanding.

"Argh. I hate it when Raul is right," Joseph chuckled.

"Maybe we can test the water. We can each go out," Gia suggested as she motioned from herself to each of the men in turn. "Maybe go to one of those events you guys are complaining about needing a date for?"

Sal jumped in with an excited tone. "You're brilliant, Gia. You can come to the grand opening of my building!"

"That works for me."

Raul nodded his head thoughtfully. "You know, that is a good idea. It would give us a chance to get to know one another with no pressure and no contract."

"I have a client dinner in a few days. Would you come to that with me?" Joseph asked.

"That works, too."

Gia turned to Raul, "So, what do you have going on?"

"Well, I do have a fundraiser to go to this weekend. But how does all this fit into your schedule?"

"I'm a maid with an early shift, so anything in the late afternoon or evening or on my days off works for me."

"Then it's decided. We'll each do something together and then get back together here to discuss the contract," Sal said, still eager to close the deal.

Gia discreetly slid the paper placemat filled with notes over to Sal and said in a quiet voice, "If you can read the chicken scratches, here's a draft of the contract." She smiled at him. "Just in case."

He smiled back at Gia, folded the paper carefully, pushed it into his pocket and patted it gently. "Yes ma'am, I'll keep it safe." He looked around the table. "Let's all exchange phone numbers."

Gia laughed. "Still with the pickup lines, Sal? You all give me your numbers, and I'll call you to arrange the details." She picked up her phone.

Raul and Joseph exchanged smiles, and Joseph raised his eyebrows.

After she put all their numbers into her phone, Gia said, "If you'll excuse me, I have a long commute home and an early morning at work."

She dropped some money on the table, stood up, and the men immediately stood up as well.

Sal helped Gia on with her coat, and she gave each of them kisses on both cheeks before she left.

As the door closed, Sal did a fist pump and said in an ecstatic voice, "I have a date with her!"

"Technically, it's not a date," Raul added.

Joseph laughed, and Sal patted his pocket. "This arrangement is way better than a date."

Raul cautioned, "If it ever happens."

Joseph tossed cash down on the table. "I bet she never calls."

"Of course, she will," said Sal cockily.

The Dates

Madrid, Spain

After the mayor's speech, the clapping died down. Gia turned to Mr. and Mrs. Medina. "You must be so proud of him." Without taking their eyes off their son, they nodded their heads, with no further acknowledgement of the attractive young woman standing next to them in the crowd.

"I hope that all who come to live here find health and happiness," Sal said as he cut the ribbon, officially opening The Peacock. "All of the condos are for sale except the penthouse, so please go up and take a look at that model. Imagine yourselves living here, in this wonderful neighborhood, in the lap of luxury. And we have agents on every floor to show those units if you're interested in them."

The cameras flashed, and Sal looked up, grinning from ear to ear with pride and excitement. He caught Gia's eye and winked. Gia smiled shyly, and Mrs. Medina stared at her.

The cameras continued to snap pictures of Sal, the mayor and the building as he invited his parents to join him.

"Mamá, Papá, please, come up here." The group shook hands, hugged and kissed cheeks.

And then the mayor excused himself. "I have another event to attend. So, I'm sorry I can't go up to see the model today. Perhaps another time." He gestured toward the building, "This makes a beautiful enhancement to the area."

"Thank you for taking the time out of your busy schedule to come to the ribbon-cutting," replied Sal as he shook the mayor's hand.

"It's a pleasure to see this area continue to develop. The Medinas have given this city so much. I wouldn't have missed it. Congratulations again, Sal." The mayor and his assistant climbed into his black car and headed off.

Sal motioned for Gia to join them at the front of the crowd. She shook her head slightly and mouthed, "No." He held up a finger for her to hang on a second.

Sal turned to his parents. His mom gushed, "Oh, Sal. I'm so proud of you and what you've accomplished." She motioned to the building, "Your grandfather would have been proud of you, too."

His dad leaned close to make himself heard over the conversations going on around them. "Son, completing this project before your thirtieth birthday is amazing. I didn't do anything on this scale until I was almost forty. You've made me proud. But I'll be interested to see what you accomplish in the next ten years."

Sal looked over his mom's shoulder at Gia and suggested, "Why don't you two go in and see the units. I'm not going to go up the model. I want people to view it without me there. It is about them envisioning living here, not their compliments to boost my ego. I'll see you both later this week."

Before they disappeared into the building, Mrs. Medina put her hands on Sal's cheeks and kissed him on the forehead. His father clapped Sal on the shoulder.

Gia stood back and watched the crowd as they began to file into the building. She noticed the loving interaction between Sal and his parents, and for a brief moment, she felt a pang of loneliness as she thought about her family. And then Sal walked over to her, interrupting her thoughts. "Let's get out of here and find some lunch. I'm starving. I know the perfect place."

"So, this is the type of event you need someone to attend with you? With such impressive people? With all those cameras? I didn't realize how successful you are, how many important people you know."

"Oh yeah. My grandfather was well known in commercial real estate in his day. Whenever he had an opening or a ribbon-cutting at one of his buildings, he invited whoever was mayor at the time. My dad continued that practice, and so have I. So, I've met all the mayors of Madrid since I was a kid." He looked at Gia and added, "I'm not bragging. It's just how I grew up, how my family does business, and I've carried on the tradition."

"What a wonderful event. Someday, I would like to see the inside of The Peacock." Gia took her jacket off as they walked down the street. "It's been a beautiful warm day for it." She looked down at her clothes, her simple dark skirt and blouse. *I'm not sure I had the right clothes for that event. And what if the other ones are more formal? I will definitely need that stipend.*

"All those cameras at the ribbon-cutting," said Gia. "I didn't want to come up to stand with you and get caught in a photo that might show up on a society page—because of the contract."

They walked down the street, side by side, in comfortable silence, and then Sal added, "Yeah, those cameras could be an issue, couldn't they?"

"Mmmm-hmmm. I don't think we want to be seen in the newspaper together like that. It could cause problems for Raul and Joseph."

"Well, then I would have you all to myself." He turned to Gia and winked and walked a little closer so their shoulders touched.

"It's been a perfect morning. And the place we are going for lunch has a wonderful little garden with outdoor seating. Let's eat outside in the sun."

They turned from the busy main street onto a cobblestone street the width of an alley. "This is so charming," said Gia as she looked around curiously.

"The buildings on this street have been untouched for centuries on the outside. But inside, they've been converted into new restaurants and clubs. It's hopping at night. I like to come here during the day for lunch when it's calm and—I guess, serene. The place we are going to is down the block."

As they entered the small restaurant from the bright, sun-drenched street, Gia squinted her eyes in the dimly lit interior. Sal placed his hand on the small of her back. Her stomach tightened at the unexpected touch of his hand. The owner crossed the room quickly. "Hi Sal, how was your grand opening?"

He took both her hands in his, pulled her to him and gave her a kiss on each cheek. "It went off without a hitch, Camila."

"Love, it's too bad I was working and couldn't be there with you."

"Ahhh, the burden of being a restaurant owner." Sal turned from Camila to Gia and said, "Gia, this is Camila, the owner of this lovely little establishment." His eyes twinkled.

Once seated in the garden, under the shade of an umbrella, Gia glanced up from her menu to look around. There was a combination of small tables, just the right size for a couple like them to have a light meal, and a few larger tables occupied by bigger groups and families. The birds, perching in the trees, twittered away happily, also enjoying the lovely spring weather.

"Wow, you know a lot of people. From the mayor to the restaurant owner," Gia commented, trying to sound off-hand.

"I've lived in Madrid my whole life. How is this different from where you come from?"

Before Gia could answer, the waiter arrived with their drinks and took their order. Then she responded, "There's nothing similar between Fregenal and Madrid. The place certainly isn't hopping at night, and there are no charming side streets filled with clubs and little restaurants and sweet little gardens for outside dining. It has changed in the past few years and is becoming a little more upscale, but it's no Madrid. The economy is based on agriculture and livestock, and fewer than five thousand people live there. But honestly, I was too young to appreciate all of that, and I certainly couldn't be seen out and about with my boyfriend, so I spent most of my free time hiking in the nearby hills and only went downtown to go to the market and to church on Sundays with my whole family."

"Do you miss it? If I left Madrid, I would miss it terribly."

"I miss the hiking and my mom. But the adventures I can have here are countless."

"Like the contract?"

"If it happens, yes."

◆

Standing at a small bar-height table, she couldn't believe she was there. She looked at all the lovely cocktail dresses worn by the women and was glad she had a key to Mari's apartment so she had been able to borrow a dress and heels. What a great best friend, to give her carte blanche to raid her closet whenever she needed to.

Raul came across the room. Gia noticed his confident walk

as he approached in his dark, well-fitted suit. He looked so handsome, and her heart rate increased when he looked at her and flashed a devastating smile.

"Did you shake enough hands?" she asked in a humorous tone.

"I'm sorry to have left you alone for so long. I brought you this as an apology." Raul set down a glass of wine in front of Gia. "Do you forgive me for leaving you to your own devices all that time?"

"Don't worry about me. I kept myself occupied. I went to every one of the hors d'oeuvre stations." She motioned around the outside of the ballroom.

"They have these little blini topped with sour cream and three types of caviar, radicchio and manchego quesadillas, shrimp and mussel salad, vine leaves stuffed with wild rice and apricots and wonderful, crisp, hot tempura vegetables. And an enormous carved ice swan filled with freshly steamed shrimp." Gia smiled in delight, "I've never had caviar before. Imagine how healthy it was, the blini were made of peas. It's my new favorite."

"You're a foodie? Me, too."

"You bet. I didn't feel like I was left alone. I was left in heaven. I chatted with lots of people, they were all so interesting, and I tried some of everything. I'm stuffed," Gia said as she patted her stomach.

Raul smiled as Gia continued, "I've seen elaborate events like these in the hotel where I work, but I had no idea they were for such important things." Gia pointed at the sign with a thermometer showing how close the hospital was to its ambitious goal of raising a million euros toward a new modern CT scanner. "And all these people are willing to donate generously to save the lives of total strangers."

Her enthusiasm is infectious, Raul thought to himself. "It's part of my job now, to go out and meet people and convince them of the importance of the new equipment we're trying to buy. These people can make a huge difference with their donations."

A man with broad shoulders wearing a well-tailored, close-fitting suit approached them.

"Gia, this is Boyd. He's a visiting physician from Melbourne."

"It's a pleasure to meet you, Gia. Thanks for attending our fundraiser," he said as he shook her hand.

"Ooooh, you're an Aussie. I love your accent," Gia said.

And before she could continue, he asked, "Do you mind if I steal Raul away from you for a moment?" He put his hand lightly on Raul's arm.

Gia stepped back and motioned with her hand. "Of course not. He's all yours."

The doctors stepped away to a nearby table.

Gia sipped her wine and looked around, noticing guests beginning to depart. A few minutes later, Gia glanced over at Raul and Boyd and observed how frequently Boyd reached out to touch Raul's arm to make a point. And each time, Raul leaned away a fraction. Finally, Raul's face turned red. He looked over at Gia, his eyes pleading with her to rescue him.

Gia took a final sip from her glass and strolled casually over to stand beside Raul. She put her hand confidently on his arm and said to him, "Raul, would you mind if we left now? We promised we'd meet our friends after this, and I'm afraid we're going to be late."

Raul looked at her, confusion on his face, and Gia continued, "Raul, the birthday celebration? The surprise for my best friend?"

"Oh, that's right." Raul recovered quickly. "Boyd, I need to head out now. Can we chat tomorrow at work?"

Boyd reached over and touched Raul's hand and looked directly into his eyes. "Of course, Raul," he said softly.

"It was nice to meet you, Boyd." Gia tucked her arm through Raul's. "I'll call her husband when we get to the car and let him know we may be a little late."

As Raul opened the car door for Gia, he sighed, "Thank you, Gia. That was a genius rescue. I was becoming very uncomfortable with Boyd's attention." He closed the door.

Once Raul had started the car, Gia turned toward him. "You were really uncomfortable? For a while there, it looked like you were enjoying his advances."

"Advances? What are you talking about?" Raul blushed.

"It was obvious to me that I was watching two people who like one another making a real connection."

"What are you talking about?" he repeated.

They began to drive through the city. Gia admired the way Raul skillfully navigated the congested streets. *Obviously, he doesn't want to talk about that*, she thought and changed the subject. "You can drop me at that bus stop over there, and I can catch a bus home."

"I'm going to drive you home, Gia, I insist. I won't take no for an answer. Which direction from here?"

"I don't want you to see where I live. I'm embarrassed. It's horrible."

"All the more reason for me to drive you home and make sure you arrive safely."

Gia argued, but Raul refused to let her out to travel home on her own. Annoyed, she turned her face away and grudgingly provided directions. She sat in silence for several minutes, her arms crossed, refusing to talk to him. Then finally, she looked at him and blurted out, "You're gay, aren't you?"

"I've been married, Gia. You know that."

"That doesn't mean anything. I saw how you looked at Boyd and how he looked at you. I saw your reaction with my own eyes. You can't bullshit me."

Raul pulled over to the side of the road and parked along the curb. He turned to face Gia. *I've done it now*, Gia thought, *I've crossed the line.* She reached for the handle, ready to open the door.

"You don't have to get out. I just can't focus on the road and this conversation at the same time."

Gia gave a huge sigh of relief. "What do you mean?"

"You just met me a few days ago, and you don't know me at all. You knew I was married, and now, you're so bold as to say there's something going on between Boyd and me? Where do you get off asking me if I'm gay?"

"Well, aren't you? I thought it was obvious. It's no big deal."

"It's a big deal for me. I know I am attracted to Boyd. However, I was married and always thought I would remarry someday when I met the right woman. Someone whom I was attracted to as much as she was to me. I don't know how I feel. I don't know what to think. But I know I'm attracted to him."

"Wow." Gia's tone became compassionate.

Raul lowered his head and fiddled with the console between them, thinking.

"Are you saying you don't know?" she pressed.

Raul turned to face the steering wheel again, his jaw muscles clenched tightly. He put the car into drive and began to pull away from the curb. Then, abruptly, he slammed the gear shift back into park and turned to look at her, his eyes full of pain.

"I *am* gay, Gia," he confessed. "This is the first time I've said it out loud to anyone, ever. I always hoped I was wrong, that I just hadn't met the right woman. I married to meet the expectations of my family. They are staunch Catholics and believe being gay is wrong. It's against the teachings of the church. But I've known I was gay since I was a teenager. I've always been so ashamed."

"It must be so hard for you, trying to live according to other people's expectations."

"Yes, it is. But I'm glad you called me out, and I'm glad I've finally said the words. I've held it in for so long. I can't talk to anyone about it. Not Sal or Joseph, no one I work with, not my family. I've felt like I'm living a lie. I don't want to pretend I want to marry a woman anymore. I don't want to sneak around to have a relationship."

"So, you've never been with another man?"

"Not yet. I've never even dated a man."

She watched him closely, sensing that there was more he wanted to say.

Then he surprised her. "I think the contract will be good. It'll allow me to maintain the illusion of being straight while I try to figure it out." He looked at her. "You're very perceptive. And you just say what's on your mind, don't you? I like that. I want to be able to be that way."

"I've always noticed things others don't, and I always say what's on my mind. My father hates that about me. My older brothers, too."

Gia gave him directions to her apartment, and they continued to chat comfortably as he drove along.

As they pulled up in front of her home, Raul looked around the neighborhood. "Gia, this is awful. It's not safe. How can you live here alone?"

"It's all I can afford. It's okay for now. You don't need to feel sorry for me. I'll find a better place eventually." She opened the door and stepped out of his old car. And then she leaned back in through the window. "Raul, I had a lovely time tonight. I've never been to an event like that. No matter what happens with the contract, I hope we can remain friends."

"I would like that."

◆

"Is that picture of Jaime?" Gia pointed to the elegantly framed picture on the wall.

Joseph looked behind himself. "He's the young man, and the other is his grandfather."

"He looks just like him."

Gia rubbed her arms, and Joseph asked, "Are you cold?"

"I didn't expect it would cool off so much tonight."

Joseph took off his suit jacket and draped it around her. His hand lingered on her shoulder before he moved it away. Gia felt a tingle on her skin.

"Thank you. You're so kind."

"You're so beautiful. And you were brilliant at the client dinner tonight."

"I was just being myself and saying what I think."

"With a bunch of traders, that's the best way to be. You can't be meek, or they'll eat you alive."

"They aren't bad, just rowdy, like my eight brothers."

"Really, you have that many brothers? That's a huge family."

"We live on a farm, and my parents believe in big families. That's why my dad wanted me to marry so young. So I could start one of my own."

"Such a contrast to how I was brought up as an only child. The burden falls on me to call Mamá all the time to make sure she and Papá are okay."

"You're a good son, Joseph." She searched for a lighter subject. "The other day you mentioned music. What do you play? Where do you play? I think that's so cool. I wish I could play an instrument. Can I come hear you play sometime?"

"Not just one question, huh?" He reached out to Gia and took her hand in both of his. Gia didn't pull away. She liked the way it felt to be touched by him. She liked the energy between them.

"Do you play the flute? The clarinet? The violin?" Gia giggled, a little silly by now from all the wine she'd had at dinner and most of the glass in front of her.

Joseph laughed at the questions and at her giggle, and his head went back as he laughed in return. "I never thought about playing flamenco on a flute. No, silly, I play the guitar."

"Finally, an answer." She giggled again. "Did you say you play flamenco?"

"I did."

"My best friend dances in flamenco competitions. She's really good. She wins quite often. Maybe we could go see her dance sometime?"

"That's impressive. I'd like to see her dance. I'd like to dance with you."

Gia saw Jaime approaching and pulled her hand out of Joseph's. Joseph gave her a little pout of disappointment.

"You know we're not supposed to be here," said Gia.

"But we don't have a contract yet." He grinned at her and picked up his almost empty glass. "Jaime, we'll have another round, please."

Gia put her hand over her glass. "No more for me. I need to head home soon. I have a long commute, and we've already drunk a lot."

Jaime asked, "So one beer and one sparkling water, then?"

Joseph quickly replied for them both, "Yes."

After Jaime returned with their drinks and walked away, Joseph looked into Gia's eyes. "Gia, I like you a lot. We're good together. Would you go out with me on a real date?"

"You know that isn't the purpose of these dates. We're supposed to get to know one another so we can decide about the contract."

"I don't care about the contract."

Chapter Three

April 2004

Maggie

Tracey took a final bite of his dinner, set down his fork and leaned back in his chair. Once again, his cook and housekeeper, Marie, had surpassed herself. He sighed with pleasure, and then stood up, slowly gathering his dinner dishes to take them into the kitchen.

"Marie, that was splendid. Lamb, new potatoes and asparagus. One of my favorite spring meals. Thank you so much."

"You're welcome, Judge. I know how much you like that combination, so when I found such wonderful asparagus at the farmer's market, I knew what I'd be making for your dinner tonight. Here we are, only the second of April, and the weather is unusually warm. You should take your cognac out into the garden and enjoy it. I hear we have rain coming tomorrow. And when you come in, if you'd please bring a few of those lovely Meyer lemons from the tree out there."

Tracey patted her on the shoulder and said, "Thanks again, Marie. I'll do that." He wandered into his study and poured himself a generous snifter of cognac. Mrs. Whiskers wound around his ankles, purring, and Tracey leaned over and scratched her head. "You're such a good girl." He carried his drink and pipe out to the garden, where he took his seat on a wrought iron chair padded with comfortable cushions and began to fiddle with his pipe.

He breathed in the fragrant evening air and stretched out his legs, his mind wandering to that night exactly six years ago, a week before Maggie's funeral. He leaned back, his heart beat harder, his breathing quickened as he recalled what had happened that night.

♦

He'd stood outside MJW Expressions, watching for her. The wind had blown hard and cold, and he'd turned up the collar of his favorite Burberry and tightened the belt. He'd watched Maggie as she set the alarm to her gallery and locked the door. As she came out onto the sidewalk, he had walked by, his head down, pretending that he was just keeping the wind out of his face.

"Oh, I'm so sorry. I should have been watching where I was going. This damned wind—" Tracey looked up as he ran into Maggie and feigned surprise at seeing her. "Maggie! Are you okay? I was just focused on getting out of this weather as quickly as possible."

"Well," she laughed as she regained her balance, "you certainly took me off guard. Nothing like running smack into someone to get your heart rate going. But really, I'm quite alright."

"So true," he laughed. "Could I buy you a drink to make up for startling you so?"

"Thanks, but not tonight. I'm on my way home. I hope to see my son before he goes to sleep. He always fusses so if he doesn't get his goodnight kiss from his mommy."

Tracey and Maggie walked along the quiet dark street for a few minutes, chatting about her gallery and her newest series of paintings.

Maggie said, "For each new series, I try to find a different perspective, a new kind of inspiration. This time, it was a piece of art my son did in preschool. He drew people with a box for the body, a circle for the head and four sticks for the limbs. So, all the pieces in my new series are combinations of those simple shapes. I decided to feature primary colors like in his piece of art. I think these new ones are quite different from what I've done before."

"I'm sure they are splendid," Tracey said. He thought, *She still hasn't recognized me. It's been a year now. I want her to know I'm her son.*

"I need to cross over here. I'm in that parking lot across the street behind those buildings over there." Maggie pointed.

"I'm parked there, too. When it's dark and windy like tonight, that lot is pretty creepy. Sometimes I wonder how safe it is late in the evening."

"It is creepy." She glanced up at Tracey with a little smile.

As they crossed the street, they continued to chat about her gallery, how amazingly successful it had become in such a short while and about the classes she had offered underprivileged women.

They approached the lot, and Maggie asked, "Where's your car?"

"Oh, it's all the way back there in the far end of the lot." Tracey motioned vaguely. "Let me walk you to your car."

"Thank you. That makes me feel safer."

Maggie stopped next to her car. "This is me." She dug in her handbag for her keys, pulled them out and held them up. "Here we go," she smiled.

It was time, the moment he'd been waiting for. Tracey pulled up his sleeve and showed Maggie the two red streaks on the inside of his forearm that looked as though he'd been scratched by a wild animal. "Do you recognize this?"

At the sight of the birthmark, Maggie put her hand over her mouth and gasped, "How could I forget it?"

"I'm your son. Why don't you recognize me? I love you. I've been trying to find you my whole life."

Maggie was stunned. She was silent. She didn't react. She didn't reach out and hug him. She didn't say anything except, "Why didn't you tell me sooner?" in a flat, emotionless voice.

"You never recognized me throughout this entire year since we met at the museum—when we talked about so many things— as we got to know each other. How can a mother not know her own child?"

Maggie stood completely silent, and thoughts raced through Tracey's mind. *Why isn't she happy to finally find me? Why doesn't she reach out to hug me? Why doesn't she say she loves me? That isn't how mothers behave. That isn't how she used to be.*

She didn't respond, not with a single word or gesture. And he felt as alone, as abandoned as he had felt that night when they had taken him and his twin sister away when they were only small children. He was devastated, he was angry that she didn't seem to care, and he leaned very close to her face and spat out, "Why did you leave us? Why?"

Maggie stepped back, threatened by his harsh voice, and put her hands behind her against the car door to brace herself. "You were taken away from me. I went out. I had to meet someone, and

I had to buy you and your sister some milk. I was only gone a few hours." She shrugged. "You'd stayed alone before when I couldn't afford a babysitter. But when I got home that last time, Child Protective Services was there, taking the two of you away. I begged them not to do it. I cried. But they didn't listen, even when I screamed at them. I felt guilty every day for years that I didn't look harder for you, but I was just a prostitute—and they'd taken my children—I thought I was no good—no good for you—no good for anyone—no good for anything."

Tracey's breath caught in his throat as he remembered how he had felt as he and his sister had been removed from the tiny apartment by big people wearing uniforms, how they had struggled, how they had called out and reached for their mother, how hard they had cried, how lonely those first weeks were, how abandoned they felt—without their mother's hugs—without her love. And how he and his sister were separated soon after and never saw one another again, how much lonelier he had felt then.

He moved even closer and continued, "But you never came and got us. I never saw you again. And then they separated us, me and Sarah. We didn't even have each other."

She said softly, "By the time I tried to look for you, you were already gone—I finally gave up on ever seeing you again." She shook her head and then went on, "My God, I'm so overwhelmed—I need to think about this." She put her hands up, palms out toward him, emotionally distancing herself. She took a deep breath, and then she shivered and said in a dull voice, "It's getting chilly. I need to go home to my family, to my husband and my son."

"You haven't even acknowledged me as your son. You haven't called me son. I used to be your family. I used to be your son. No mother gives up on finding her child—not ever! You should at least invite me to go home with you, to meet your family and my little brother."

"What about *your* new family? You belong to them now, not to me. You're not mine anymore."

"This isn't about them. *They* welcomed me from the first day. *They've* always loved me. *They* never abandoned me."

The wind was blowing harder. Tracey stood so close to her that she couldn't open her car door. Maggie's eyes dilated in fear. She pushed him abruptly, and he stepped back. "Excuse me." She said and brushed back her beautiful red hair with her hand.

Forgotten memories came flooding into Tracey's mind.

That's what she would always say when she was angry and would put me in my room for punishment. That's what she said to me that night. That's what she did. I only wanted a glass of water. I walked out of my room in the dark. I was trying to be so quiet and not bother her. One of Mommy's friends was sitting on the couch. He called me over and lifted me onto his lap. He slipped his hand down my pajama bottoms and began rubbing me. It was scary. I couldn't move. It made my penis grow. I didn't like the way it felt. I didn't know what to do. The man had his head back. He was making noises. I thought it would never end.

Then Mommy came in. "What are you doing out here?" she yelled at me. She grabbed me hard. It hurt. I started to cry, and she put her hand over my mouth to make me be quiet. She pulled me down the hall by my arm. She pushed our bedroom door open with one hip. She took me by the shoulders and gave me one hard shake and shoved me backwards a little and then leaned over me. Our noses were almost touching, and she clenched her teeth and said quietly, "What did I tell you about coming out of your bedroom at night when my friends are here? Never. Come. Out. Ever!" My lips quivered as I held back my tears. Mommy stood up and said, "EXCUSE ME! I need to go make money to feed you and your sister." She shoved her hair off her face and slammed the door. I heard her yelling at her friend, and his deep voice, and then they started to make noises.

Tracey took a deep breath and ran a hand over his face, surprised at the memories that had come out of nowhere.

I found her. I sought her out. I told her who I was, that I loved her.

Maggie interrupted his thoughts. "I really need to get home to my family."

He said bitterly, "Weren't we your family?"

Maggie still didn't respond. She still didn't acknowledge him.

The wind gusted again and blew her hair back into her face. She used both hands to pull it out of her eyes. "Excuse me," she said again and turned her back on him and opened her car door.

His anger turned to rage, uncontrollable rage. *She's rejecting me.*

She's abandoning me. Again.

And something inside him finally broke—something snapped. He stepped in close behind her and put one hand over her nose and mouth to stifle her screams. He buried his face in her soft hair and smelled her familiar scent—this had been his mother. Then he put his left hand around her throat and choked her. He choked her life from her, he was aroused when he did it, when he felt her struggle against him, when he heard her moans, moans like he'd heard from the room next door as she entertained her friends when he was a small child, sounds like he heard from the man on the couch.

At last, her struggles stopped, and Tracey laid her gently in her car. He carefully brushed her hair back from her face. She was still a beautiful woman, perhaps even lovelier than she'd been many years before. An earring had caught in her hair, and as he untangled it, it came away in his hand. Without thinking, he slipped it into his pocket, and he walked away.

♦

The scent of lemon blossoms wafted through his garden. Tracey's thoughts slowly returned to the present, his breath coming in hard, sharp bursts. He clenched the armrests to the ornate wrought iron chair and absentmindedly rubbed one thumb along a rough spot, gently at first and then harder and harder until he felt it draw blood. He put his thumb to his mouth, tasting the salty liquid, feeling the pain of the cut. He breathed deeply and slowly, calming himself.

Chapter Four

April 2004

The Contract

Madrid, Spain

Jaime took down the bottles so he could clean them, one shelf at a time. It was late on a Sunday afternoon. He had put on some traditional Spanish music, and he sang along as he took advantage of this quiet time to do his regular cleaning. He polished the shelf and then wiped each bottle carefully before putting it back in its place. The bottles glistened in the light, proudly arrayed at exactly the same distance from each other.

Perched five steps up on his ladder, he glanced over his shoulder to see who was making all that noise. Raul, Joseph and Sal, talking and laughing as usual, walked through the taberna to the same table they'd occupied the previous week with that attractive young woman. *What was her name?* He thought for a moment. *Ah, yes. Gia. She's a pretty young thing. And Sal certainly found her attractive. But then she came in with Joseph the other night. And they seemed to be more than just friends. Hmmm?*

Jaime was always curious when his locals changed their routines. He continued to watch them as he set down his cloth and carefully backed down the five steps. *It's very odd for them to sit at a table and not come to the bar. I wonder what they're up to.*

"Will you be eating this afternoon or is this only a stop for drinks?" asked Jaime as he stood beside them at the table.

"Jaime, how are you?" Raul said. "We'll have some tapas and our usual drinks."

Sal added, "We'll need a third wine glass as well." He motioned to the empty seat.

"I'm doing fine, but I'm wondering what you guys are up to," he pointed at the table, "here," he gestured toward the long bar, "and not there."

"Oh, it's nothing illegal, Jaime," said Joseph with a grin, and Sal snickered.

Those boys. Jaime shook his head fondly and walked away.

He placed their food order, and while he was preparing their drinks, he heard the door open. He looked up and saw Gia approach the table. *Aha, that's who the third glass is for.* Jaime nodded and raised a mental eyebrow. *Something is going on there. I'll just have to keep my eyes open,* he thought.

Sal stood up immediately, gave Gia a wink and a kiss on the cheek, helped her take off her jacket and pulled out a chair for her. Before she sat down, Gia walked around the table to give Raul and Joseph each a kiss on the cheek. She sat down and adjusted the red patterned scarf around her neck. Sal looked at her, admiring her simple stylish look.

"Thanks," Raul said as Jaime poured the dark red wine into three small glasses and set a tall glass of beer in front of Joseph. "You remember Gia?"

"Hi, Gia. Welcome back." Jaime smiled at her.

She smiled in return. "Thanks, Jaime. I think I made it just in time to miss the rain."

A customer who had just entered called out a greeting to Jaime from where he stood at the bar. "Excuse me. I'll be back in a few minutes with your tapas." He bustled off to take care of the new customer.

Gia said nervously, "So, here we all are."

Ceremoniously, Sal pulled out a document from his pocket. "I typed up all the notes from Gia's chicken scratches so we can talk about this."

Raul had taken a sip of wine and was holding it in his mouth, savoring it. He put his hand up for Sal to slow down, and after he swallowed, he said, "Why don't we discuss how our dates went before we jump to that?"

"But we're not supposed to talk about our dates with each other," Sal reminded him.

Raul stared at Sal. "We need to at least know how they went, if we are compatible so we can decide if we are going to move forward with this arrangement."

Joseph smiled at Gia. "Ours was great."

Sal scowled at Raul. "Are you in or out of this? I'm in."

"Sal, be nice! Stop pushing Raul." Gia said with a little frown at Sal.

Raul sat back in his chair and answered, "There are no rules yet. We have to know if this is going to work for all of us first."

Slightly annoyed, Sal paused, and then he realized there was something important they all needed to talk about. "There were a lot of photographers at the ribbon-cutting. Gia was careful to stay out of their way," he continued with an admiring look at her. "And later she pointed out that we need to be careful not to be photographed when we are on our dates. We don't want pictures of one of us with Gia showing up in the paper, and then she is seen later out with another one of us."

"We need to be careful about that. Nice catch, Gia," Raul said with a quick smile at her. "As for our date, Gia was very impressive. She was a little nervous when we first arrived. And then I left her to her own devices for a long time because I had to go off and twist arms for donations. She jumped right in on her own. Since then, my colleagues have been saying to me that they hope I bring my 'new girlfriend' along again. She was amazing."

Gia's cheeks turned pink, and she stared at her wine glass and twisted it by the stem, a little embarrassed by their praise.

Joseph added, "This is definitely going to work for me." *At least I can sleep with her once a week*, he thought. "My clients were quite impressed by her. They said it felt like she had been going to these dinners forever."

Sal looked at Gia and thought, *I really don't want to share her, but if this is the only way—*

Gia finally interrupted them, "Guys, you do know I'm sitting right here?"

"Sorry. We aren't ignoring you, just comparing notes to see if this could work from our perspective." Raul gave Gia an apologetic look and reached over to pat her hand.

At the same time, Sal and Joseph said, "This works for me," and they both laughed.

Jaime carefully arranged the plates of tapas in the center of the table and set small plates and forks in front of each of them. With a quick smile, he walked away quietly. He glanced out the large window on his way back to the bar and noticed that the heavy clouds had come in again, and it was getting dark. He paused near the door to turn on the lights and then stepped back behind the bar to wait on a group of customers who had gathered there.

Once Jaime had moved away, Raul picked up the document Sal had laid on the table, and they all fell silent as he read it carefully. Joseph tapped his thumb on the table impatiently, and Sal rolled his eyes toward Raul as if to say, "There he goes again." Anxious to hear his comments, Gia shook her head at them in mild rebuke.

Raul looked up and asked Gia, "How do you feel about this? Can you negotiate these three different worlds?" He gestured around the table. "And how about the sex part of this arrangement? Are you okay with it?" *I'm glad Gia knows about me,* he thought. *No illusions. No pretending between us. She could be a good friend and a good cover for me. And she needs to get out of that horrible place where she lives.*

"Really, Raul? Are you serious?" Sal said and pushed back from the table, crossing an ankle over his knee.

Raul ignored Sal and tapped the paper on the table. He looked at Gia. "If you believe you can deal with the three of us and all our needs, it looks like this covers everything we discussed." He handed her the document. "Look it over carefully and tell us what you think."

Gia looked it over for a few moments while she nibbled on an olive. "It covers everything we talked about," and she handed the document to Joseph.

Joseph flipped through the pages quickly, not paying attention to the details, and said, "Fine by me."

Gia finally answered Raul's question, "I can definitely do the professional side of the arrangement. You've all seen that. As far as the sex," she looked at each of the men before she continued, "we'll have the four-month trial, and the rule is that any of us can back out at any time."

They all looked around at one another.

Joseph said quietly with a smile, "Good plan."

"So, it's decided?" asked Sal, pressing them.

And then Gia surprised them again, "But I need more time to think about this."

Raul smiled at Gia, at her willingness to stand up to the

pressure from Joseph and Sal and not just sign the contract without really thinking it through.

Sal asked, "What's there to think about?"

Gia replied, "I know it was my idea. It was fun talking about this arrangement and it was nice to go out with each of you, but this is my future. Up until this point, I didn't know what you all thought about our dates, about me, how serious you all were. I just need more time."

Raul nodded, ran his hand through his hair and smiled at Gia.

"Why are you dithering?" said Sal impatiently.

Raul defended her. "This will change Gia's life. Let her take all the time she needs."

♦

Tired, but excited at the possibility of this commute being over soon, Gia boarded the first of the two buses she had to take. After all the drinks and tapas she'd consumed, she was anxious to get home, make herself a cup of hot tea and think over what she had proposed to these—these—these strangers.

"What was I thinking?" she whispered to herself.

Gia thought about her unusual week and the three men she'd met. *How charming they all are, and how different each one is. Observant and sensitive Raul, mischievous Joseph with his irreverent sense of humor, and Sal, cheeky, impetuous Sal. What fun it will be to get to know them all. But the contract, what will I do about the contract? Is it really a good idea?*

It was dark, and the streetlights were already on when she got off the second bus and walked up the shadowy street to her building. Only one of five lights on the front of the building was still working, and the windows were painted with the grime of years of neglect. Gia wiggled her key in the lock to the outer door and shoved hard with her shoulder to open it because, as always, it had stuck. Once inside, she slammed the door to ensure it latched.

The entry was dimly lit, and as she walked up the four flights of stairs to her tiny flat, there were patches that were in complete darkness. "I wonder if the building manager is just too lazy, or if the owner won't pay for enough bulbs to light this stairwell properly," she grumbled to herself. Out of the corner of her eye, she saw movement on one of the landings and shuddered at what it might have been—a rat, a giant roach, or something else equally disgusting.

Gia entered her single-room flat and leaned against the closed door with her head tipped back. She sighed deeply and said out loud, "I'm adventurous, but eeeessh, that contract would be a whole new level of adventure."

She put the kettle on for tea and changed into her pajamas and slippers and then took her drink over to the window seat to relax. *This seat and this cup of tea are my only luxuries for right now,* she thought morosely.

If I go through with this proposal, will I be a kept woman? Probably, but in a limited way with only three clients. Well, I won't be sleeping with Raul, even if we pretend we are. Gia sipped her tea. *And they won't really be paying me. Do courtesans have contracts? Hmmm, I wonder.*

A lot of women date three men at the same time and sleep with them. Maybe that's just how I should think about it.

Gia looked into her teacup and murmured, "Mamá wouldn't be happy with this, but I have to make my own decisions now."

She said suddenly, "But what about Mari? She's my best friend, and I'll have to explain this to her. Hmmm."

She blew into the hot tea and took another sip.

She nodded her head emphatically. "No matter what they think, I have to forge my own path in life and do what's best for me."

She looked around at the bleak room, the peeling wallpaper, the uneven floorboards. As she heard the neighbors below start their nightly shouting match, she thought, *I haven't been here very long, but I already know I can't go on living like this.*

"God, I need to get out of this place!" Frustrated, she banged her heel against the window seat and looked down at the floor.

Was that day at Jaime's fate? Everything happens for a reason, right? If we did a four-month trial, then I wouldn't have any long-term commitment to this. I feel like it's right. And I'm glad I went out with each of them. Now I can sit down and confidently list the pros and cons and make this decision like an adult. But it does feel right. Hmmm, I wonder?

Gia sat for a while, peering through the dirty window at the street below, as she continued to ponder her options. Suddenly, she realized how late it had become. She needed some sleep so she could get up at three-thirty and get ready and make the long commute to work.

"I'll make a decision tomorrow."

♦

Gia took a seat at her usual table in the window of the small café that had become her refuge in her neighborhood. The café wrapped her in its warmth. It was a cozy place where she could escape her bleak apartment and the scary streets. In the short time she'd lived here, she'd noticed that this was the only place in the neighborhood where the owners seemed to care about their business. She liked how proudly they kept up the café—the tables, counters and display case were all older and worn, but it was well lit and so clean, the floors were free from crumbs and sticky spills, even the bathrooms functioned. Each morning, the husband swept the sidewalk, and he washed the windows weekly, cleaning away the dirt from the city that permeated the area. On every table inside, the wife placed a fresh flower in a reused glass container—perhaps a jam jar or a small olive bottle or a glass with a tiny chip that was no longer safe for drinking but too good to throw out.

The streetlight directly opposite the window had just come on, and she watched people sheltering themselves from the rain under their umbrellas as they scuttled by on their way home from work. She thought about how different it was from the scene outside the window at Jaime's Taberna. Here, there was none of that quaint charm, inside or out. Her thoughts drifted to the three men and the proposal she'd made so spontaneously.

She'd been thinking about the contract constantly since her alarm had woken her in the early hours that morning—throughout her daily routine at work, as she changed from her black-and-white uniform back into her regular clothes at the end of her shift and on her extra-long commute home. The trip had been brutal today—with the rain and accidents, the buses had crawled, and Gia's normal hour-long commute had stretched to more than two.

As a treat, Gia often stopped on her way home for coffee and a pastry at the café, where the morning's leftover baked goods were reduced to half price in the middle of the afternoon. However, since she was later than normal that day, she decided to relax over a glass of wine and the early dinner special. She always enjoyed their inexpensive, simple food. It appealed to her sense of frugality and the flavors reminded her of home.

After she ordered her dinner, she told herself, *I need to use this time while I'm sitting here to decide if I will accept the contract with them or not—but to be honest with myself, I'll probably go for it.* Gia continued to gaze outside and tasted her wine. She knew she tended to make quick decisions. *I need to be an adult about this. This is the first life-changing decision that I've had to make totally on my own, so I need to do my due diligence and weigh the pros and cons.*

She pulled a piece of paper and pen out of her bag and placed them on the table. As she did, she looked around the café and saw the pensioners, who were also taking advantage of the dinner special and seeking refuge from the grim neighborhood and the weather. They were the same people she saw in the café and on the streets every day. *I don't want to be here still when I'm their age, with nothing to look forward to except a cheap dinner at the local café and then a night listening to my neighbors argue.*

Gia propped her chin in her hand and took another sip of her wine. When she looked back out the window, she noticed the rain had stopped, and a woman and her four boys were walking by. The boys looked like they were all younger than seven years old. She smiled as she watched them stomping in the puddles and kicking water at one another as their mother tried to keep them moving along. They reminded Gia of her family back in Fregenal de la Sierra. She'd only been in Madrid for a few months, but it seemed like a lifetime since she'd last seen them.

Gia sat back, reminiscing about the train ride to Madrid. Overwhelmed by the impact of the move, she'd cried silently behind her large sunglasses. The farthest she'd ever been from home before was when she and her mom would make the train trip to see Mari and her family in Seville. But Madrid was much farther from Fregenal. She'd left behind everything that was familiar for this new adventure. While she was glad to have escaped the marriage her father had arranged for her, she was sad to have left behind her eight brothers, her mother, and, yes, even her father. She missed her big family. And although she and her mom had planned her departure secretly for months, she'd never had an opportunity to say a proper goodbye to her brothers. She'd needed to keep it a secret from her dad, and one of them surely would have run to tell him immediately.

Gia swallowed the last sip of her wine and caught the eye of the waitress to indicate she'd like another. She gazed out the window at the city street and the dingy buildings, crammed together around the café, and thought about how much she missed the verdant countryside where she'd spent her free time hiking and reading outdoors or in the hills with Pierre.

It'd been many months since she'd last seen him, and, oh, how she still missed him. He'd looked so funny when they were in primary school. *He was skinny as a rail and his hair was never combed back then. But we had so much fun growing up together, roaming the countryside—and he became so handsome as he grew older, but those last years were the best, when we learned about love with each other—we didn't know anything at first. We were just two innocent teenagers.*

Gia's mind shifted to the three men from yesterday. *I bet they aren't innocent, and that could be exciting. But the "don't share anything" clause in the contract will make my relationships with them just as secret as my love affair with Pierre.*

She smiled as she recalled that last hot September day, before his departure for the university. *We met at our usual hidden spot under the huge tree in the hills. I remember the still air, how it smelled of dry, late-summer grasses crushed under our blanket—it would have been perfect except for his departure hanging over us. I brought that wonderful picnic lunch with fresh bread, fruit and local cheese. He brought a blanket and a bottle of wine. We read poetry and laughed and ate and drank. And in the late afternoon, we made love one last time. And then he was gone.*

The waitress set a glass of wine in front of Gia. "Thanks," she said absentmindedly, still lost in her memories. She took a small drink. *I miss Pierre, and I wish he had written. I wonder why he hasn't. It's been hard, never hearing from him. Maybe he just wanted to start*

*fresh in his new life. I wonder if he found another girlfriend? Maybe he did me
a favor because it was certainly easier to leave home without ties to him. I never
thought I would leave Fregenal. But things change.*

*Even my relationship with my mom changed in those last few months
before I left, when we became co-conspirators. That third time my dad tried to
arrange a marriage for me, I told her I needed to leave, and we planned how
to make it happen. She saved money from her household budget, and I did odd
jobs for the neighbors and merchants in town. Thank God Mari was able to
get me a job here. She's more than just the sister I never had. She's a great
best friend, and I couldn't have escaped without her.*

Gia's dinner arrived, and she slowly began to eat. She pulled
her attention back to the piece of paper, picked up the pen and
began:

Pros:

- o   *Clean and nice condo – MOM*
- o   *Safe neighborhood close to Mari – MOM*
- o   *Free condo – ME*
- o   *Save lots of money – ME*
- o   *The stipend for clothes – ME*
- o   *Travel and adventures with the money I save – ME*
- o   *The men are lifelong friends – SAFETY*
- o   *They talked about their moms – SAFETY*
- o   *They gave me their phone numbers, and it didn't bother them
  that I wouldn't give them mine – RESPECT*
- o   *Bartender knows them well – SAFETY*

Cons:

- o   *Complete strangers to me*
- o   *Are they trustworthy?*
- o   *Are they going to rape me? Even though that's covered in the
  contract?*
- o   *Are they going to take me and sell me into the sex trade?*
- o   *Are they going to hold me captive?*
- o   *Will they kill me?*
- o   *Will this make me a whore?*

Gia knew her mom wouldn't approve of the horrible
apartment she'd found in this crime-ridden area of Madrid, but it
was all she could afford if she wanted to save any money at all.

And her mom would definitely not approve of the arrangement with the three men, but the contract would help keep her safe, and she'd be able to save money for travel and other adventures.

As Gia looked at the list, she laughed to herself—some of the cons were pretty extreme and unlikely.

As much as she loved her family and missed them, she was ready to move forward into this next part of her life. *If I don't do this, will I regret not jumping on this opportunity and not giving myself an advantage to get ahead?*

She knew that even though she could talk herself into or out of this contract, she'd already made her final decision. She'd follow her gut and do it—and then she'd convince Mari. And she still had two weeks to figure out how to tell her before she returned from her vacation. She'd deal with that later.

She'd call Sal as soon as she got home.

The Peacock

He grabbed his phone in excitement as Gia's number flashed on the screen.

"Hi, Sal. This is Gia."

"Well—hello there," Sal replied in his deep, sexy voice, and he smiled. He'd known she would call him. He paused.

"I've given this contract a lot of thought. I thought about it all day. I wrote down all the pros and cons. I weighed my options. It's definitely been a hard decision but—"

"And?" Sal pressed.

After a moment, Gia said nervously, "I'm in."

Sal laughed. "I figured that because otherwise, you would have deleted my number from your phone."

Gia giggled.

"You're agreeing to this without seeing the condo?"

"I've seen the outside and the neighborhood. Trust me, it will be better than where I live now."

"You're trusting a bunch of men you just met a week ago?"

"That's why we'll have a trial period and why I insisted on the contract for my protection. It's not to keep anyone in this relationship, it's to protect all of us. Anyone can walk away."

"True."

"Not to mention, if you guys don't behave, I'll go tell Jaime." She laughed, and Sal joined in.

"He's your safety net?" Sal replied, enjoying their banter.

"Absolutely. He probably knows your mothers."

"Ouch, that's a low blow. So, the condo is ready. Let's meet tomorrow afternoon at three o'clock to take a tour of The Peacock, and you can make your final decision."

Well, this will certainly be an interesting adventure, she thought.

Then Sal said in his sexiest voice, "I'll look forward to seeing you there."

"Me, too. I'll see you there." She hung up. Butterflies of nervousness and excitement did battle in her stomach. But she was sure she'd made the right choice.

◆

Early the next morning, Gia dressed in her nicest skirt and blouse for her meeting with Sal. She slipped her feet into her carefully polished heels, and after ensuring the door was tightly closed and locked, she started down the stairs, shoving her arms into her jacket sleeves as she went. She'd need to hurry, she thought, so she wouldn't be late for work. She ran toward the bus stop.

All day, as she cleaned rooms, scrubbed bathrooms and vacuumed the hallways, Gia couldn't stop thinking about the condo she was about to move into, the contract, the men and seeing Sal again.

She walked to the building from work slowly so she wouldn't be too early and seem too eager. Strolling along the broad boulevard, she admired the mixed facades of old and new buildings and browsed in the shop windows along the way.

It was just a few minutes before three when Gia paused and admired the building again. Her eyes opened wide. "Oh, this is lovely," she murmured. She envisioned living there and stepped back and tipped her head to better appreciate the charming architecture, the cream-colored paint, the art deco detailing. She imagined standing, people-watching from one of the narrow step-out balconies or sitting outside at a tiny table, sipping a refreshing glass of sangria on one of the covered balconies with black iron railings in a traditional sunburst pattern.

Then the large brass plate to the right of the door caught her eye, and she moved closer to study it. "The Peacock," she read aloud, and ran her fingers over the intricate feathers, and then the beak of the bird embossed on the brass. "I wonder about the history behind that. I'll have to ask Sal."

"Ask me what?" he said from close behind her.

Gia jumped. "Sal, you shouldn't sneak up on a girl like that," she giggled and then gestured at the building. "This is so beautiful, but you need to tell me about that." She pointed to the brass plate.

He put his hands on her shoulders and gave her a kiss on each cheek. "Last time we were here, there were so many other people that I didn't get a chance to personally welcome you to The Peacock," he said with a grin. "You'll understand when you get inside."

"I can see why you bought it. I'm in love with it already, and I haven't even seen the interior. Tell me, how did you find it?"

Sal smiled at Gia's passion for the building, which matched his own. "I can't believe we didn't talk about all of this last week. I guess we were so busy getting to know one another that we didn't even think about the building." Sal winked at her. "Anyway, the exterior attracted my attention first, but when I saw the interior, I knew I had to buy it. In high-end real estate, you stumble across all kinds of gems. Some just need a lot of polishing. This was one of those. It was a total disaster when I bought it, and that's why I got such a good deal. If you had seen it before, you wouldn't recognize it now. Just wait until you see the inside." Sal unlocked the entry door and held it open and gently took her elbow to guide her.

Gia's heels clicked sharply as they walked across the marble floors of the spacious lobby, past perfectly placed, lush plants and a few low chairs, and she quickly peered down the hallways leading toward the units on either side. Awed by the elegant decor, Gia stopped and looked around. "You know, it's like the lobby of a very upscale boutique hotel."

Sal grinned at her. "Yes! That was exactly my intention. I want the residents to feel pampered the moment they enter that door."

Gia paused to admire the walls decorated with old art deco murals of peacocks. The background colors were muted, the birds' lapis and turquoise plumage glowed in sharp contrast. "Wooow! I get it now. *El Pavo Real*—The Peacock. That was clever to use the English translation for the name. It makes your building stand out."

"Precisely," said Sal.

She pointed to the murals, "Are these original?"

"They were, though they were very badly neglected. I had

them restored. It was quite expensive to hire the right artist, but I couldn't bear the thought of covering those glorious birds with wallpaper or paint, or even worse, ruining them with a botched restoration."

They continued through the lobby and up the two steps to the elevator landing. Gia said, "Nice touch," as she ran her hand along the railing next to the steps. "Same pattern as the railings out front but silver. You've really stayed faithful to the deco style of the building."

Sal smiled and nodded. "Actually, those exterior railings are reproductions. I wasn't able to save the old ones. But these are originals. I used them as inspiration for the outside."

"I never would have known."

When she saw the marble facade surrounding the elevator, she reached out and gently stroked the polished surface with her fingertips. Sal pushed a button, and when the elevator arrived, he pulled back the ornate iron gate and the old-fashioned, double doors slid open. He let Gia in and closed the gate behind her. And as he pushed the top-floor button, the inner doors closed quietly.

While the elevator rose, Sal said, "Isn't this wonderful?" gesturing around the elevator. "We kept all the original architectural and structural details when we renovated it, but we replaced all the mechanical bits, so there's no danger of it failing. It's another one of the many things about this building that attracted me."

"I imagine that was another expensive renovation, but how could you not keep this wonderful elevator, Sal? You've done a marvelous job, maintaining a perfect balance of old and new. It's one of the things that I love about Madrid, that juxtaposition. Where I come from, it's just all old," she laughed.

As they stepped out of the elevator at the top floor, Gia said, "Aaaahhh, the same wall sconces from the lobby are up here, too." She looked from side to side at the landing walls. "Oh my, I just noticed that the pattern they cast is the same as the ironwork on the railings. It's so much easier to see up here."

Sal nodded. "Mmmm-hmmm. It was all part of the plan."

He unlocked the condo, stepped in and turned to hold the

door for Gia so he could watch her reaction.

Gia stepped inside, took a deep breath, and as she breathed out, she clasped her hands in front of her chest. "Oh—my—goodness." Sal smiled, pleased at her reaction.

She was speechless as they crossed the spacious foyer and entered the living room. Sal removed first her jacket and then his and laid them carefully on a chair.

He's such a gentleman, thought Gia with a happy little smile.

All the details of the long, gracious room distracted her for a moment—the tall ceilings, intersected by dark beams, the bar near the entry, the furniture perfectly placed for comfortable conversations—but then the light filtering through the doors at the far end of the living room caught her eye. She turned to Sal. "I love those French doors. They're so beautiful."

"Almost as beautiful as the view from the terrace. Come see."

Sal guided her across the living room with his hand on the small of her back, and as they stepped out, Gia said, "I love this terrace."

Sal laughed. "So do I. It's a beautiful day to enjoy it."

They stood gazing out across the city. Sal watched Gia tip her head back to enjoy the sunshine on her face. Reveling in the momentary warmth of the sun and the cool air, washed fresh by the recent rain, they stood quietly enjoying the view and one another's company for a few minutes.

When Gia shivered, Sal put his arm around her. They walked down the terrace to their left and entered through another set of French doors into the open dining room and kitchen area. Sal took Gia's hand and drew her past the long table in the dining area and on into the kitchen. He opened the refrigerator and took out a bottle of local sparkling wine. "Shall we celebrate?"

"Well, we haven't signed the contract yet—" She looked around. "But I suppose we—oh, yes!"

Sal smiled and then opened the bottle with a flourish and poured two glasses of the crisp, bubbling cava.

"Wow, you've thought of everything!"

"Oh yeah, this place is completely furnished, down to the bubbly and the glasses."

Sal handed her a glass and then raised his. "To a successful partnership."

"To our partnership." She blushed and he smiled. They clinked glasses and took a sip of the wine.

As they drank, Sal watched Gia wander around the kitchen, peering into cabinets and drawers. She opened the door to a spacious pantry. "Oh my! This kitchen has everything I could possibly need to cook."

"You cook?"

Gia smirked, her dark brown eyes twinkling at Sal as she said, "Only daughter, eight brothers. What would you expect?"

"This contract has benefits, then."

"That wasn't in the contract! If you're lucky enough, you might convince me to cook for you now and then."

Sal smiled, and as she continued to explore, they sipped their wine and chatted comfortably.

Gia gestured widely with her free hand. "I know I'm gushing, but I love this place!"

Sal refilled their glasses. "Well, come on, there's more to see."

She smiled to herself as, once again, he put his free hand on the small of her back, and they walked together into the living room. Gia stopped abruptly as she noticed the fireplace with built-in bookshelves on either side. She pointed. "Another thing I love. That—is it new or original?"

"The insides are all new, but again, I was able to keep the original facade and bookshelves." Sal grinned. "Let's continue the tour." He guided her across the living room into the foyer. And then through another doorway. And to the left into an airy, spacious bedroom.

Gia paused and looked around—at *her* bedroom. *Wow!* she thought, *this is mine?* To her right stood a lovely bed, its headboard upholstered in intricately pleated heavy cream silk, white bedding piled with soft pillows. The nightstands on either side of the bed were silver with mirrored tops, and polished silver lamps with white shades glowed softly. She walked into the middle of the room and turned slowly, taking in the coral jacquard chair, tucked in the corner to the left of the bed, and the pale silver dresser, topped with bold coral roses in a Chinese bowl on the opposite wall.

"Those roses perfectly match that chair. Coral is my favorite color," she said. *He has such wonderful taste. I wonder if he actually chose all this himself.* She tipped her head back to admire the high ceiling, white, like the walls, enjoying the way the exposed dark beams interrupted the smooth surface. "I bet those beams are original, too," she murmured.

Gia's gaze drifted across the room, caught by the gentle movement of the gauzy white curtains. "Another set of French doors? How romantic this room is," she sighed. "Sal, this couldn't be any better."

As Sal walked over to stand near the French doors, he set his glass on the dresser and turned to watch her. "Come see the bedroom from this angle," he said to Gia, who was standing still in the middle of the room, looking about in wonder.

She slowly walked over and took another sip of her wine before she set it next to Sal's. She looked around and then up at the beams again, turning, trying to take it all in. She stumbled slightly, accidentally bumping into Sal. He put his arms around her. "I've got you."

She turned to thank him. Their faces were almost touching, and he kissed her gently. He couldn't believe his luck. She had literally fallen into his arms. Gia's eyes opened wide. He smiled and slightly tightened his arms around her. She leaned against him, and he kissed her again. And when she began to respond, Sal intensified the kiss.

"Mmmm," she purred and slid her arms around his neck and threaded her fingers into his curly dark hair. He stroked her back sensually as the kiss continued.

Then he stopped. Gia was caught off guard. Sal bent down and picked her up. She rested her head on his shoulder, took a shaky breath and whispered, "Ooooh."

"You okay?"

"Yes," she giggled lightly. "I think I'm just a little lightheaded." She giggled again.

He took a couple of steps and gently placed her on the bed

and then sat next to her. He slipped off his shoes and reached over to push her hair back from her face. He kissed her again—lingeringly. When he drew away, he smiled at her and took her hand and brushed his lips across her fingers. Then he put his arms around her and drew her in and held her close.

After a few minutes, Sal leaned back from her and pulled her feet into his lap. He turned, and holding her gaze, his eyes gleaming with passion, he took her foot in his hand and slowly slipped off her shoe and let it fall to the floor. He skimmed his hand down her calf and massaged her foot tenderly and ran his thumb along her arch. Gia gave a long moan. Then he slowly removed her other shoe and ran his hand down her calf, holding her foot as he dropped the second shoe to the floor. Gia moaned again in anticipation, and he began the same lovely treatment of her foot.

Gia's mind went blank. All she could do was wait eagerly for his next touch—

He stroked his hands up and down the outside of her legs, up and down and eventually up and under her skirt, and Gia sank back into the pillows, her heart pounding, her breath coming faster. He slipped off her thong in one—long—slow—tantalizing motion.

Sal lay down beside Gia and caressed her neck gently. He began to tease open the buttons on her shirt—slowly—from bottom to top—button by button, following each button with a light kiss on her bared skin. He watched her squirm with excitement and smiled at how thoroughly she was enjoying being seduced.

And then, with two buttons to go, Gia surprised him by putting her hand on his. "Wait," she said and paused. Sal wondered for a moment if she was going to stop him—now.

Then she sat up and slid her hands down his chest and slowly unbuckled his belt. Sal turned onto his back and propped himself up on his elbows, watching Gia teasingly, slowly, slowly pull off his belt and unbutton and unzip his trousers. She pulled out his shirttail and then unfastened his shirt—from bottom to top—touching his skin with her lips as she uncovered it—one button at a time.

Sal watched her—his breath ragged. Gia looked up and smiled slyly at him, taking pleasure in his reaction to her touch. She ran her fingers through the soft hair on his chest. *Oh, I do like the way he feels,* she thought.

Finally, his shirt open completely, she straddled his waist, leaning forward to nip gently at his earlobe—down the side of his neck—along his collarbone. She sat back, provocatively unfastened the last two buttons and removed her blouse—and giggled.

Sal loved that giggle of hers. He put a hand on each side of her face, drew her to him and captured her mouth with his. He slid one hand around to cradle the back of her head, and with the other, he unclasped her bra and slipped it off. He stroked her breasts, with the back of his hand and then the tips of his fingers. Her nipples hardened, and he pinched them gently.

Gia gasped and cried out into his mouth. Sal deepened the kiss, his tongue probing, exploring her mouth, and he felt her wetness against his belly. He moaned deep in his throat, enjoying her arousal—his arousal—anticipating—

Then he grabbed her waist and quickly flipped her onto her back.

Giggling with delight, she thought, *Oh, this is so different than it was with Pierre. This is going to be fun!*

Sal stood up next to the bed and slowly took off his shirt and dropped it on the floor while Gia watched. But when he put his hands on his waistband to slip off his trousers, she sat up quickly, "Whoa, whoa, whoa, that's my job," swung her legs off the bed and moved his hands.

Sal gently laughed and raised them in mock surrender.

Gia knelt on the floor in front of him. Her eyes widened as she quickly yanked down Sal's trousers.

He looked down at Gia. "Ohhh my God!" he sighed. "You are the sexiest woman I've ever met." Then he pulled her up to her feet and looked at her slowly from head to toe. "Seeing you in only a skirt is making me crazy."

"I can take care of that." She unfastened her skirt and let it fall to the floor.

"Oh, you little minx," groaned Sal.

They both laughed. She looked down. "Mmmm, I think we have something important to take care of," and stepped closer, pressing her body against him—her mouth against his—a heated kiss—her tongue flickering against his, tasting him, tasting his desire. She ran both hands down his back, slowly slid them into the back of his briefs and squeezed the firm muscles of his buttocks. Sal pushed against her as he groaned again with pleasure.

She took the waistband of his briefs and looked him playfully in the eye. "I think it's time to release the beast," she whispered as she slid them down to his knees.

Sal drew a ragged breath and then grinned broadly. "Can you tame him?"

Gia smirked. "I'll try my best."

◆

As the late afternoon sun shone through the curtains, Gia lay back against the pillows, completely content, watching Sal dress. She admired his narrow hips, his broad shoulders, the defined muscles on his chest. And as he buttoned his shirt, he winked at her. "Thanks for helping me christen the condo, Minx." Gia giggled at the nickname.

He leaned over, and they enjoyed one long, final kiss. Then Sal pulled a set of keys out of his pocket. He placed them in her hand, wrapped her fingers around them. "Welcome home," he said and kissed her on her forehead.

Gia caught her lower lip between her teeth as she took a slow, deep breath.

Sal strolled out of the room.

He left in a hurry. Hmmm, I wonder what that's about? She heard the front door close.

With a smile on her face, Gia let her mind wander, *Sex with Sal was amazing! I wonder what it will be like with Joseph.*

After a moment, she sat up quickly, threw her arms out wide and said out loud, "What an awesome arrangement! The beautiful condo! The gorgeous men! Everything!"

Gia stood up and put on her thong and her shirt. She fastened a few buttons as she wandered into the bathroom. She ran her hands along the Carrara marble counter, admiring its cool, smooth surface, fingered the soft, fluffy towels and lifted the scented soap that Sal had left on the counter and inhaled its perfume. The separate glass-enclosed shower, large enough for several people, the oversized soaking tub under the tall windows that let in so much sunlight—she put her arms out and spun around in front of the mirror, smiling with happiness. She had never experienced luxury like this outside the hotel where she worked. Now she lived in it!

Gia walked across to the dresser and picked up the two glasses. She took them into the kitchen, poured the last of the wine into her glass and began to examine the kitchen more thoroughly, picking up plates and glasses and then replacing them in the cabinets. "I'm going to really like cooking here." She toasted the kitchen and then walked through the dining room to the terrace doors. "It's mine, all mine! No screaming neighbors, no dirty windows, no rowdy brothers, just mine, all mine."

An hour later, Sal called Gia. "Hello, Minx. I'm in a bit of a rush to a client appointment but wanted to let you know I touched base with Joseph and Raul. We'll be over tomorrow night at eight to sign the contract."

Gia said saucily, "See you then, Beast," and Sal laughed.

♦

Gia sat on the window seat in her dingy little apartment and looked through the glass one last time. She watched the traffic as it crawled slowly past on the narrow street four floors below. "I'm so glad to be out of here. Financially, it was a good place to land when I first got to Madrid, and the week-to-week rent was low. But living here, ugh—what a dump! And the building manager—a total creep! It's definitely time to get out."

She took a quick look around to make sure she hadn't left anything important behind. Sal had furnished the new condo so completely that she wouldn't even need the little espresso pot, her single cup, or her tea kettle. She'd leave those for the next tenant.

"Poor thing, whoever you are," she said. And then she picked up her single suitcase of belongings and closed the door quickly behind her.

On her way out, Gia stopped by the building manager's apartment to drop off her keys and let him know she was moving. He opened his door, and seeing who it was, he leered at her and licked his lips. But his tone changed abruptly as she gave her notice.

"Notice, eh? Well, I'll be glad to see the last of you and all your complaints. 'Ooooh, I saw a rat on the stairs! A cockroach ran over my foot—eeeew! The light bulb is out. The door sticks.' Complain, complain, complain." He stretched out his hand to take the keys, black dirt rimming his fingernails and ingrained in every crease. She held the keys between her fingertips, dropped them onto his filthy palm and turned away quickly.

"Yikes, there's someone I really won't miss," she said to herself as she walked out the front door, a smile breaking out on her face. "New life, here I come!"

♦

Gia turned the key to unlock her new door, a little flutter of excitement in her stomach. She set her suitcase in the foyer. "Mine! All mine," she said and twirled through the foyer and into the living room. After walking through the entire apartment to reacquaint herself with the details of her new home, she said, "I'm eighteen years old, and I live here. Oh. My. Goodness!" She ended up in the kitchen. "Now, to get all the ingredients for tapas for tonight's contract signing." She made a quick list of what she'd need and headed out to explore.

She wandered around her new neighborhood—there was Jaime's over there, she noticed, and some wonderful-looking little boutiques that she'd have to check out later. But right now, she was on a mission.

A thrill of anticipation ran through Gia as she turned from the broad boulevard filled with traffic and the sound of cars honking vigorously into the covered market that had been converted from a narrow alley. She drew in a deep breath—all those wonderful smells. She wandered down an aisle to find fresh flowers and herbs and then, following more delicious smells, discovered a bread stall—rolls and loaves of newly baked bread. Then a woman selling poultry, a man selling fresh fish and the vegetable area—fresh, pickled, dried—row upon row of stalls with every type of vegetable you could possibly want. And the cheeses, oh, the cheeses—cheeses of all kinds! It was a cornucopia of edibles. She wandered around the market, taking her time, touching and tasting everything. She felt like she was in heaven.

As she got off the elevator on her floor, her phone, which she'd stuffed into her jacket pocket, sounded with Mari's special ringtone. She set down her heavy bags and immediately answered it.

"Hey, you. How's your time been in Seville?"

"It's been wonderful to get away from work and the bustle of Madrid."

Gia peppered Mari with questions. "Where are you staying on this trip? Your parents' house? Their inn? The casita? How're your parents? How's your brother? When will you be back? I have so much to tell you!"

That's Gia. Not just one question for me, Mari thought.

"Well, I'm staying at the inn, in one of the rooms that hasn't been renovated yet because Leonardo has moved back to Seville and he's staying in the casita," Mari explained as Gia started to carry one bag at a time from the hallway into the kitchen.

"Not much privacy for him being right behind your parents' house. But he gets to be spoiled by your mom."

Mari chuckled. "He's only staying there until he can find his own place close to the inn."

"So, he's planning on settling in Seville permanently then?"

"Yes, he's here for good now. And we're all so excited to have him back. I didn't realize how much I've missed my big brother. Now I'll see him more often." Gia could hear the love in Mari's voice. "He thought he wanted a change of scenery, to get away from family and to make new friends, but he's decided he misses the family too much and has come back home."

"Why does Leonardo need to be close to the inn?" Gia asked

as she took the final bag to the kitchen and with one hand, began to put the groceries away, holding the phone to her ear with the other.

"My dad offered him the position of head chef. It's not a big kitchen, just a small staff, but he can call it his own. I'm sure the reputation he's established as a chef will attract the type of clientele that my parents are looking for."

"Good for everyone then. How is your mom?"

"My mom is over the moon to have him back home, and so on this trip, I'm not getting the love I normally do," Mari joked, and Gia chuckled in response.

"She and Papá are busy with the renovations to finally update the inn and make it more luxurious."

"It must be chaos right now."

"It is. Sometimes the construction noise is really bad."

"Is that what I'm hearing in the background? It is pretty loud."

"Just part of the renovation experience," Mari laughed.

"But having my brother, with his credentials, as the new chef takes the pressure off my dad to go out and find someone to fill that spot. With the following he already has, they've decided to open the restaurant first."

"Food first. That's a good decision. I can hardly wait to taste his cooking. Yum." Gia smacked her lips.

"Exactly. He just started creating the menu. I've been his guinea pig, sampling his dishes, and he's fantastic." Mari smiled. "They'll reopen this summer. Between now and then, they'll advertise in food and travel magazines and target young professionals and more affluent clients from Madrid and other cities throughout Europe."

"I can't wait to see the place on my next visit!"

"I'm very excited because this strategy should really increase business for them. This is exactly what they've been working for."

"I know. They've wanted to do this for years."

"They'll love to show it off to you. What's new back there in Madrid?"

Gia continued to put her groceries away as she and Mari

caught up on gossip. Her mind was on that evening and so she was only half-listening to their conversation until she heard Mari's voice change.

"Well—hmmm—"

"What? What's wrong?"

"Nothing's wrong."

"What then?"

"Well, I applied to Spectrum." There was a pause on Mari's end, while she waited for Gia's response.

"What's Spectrum? What did you apply for?"

"I was flipping through one of the magazines my mom gets, and I saw an advertisement for the Spectrum River Cruise Line. They do cruises all over the world."

Surprised by Mari's news, Gia asked, "What?! River cruises? All over the world? What?! What have you done?"

"I've applied for a concierge position with Spectrum."

Gia paused, a final bunch of herbs in her hand, and waved them about excitedly. "Concierge, that's amazing. That's your dream job, and all your experience and education should mean you're in a good position to get it. That's wonderful. Wow, you could end up anywhere!"

Mari relaxed when she heard the enthusiasm in Gia's voice. "Hang on—I haven't gotten it yet. I just sent in my application this morning." Mari tried to temper Gia's excitement. "So, we'll have to see. It could be a job on a river here in Spain, or halfway around the world in Asia. We'll see. If I even get it."

"Wow, world travel. That would be fun." Gia's eyes landed on the serving dishes she had placed on the counter, ready to fill with tapas that evening, and her attention drifted away to Sal and the other men and the contract they'd all sign that evening.

"How's the hunt for a new apartment coming along?"

Gia replied, her voice deliberately casual, "Oh, actually, I've found a new place to live, and it's much better than the old one, and it isn't too far from you, and I know you'll like it."

"A new place? Anything's gotta be better than that dump you've been living in. I wish I had time to hear all about it, but I have to go meet up with my family."

"This place just fell into my lap since you've been gone. I wasn't going to tell you about it anyway because I want it to be a surprise when you get back," laughed Gia.

◆

As Gia cooked, she swayed and sang along to a song about love and life's experiences. Suddenly, she realized how dark it had become outside. She flicked on the lights in the kitchen and then walked into the living room to turn on a couple of lamps in preparation for her guests. "They'll be here soon," she murmured to herself, pleased by the welcoming atmosphere of the room.

She came back and paused in the doorway, admiring the kitchen, the counters covered with platters, food preparation underway, pendant lights glowing softly, music playing in the background. *Making tapas in this kitchen is such a pleasure. I hope they like these as much as the ones the other evening at Jaime's.*

As she walked around the island, she stopped to take a swallow from her glass of local red wine, thinking about the carefully planned selection of tapas that she would serve at room temperature. She didn't want to be tied to the kitchen once the three men arrived. And, based on what she'd observed at Jaime's, she knew they would eat a lot, so she was preparing large quantities of seven different dishes, all favorites of hers.

"*Papas arrugadas*, with those very small, new potatoes boiled in saltwater and then roasted—oh yum! I think I like this one best of all," she said as she sniffed the air appreciatively. The tiny potatoes were roasting in the oven, and Gia prepared the mojo sauce she'd serve with them. Carefully following her mom's recipe, she blended fresh garlic, paprika, red pepper, cumin, olive oil and wine vinegar, all finds from her morning excursion to the local market. Then she tasted the mixture. She tipped her head, examined it critically and thickened it ever so slightly with finely ground breadcrumbs.

As she headed to the refrigerator, she danced to another song on the radio. She took out the olives and smiled as she placed them in a beautiful bowl. *That market has such a fabulous selection of olives, and they are all so delicious. I didn't even need to eat any lunch after all the different types I tasted.*

"Now for the anchovies," she murmured to herself as she opened the door again. "My entire refrigerator smells of vinegar and olive oil and parsley—but mostly of that lovely, lovely garlic." Gia dipped her finger into the marinade the anchovies had been resting in and touched it to her tongue. *Almost as good as my own,* she thought, *and I'm so glad I found them pre-made since I didn't have the entire day to let them marinate.*

She arranged them on another of Sal's beautiful plates and sprinkled some pieces of garlic on top. *Wow, Sal provided enough serving dishes for a feast. He really is amazing. Engineer, realtor, fantastic interior designer and*— She giggled to herself and blushed slightly as she thought of just how amazing he had been the previous day.

"Time for the *banderillas,*" she announced and took out the pickled baby vegetables she had bought in the market and threaded them onto tiny Japanese bamboo skewers. Then she added her personal twist, the pickled quail eggs she had been so fortunate to find that morning. "I wonder if anyone will notice this little touch I learned from you, Mamá. Here's to you! I love you and miss you so much. I think you'd be proud of this spread." She lifted her wine in a toast to her mom.

Gia arranged the tapas and bread carefully on the dining room table and then added four place settings—small plates, forks, napkins and glasses and stepped back to admire it all. "It's perfect," she said with a satisfied nod.

That morning, she had made sure there was enough sparkling wine in the bar refrigerator before going out. "I'll ask Sal to bring it in and pour it once they arrive. Can't let it get warm!" she said checking off her mental to-do list.

With a few minutes still remaining before they arrived, Gia turned off the radio and stepped outside into the cool evening air to admire the view of the city. She shivered as she looked at the twinkling lights, drew in a deep breath and let it out slowly. "Outdoor living space. I haven't had that since I left Fregenal. Oh, I am the luckiest girl on earth." Gia shivered again and rubbed her arms as she turned to go back into the warm apartment.

She heard a key in the lock, and the door opened with a burst of sound. It was obvious that they had arrived together and were, as usual, discussing something "very important". Gia walked over to greet them, and they all greeted her with kisses on both cheeks.

Joseph and Raul toured the condo quickly, ending in the dining room, and called out, "Gia, is this food for us? It looks and smells wonderful."

She smiled at Sal, who had remained standing next to her in the living room. "Yes, it is," she replied. "Save some for us. Sal, would you please bring the bubbly from the bar fridge?"

She walked into the dining room where she overheard Raul say to Joseph, "This is impressive," as he looked at the table.

Joseph replied quietly, "And quite an added benefit." When Sal walked in, Joseph slapped him on the back. "Great place. Well done, my man."

They sat down and immediately dug into the tapas and wine as though they hadn't eaten in days.

"Always hungry. You're just like my brothers. I love all this chaos."

Raul asked Gia, "Quail eggs with the *banderillas*? That's a nice touch."

"You're observant. I learned it from my mom." They smiled at one another.

They all talked non-stop as they ate, the men, as usual, interrupting one another, completing each other's sentences, laughing and joking. Gia quizzed them about their lives, and they asked her about her life growing up in Fregenal and how she liked living in a big city.

After they ate, the four of them carefully reviewed the contract. Sal looked around the table. "Is it missing anything?"

Simultaneously, the other two replied, "Nope."

Sal looked at Gia. "And you?"

Gia, realizing this was the last moment before signing, slowly shook her head. "I can't think of anything else." And immediately qualified, "There is a trial period, after all."

Raul said, "Yes, that trial period is important."

Sal grinned and was the first one to sign before passing the contract around. As the others signed the papers, he refilled their crystal glasses and raised his in a toast. "To our contract."

Joseph added, "Hear, hear."

And Gia chimed in shyly, "To new friendships."

Raul smiled as he looked around at the group of friends.

Then Sal made a big deal about handing out keys, which he had put on special keyrings with a "G" on each. Joseph snickered as he held the keyring, "'G?' Really? Come on, now."

Sal replied a little defensively, "I saw them and couldn't resist."

Gia teased, "Hey, Sal, why didn't I get a "G" on my keyring?"

Raul said, "Yeah, Sal, why not?"

Sal shook his head and ignored them both. "Let's move to the other room, and I'll get you all another drink." He headed to the living room bar.

As they followed him, Joseph said to Raul, "I bet Sal has stocked that bar with all our favorites." Raul laughed and nodded his head.

Sal, already standing by the bar, put his hands up and shrugged, "Of course I did!" and they all laughed.

"But we haven't finished our bubbly," Gia said.

"You never will," Joseph chuckled, knowing that Sal always kept their glasses full.

After they'd settled in the living room with their drinks, Sal handed Gia a flat white box, tied with coral ribbon. "A gift? For me? You shouldn't have. How sweet. Can't be a keyring, it's too big and heavy." She gave him a smug little smile.

"Open it, would you?"

She pulled the ribbon slowly, took off the lid and lifted a dark coral, leather-bound calendar from the box.

"This is for you to keep track of our 'appointments'."

Gia touched the soft leather and turned it in her hands, admiring the gold edges of the pages and running her fingers along the embossed letters on the front, "'Appointment Diary', ohhh, this is lovely."

Joseph said glibly, "Well at least *that's* useful."

"Useful? It is absolutely beautiful. Thanks, Sal." Gia leaned over and lightly touched his hand. As she did, she felt the electricity between them again. Sal turned his head toward her and winked so the others couldn't see it. Gia blushed and suppressed a giggle.

Then she took over, with her new diary and her work schedule in one hand and a pen in the other, and they agreed on their "appointments" with Gia: Joseph on Monday, Sal on Tuesday, Raul on Thursday. She diligently marked them down.

"So, in addition to the appointments, what else is coming up? Any special events needing a date?" Gia made meticulous notes:

Raul – dinner & fundraiser at the children's hospital.

Sal – dinner with business colleagues.

Joseph – pub crawl with work colleagues for the spring festival.

Joseph watched Gia as they threw dates around. *She's beautiful, she's kind, she's smart, and she manages us all so well. I like her. It could be easy to fall for her. But there's that contract, so I'll need to be careful.*

After they'd finished with the schedule, they relaxed. The atmosphere was friendly, light-hearted and warm.

At eleven, Gia stood up and announced, "As much as I hate to break things up, I have to work in the morning, so you all need to let me get my beauty sleep."

She won't let us walk all over her, that's for sure. I like that, thought Raul.

On the way out, Sal dawdled so he was the last to leave. He leaned toward her and whispered, "Shall I stay, Minx?"

"You'll have to wait for your appointment."

Sal's head went back in disappointment, and he groaned.

"I'll see you then, Beast—off you go." She motioned him out with a flick of her fingers and gave him a sassy smile.

As Gia closed the door, she heard Joseph at the elevator. "What are you up to, Sal? What did you say to her? You always have an angle. I think we have a good thing here. Don't mess it up!"

Gia cleaned up the kitchen and poured herself another glass of wine. Then, to unwind, she curled up in a large chair next to the fireplace and pulled a wrap around her shoulders. "Now I just have to break the news to Mari."

Appointments

Madrid, Spain

Gia strolled along the wide boulevard, separated from the heavy traffic and exhaust by the row of trees planted near the edge of the sidewalk. She'd just finished work and was enjoying the early afternoon air, cool in the shade, warmer in the sun.

This is lovely. I can walk home from work every day and still have some of the afternoon ahead to enjoy. This is the life. Her mind wandered to her contract with the men, and she wondered, *but how much sleep will I get with three men in my life when I have to get up at four-thirty for work? I guess I'll figure it out and catch up on sleep when I can. Lack of sleep will not force me to give up my lovely apartment.*

As she passed Mari's apartment, she looked up to admire the new, modern building and murmured, "It'll be so nice to live closer to Mari. We can pop in to see each other more often. Another pro to this arrangement!"

Gia continued to stroll along, admiring the well-dressed shop windows with their enticing displays of jewelry, clothing and shoes. *My new neighborhood has really nice shopping,* she thought as she paused in front of the windows of a lingerie shop. Recalling her encounter with Sal, she bit her lip, *I need to buy new underwear. Mine is old and shabby, which was fine before. But since the men will see it, I really need some new, lacy, sophisticated things,* and she walked into the shop.

As she stepped onto the lush carpet, Gia inhaled deeply, breathing in the sweet perfume from the vases of roses and lilies on the counters and low tables. She looked around at all the merchandise, arranged by color, and smiled as she heard soft romantic music playing in the background. She whispered to herself, "Wow, this is so nice—no, it's lovely."

The saleswoman approached her. "Would you like a glass of champagne while you shop?"

"Yes, please."

After the woman turned away, Gia thought, *I could get used to this. It's so different from where I used to buy my underwear. Our local store in Fregenal sold everything from underwear to toasters and lawnmowers. And they certainly didn't offer French champagne.*

She moved around the shop, glass in hand, fingering the fine material and soft lace. From time to time, Gia picked up an item, enjoying the way the light filtered through the sheer fabric. *It's so hard to choose. I could buy everything here.* She giggled at the thought. *But that would destroy my budget!*

An hour later, Gia left the shop carrying a pretty, tissue-filled bag with three delicate negligees and several sets of dainty new underwear. *I've never spent so much money on myself before, but what fun it was!*

Pleased with her purchases, she glanced at her watch, "Yikes, I didn't realize how long I was in there. Now I really need to hurry if I'm going to get to the market to buy some food so I can make dinner for Joseph this evening."

Back home, Gia showered and changed into her new undergarments and carefully hung a sexy satin gown in the bathroom. *Just in case I need it.*

She dressed in her favorite worn jeans and a soft, white t-shirt that molded itself lightly to her torso and stopped just above her hipline. She wondered, a little nervously, how the appointment would go. She'd never dated more than one man at a time.

She wandered into the kitchen in her bare feet, pulled out fruit and a knife and the big cutting board and began her afternoon ritual of preparing sangria. Her sharp knife sliced through the crisp apple, and Gia smiled, enjoying the sound. She inhaled the scent—oranges, apples, grapes, blackberries, lemon and her favorite, lime—and mixed them gently with simple syrup. *I think preparing my sangria gives me at least as much pleasure as the drink itself.*

Thoughts of Joseph floated through her mind. *He's so handsome—hmmm. What will we talk about—maybe more about his music—I wonder what he'll be like in bed?* She smirked.

Gia took the pitcher of fruit and went to the bar. She carefully measured her favorite local *crianza rioja*, triple sec and brandy, added them to the pitcher and poured herself a glass that she topped off with soda water for the fizz that made it special.

"Ahhh," she sighed as she took the first sip. "My first sangria in this lovely apartment. And a fine one, if I do say so myself!"

♦

As soon as the stock market closed, Joseph rushed away from work and sped across Madrid for his first Monday appointment with Gia. Soon he was knocking on her door.

She opened the door. "But you have a key."

"Hello to you, too. Does that mean I have permission to just walk right in every Monday evening?" He set down his bag, took her face in his and kissed her lingeringly on both cheeks. And when he pulled away, he grinned.

"That's why you have a key."

He took a deep breath of her perfume. "You smell delightful, and you look incredible!"

Gia stepped back with a big smile. "Why, thank you, kind sir! You don't look half bad yourself. Here, let me help you." She stepped behind him and helped him take off his coat and hung it alongside hers on a hook in the foyer. He set his bag below it.

"Your suit, tie and overcoat—they're such a contrast to your jeans and leather jacket from last week. I think I kinda prefer the casual look for you."

"Let me take care of that." He took his bag and stepped into the powder room to change.

Gia went to the bar. "Do you drink sangria?" she called out to him.

"Not on your life!" Joseph exclaimed in mock horror, as he came back into the room, hung his suit up with his coat and set his bag back below it.

He came over and stood next to Gia and bumped his hip into hers. "Oh, that's much more you," she said, looking at him. She giggled. "Let me get you a *Cerveza la Cibeles.*"

"You knew that all along, you sly wench! I'll have the pale ale if you have it. What am I saying? Of course you do, since Sal stocked the bar." They both laughed. She handed him the bottle, and he took a swig.

"Let's get business out of the way so we can concentrate on pleasure afterwards!" She picked up her drink and leather-bound calendar and motioned toward the sofa, smiling. "The spring festival. How do you celebrate it?" Gia sat down and tucked one foot under her, touched him on the shoulder and thought briefly about her new lingerie.

She asked Joseph more detailed questions about the event. "Where do you go? What do you do?"

"Instead of the parades and street parties, we'll do a pub crawl with my fellow traders and their dates or wives. It's always an adventure!"

She paused and then asked, "But what about Raul and Sal? Don't you celebrate with your best friends?"

"They hate the whole crowded pub scene. They are such snobs!" He laughed. "The pubs are packed and loud and rowdy, and I love it, so I'm on my own."

"Okay," Gia nodded. "What do I wear?"

"For what?" He poked her in the side and leered at her in mock lechery.

She giggled. "For the pub crawl, you goof," and she nudged him back.

"Jeans and t-shirt. Super casual. What you have on is perfect, but you'll need some shoes," he laughed. "And a jacket. Be prepared for a long night." Joseph wiggled his eyebrows. Gia giggled, excited about her opportunity to experience Madrid's nightlife and about sharing it with Joseph.

They chatted about the upcoming celebration, and then she touched Joseph lightly on the leg and stood up and took his hand. "Come on, help me with dinner. A meal is about family, and everyone's involved with the prep and the clean-up afterwards."

"So, I'm just family now?"

"Family, meaning you need to help me. Other than that, we'll see where the evening goes." She giggled again charmingly.

Joseph followed her. *I like her quick wit. And her giggle. She is such a lighthearted person. This is going to be even more fun than I expected!*

While they were making dinner, they laughed and joked around and shared tidbits about growing up. Their playful mood continued through dinner when they snuck food off each other's plates and then pretended to be annoyed.

After dinner, they cleaned up, deliberately bumping into and getting in the way of each other, enjoying their closeness.

Then, suddenly, Joseph looked at his watch. "Let's go out."

Gia whipped her head around. "But we can't."

Joseph smiled impishly. "No one will know. There's this great underground place where we can go to listen to all kinds of indie music. My buddy is playing there tonight. I really want to hear him."

"Buuut—"

"Raul and Sal and all their colleagues wouldn't be caught dead at this club."

"Are you sure?"

"You'll love this place. You'll see. Pleeease, just go with me." He looked at Gia with soft puppy eyes.

"But what about the contract? It says we can't go out for appointments."

Joseph leaned over, kissed her lightly on the lips and teased, "You're a coward, huh?"

"Oh no, not me," she softly whispered against his mouth as she began to respond to his kiss.

"Mmmm—" He brushed her face with the back of his hand, looked at her quizzically and raised his eyebrows, "—let's be adventurous, okay?"

"Here?" she grinned, "or out?"

Joseph grinned back. "Out—then here."

Gia couldn't resist the temptation. She replied excitedly, "What the hell. Adventure it is," and looked down at the dishes in the sink. "Those can wait."

He smiled, wiggling his eyebrows again. "Let's do it." She quickly shoved her feet into her favorite heels, pulled on a casual blazer and took a light coat from its hook by the door. Joseph grabbed her by the hand and pulled her out.

At the club, they wove their way through the tables, chairs and people to the stairwell at the back of the room. As they came down into the basement, Gia broke into a wide smile, drawn to the energy and the music. Joseph leaned in close to her and said loudly into her ear, "This is the place where almost anything can happen."

The band at the far end of the room was in mid-song. Joseph waved at people as, hand-in-hand, they wended their way through the crowded space to a small bistro table against the wall. He pulled out a chair for Gia and tossed their coats on the other. "Guard this table with your life. And don't let anyone steal my chair either. They'll grab it in a heartbeat." And off he went to get drinks.

Gia looked around, wide-eyed, as she took in the scene. She'd never been to a place like this, but somehow, she was totally comfortable. The beat was loud, the music contemporary, and she tapped her feet in time to the rhythm. She watched people coming and going from the stairs, the bar and the dance floor and laughed delightedly.

When Joseph returned, she asked, "How did you get these so quickly? That bar is packed."

"It pays to be a regular. Samantha saw me coming over, and when she's working, I always get served immediately," he smiled.

Gia felt a twinge of jealousy. *He is so hot and handsome, and he knows the bartender, and she gives him special treatment.* But then she reminded herself, *this is a contract.*

Gia turned to the table to set down her drink and pointed to the "Reserved" sign. "This was presumptuous of you," she laughed.

"I knew you would come out with me. You love adventures." Gia looked confused, and he went on, "That's a good thing, in my book."

"Oh—okay, I do love adventures. But that I would break the contract?"

"Isn't that part of the adventure?" He reached over and took her hand.

"You've got your own moves. They are just not as transparent as Sal's pickup lines."

Joseph laughed at her perceptiveness.

An older man with a grey ponytail, dressed in the ubiquitous jeans and white t-shirt worn by almost every patron, approached the table, interrupted their conversation and immediately shook Joseph's hand.

"Hey, Juan. Let me introduce my friend, Gia. Gia, this is Juan, the owner of this fabulous club."

Juan turned to her, took her hand and slowly kissed the back of it as he rubbed her palm with his thumb. "Gia, you're a beautiful friend."

Gia blushed uncomfortably. "Juan, I love your place. The music is fabulous. It makes me want to dance all night."

He turned back to Joseph, "Can you play next Monday night? Fernando canceled on me—again."

Joseph looked at Gia. She nodded vigorously, excited at the thought of coming back again the following week for their appointment. "You can count on me, Juan," he said.

"I'll let you kids get on with it." Juan kissed Gia's hand again and then shook Joseph's goodbye before gesturing toward Gia. "You need to get your *cariño* out on the dance floor."

As he walked away, Gia leaned toward Joseph. "You let him call me 'sweetie'? Really? He just met me."

"It was a compliment."

"Really? Are you serious? It doesn't sound flattering to me. It sounds degrading."

"Don't read anything into it, he calls everyone *cariño*. You need to get out more—*cariño!*" he laughed.

She laughed back. "I've never been to a club like this before. I guess I do need to get out more. I have a lot to learn." Gia could feel the beat through her whole body, teasing her to move. She jumped up, moving to the music, "Let's dance!"

She grabbed Joseph's hand as he was taking a drink. He set it down just before it spilled. "Slow down—*cariño!*"

She pulled him out of his chair and onto the dance floor. "Come on, slowpoke!"

"You're a strong little thing."

"I was raised on a farm with brothers. I'm probably stronger than you!" They both burst out laughing.

They danced until the band announced they were taking a break. Holding her hand, Joseph led Gia up to the stage and introduced her to the band members, who all greeted her with admiring looks.

"I'll be filling in next Monday for Fernando. See you then, my brothers." They all bumped fists. Joseph took Gia's hand as they walked back across the dance floor toward their table.

"You know *everyone* here."

"It's my favorite hangout."

As the evening went on, Joseph and Gia continued to dance, every now and then taking short breaks at the table.

"It's easy being with you, Joseph," she said as they danced.

He paused, leaned down and gave her a sensual kiss. She responded.

"Oh my, that was nice. I'd like another, please." They kissed again.

The band changed to a slow song. Joseph held Gia close, running his hands along her back, down onto the curve of her hips. She pressed her whole body against his. He kissed her again, more deeply this time. She broke off the kiss and whispered in Joseph's ear, "Let's get out of here."

As they walked back to the apartment, Gia shivered. "It's a bit nippy out here tonight."

"It's April out here tonight." Joseph pulled her close to him, "Let me warm you up." He maneuvered her into a doorway and kissed her as they pressed up against the wall. Their hands began to explore, and the kiss went on and on.

When they finally got back to the apartment, Gia said, "Light the fire, please. I'll be right back."

In her bathroom, nervous, giddy with excitement, a little tipsy from all the alcohol she'd consumed, she put on her new negligee and quickly checked her hair and makeup. She came out slowly and a little shyly and went over to Joseph, who'd made himself comfortable in front of the fireplace.

She looked around. "How romantic, you lit the fire—and candles, too."

Joseph nodded, "Mmmm-hmmm." He stood up, handed Gia a glass of wine and said in a voice hoarse with desire, "Here's to how amazing you look. I want to be with you."

"Is that the alcohol speaking?" Gia teased, as they both took a sip.

"Oh no, we danced too much for me to be drunk."

Gia giggled and took another, larger sip.

Joseph took both glasses and set them on the table at the end of the couch.

"You give, and then you take away?"

"Oh—I'll give again, *cariño*," and he pulled Gia close against him and kissed her passionately.

He stepped back. "You look lovely in this, but—" He slipped the straps off her shoulders. "—you look even lovelier like this."

As the satin gown slid to the floor, Gia giggled, and she whispered, her fingers at his waist, "And yours—they need to come off, too."

In the morning, Gia got up extra early, slowly drew the huge glass-paneled doors to the kitchen closed, finished cleaning up the debris from dinner and then got ready for work while Joseph snored very softly on the couch. *Last night was so much fun!* she thought. *We didn't even make it to bed. What a wonderful surprise.*

Before she left, Gia fixed Joseph an *ensaimada*, a plate of fruit and juice. She carefully placed the tray on the coffee table with a note, *"Hope you enjoy this as much as I enjoyed you last night,"* and tiptoed out of the apartment with a grin on her face.

♦

Later that day, at precisely five p.m., Gia heard Sal's key in the door.

Well, he's prompt for his appointment, isn't he? I wonder if he's looking forward to it as much as I am.

Sal walked in and dropped a box on a chair in the living room. He playfully called out, "Minx? Where are you?"—silence.

He looked toward the bedroom and chuckled as he saw the trail of rose petals that disappeared around the corner. "Is she trying to seduce me?" he said to himself quietly.

Gia lay in the big bed with the covers pulled almost to her neck and her dark hair spread carefully, artfully, casually across the pillows. She listened to him slowly removing his clothes in the living room—the thud as he dropped his shoes, the clink of his belt buckle, the rustle of his shirt and pants.

Why is he taking so long? This waiting is killing me!

Following the petals, Sal strolled slowly into the bedroom, wearing nothing but a smile. Their eyes met, he winked at her, and her breath quickened as he crossed the room.

At last, he arrived at the bed. He stood, looking down at her, his eyes half-closed, a smile tugging at the corners of his mouth. He slowly pulled back the covers with one hand to reveal Gia lying there in a sheer negligee. He raised his eyebrows, cocked his head to one side, appraising her, and let out a long breath. He lifted his other hand and let the coral rose petals he'd picked up on his way in drift down onto her, one by one.

She stretched with a long, contented sigh, "Mmmm."

Sal lightly touched her face and gently stroked his fingers over her nipples. He paused to watch them harden in excitement. Then he trailed his fingers between her breasts, down her belly— Gia reached over and eagerly reacquainted herself with the Beast.

Later, as they lay catching their breath, Sal said softly in Gia's ear, "I have something for you, Minx."

"Ahhh, again—so soon?" She slid her hand under the covers and down his chest while she nuzzled his neck.

Sal took her hand and kissed her fingers one by one. He laughed lightly. "No, Minx, not yet. I have a gift for you, and it's in the living room." He swung his legs out of bed, and Gia watched his self-confident little strut with pleasure as he left the room. He came back in, a large white box tied with a coral bow balanced on his hands and set it on the bed beside her.

"Oh, I love prezzies," she giggled as she sat up and untied the ribbons and let them fall to the bed. Gia lifted the top, pulled back the tissue paper and saw a beautiful robe nestled inside. "Ooooh," she said in delight, stroking the pale apricot velvet with her hand. "It feels divine."

I'm glad I didn't buy one last week on my shopping spree, she thought with a little giggle.

She lifted it from the box and raised the velvet to her cheek. She turned to look at Sal. "This is sooo lovely. This is the sweetest gift I've ever received," and thought to herself, *I could get very spoiled by this man.*

Sal pulled her to her feet and wrapped her in the robe and led her by the hand into the living room. He lit the fire while Gia curled up on a chair and admired his beautiful naked body. They chatted about their upcoming dates as he got dressed, and then he walked over to the bar and poured her a glass of rich red wine. He handed it to her and said, "I need to run, Minx." He gave her another long kiss that left her heart pounding, her body already wanting him again. As he drew away, he said, "See you next time." He picked up his coat from the chair, and just before he walked out the door, he turned and gave her one final wink.

Gia was astounded by his quick departure and said out loud, "Just like last week. I wonder what that's about?" After a moment, Gia reminded herself, "This is a contract, not a relationship. But I wonder if it will be like this every time?"

♦

Raul peered through the fogged-up windshield and rubbed it again to clear a spot to see through as he drove from the hospital to Gia's apartment. Work had been particularly hectic that day, and the pouring rain had snarled traffic beyond belief. Fortunately, Gia had sounded okay about it when he called to let her know he was running late.

As he pulled up to the building, he said, "Thank goodness Sal had the foresight to dig out below the building and put in a garage for the owners. At least I won't be soaked again on top of everything else."

Raul smiled as he thought again about their brief conversation, how she wasn't at all irritated that he'd been delayed, how easy it was talking to her. He was looking forward to getting to know Gia better, but still, he wondered about the evening ahead. He wondered what their relationship would be like. He already knew she was beautiful, articulate and strong-willed.

Gia opened the door when he knocked and looked at him quizzically. "Why didn't you use your key?"

"I knocked because I respect you. I'll always knock."

"Always?" She smiled at him a little shyly.

"Yes, this is your home, not mine," he replied. "I wanted to stop and get you flowers, but—" he gestured at his raincoat that was still wet from his walk from the hospital to his car. "Weather—"

"How kind, but that's not necessary," she said.

He took off his coat and hung it on a hook to the left of the door. Gia noticed how careful he was not to let his wet coat touch any of hers.

He gave her a kiss on each cheek, and Gia hugged him in response. Surprised, Raul hugged her back. As she pulled away, Gia said, "You give good hugs—yum—you smell nice, too."

She held out her hand. "I was in the kitchen making dinner for us. Come. Help me."

"Well I'm no cook, but I can certainly follow instructions."

"That works. You can be my sous chef." They both laughed. She tucked her arm into his, and they walked into the kitchen together.

"Help yourself to some wine and top my glass off while you're at it, please."

He looked at the label and read out loud. "'Ten-year-old *Rioja Gran Reserva*, aged in Hungarian oak.' Good choice."

"You know Sal. In fact, another carton of alcohol was delivered this afternoon. I don't know what he thinks I am, a lush or something?" They both laughed again.

"I thought you would be drinking sangria."

"I like to enjoy it as an afternoon drink or when I go out. Besides, I don't have all the ingredients, and it's not worth making it if you can't make it right."

"All the ingredients?" he laughed as he pointed to the fully stocked bar in the living room.

"I don't have all the fresh fruit that goes into a sangria, a real sangria."

Raul nodded. "I don't know enough about it to know what's real or not. Perhaps you could educate me some time."

They made dinner together, Gia giving orders and Raul obediently following her instructions.

"This reminds me of being in the kitchen with my mom and sisters. They just bark orders," he said humorously.

Gia smiled and teased, "I hope you're not looking at me like I'm your mother."

"Oh, no, you are definitely NOT my mother," he laughed.

"How many sisters do you have?"

"Two older and one younger."

"Any brothers?"

"You know my brothers, Joseph and Sal." He looked at her and grinned. "I'm the only boy."

"And I'm the only girl, with eight older brothers. Do you ever miss the traditions and chaos of a big family?"

"Absolutely." They smiled companionably at one another across their cutting boards.

Gia's mind wandered. *He loves to be in the kitchen—he is so easy to talk to—he has such a great smile—too bad he's not available.*

After a moment, Raul said, "Family dynamics are always—interesting."

"Secrets?"

"Of course. My family has always condemned people who live a gay lifestyle. And my dad died without ever really knowing who or what I was."

"Will you tell your mom and sisters now that your dad is gone?"

"I don't know what I'm going to do. Tell them? I want to. I'm so tired of hiding it, but if I do, they might reject me. I have to figure out if I'm strong enough to deal with rejection from my family."

"That must be so difficult, Raul." Gia walked around the island and gave him a hug.

Raul hugged her back, resting his cheek on top of her head. She was the first person on earth who knew his dilemma. Her simple acceptance and her lack of judgment was so comforting.

Gia realized how difficult this conversation was for him. As she walked back to her cutting board, she changed the subject. "Carlos, the youngest of my brothers, and I are four years apart and then there is a gap of seven years between us and our older brothers. We were almost a separate family and much closer to each other than to them. We told each other everything. He would cover for me when I sneaked out to meet my boyfriend, Pierre, after school. I just got off the phone with him before you got here."

As Gia said this, she turned to the stove so Raul couldn't see her face. She turned on the burner and poured a little olive oil into the pan. After a few minutes, as it began to shimmer, she asked Raul to bring over the vegetables he'd chopped.

With serving dishes and the bottle of wine in front of them and soft music playing in the background, they sat at one end of the dining room table, listening to the rain blowing against the French doors as their conversation flowed easily, shifting back and forth between lighthearted and serious.

As dinner wound to a close and they finished the bottle of wine, Raul asked suddenly, "What's bothering you?"

"What do you mean?" Gia asked, caught off guard.

"I've noticed that occasionally this evening, your mind seemed to wander off to some sad place."

Gia's eyes welled up. "I'd hoped you wouldn't notice—" she sniffled. "The phone call with Carlos earlier was not good news. I'm so sad for him. His wife was killed this afternoon. She was crossing the street when a scooter—a Vespa—just came out of nowhere, didn't see her in time and—and plowed into her. The four of us—the two of them and my boyfriend and I—grew up together. I can't believe she's gone. I'm so sad for my brother. He's devastated. And I can't be there for him.

"I don't even know if I'll go to the funeral." Gia explained her complicated relationship with her dad. "I sneaked away without saying goodbye, and I haven't spoken to him since then. He doesn't treat me like an adult, and if I go back, I'm afraid he'll try to pressure me to get married. So, I'm not sure I should go to my sister-in-law's funeral if I'm going to have to face all that on top of our families' sadness."

Raul listened quietly. "You're not thinking about what you need, Gia. You need to go because you need closure. You obviously loved your sister-in-law, and Carlos needs you."

Raul took her hand and said, motioning to the remnants of dinner, "Let's leave this, get another bottle of wine and go into the living room and talk."

"I'd like to clean up beforehand, so then I can relax and not think about the mess." Raul nodded and followed her into the kitchen, his hands full of dishes. They continued to make light conversation, Raul bringing in the remaining dirty dishes and Gia scraping the plates. She made quick work of loading the dishwasher while he cleaned the table, the stove and the counters.

Once they were done, Raul looked at her and said, "The kitchen is closed." Gia laughed.

On the way to the living room, Raul hugged Gia and kissed the top of her head. *Like a brother*, she thought, *he's so easy to be with*, and she leaned against him as though they'd known each other for a long time. *Raul is such a sensitive soul, and he's so different from the others.*

He handed Gia another glass of wine, and his hand lingered on hers in comfort. He sat on the long, low couch and pulled Gia close to him. He left his arm around her shoulders, "Are you okay?"

Gia nodded and sniffled. "Sorry I'm so full of doom and gloom." She turned toward Raul, and he tenderly wiped the tears from her cheek with his thumb.

"Doom and gloom, no, you're not. You just found out about this, so of course you're sad—it's important to go through the process of mourning. This is part of it. Ups and downs, laughter and tears, memories—"

They sat close together in companionable silence. Then Raul motioned to the architecture books piled on the coffee table and asked, "Are you studying architecture?"

"No, I love to read anything and everything—classical fiction, novels, travel books, biographies, even newspapers—" she chuckled, "—or the back of a cereal box. But I especially love architecture. I love reading about it. I love looking at it. I want to see it all."

Raul smiled at her passion. "Speaking of architecture, I can't believe the great work Sal did on this renovation." He looked around. "He did a fabulous job modernizing the building and this apartment, but I like that he kept all these original features, like the fireplace with that antique mirror above it and those built-in bookcases on either side."

"It's hard to tell, isn't it, which parts are restored and which are new? Sal pointed out some to me, but he's tormenting me by making me guess about the others," said Gia. "I absolutely love this building and this apartment."

Their conversation meandered across books that they had read, food they liked, places Raul had visited for medical conferences.

"I've only traveled a little and only in Spain, but I've read so much about other places, and someday, I want to explore them all," said Gia earnestly. "Someday, I intend to visit all those wonderful places."

Raul picked up the bottle, tipped it to the side and, seeing that it was empty, looked at Gia and smiled. "Do you have to work tomorrow?"

"Nope."

"Me either. Another?"

"We have all night," Gia smiled.

While Raul opened another bottle of wine, Gia excused herself, "I'll be right back."

She came back into the living room and stood quietly, watching Raul who was sitting on the couch, his long, long legs stretched out, the lamplight gleaming on his dark hair, his head tipped back, his eyes half closed, so easy and relaxed.

As she walked over to join him, she paused and picked up the picture of her brother and sister-in-law she'd placed on the table next to the couch. She put a finger to her lips and then touched it to the glass. She felt her stomach clench in sadness, and she set the picture very gently back on the table.

"You're back in your sad place again."

"She died so suddenly. She was only in her twenties. I wonder if she had everything she wanted in life?"

"It's hard to say. Do you have everything you want in life?"

"Wow, that's a hard question. I love the direction my life is going right now. Getting to know the three of you, the apartment, living close to my best friend. It's all come together. I'm happy.

I'm content. I'm not longing for anything right now."

"Is this all you want in life?"

"I'm going to be able to save money to travel. See the world."

"I hadn't thought about that advantage. That'll be fun for you, but then what?"

"What more would I need?"

"A family? A career? Something that fulfills you? What do you dream about?"

Gia began to wander around the room, touching ornaments on the mantel, straightening pictures. She turned to look at Raul. "No one has ever asked me about *my* dreams. My dad never asked me. He was too busy thinking about getting me married. My mom never asked me. She was too worried about taking care of my dad and the nine of us kids. My brothers never asked. They were all too involved in their own lives. My best friend never asked. She's focused on her own career. She's ten years older than me, and sometimes it seems like she still thinks of me as just a kid. Do you really want to know?"

"Well, I'm asking you about it."

Gia sat down again next to Raul and looked at him. "I'm amazed you care. We just met."

"You're a special woman, Gia. I recognized a kindred spirit in you when we were together last week and even before that, when you defended me to Sal."

Gia moved over next to him and put her head on his shoulder. "You're a special man, a kind person."

She took a deep breath, and she let it out slowly. Then she sat up straight and turned to Raul. She waved her hands around, her voice excited, her words tumbling out. "I do have dreams, I guess. Lots of them. I think I want to be an architect. It's weird to finally say it out loud. I'm really interested in urban development, city planning. I want to make crappy places into better places to live. I want to make the world beautiful."

"Now that's a dream worth chasing."

Mari's Tour

Madrid, Spain

She paced back and forth impatiently. It was Saturday, Mari was finally back, and she'd arrive any minute. Gia had already checked her watch for the umpteenth time when she heard the buzzer at the outer door. She ran over and pressed the button to release the lock and stepped out of her apartment. The elevator was moving upward, so, so slowly. Gia stood on the landing, eagerly awaiting her friend.

When Mari exited the elevator, Gia ran over and gave her a big hug then grabbed her by the wrist and pulled her into the apartment, saying over her shoulder, "I'm so glad you're back. I missed you so much!"

"I missed you, too," she smiled.

Mari stood in the foyer with the door still open to the hallway behind her. She looked into the living room and through to the terrace, "Oh, my! Before I left, you were living in that squalid apartment, and now, you're living in the lap of luxury only five blocks from my micro-apartment!"

"But I love your apartment."

"Gia, that's not the point. How can you afford this? What happened? I was only gone three weeks. Did you rob a bank? Did you win the lottery? What's up? Seriously, how can you afford this? You're a maid, for God's sake. How can you afford it?"

"Wine first." Gia motioned toward the bar on her right in the living room. "Then a tour. You've gotta see this place."

"And then, my friend, *you* have some explaining to do."

Gia poured from an already opened bottle and handed a glass to Mari. Mari raised her eyebrows as she saw the label and then the well-stocked bar in the living room. She took a sip of her wine. "Mmmm, that's nice," and she pointed at the bar. "How can *you* afford all this?"

Gia ignored her and led the way through the living room and out the French doors onto the terrace. Mari looked around her and quietly said, "Niiiccce."

"I know, it *is* lovely, isn't it?" she said as she waved her hands at the view of Madrid. Mari looked at her, opened her mouth to ask again and, thinking better of it, just agreed, "Yes, it is lovely."

They entered the dining area through the second set of French doors. Mari crossed the open space into the kitchen, which had caught her eye immediately, "Niiiccce. We can really do some serious cooking here!"

"I know, it is lovely, isn't it? I think it's my favorite part of the apartment."

Mari looked at her, questions wrinkling her forehead, as Gia walked past her and slid open the oversized doors separating the kitchen and dining areas from the living room. She reached out to touch one of the panels. "See all these ripples in this glass? That's because these are all the original glass panes," she said as they walked through into the living room.

"The flow of this space is incredible. How clever the designer was—those doors keep the visual connection between the living room and the dining and kitchen area," said Mari.

"They are fabulous, aren't they? I'm so glad Sal kept them."

"Sal?"

Gia didn't answer.

They circled back through the living room and across the foyer toward the bedroom. Gia waved her right hand and casually said, "Oh, and there's a powder room over there."

Mari stopped and shook her head in disbelief. Gia was already waiting impatiently in the bedroom doorway. "Mari, come on in here. This is the *best* part."

Mari murmured, "The best part? I thought that was the kitchen." She entered the bedroom, glanced to the right and saw the marble bathroom. She frowned and shook her head again. Gia grabbed her by the hand to pull her farther into the room.

"This is the bedroom. Isn't it lovely and romantic?"

Mari responded impatiently, "I know it's the bedroom. I still can't figure out how you can afford it."

"And LOOK! There are more French doors that go back out to the terrace again." And through them she went.

Looking around, Mari shook her head and muttered,

"There's got to be a catch. Nothing comes for free. Is she living here with this Sal?" and followed Gia onto the terrace and then back in through the living room doors.

Finally, Mari had had enough. "Gia Delgado, we have to talk about this. Now. Sit. There!" She pointed at the couch.

Gia knew she couldn't avoid the conversation any longer and raised a hand in surrender. "Okay, okay, okay." She tucked one foot under her as she sat down in the middle of the long couch. Mari sat at the end and looked at her, waiting. Gia paused for a moment and took a deep breath. "I promised my mom I would live in a safe place, and where could I be safer than here?" She tried to figure out where to start.

Mari said sternly, "Gia?"

Gia continued, slowly backing into the story because she still hadn't figured out how to tell it. "I have a contract. So, it's all legal."

"Gia—start at the beginning," Mari said.

"Promise me you won't say anything until I'm finished?"

Mari repeated impatiently, "Gia?"

Gia gave an exaggerated sigh. "I met these three guys in your bar when you stood me up because you needed to pack for your vacation. So, I guess it's really your fault," she giggled nervously.

"My fault? Gia, what are you talking about?"

"They're childhood friends, and everyone there knows them. You probably know them."

Mari rolled her eyes and shook her head.

"They are all very busy professionals with very respectable jobs—a stockbroker, a real estate agent and a pediatrician."

"Aaaand?"

Without thinking about how it might sound to Mari, Gia shrugged, waved her hands around and said, "They needed help."

Mari tilted her head quizzically, "Exactly what kind of help?" she said, trying hard to be patient. "What have you gotten yourself into?"

Gia jumped up, turned toward Mari and stomped her foot. "Stop acting like my mother. You're only ten years older than me, and you're my best friend. So, stop acting like my mom!"

Mari reached over, pulled Gia back down onto the couch and gave her a quick hug. "Awww, Gia—just tell me what this is all about. I promised your mother I'd look out for you because you're new to Madrid."

Gia paused a moment and took a deep breath.

And after taking another deep breath, she blurted out, "I know this is going to sound ridiculous. I met these three young professionals in your bar. We got to talking about how busy they are. They don't have girlfriends they can take to their various functions—ribbon-cuttings, fundraisers, department dinners, you know. They just need a date from time to time."

Mari motioned around the room, "And this—?"

Gia gulped. "And I've agreed to be their date, and if we want, I'll sleep with them at their allotted appointment times."

"WHAT? Appointment times? Sleep with them? And what about this?" She gestured around the room again.

"It's no different than dating three guys at the same time and sleeping with them."

Mari thought, *Well I've done that,* and said, "Ooookay, that's a valid point, but what about this?"

"We have a contract. They want to take care of me. And one of the guys owns the building. He renovated it, and didn't he do a fabulous job keeping the charm?"

"Yes, he did, but what are YOU doing here?"

"It's better than that crappy old apartment. This is a good neighborhood. The shops are great. It's closer to work, it's close to you. The men love it here. I couldn't entertain them in that awful old place!"

Mari finally pieced it together. She said slowly, "Sooo, you're sleeping with them, and in return, you live here?"

"Yes."

"Do you pay rent?"

"Nooo—and they give me a stipend for clothes so I'll look nice at the events I'll be attending with them."

"And you're okay with being a kept woman?"

"We're all adults. It meets our needs, and we wrote everything down in the contract. Not to mention, I can save almost all my money, which I never could before."

"Saving money is good. But a contract? What's in this contract?" *This is weird, but she is an adult,* Mari thought. *She's eighteen years old—she has to make her own choices and her own mistakes—and she seems to have thought this through—I'll just have to keep an eye on her.*

Gia smiled in relief that the hardest part of their conversation was over, and while it hadn't gone smoothly, at least she hadn't botched it too badly. And Mari finally seemed to be on board.

"All the important stuff is in it." Gia picked up the contract from the coffee table while Mari stood up to turn on the lamp at the end of the couch. She sat down close to Gia, and they leaned against each other and read through it together.

Afterward, Mari said, "Well, this is the most unusual contract I've ever heard of, but I'm impressed with the detail and particularly that you put in there that I need to know everything for your protection. I just hope this isn't long term." Mari began to relax about the arrangement.

"It's what I need right now, and you saw the trial period." Gia smiled, happy that Mari finally got it. "The guys are so handsome," she sighed.

"All the best features of Spanish men?" They both laughed.

"Definitely. They all have black hair and black eyes."

"Of course."

"Raul is the tallest, and Sal is the shortest. Joseph plays guitar in a band that plays all sorts of music, including flamenco. I went with Joseph to this amazing indie music club to hear them play. They were awesome."

I'm pretty sure I know these guys, Mari thought, *but I'll wait to bring that up.*

"And he likes bullfights, but I told him I'm not interested in watching bulls being tormented." Gia made a little face of disgust at the idea. "Joseph's a trader and looks hot in his business suit. And Sal wears tight jeans and a leather jacket and makes me laugh. He looks fabulous with clothes and without. I could easily fall for him."

"Too much information, my friend," and they laughed.

"Raul is the pediatrician and loves kids. He asks me really

hard questions about what I want to do with my life." Gia took a quick sip of her wine.

"What do you think about that? He could be good for you."

"Well, you know me. I don't like all those hard questions. I like to be in the here and now. I'm not so much into that long-term stuff. Raul and I had a wonderful evening, even though I was really sad about my brother's wife dying."

"I know—I'm so sorry—"

"I found out about it on Thursday, just before Raul came over."

"Oh, Gia, I'm so sorry." She reached over and took Gia's hand in hers and squeezed it.

"Yes, and that's why I was so sad when Raul was here for his appointment. He was so kind and gentle. He understood that it was a tough time for me."

"Are you going to the funeral since your dad's probably going to be there?"

"Raul and I talked about that, and he convinced me I should go."

"Right answer," said Mari and thought, *Raul could be a good boyfriend for Gia. Maybe even more. Get her thinking more about her future. I know her too well. Being a maid is not a job that will make her happy in the long term.*

"I leave Monday, and I'll be back Friday. I've had to cancel my appointments and take time off work. It will be a tough trip in so many ways. Carlos is devastated, and I'm sure there'll either be drama or a cold shoulder from my dad, since I left without saying goodbye. But it'll be wonderful to see my mother. I miss her so!" She paused for a moment and then looked at Mari with a question on her face. "How did you find out about the accident?"

"Carlos called me."

"He called—you?"

"Yes, we talk from time to time." Gia frowned. Mari noticed but continued, "Anyway, it's very sad. They were so in love with one another, even though they couldn't have children."

"What?"

"What do you mean, 'what'? I thought he told you that they

couldn't have kids. They did tests and found out that the problem is with him."

"I didn't know that," Gia said very sadly.

Mari was surprised. "You didn't? Oh no. I thought he would have told you. But he did say he wasn't telling the family about this because of your dad. Maybe he was going to tell you later. I only found out while I was in Seville, just before the accident."

"My dad would not be happy to know one of his sons couldn't have children. He's so traditional—but why would Carlos share that with you and not me?" Gia said in disappointment.

"I don't know, Gia. Maybe timing? Maybe he didn't want to admit it yet? He said he feels inadequate, so maybe he's embarrassed?"

"But I thought he and I shared everything."

The clock on the mantel struck the quarter-hour, startling Gia out of her mood. She looked at the time. "Oh, my goodness! It's almost three, and we have to meet the guys. They're expecting us at Jaime's shortly. We have to go!"

Wow, that was awkward, thought Mari, relieved by the abrupt change of subject.

As Mari and Gia walked arm in arm over to Jaime's, they talked about how nice it was that now they lived close to one another and all the things they would be able to do together.

Mari said, "Actually I think I do know 'the boys'. We've all hung out for years at Jaime's."

"The boys?" Gia giggled, "Really? Tell me what you think before we get there." She slowed down slightly and looked sideways toward Mari.

"You're right, they're really nice guys."

"What about Sal?"

"If he's the one I think you're talking about, he's a playboy, and it's all about drugs, alcohol and fun, so be careful there."

"Of course, I will. And we have a contract."

Quickly, before entering the bar, Mari asked, "Do they know about me?"

"You saw it. I put your name in the contract."

When they walked in, the boys were standing in their usual

place, next to the bar. As Gia and Mari walked through the room toward them, Joseph slapped his hand on his forehead. "Of course. Marilyn Oliver is the name in the contract, but she is the Mari we've known for years."

The other men looked over at the two women, and they all laughed.

Raul asked, "What are the odds?"

"Well, technically speaking," said Joseph, "the odds are pretty good. We all hang out here."

Sal punched Joseph on the arm and said sarcastically, "Ah, that would be no degrees of separation. This will be fun," and winked at Gia. Mari rolled her eyes.

"This is Mari, my best friend."

Mari said with a straight face, "It's nice to meet you all."

Then the boys and Mari laughed. Raul said to Gia, "We've run into each other regularly ever since she started coming here."

Mari and Gia gave each of them a "hello" kiss on the cheek. When she kissed Sal, Mari said to him quietly, "Don't break her heart."

Mari nudged Gia and gestured toward Sal with her thumb. "He's such a playboy. Watch out for this one," she smiled.

Simultaneously, Gia and Sal said, "It's just a contract," and the two of them looked at each other and laughed.

Sal continued, "I can't count the number of times Mari has turned me down."

Gia said lightly, "You've got to work on your pickup lines, Sal," and everybody laughed again.

Mari watched their banter with an amused smile on her lips. *They're a good bunch of guys. I think Gia will be okay with them.*

Sal and Gia stepped away from the group, and he took her coat off slowly. Raul turned to the bar to ask Jaime something. Mari turned her back toward the others and said quietly to Joseph. "Gia can never know about us. It was great, but it can't happen again now that you're with Gia."

Joseph grinned and wiggled his eyebrows at her, "Why not? The contract doesn't say we have to be monogamous with Gia.

Chapter Five

New Year's Eve 2004

The Bartender

Raleigh, North Carolina

The driver negotiated the final corner in Raleigh's warehouse district and approached the museum. Tracey's grandparents had purchased and renovated the building in the late nineteen seventies. From the outside, just like its neighbors, it still looked like one of the original warehouses, complete with aged red brick and large windows. But by the time it opened in nineteen eighty-four, the inside had been transformed from a dirty, neglected warehouse into a stunning art museum.

His car joined the line of limousines and town cars dropping off guests for the New Year's Eve gala. No one drove—it was an elaborate event, in the best venue with the best food and drink at any party in the city. Slowly, the car crept forward, and finally, they arrived. Tracey felt the same thrill every time he came there, a sense of pride to be part of this history and this wonderful family who had adopted him. His grandparents had built the museum out of a desire to recognize Raleigh's emerging artists and to display their work alongside that of well-known contemporary artists.

This fundraiser is the event of the holiday season, Tracey thought. *The most elite members of Raleigh society, the crème de la crème, the patrons of the arts—every year they choose to spend their New Year's Eve here, supporting this endeavor. How wonderful.*

As they stopped in front of the heavy double doors at the main entrance, his driver said, "Have a good evening, Judge Lauch."

Tracey smiled. "Thanks. I'll call you when I'm ready to leave."

A doorman approached and opened the car door. "Welcome to the Lauch Art Museum gala, Judge."

Tracey murmured his thanks as he stepped out of the car and looked approvingly at the heavy doors, decorated with massive green wreaths, each tied with an enormous silver bow. He paused at the cloakroom to check his coat and scarf, tucked the coat check in his left pocket and ran his hands over his tuxedo jacket and straightened his tie. Then he proceeded through the doorway to the grand hall that stretched from the front almost to the back of the building. He stopped again briefly to admire the scene before him, in particular, the large Chihuly glass chandeliers hanging from the rafters. They were a new purchase that year, one that he had personally overseen as a member of the board of directors. Tracey nodded his head in satisfaction.

He glanced around the room and smiled with approval. Once again, the committee had outdone itself with the holiday decorations. The same greenery that formed the wreaths on the entrance doors was wrapped in tiny twinkling lights and swagged over every large window and up the ornate railing of the grand staircase leading to the second and third floors. A dark green velvet rope blocked entry to the upper levels for the night. And nestled in the large curve of the stairs stood a majestic twenty-foot tree, sparkling with the same fairy lights that lit the holiday greenery. The glass balls on the tree shimmered in the colors of the chandeliers—greens, blues, creams and reds. Again, he nodded his approval. It was precisely as he had expected.

As Tracey moved on into the room, he began to greet the guests by name. He paused to give air kisses to the women and shake hands with the men, exchanging a few words with each before he moved on. He always admired how lovely the women looked in their long gowns and elaborate jewelry, each piece as unique as the woman wearing it. *They are like pieces of art on these festive evenings,* he thought as he moved slowly through the room.

The gala always began with a reception where the guests caught up with one another. They discussed politics and their family vacations, exchanged gossip and admired the changes to the hall and that year's holiday decorations. Waiters circled the room, balancing trays topped with glasses of champagne and sparkling water, and guests who wanted something stronger found drinks at one of the spacious room's three bars. Other waiters moved through the crowd, carrying trays of light hors d'oeuvres—tiny mushroom caps, shrimp on thin lemongrass skewers and little toasts topped with country pâté or caviar. Only the best was served here, and the guests indulged.

The muted tone of a Chinese gong sounded, and Tracey's father took his place at the front of the room. "Welcome to the Lauch Art Museum's annual fundraising gala." Everyone grew quiet and turned to face him. With a broad smile, he continued, "This is my first time hosting this event. As you know, my parents died this spring, so let's raise a glass to them and all they did to establish this wonderful art museum." He paused, lifted his glass and everyone followed suit. "This is our twenty-year anniversary, and I'm humbled to see many of the same faces in the crowd that I saw at our first event when my father made this speech. Thank you for your continued support. *You* make this museum possible." He set down his glass on the table beside him and extended his arms to clap at the crowd of two hundred people. They all joined in. Once the applause died down, he concluded, "You aren't here to listen to speeches, so I'll just welcome you all like my father did and let you get on with the festivities."

And someone in the crowd said loudly, "Please do."

After the laughter died away, he continued, "Please be seated. Dinner is being served. Dancing, of course, will follow. Again, thank you and enjoy your evening."

Tracey's mom, who had her finger on the pulse of society, had carefully arranged the seating so no one sat next to someone else with whom they were at odds or not on speaking terms. Tracey wandered up to the two tables at the front of the room reserved for his family, the board members, their guests and the mayor. He sat down in his assigned seat and noticed the empty chair next to him with no name card. He leaned over the empty chair to his mom. "Who is this seat reserved for?"

"I was hoping you would find someone to bring. It's been six months since Helen moved away. With all the dates you've been on, I had hoped you would be seeing someone by now."

"I haven't found anyone I was interested in having more than one date with. Helen and I had a special relationship. We had similar expectations about each other. I haven't found anyone since her who measures up to that."

"Sometimes, it takes more than one date to really know someone, my dear. You know, we want grandchildren. And you're already thirty-four. You can't wait forever."

In a soft voice he said, "Mom, not here." He raised his hand slightly to stop the conversation.

She took his hand, pulling him toward her as she leaned over and whispered very softly, "The mayor is single. She's beautiful. She's smart. She's available. Talk to her." She smiled and quickly pulled away, looked over at the president of the board and joined into his conversation.

Tracey sighed and took a sip of his scotch.

After a few moments, the mayor, seated on the other side of Tracey, turned to him and said, "I have to apologize. I was so preoccupied with the November elections, I haven't had a chance to congratulate you on your appointment as a family court judge. That's an amazing accomplishment for someone your age. How have your first six months been?"

"Interesting. You know, our families have known each other for a long time. So, I should have called you to congratulate you on your election. Your accomplishment is so much greater than mine."

The live band played an eclectic mix of music, and people filled the dance floor. Finally, midnight had come and gone, and after too many dances with the mayor and the wives of other patrons, as well as all the single women vying for his attention, the evening began to wind down. Tracey made his way to the bar by the front windows for a final drink before calling his driver. As he stood, gazing out at the street while he waited to be served, he overheard a guest who obviously had had too much to drink. "I cannot believe I've had to pay for drinks after I paid fifteen hundred dollars for this event."

Tracey put his hand on the gentleman's shoulder and said in a slightly condescending tone, "This must be your first gala."

Surprised, the guest turned around quickly. "Yes, it is. How do you know?"

Tracey shook his hand and said, "I'm Judge Tracey Lauch, and my family hosts this event every year. I've been coming here since I was fourteen years old when my grandparents opened this museum. The donation for dinner is, in part, what runs this place and allows Raleigh to have another museum to celebrate the arts and local artists." Tracey gestured around the room with a well-manicured hand. "Please know we appreciate your contribution and participation in this fine event—the liquor is worth the price alone. It's only the best. And all the profits from the sales of alcohol are also donated to the museum." He reached out to shake hands with the guest. "I look forward to seeing you at these events for many years to come."

Tracey smiled and thought, *Only the wealthiest would complain about having to pay for booze at an event like this.*

He turned to the bartender when the obnoxious guest had left. She smiled as she recognized Tracey and mouthed, "Thank you." And then she said, "Your usual, Judge?"

"Yes, please, Zoe."

She poured his cognac into a large snifter and leaned over to place it in front of him, her low-cut dress showing off her deep cleavage.

He paid her. "I'm so sorry I don't have anything smaller."

"For you, it's not a problem—Judge." Zoe smiled flirtatiously at him.

Tracey smiled back and watched the attractive, thirty-something, red-headed bartender lightly swinging her hips as she walked away in her form-fitting black dress. At the register, while she was making his change, she was distracted by another guest who wanted a drink—now.

When Zoe finally returned, she began to count out his change. Suddenly, she realized she was short. "I'm so sorry, I'm so sorry, I'm so sorry," she jabbered nervously and grasped her hair, twisting it, pulling it to the back of her neck. "I'll be right back. Please excuse me."

Excuse me, he repeated to himself. *Excuse me.*

She spun around quickly to get his additional change, and as Tracey watched her, he felt a tightening in his groin. And then he calmly finished his drink and went back to say goodbye to his parents and the other guests.

He slipped on his coat, scarf and gloves, stepped outside into the cold air and called his driver to cancel his return car home.

Then he stood and waited for Zoe to leave.

♦

Tracey looked around the cold, poorly lit parking garage as he followed quietly behind the bartender. No one was there, all the cars were gone from that level. He moved closer and then reached out. One hand covering her nose and mouth, the other around her throat.

His heart pounded, his breathing was shallow and rapid. Zoe drew a final ragged breath, and then he laid her on the ground in front of him. He looked down at her sadly. *You look so much like my mother,* he thought. He looked around again. No one was there. Like a lover, he gently pushed her red hair back from her face and removed one of her dangling rhinestone earrings. He looked down at her one final time.

This time was different. This time I planned to kill her. This time I waited for her. This time, I followed her. Then I killed her. Now I've killed three women. What's happening? I need to stop.

Chapter Six

January 2005

Mari's News

Mari waved the bottle of cava about as she entered Gia's apartment. She began to open it, and in her excitement, she twisted the cork out with a jerk. The wine frothed over onto the floor.

"Whoopsie!" Gia rushed to the kitchen for a towel to mop up while Mari just stood, watching the bubbles spill from the bottle, laughing as they ran over her fingers. Gia took the bottle and poured two glasses. "What are we celebrating?" she asked as she handed one to Mari. "It must be really special because this," she gestured to the floor, "is so not you!"

Mari's words tumbled out in excitement, "D'you remember ages ago I sent an application to Spectrum, that river cruise company? Well, they have an extremely low staff turnover, so they hardly ever need to hire, but they finally had an opening for a concierge. I can't believe it, but I got it! They didn't hire internally. I'm so glad I kept in touch with that woman in human resources because she thought of me when the position opened up. Me! My dream job! A concierge on a riverboat! Me!"

Gia took their glasses and set them on the coffee table. She threw her arms around Mari, hugging her tightly, and they jumped up and down in excitement. "I'm so happy for you! I'm so happy for you! Congratulations! That is wonderful news! Wow! Congratulations!"

Out of breath, Mari picked up her glass and noticed the bowl of vibrant pomegranate flowers on the coffee table. "Oh, my favorites!"

"Of course. Except for coral roses," Gia said, shyly thinking of Sal, "they've become mine, too, because they always make me think of you. I'm so happy for you, Mari!" Gia walked around the coffee table, sat down and patted the cushion beside her. "Come, tell me more about the job." Mari sat right next to Gia and gave her a big hug.

"Buuut I'm going to miss you so much. We've had so much fun since I moved here. You are my best friend and the sister I never had." Tears rolled, one by one, down her face.

Mari touched the tears on her cheek. "Oh, but look how far you've come this last year. You have a great apartment, a great sex life, the boys are wonderful friends and then there's your architecture program you've signed up for."

"I know, but I'm going to miss you," sniffled Gia.

"I'll miss you, too. But every chance we get, we'll see each other, I promise. I'm not going so far away, after all. As it turns out, I'll be here, in Europe."

Gia wiped her cheeks with her sleeve. "It's just that you're the reason I adjusted so well to living here, and Madrid will feel a little empty without you here."

"Ah, you're so sweet." Mari reached down, pulled Gia's feet onto her lap and began to give them a slow, satisfying massage. "But you'll still have the boys." She smiled at her.

Gia gave Mari a watery smile. "But they are boys," and they both laughed. She wiggled her toes. "Ooooh, that feels so good. You always give the best foot massages. I'll miss those, too."

The two women sipped their wine, lost in their own thoughts. And then the architecture books on the coffee table caught Mari's eye. "So, have you started your course yet?"

"It starts Wednesday night. I can't believe I'm going back to school. I never thought I'd be a university student. I was perfectly content to be a maid forever and just enjoy life and live in the moment."

"Dreams and goals. Raul helped you think beyond today."

"He's been a wonderful friend and mentor. He's been so good at asking questions and helping me figure out my goals, what I really want to do with my future, and then we talk about the steps I need to take to get there. The whole process has been so much fun. And we're so relaxed, it's like hanging with my brother. I just love my time with him. Did I ever tell you that he was married, while he was still in med school?"

"Really?" Mari stopped rubbing her feet and looked at Gia with her eyebrows raised.

"Oh, don't stop!" She wiggled her toes again. "But it didn't last long, and they were divorced before he finished his program.

He said he could never get close to her. He had an internal struggle with himself all his life about not wanting a girlfriend, not even feeling particularly attracted to women. He said when he admitted to me that he's gay, he felt so relieved to be able to talk about it with someone. But he is still very guarded about his lifestyle."

"I don't blame him. I know his family would be devastated, and that's why he doesn't visit them very often and always asks Joseph how his mom is instead."

"I know how hard it's been for Raul to accept it himself, much less to admit it to anyone else, even to us. And as a doctor who wants to be head of pediatrics at the hospital here in Madrid, I can understand why he felt the need for such secrecy. But now he has David, who's really special. I'm so happy for him," Gia said.

Mari nodded her head in agreement.

"Raul told me that David loves his charm, and Raul really loves David's impish, outgoing personality. Apparently, he's quite a practical joker. He says they are the perfect match."

"But Raul is so private. I would never have known he was gay if you hadn't told me. I can't imagine him ever coming out publicly."

"Raul says David understands his desire for privacy. But he still pushes Raul to get out of his comfort zone," Gia went on. "I really hope I get to meet him someday soon."

"Me, too. At least Raul can meet up with David at medical conferences outside Spain. Hmmm, I wonder when he'll finally tell the other boys?" Mari said.

"I dunno. That's going to be a hard one for him."

As they sat there comfortably, sipping their bubbly, Mari suddenly sat straight up. "I just had this fabulous idea!"

Gia pulled her feet off Mari's lap and sat up cross-legged, "What?"

"Since Raul and David have only been able to meet at conferences, why don't you and Raul cruise with me—the other boys still think you are sleeping with him, so the two of you going on vacation at the same time wouldn't seem unusual, and then Raul can meet up with David on the boat. They've been 'dating'," she made air quotes with her fingers, "for a year, and they haven't had any vacations or spent a significant amount of time together. And you, my friend, haven't traveled much at all. You need more adventures."

"Like this contract with the boys hasn't been enough of an adventure?" Gia grinned and raised her eyebrows at Mari. "But the idea of traveling is pretty exciting. I think you may be onto something. And it would be my vacation after all." And then, as she and Mari giggled and planned the trip and finished off the bottle of wine, they heard a key in the door.

Sal entered, and they stopped their conversation abruptly. They both jumped up from the couch, and Gia said, "Oh, my goodness, I completely lost track of time. Mari and I were just celebrating her good news. She has a new job working as a concierge for the Spectrum River Cruise Line! Isn't that fabulous!?!"

Sal gave Mari a hug. "Congratulations. I'd say that this calls for a drink," Mari and Gia looked guiltily at the empty bottle and giggled, "but I see you've already started. I think I'll join you." He walked over to the bar and opened another bottle.

Mari put up her hand. "No more for this girl. I've probably had enough for now since I had no lunch." She put on her coat. "I'm off." She gave Gia a quick hug and waved at Sal. And as she closed the door, she said, with a wicked laugh, "Have fun, you two!"

As soon as the door closed, Sal grabbed Gia around the waist, lifted her up and twirled around in a circle. Gia giggled. As he set her down, he said, "Grab your glass, Minx, and follow me," as he picked up the fresh bottle and a glass for himself from the bar and headed into the bedroom.

118

Chapter Seven

March 2005

Tensions

The pungent smell of marijuana wafted up the stairs. Gia wrinkled her nose as she walked down into the bar. *How can people smoke that stuff? The smell is as overpowering as cigarette smoke,* she thought, pausing at the bottom of the steps and glancing around for Joseph. She noticed that their usual table was available and went over quickly to drop her coat on one of the chairs.

"Hello, *cariño*, where have you been?" Juan took her hand in his and raised it to kiss her fingers. He stroked her palm as he always did. Gia had to struggle not to pull her hand away. She knew it was just the way he was, a little too touchy-feely, a little too close and personal. He was like this with all the women, young and old, but nonetheless, it made her uncomfortable.

"I've been pretty busy, so Joseph has had to come without me." *But the truth is, he's been avoiding me lately, and I'm here to find out why,* she thought. She smiled, "It's so nice to see you again, Juan."

"Whenever you're not here, I miss you."

"Juan, you're such a flatterer. Look at all the women here."

"But you are my only *cariño*."

"Awww, aren't you the sweetheart?"

Samantha called out from the bustling bar, raising her voice to be heard over the din, and beckoned at Juan. "I have to go, but I'll bring your drink right over. The usual?"

"Yes, please."

They kissed each other on the cheek. Gia remained standing alone by the table and watched Joseph play his guitar with the band.

After Juan dropped off her drink, she sat and sipped it slowly and watched the people out on the floor, dancing. Her eyes drifted back to the band. *He is so handsome and so talented,* she thought. *And this is where he's happiest, up there with the band, playing his heart out. Everyone loves their music. I wish I still made him that happy.*

One of the patrons approached and took Gia's hand, pulling her onto the dance floor. During the past year, she'd found a few regulars to dance with whenever Joseph was performing. Coming there had always been such fun, but that night, even when she was dancing, somehow, it felt different.

After a few songs, the band took a break. Joseph glanced at Gia and quickly slid his eyes on past her. And when he stepped away from the band, instead of coming over to greet her, he went up to the bar for a drink. When Juan tapped him on the shoulder and motioned toward her, Joseph lowered his head and shook it. Gia watched him impatiently as he turned to talk to Samantha again.

Will he come over here tonight or just ignore me? She tapped her fingers on the table.

Finally, just minutes before the break ended, drink in hand, Joseph came over slowly. *Reluctantly?* she wondered, irritated by his behavior.

"Hi, Gia."

"Nice of you to come by," she said in a voice heavy with sarcasm.

"What's up?"

"I think that's my line. We need to talk." She kicked her foot against the table leg in frustration.

"You know I'm working here. I can't just stop and talk."

"Of course, I'm not that naive. It's obvious you're working." Joseph looked away and took a sip of his drink before turning back toward her. "How long do you plan to stay here tonight?"

"Until the end of your gig. Then we'll go somewhere to talk." She stuck her chin up in the air and narrowed her eyes slightly.

"So, you're just going to sit here and wait for another couple of hours?"

She glared at him. "No. I'm going to dance and drink and have fun. I'm going to enjoy myself. We'll talk when you're done."

"Talk? Whatever—I have to go." Joseph spun around and walked away.

How dare he?

As Gia stewed, another regular stopped by and dropped into the empty chair. "So, Joseph didn't look too happy. What's going on?"

"It's not a big deal. Just a little misunderstanding between us. We'll work it out."

The two women chatted for a while before they got up to dance with each other. *Dancing is a good distraction,* thought Gia.

At the end of the evening, she watched Joseph pack up his equipment. She noticed how very slowly he was going through his usual routine, one that normally took only minutes. And once he stepped off the stage, he stopped and chatted with a few people and then a few more before he finally came over to the table.

"You've avoided this—and me for too long now. Let's go." Joseph raised his eyebrows at her curt tone.

They went around the corner to a little bar and found a quiet table where they could talk. Joseph ordered a bottle of local red wine. They hadn't exchanged a single word on the walk over. Gia finally said, "So, you're drinking wine now?"

"I know you love wine."

"Why do you care about me now?" she said bitterly.

"Gia, if we're going to talk, let's do it in a civilized way."

"So now you want to talk?"

His voice became heated. "Give me a break, will you?"

"You have been frustrating the hell out of me, you know."

He was astounded by the ferociousness in her tone. "What's so frustrating?"

"For months now, you've been canceling our appointments. You blew me off again last week, and it was your birthday. I'd even made your favorite brownies. And I thought we would be doing your St. Paddy's Day pub crawl."

"Well, I've been busy, you know," he said sullenly.

"Come on, we've gone from seeing each other every week since last April. Going out dancing, having fun, having great sex. And then, out of the blue, in the new year, you've become distant and then canceled appointment after appointment with me. Something is up, and I deserve to know."

"The contract didn't say we had to keep our appointments. So, what's the problem?"

"Argh—the contract doesn't excuse your rude, insensitive behavior."

"Gia, we had a lot of fun, but I don't owe you anything."

"Respect, Joseph. You owe me respect. I'm a human being, and I thought we were friends." Gia's eyes welled up.

"Gia, I don't want to hurt you."

"You already have."

Joseph's head jerked as though she had slapped him across the face. He reached over and took her hand and held it between his. He gazed into his drink for a moment and then looked back at her with a solemn expression on his face. "I never ever meant to hurt you. You don't deserve that."

"Then please, tell me what I did wrong. Why you're treating me like this."

"Oh, shit. You haven't done anything wrong. You're wonderful."

"Yeah, right. Wonderful enough to be ignored." Gia wiped away her tears with the back of her free hand.

Joseph took a huge breath and exhaled slowly. He was still holding Gia's hand and looked away, thinking before he replied, "Gia, I've met a girl."

"And you didn't think you should tell me?"

"I wanted to, so many times, but I didn't know how."

"What's her name?"

"Anusha."

"How long have you been with her?"

"We just started dating last week."

"But you've been ignoring me for ages."

"She and I have been friends for about a year. And then a few of months ago, I realized I have really strong feelings for her. Our dating is a secret. Her parents—or her father, I should say—are very traditional, and while they support her having a university education, even getting her doctorate, they want her to marry a Muslim. So only a few people know we are dating."

"Okay. How come I'm not one of those 'few people'?" she said angrily.

"Gia! Please—stop beating me up. You're right, I should have told you. I'm sorry. But I'm telling you now."

Gia nodded at him, stony-faced, and Joseph went on,

"Anyway, Anusha has three brothers. Yani's a doctor. He works with Raul, and he agrees with her parents that she should only marry within their faith. Her second brother, Ahmed, does chemical research. He's very open-minded and believes that Anusha should pick her own husband, regardless of religious beliefs. Her third brother, Haidar, is a professor at the university. He knows about us, and he agrees with Ahmed."

"So, Anusha is comfortable defying her parents and dating you?"

"Yes, she is. And Haidar not only supports us dating, he even drops her at the library to 'study' on Saturdays."

"Okay."

"So, we can do pretty much what we want as long as we stay on campus."

"Have you slept with her?"

"I haven't slept with anyone since you and I were together just after the new year," Joseph said with a wry little twist to his mouth.

"Why did you stop sleeping with me?"

Joseph finally opened up. "She is so special to me, Gia—not that you're not special. Oh, shit. How do I say this? I've never felt this way about anyone. Please understand—this is so different for me. I think I want to spend the rest of my life with her. Things between you and me were always great, from that very first night. We always had so much fun—we're such good friends, and I hope we'll *always* be friends. You are a wonderful woman."

Gia looked away. Her face crumpled, and tears streamed down her cheeks. "I'm glad you finally told me this. I wish you and Anusha all the best. However, I have to tell you I'm hurting. I'm hurting. I need to think about all of this—I need to figure it out. I'm going home." She stood up abruptly and began to put her coat on.

"I'll walk you to your apartment." Joseph dropped some money on the table, and they departed without another word.

They walked slowly toward Gia's apartment, and she said sadly, "I'm going to miss you, Joseph."

"But we'll still see each other when we go to functions

together."

"What? Functions?"

"I know it's asking a lot, but I can't take Anusha to work functions because no one can know we're together."

"So, you expect *me* to do that?"

Joseph stopped and faced Gia, taking hold of her by the shoulders. "If you don't want to, if you want me to back out of the contract, I'll respect that. But I would love to see you—as friends. I don't want to lose that. Am I asking too much?"

"It's part of the contract, so let me think about it," Gia said as Joseph kissed her forehead.

She met his eyes and leaned in to kiss him. She was so close that Joseph could feel her breath on his lips when he caught her face between his hands and moved her away gently. "I can't."

"You must really love this woman," Gia said softly.

"She's the one."

Gia hesitated before she silently slipped her hand into the crook of his arm. Joseph smiled at her gesture, covered her hand with his, and they turned to walk on to the apartment together.

Gia unlocked her apartment door, stepped inside and leaned against it. She felt lost and lonely, and she inhaled shakily, willing herself not to cry again. Then she went into her kitchen and made herself a cup of tea. She put her drink and one of the brownies she'd made for Joseph on a tray. "Well, I have all these to myself now," and she went out to sit on the dark terrace. She put a piece of the brownie into her mouth. "I wish I were sharing them."

It was unusually warm for March. Gia laid her head back and snuggled under her throw and closed her eyes. She dozed, off and on, until the sky became lighter.

She sat up and grabbed her phone from the small table beside her. *Hopefully Raul's home and awake.*

"Gia, is everything alright? It's so early."

"Ra—Ra—ul. Can you come over? Now that Mari's gone, I need someone to talk to."

"Of course. Are you okay?"

"I—I guess so. I just need—someone to talk to," she said in a small, sad voice.

"Okay. I'm on my way. I'll be right there. And I'll pick up some pastries from the bakery—"

"Let yourself in when you get here." She went inside and washed her face and brushed her teeth and looked at her negligee, hanging hopefully on the back of the door as it had for so many Mondays. Tears welled up in her eyes and she blew her nose. *I won't cry, I won't cry,* she thought as she changed her clothes.

She was in the kitchen making coffee when she heard the door open.

"Gia, where are you?"

"I'm in the kitchen."

Raul set down the bag on the island and wrapped Gia in his arms. When he let go, he looked at her. "You've been crying. What's the matter, sweetheart?"

"Joseph broke up with me."

"He broke the contract?"

"Nooo."

"Ohhh—this sounds complicated. Let's take our coffee and pastries and sit in the living room where we can be comfortable. You can tell me the whole story."

After they sat down with their cups in their hands, Raul asked gently, "So, what happened with Joseph?"

"You're asking me to break the rules?"

"Oh, I guess I am." He drew a long, thoughtful breath and stood up to open the French doors. Looking out over the terrace, he took several more deep breaths and shivered slightly in the cool morning air, "Without Mari here, someone has to know what's going on with you. Talk to me."

"Are you really ready for me to break the rules?" she replied sadly.

Raul turned toward Gia, saw the sadness in her eyes and the anger lurking behind that. "Yes, I am. Please, tell me."

Slowly, Gia got up and wandered out of the room and into the bedroom.

When she didn't return, Raul followed her. There she lay, flat on her back, staring up at the ceiling. He walked around to the far side of the bed and lay down close to her, staring up at the beams.

After a moment, he inched his hand over, took hers and pressed it lightly, "Start at the beginning."

She gripped his hand. "Joseph has been avoiding me. He wouldn't tell me why."

"What are you talking about? Please—start from the beginning, Gia."

She turned on her side and propped herself on her elbow and looked at him. "You have to promise not to share any of this with anyone."

"Okay, I promise. It's just that it's obvious you need to talk about it."

Gia breathed in, paused and began, "Until early this year, we had an awesome time—on his appointment night, we would sneak out and go clubbing—I'd never been before, and Madrid's nightlife is so much fun. We listened to music, we laughed and danced—every week. He'd call me his *cariño*—it was so sweet— we would have our hands all over each other when we danced— the sex afterwards was fun and carefree—I would leave him breakfast in the morning before going to work. It was such a happy way to be." She paused again.

Raul thought, *This is way more than I wanted to hear*, but he stayed silent, waiting.

She looked across him toward the window and collected her thoughts. "Then one week, everything changed. We would go out, but it wasn't as much fun, he barely touched me, and he was distant—then he started to cancel—every week—without an explanation. This went on for weeks, and I had no idea why it was different—" Her voice became quieter, and she continued, "I kept asking what was going on, what was wrong, but he just ignored me."

"It is a contract, Gia," Raul said and thought, *I hate to see how he's hurt her.*

"Finally, last night, I made him tell me—it turns out he has a girlfriend. So, what did all those wonderful times mean? What was I? Nothing to him?"

"He should have been upfront and told you. But it is a contract."

"I wasn't in love with him, it's just that we had such good times, and I felt like we were so close—friends don't treat friends like that. He didn't even feel like he could tell me—that's what hurts so much."

After a pause, Raul asked, "So who is this person Joseph is dating? What's her name?"

"Anusha. They met at the library. Their dating is a secret. Her parents will only let her marry or even date a Muslim."

"Okaaay—"

"Joseph said you work with her brother, Yani."

"The pediatrician? I do—so Anusha and Joseph, huh?"

"Yeah. They can only date on campus, when her brother drops her at the library to 'study' on Saturdays."

"Okaaay—so what do you want to do?"

"I don't know." Gia closed her eyes and sighed. "You always ask the hard questions—" Raul smiled. "I don't want to walk away. I'm just hurting now because of Joseph's behavior. He didn't talk to me about it. He didn't trust me. And he wouldn't even kiss me one last time—" They lay quietly for a while. "Thank you for listening, Raul—for letting me talk it through." Gia sighed and stood up. "Come on. Let's go get some more coffee."

"And let's eat those pastries. I'm starving."

Gia brought two fresh coffees into the living room and saw Raul already shoving a soft, freshly baked *ensaimada* into his mouth. "Mmmm."

"Hey, leave some for me." She dropped down next to Raul, grabbed one from the plate and took an enormous bite. "Ooooh, I didn't realize how hungry I was."

When Raul was content, he leaned back and asked, "So, how's it going with Sal?"

"Really? You really want me to break the rules again. Twice in one morning?" They both laughed. Gia set down her half-eaten pastry and turned toward him. "Everything with Sal started the day before we all signed the contract. It was the day he showed me this place. He seduced me."

"Did he hurt you?" Raul asked in a harsh voice.

"Oh, no." She touched his arm. "It was wonderful and gentle

and funny and romantic and everything I ever wanted. It's always that way."

"Sooo?"

"I thought it was strange that he left immediately after we finished. I thought maybe it was just that day. But his 'wham, bam, thank you, ma'am' approach to sex has continued—every visit. We have sex, and he leaves—we have sex, and he leaves—and I'm sure he arrives stoned sometimes. I worry about him."

After a deep breath, she continued, "I know. I know I'm not supposed to care. It's just a contract. But contract or not, I feel like I'm just a sex object to him."

Raul muttered under his breath, "That's Sal."

The conversation went quiet.

"If you're not happy with things, with Joseph, with Sal, why don't you end the contract?"

Gia paused to think about his question. She stood and walked over to the fireplace and stood, idly rearranging things on the mantel. "I don't know. More hard questions—" Raul smiled again, and Gia turned toward him. "It never occurred to me to end it. I love the apartment and the lifestyle I have. But even more, I love our friendships, and I love each of you—for different reasons. You're my Madrid family, especially with Mari off to her new job—how could I walk away from all this?"

"But it seems like you're so unhappy. I'll always be your friend. This apartment is just a place, and you've saved enough money to get a nice place on your own."

Gia sat down on the couch again and dropped her face into her hands, sighed heavily and ran her fingers up through her hair. "Being an adult is overrated."

Raul laughed, reached over and rubbed her back, and Gia laughed, too. She turned to look at him. Her face softened. "I think I'm falling in love with Sal. It wasn't supposed to happen, I know." Her lip quivered.

Raul hugged Gia. "I guess you're a human being." Gia chuckled wryly. "So, what do you want to do?"

"I don't want to change anything—other than my expectations of Sal."

"Wow. I thought you would want to tell him you love him."

"That would drive him away, I'm sure."

"Maybe not."

"I'd have to think about that. There's no need to rush into any decisions."

"You've always been one to look before you leap, haven't you?"

"I try, but sometimes, it's hard not to act on impulse."

"Well, you didn't allow Sal to rush you into the contract, and now, despite everything, you're not prepared to let him push you to end it."

Chapter Eight

April 2005

The First Cruise

Spectrum Cruise, *The Rosé*

Seated beneath the Paris café's red-and-white striped awning with the morning sun peeking through the trees, Raul and Gia were served their breakfast by the very proper waiter in his white shirt and black waistcoat. "Au lait for *madame*, and coffee for you, *monsieur*," he said, as he put their drinks in front of them and then placed a basket of croissants between them with a flourish.

"Merci," said Raul. Meanwhile, unable to resist the temptation, Gia had already reached out to touch the fragrant buttery croissants in the basket. "Ooooh, these are still warm from the oven." She pulled a piece off of one and dunked it into her coffee. "Yum."

Raul reached under the croissant Gia had just ripped apart, took one and put it on his plate. He carefully pulled it apart and slathered it with fresh butter and homemade jam from the small glass bowls in front of them. Gia watched him. "What a sweet tooth you have."

He grinned, "Sweet tooth? I'm sweet all over, just ask David," and he took a huge bite. "Yummy is right!"

Gia laughed at him and reached over to brush a crumb from his cheek. "So, you're finally going to have a real vacation with David."

Raul smiled, his hands and mouth still full, and nodded.

"Are you as nervous as you were before your first date with him?"

He picked up his napkin to wipe his mouth and thought for a moment before answering. "Nervous, no. Excited, yes. My date with David was the first time I had been out with a man. I didn't know what to do, I didn't know what to expect, I didn't know how to behave, and we had to sneak away to avoid our colleagues at the conference. I felt like a teenager."

"I never realized he was your first date after your divorce. I thought you would have gone out with that Aussie—that hunk who tried to pick you up at the fundraiser."

"I wasn't ready for dating then," he said with a grin as he remembered how Boyd had chased after him before he went back to Melbourne.

Raul finished his pastry and licked his fingers and rubbed them around his plate, chasing the crumbs. Gia raised her eyebrows and giggled.

"I have to get every last crumb. These are fabulous, darling. Absolutely scrumptious," and they both laughed.

Gia teased, "You're channeling David now. Will I ever see you two love birds on the cruise?"

With a shy smile, Raul said, "We'll need to emerge from time to time and eat to regain our strength."

"Or you could just send out for croissants!"

"Ha, ha! Let's hope the ones on the boat are as good as these."

Gia reached over and squeezed Raul's hand fondly. "I'm so happy for you two."

As Gia finished her coffee, Raul quirked an eyebrow at her. "Ready?" When she nodded, he stood up and dropped a handful of euros on the table to cover their bill and then pulled out Gia's chair. "After you, *madame*."

"Oh, you're so polite," Gia giggled as she stood up and tucked her arm through his.

He hailed a cab and held the door for her before going around to get in on the other side. "I'm glad we'll be able to get to the boat early, so we'll have a chance to say hi to Mari before she gets too busy," he said. "I'm interested to hear how she likes her new job."

Mari was in the boat's reception area, waiting to greet passengers as they boarded. Gia saw her from the bottom of the gangplank and ran up and threw her arms around her. "Oh, I've missed you so much. How's your job? You look wonderful! Oh, and you smell wonderful, too! Where did you get that new perfume? Oh, I really missed you."

Mari laughed and hugged her and then untangled herself from Gia's arms, "I love my new job, but I miss you, too." Mari wiped a tear off Gia's face.

Then Mari turned to Raul and gave him a big hug.

"Welcome to *The Rosé*, one of our newest riverboats in the Spectrum Cruise Line," Mari continued her welcome spiel.

Gia began to giggle, and Mari smiled. "I have to tell this to all the passengers, including you."

"Bring it on. I want the whole experience," Raul smiled back at her. When she finished her welcome-to-Spectrum speech, he said, "David will be coming on board, so look out for him, please." Raul pulled out his phone and showed Mari a picture of David.

"Oooo-la-la, I'm sure I won't miss *him*! Tall, handsome, blond men never get by me."

The three of them laughed out loud. Then Mari went to the desk and came back with two keys.

Mari handed one to Gia. "This is yours. Your luggage is already in your room."

Then she turned to Raul and handed him a key. "We put David's and your luggage in here. You two are across the hall from Gia. When he arrives, I'll let him know you'll be waiting for him there."

Raul blushed. "Everyone is so casual about this."

Gia replied quickly, "It's your first time together publicly. Of course, you're uncomfortable. But just relax, we all love you, and we're here to support you and David."

They chatted for a few more minutes, and then, as more guests came on board, Mari excused herself. Gia made a comical "so-sad-you-have-to-work" face and went with Raul to look around the reception area. She pointed. "Look, they have a library. It's not very big, but I'll definitely take a closer look at what they have. Especially since I'll be on my own when you two lovebirds are otherwise engaged." She nudged Raul with a grin, and he nudged her back.

Raul looked around. "This area isn't very big. Let's move along so other guests can board. Our rooms are on the upper deck," he moved toward the wide staircase, "so let's use these stairs."

Standing in the hallway between their rooms, Gia turned to

Raul, "Let's meet for dinner in front of the dining room. That will give you time to unpack and 'greet' David properly when he arrives," she said with a sly smile. Raul blushed, and Gia continued, "Aww, sweetie, it's no different than if I were meeting my boyfriend on board." She gave him a quick peck on the cheek. "Get unpacked before David gets here. That way you can hog all the hangers and drawer space. Off you go."

♦

After all the passengers had boarded and the ship's gangplank had been pulled in, Mari went to the lounge for a quick drink. It was quiet because people were still settling into their rooms. One couple sat at the bar, leaning affectionately against each other, chatting with the bartender, and another couple sat on a loveseat by the window, deep in conversation, watching the shoreline recede as the boat got underway.

Mari walked up to the bar as Sasha, the master bartender, was telling the two passengers there, "No, I'm not working the Asian river cruises anymore. I'm here in Europe permanently now. I had the opportunity to make the change, and I jumped on it."

Sasha turned to Mari. "Whew, I'm parched," she said and reached into her pocket, pulled out a brooch and began to pin it on her lapel.

"A Perrier with lime and just a little ice?" he asked.

Mari nodded. "My favorite," she said as she fiddled with the clasp on her brooch.

The woman at the bar turned toward Mari. "Perrier's my favorite, too, and that's exactly how I drink it." She picked up her glass, tipped it toward Mari and smiled.

Sasha put down a glass in front of Mari. "Let me introduce you. Lee and Daniel Fong, this is Mari Oliver, our concierge. You probably met her when you boarded. She came to us only a few months ago." Sasha said to Mari, "Lee and Fong are two of our most loyal passengers."

Lee smiled and said, "Dear Sasha, she already knows. When she greeted us, she also knew that we travel on Spectrum every year." Mari smiled back at her.

Fong leaned forward and looked across Lee to Mari. "Everyone calls me Fong, and Spectrum Cruises feels like a second home to us. And, by the way, Sasha is also a dear friend of ours." Fong picked up his scotch in a toast to Sasha.

"How do you like working for Spectrum?" Before Mari could reply, Lee continued, "What a beautiful brooch. Is that a Schiaparelli?"

"I love working for Spectrum, and this treasure? I just found it in Paris yesterday." She fingered the brooch. "It's a piece of vintage Schiaparelli, and it was quite a steal."

Lee said, "It sounds like there's a story behind that gem. Do tell!"

"I can't believe my luck." Mari became animated as she told the story. "During my time off, I love to poke around the little shops on the Left Bank, looking for vintage jewelry and handbags. Yesterday, I came across this small pawnshop on a corner. When I went in, the pawnbroker was haggling with a young woman over the price. From the way they talked, I think they knew each other. Anyway, I heard them mention a pomegranate flower brooch, and my ears perked up because it's absolutely my favorite flower. I was intrigued to see what this brooch looked like, so I walked over and stood next to the young woman, and when I saw it was actually a perfect coral and white, enamel, pomegranate flower, I just knew I had to have it."

By then, Lee had turned her full attention to Mari and nodded and smiled as the story unfolded. Fong interjected, "You never know where you'll find a treasure."

"I know! And it gets even better! I know how this works, with pawnbrokers marking things up ridiculously. So, I asked him, 'What will you sell it to me for?' He glanced at the young woman and hesitated and then said to me, 'One hundred euros.' The young woman was outraged and said in a charming Irish accent, 'How dare you!! You only offered me thirty-five euros for it.' She was clearly offended that he would do this right in front of her."

Sasha muttered under his breath, "Bastard!" and all four of them burst out laughing.

"I told him I'd buy that brooch for one hundred euros on

one condition. He needed to pay the young woman seventy euros because he didn't even have to write out a price tag. The young woman immediately said, 'I'll take that!' and nodded at me."

Lee said, "Well done! We women need to look out for one another."

"Absolutely. I followed her out of the shop where she broke out into a big smile and thanked me profusely."

"Awww, I can imagine how grateful she must have been. Twice what that guy was offering."

"Well, this brooch," Mari touched her lapel, "is worth way more than I paid for it. Even though I gave her another hundred euros, it was still a bargain. Her eyes popped in surprise, and I told her that she deserved to get a good price for it."

"You have a lot of integrity."

"I just had to do what was right. After she thanked me again, we got to talking, and I learned that she is a seamstress. Well, to make a long story short, next time I'm in Paris, I'm going to see her about making a flamenco dress for me. I'm so excited to see her."

She smiled at Lee. "Unfortunately, I need to get back to work. I look forward to seeing you and Fong around the boat. Please let me know if you need anything." Mari finished her drink and handed the glass back to Sasha, and then she walked briskly away, her fingers straying to caress her brooch.

After Mari left, Lee said, "Sasha, what a very interesting woman."

"I know. We were lucky to hire her here at Spectrum." Sasha smiled gently at Lee. Quietly he said to himself, "What a delightful story. It will definitely go into my journal."

Lee asked, "While we have a quiet moment to chat, Sasha, how are you doing? How is Kisho? How's Tokyo? How's life?"

Sasha looked around to make sure everyone was taken care of before he replied, "Life repeats itself, but I love it. Every cruise has a sameness, a rhythm to it, but is also unique, as the passengers change, and we change locations. And every chance I get, I head to Tokyo to see Kisho."

Lee said, "I'm sure you both really miss each other."

"We do. He tries to spend as much time as possible with me when I'm home, but his business has really grown in the past few years and so it's become harder and harder for him to take time off."

Fong jumped in, "Good for him—IT consultancy is a growing industry these days. I was honored that he could spend a few days with me while I was in Tokyo doing those appraisals last year."

Sasha smiled at Fong before turning around to make a drink for another passenger. Fong and Lee watched him mix it and fold something, which he handed to the passenger along with the glass.

Sasha turned back to their conversation, and Fong asked, "Was that origami?"

"Yes. Kisho got me an origami book for my birthday last July to help me manage stress. Once I tried it, I was hooked, and I've really gotten into it." He grinned. "It's kind of like knitting, I guess."

"Really?" said Lee.

"Yep—you know, Kisho had a minor stroke this past winter. Ha—look who's talking about stress. Anyway, he's better now, thankfully."

"Oh dear, that must have been such a scare. I'm so glad he's okay."

"Yes, it was. I folded cranes like a madman while he was in rehab, and I'd like to think that they helped with his recovery."

Fong said, "Ah yes, the ancient Japanese legend that promises that anyone who folds a thousand cranes will be granted a wish."

"Precisely, and of course, my wish was for Kisho's good health."

Lee said, "Make me one." As Sasha folded the paper, she asked, "When will you see him next?"

Sasha looked around to check on the other passengers again as he answered, "We're meeting in Slovenia next month. We've begun to look for a vacation home that we can also retire to. With Kisho's health scare, we've decided we need to plan for our next step in life sooner rather than later."

"And real estate is always a good investment," Fong agreed.

A few moments later, Sasha handed each of them a butterfly. "Two butterflies dancing around each other is a symbol of marital happiness."

Lee smiled and leaned against Fong affectionately. He put his arm around her and gently tugged a lock of her luxurious auburn hair as she asked, "But what about the cranes?"

"The butterflies are for you two."

♦

Sasha turned around as Gia walked up to the bar after unpacking and checking out her room. "Hi, I'm Sasha Martinescu." He reached over to shake her hand.

"I'm Gia."

"Mari's Gia?"

"Well, as a matter of fact, yes."

"Mari is so excited to have you on this cruise. She's been talking about you non-stop. What can I get for you?"

Gia grinned at him, "I'm normally a sangria type of girl. I love the ritual of creating it. The sound of the fruit as I cut into it. The smell, the taste of fruit and wine." She giggled. "But since we're in France, I'd like to learn about French wines. What do you recommend?"

Sasha smiled and tilted his head to the right and thoughtfully tapped a finger against his lips. Then he carefully removed a bottle from the large wine cooler.

"I'm quite passionate about Bordeaux wines, but I promise not to bore you." He pulled the cork from the bottle with a satisfying pop. "I'm going to pour you a glass of one of my favorites from the Right Bank of the Bordeaux region. This is a very good one to ease into learning about French wines because wines from this area are quite easy to drink. They're very round and lush and silky and generally a little softer than those from the Left Bank." Gia smiled at his passion as he continued, "To keep them at the optimal temperature, we store them in the wine cooler back there." He gestured toward the area at the back of the bar.

"This is a 1998 St. Emilion Grand Cru from Chateau Larcis

Ducasse. Take a tiny sip and hold it in your mouth, and then as you breathe in across it, you should be able to taste spice and flowers, fresh herbs and perhaps even a hint of truffle."

He poured a sip into a glass and demonstrated. Gia tipped her glass and took a small amount into her mouth, carefully following Sasha's instructions. "Mmmm—that's delicious. I think I'll need to come back and spend some time with you and learn more about French wine. You might even make me a convert."

"I would be honored."

Gia took her glass of wine to the front of the boat and stood, momentarily surveying the outdoor area, scattered with tables and chairs. She tilted her head back to enjoy the fresh air and sunshine. Then, after a moment, she noticed the stairs to the upper deck and decided to go up where she'd have a better view. She walked along the upper deck slowly until she found a lounge chair set at just the right angle. She spent the afternoon there, watching the shoreline pass by and reading the book she'd picked up from the boat's small library as she sipped her wine.

The weather was perfect, and the movement of the boat lulled Gia into a nap. When the sun moved lower in the sky, she woke up, slightly chilled by the shade and the cooler air. She picked up her book and went off to get ready for dinner.

Back in her cabin, Gia went to the sliding glass door and opened it wide to let fresh, cool air into the stuffy room. She stood at the French balcony, looking at the countryside. "What a life. And Mari gets paid to experience this every day." After inhaling deeply, she watched the sunset. It was glorious that evening, bright pinks, mauves, light peach and softer purple hues reflected in the still water of the river. After a few minutes, she sat down at the dressing table to refresh her makeup and brush her hair.

◆

When she was ready, Gia walked to the dining room, her shining dark brown hair spilling down her back, wearing slim black pants, a black silk shell, her favorite emerald green shawl and high, strappy black heels. She saw Raul already standing there with a tall, blond man. She paused before they saw her, nodded her head in appreciation and said to herself, "Mm-mm-mm, they are quite the couple."

As she smiled and walked toward them, Raul saw her and opened his arms, wrapping her in a big hug, giving her a kiss on the cheek. He was *so* excited as he introduced David.

David took Gia's face in his hands and looked into her eyes. "Darling, I'm so glad to finally meet you. Raul and I are grateful to you and Mari for making this trip happen," and he kissed her warmly on both cheeks.

Gia's eyes opened wide for a second, "Oh yum! You're exactly like I thought you would be," she said, and she smiled her approval at Raul.

Gia slipped her arms through theirs. "Let's make an entrance, boys." They all laughed, stood their tallest and strode into the dining room, a matched set, all three dressed in black, all three almost the same height—David, five feet eleven and a half inches, Raul, six feet, and Gia also reached six feet in her new, four-inch heels.

Passengers already seated at their tables turned to admire the trio as they made their grand entrance.

Raul pulled out Gia's chair and seated her, and he whispered in her ear, "My, what a presence you've developed over the last year." After they sat down and got settled, he looked at Gia and said, "Remember that very first hospital fundraiser we went to? I was holding your hand, and you were shaking like a leaf. Now just look at you!" They smiled at one another.

Gia looked at the local French cuisine on the menu and then ordered pâté and steak with frites and a little salad to accompany it and a *Tarte Normande aux Pommes* for dessert. Raul and David laughed at her, "Where are you going to put all that food?"

Gia replied, "It all looks so good. I have to try everything! And the dessert is healthy—it's full of apples."

"And cream and calvados," said Raul, laughter twinkling in his eyes as he looked at her affectionately.

"What wine shall we drink tonight?" David asked.

"I had a lovely glass of Bordeaux earlier, but all I remember is that it was from the Right Bank," said Gia.

"One glass?" teased David as he called the wine steward to their table. Gia described the wine, and he went to get a bottle.

While they were waiting for their appetizers, Gia turned to David. "I hear your house in Rotterdam is very—interesting?" and giggled.

David laughed out loud. "Interesting? Raul hates it. He says they look like a bunch of boxes set on their corners, balanced on top of a column. Not to mention they are yellow, the color he hates most."

Raul said quietly, "I just prefer *traditional* Dutch architecture."

"I've seen those," said Gia. "I really admire Piet Blom's concept of homes as an 'urban roof' with the space below available for a variety of other uses. I read that the Rotterdam houses are supposed to represent abstract trees, and the whole village becomes a forest. They look fascinating."

"It's actually quite comfortable and has a wonderful view. So, as a single person, it suits me," said David with a grin.

"They appeal to the geeky part of me that's into urban planning," Gia said, "but I don't know if I would want to live in one. I agree with Raul—I prefer the warmth and character of older architecture."

Gia looked at Raul as he shook his head fondly. She pointed at herself. "Hey, you helped create this monster."

"And I can bicycle to and from work," David added.

Raul bragged, "David is an avid cyclist, and in addition to commuting, he competes in long-distance races."

David smiled, "That's why I have awesome legs and glutes." Everyone laughed.

Gia said, "I wasn't going to comment, but now that you mention it, I did notice!" More laughter.

They chatted and laughed throughout dinner. As their dessert was delivered, Gia remembered, "David, congratulations on completing your residency. You're a real doctor now. It's so cool knowing two pediatricians for the day that I have children."

"Thank you. I know, I want kids myself someday." David reached over and took Raul's hand in his. Raul blushed but didn't pull his hand away, and David smiled.

Once dessert was over, Raul said, "Let's head to the lounge and find good seats before everyone else is done."

They walked up the curved staircase. The automatic door opened with a swoosh, and Raul went off to find a place for them by the window while Gia and David went to the bar. David picked up the drinks menu, and Sasha came over, smiled at Gia and asked, "I heard you liked the Bordeaux this afternoon. Did it go well with dinner, too?"

"Yes, it was lovely. In fact, I'll have another glass, please."

Gia introduced David to him, and Sasha said, "In addition to the drinks in that menu, I make custom drinks."

A wicked gleam came into David's eye, and he grinned. "Can you make a rainbow drink for me and my partner?"

Gia playfully punched David on the shoulder and said, "You really like pushing Raul out of his comfort zone, don't you?"

"*Moi*, darling?" said David, feigning innocence. "*Moi?*" and then he grinned at her and nodded vigorously.

With an inscrutable look on his face, Sasha said, "I'll bring your order right over." As he turned around to make the drinks, Gia noticed his shoulders shaking as he laughed to himself.

He approached the table with Gia's wine and two glasses filled with an elaborate cocktail, layered with a rainbow of colors, and set the glasses in front of them and handed each of them a crane. Raul looked at his drink and then his partner, raised his eyebrows and, shaking his head, said, "David, David, David."

Gia said, "Raul, this is Sasha. He is truly a master bartender," and broke out laughing. David and Sasha—and eventually, even Raul—joined in.

Both men tasted the drinks and together said, "Delicious."

Gia turned the crane between her fingers. "I read that origami cranes grant happiness and eternal good luck. Are you making them for someone?"

"For my partner," Sasha smiled. "Do you need anything else?"

"Only a question for you. How did you learn to make such fabulous drinks?" David asked.

"My mixology instructor at bartending school in Romania

told me, 'If you want to stand out in your field, you need to master the art of making unique drinks,'" Sasha said in a very thick Romanian accent. "And so, I did!"

David continued, "What do you like best about being a bartender?"

"The people I meet and the stories they tell."

Gia said, "You must have heard hundreds of wonderful stories. You should write a book."

Sasha glanced around to see someone waiting at the bar, and before walking back, he replied, "Maybe I will someday."

Chapter Nine

March 2006

Break-up

Madrid, Spain

Anusha stormed out. "You should have told me," she yelled, slamming the apartment door in Joseph's face.

He stood, frozen, in complete shock at what had just happened. From behind him, Gia yelled, "You said you would tell her. You stupid idiot! You've been dating her for a year, and you never told her?"

"I meant to, but I never found the right time," he said miserably as he stared at the door.

"Go! Now! Go get her and bring her back."

Joseph opened the door and saw Anusha in the elevator, head bowed, crying as the door closed. He ran to the stairs and raced down them, nearly tripping over his feet in his hurry to get to the lobby before her. The elevator crept slowly downward. And when the doors finally opened, Joseph was standing in front of them, tears running down his face, his hands outstretched as he pleaded for her to reconsider.

"Anusha—"

She pushed him aside. "Get the fuck out of my way. I don't want to see you again—ever!"

Shocked by her language, he stepped back and let her pass. But then he rushed to the front door and blocked it.

"Please, just let me go. I can't be with you."

"Don't go. I can't live without you." Joseph took her hands in his and looked into her eyes. "We have to talk, Anusha. We can't just leave it like this. Please!"

She turned her head away and tried to pull her hands out of his, but he held them even more tightly. "Let me go. You're hurting me. Let me go!"

"Please—please—please, I need to explain. You need to understand. Please?"

"There's no excuse for what you did."

"What I *did* was procrastinate about telling you everything, and I shouldn't have. Please let me explain."

"Why should I? I'm done with you! I'm leaving."

Joseph sobbed, "Please, Anusha. Just listen."

His tears finally moved her. She turned her head away and said, "I'll listen but not talk." She moved abruptly toward the elevator. "Let's get this over with."

Joseph whispered, "Thank you. Thank you." *That's my girl*, he thought as he followed her.

Joseph pushed the button for the fifth floor and took Anusha's hand. "I can't stand to see you so upset. It breaks my heart." She tried to pull away. Joseph held her hand in both of his. Anusha glanced at him from the corner of her eye. His face was strained and white, his hands were shaking. She stood impassively.

Once they were back in the apartment, Gia poured each of them a glass of wine.

Anusha and Joseph sat on the couch at opposite ends. Gia angled the chair by the fireplace to face them and sat down. She sighed deeply.

Anusha sat, her face hard, completely shut down. Joseph took a huge gulp from his glass and sat silently. He didn't know where to start, how to tell his story without bringing on a repeat of her anger and tears.

Finally, Gia broke the silence. "Anusha, I thought Joseph told you about all this last year when you officially started dating."

"So, you slept with Gia, or are you still sleeping with Gia?"

"Oh no, no, no, no. Even before you and I agreed to start dating, we stopped."

Gia glared at Joseph. "Yeah, and you didn't handle that very well either."

"That's true, oh, jeez, sorry."

"Why don't we back up and tell her everything, Joseph. Anusha deserves to know the whole story."

"It doesn't matter, it's still over," said Anusha stonily.

"Please hear us out first. I should have told you this last year. I'm so sorry."

Gia began, "It all started two years ago. I met the boys in Jaime's bar. They were having problems finding dates for business functions, and I was living in a vile apartment and was desperate to move to a better place. We talked and talked. And in the end, we decided to pull together this bizarre contract. Wow, saying it out loud after keeping it a secret all this time is really strange."

"In hindsight, it does look like a very strange arrangement, but in the moment, it seemed like the right thing to do," Joseph added.

"This is sick. You are both sick. I don't want to have anything to do with you."

Gia continued to try to explain. "Anyway, I would be their date, and they would provide me with this place to live. In return, they would have weekly appointments and if we chose to, I would sleep with them on those days."

Anusha gave her a look of disgust. "That makes you nothing but a whore."

Gia drew in a sharp breath, hurt and shamed by the accusation. Joseph defended her. "She is not. She is a decent woman. She was just trying to help all of us."

"I know it sounds strange, but it was no different than dating and sleeping with more than one guy at a time."

Anusha snorted in disgust. "But you got paid to do it. Definitely not something *I* would do."

"Anusha! Please don't judge Gia. She lived in a really bad place, and she needed out. We were all single, and we all agreed. We even wrote up a contract to make sure everyone was protected."

A look of revulsion crossed Anusha's face, "I'm still not buying it."

"A couple of months before we started dating, I stopped sleeping with Gia. I knew I was falling for you, and it didn't feel right anymore."

"I knew Joseph was up to something when he drew away from me, even though he didn't tell me until I asked him," continued Gia. "I was very hurt and angry at him, but we had become friends as well. He told me he loved you then, and I know he loves you even more now."

Anusha looked at Joseph angrily. "You told *her* you loved me, but you didn't tell *me?*"

"Anusha, please, just because he is messing this up doesn't mean that he doesn't love you. I *know* he loves you. Look at him. You can see it in his face."

Anusha glanced at Joseph and huffed, "Oh yeah, right. Your ex-lover *would* know that."

Joseph went over and knelt in front of Anusha. He took her hands in his. He looked directly into her face. "Anusha, I love you. I truly do. I think I fell in love with you when we first started spending time together."

Anusha said harshly, "And then you plotted behind my back to have your ex-lover pretend to be my friend?"

"It was my idea, not his. It was to help both of you. And I wasn't pretending. I thought that we had become friends, you and I. And Mari has become your friend, too—we've had some great times together, no one could put on an act like that."

"She did it so we could spend more time together. And she's my friend, Anusha, nothing more."

"*That* whole arrangement is twisted and strange, and I don't want anything to do with either of you."

Anusha stood up and shoved Joseph backwards onto the floor in front of her. She looked at Gia and spat, "You two have this weird relationship, but I will not be a part of it."

Anusha looked down at Joseph. "To think I was going to tell you that I love you, but now, you make me sick." She put her hands up to her mouth as if she were going to throw up and ran to the door.

"Please, don't go," Joseph pleaded. He stretched his hand toward her and began to cry.

"Leave me alone! Don't follow me. I can't even stand to look at you. I need to go home."

As Anusha slammed the door, Gia asked, "Should I go after her?"

"That'll make it worse. She's very stubborn, and when her mind is made up, it's made up."

For a long while, Joseph and Gia sat in silence as Joseph tried to compose himself. He finally stood up from the floor. "I really love her. This is breaking my heart."

"I know. I can see it on your face. You poor thing." She paused and then said, "All this time, you've never told me about how you met." She moved to the couch. "Come, sit beside me and tell me about her."

Joseph sat down next to Gia and said despondently, "Not that it matters now." He looked at Gia, despair contorting his face. "Shortly after we signed the contract, I was in the university library doing some research about a new client. I pulled out the chair across from her and dropped an armload of books on the table more heavily than I expected. Anusha looked up, put her finger up to her mouth, smiled and said, 'Shhh, this is a library, some of us are studying here.'" He smiled as he recalled their meeting. "Anusha was studying for her masters in chemistry."

"She is so smart."

"I was immediately attracted to her. I was astounded by my attraction. All my life, I have been focused on money, and all I wanted was to be a multi-millionaire by the time I was forty. And all of a sudden, there was this woman."

"Things will work out. It might take time, but things will work out. I know they will."

"You saw how angry she was. How can it ever work out?"

They sat silently for a while before Joseph turned to Gia and said, "I'm sorry for how I handled this. I should have treated you both better." Hunching over, he added miserably, "There's no one to teach us how to handle these situations." He paused. "Ignoring you was the wrong thing to do, and I am so sorry. And then, you were still so gracious. You came up with the idea to become Anusha's friend so I could see her off-campus and more often."

"You're a good man, Joseph. So what if you screwed up telling me? I could see how much you cared for her. I'm a romantic, and I wanted you two to have a happy ending—what's important is—what's going to happen now between you and Anusha."

"I don't know. She has every right to be angry with me. First I hurt you, and then I hurt her. I'm such an asshole—I miss her already." He started crying again.

Gia stood up and pulled him up off the couch and gave him

a big hug. "You're too hard on yourself. It will be okay. Honest."

He buried his face in her shoulder. "I just lost the love of my life."

Chapter Ten

April 2007

Vacation in Seville

Seville, Spain

Mari paused under the arches on her parents' spacious veranda and admired the afternoon sunlight dancing across the pool's surface. She sighed—it was warm for April, but not quite warm enough to swim yet. And besides, there were other things she had to do that day. She stepped off the terrace.

As she meandered along the gravel path, through the garden to her casita, the final satsumas on the tree near the fountain caught her eye. Mari walked over to pick a few. *It's so unusual to still have any of these left by this time of year,* she thought as she put them inside the hat she was carrying. *They'll be a nice treat for breakfast tomorrow.*

She paused again to watch her friend, working away at the bistro table on the sunny patio outside the casita. Gia's sketchbook was propped on her lap, a pencil in her hand and her notepad open on the table in front of her. Her sunglasses had slid down and were perched on the end of her nose. She was completely engrossed in her work, moving her hands as she read to herself in a quiet murmur, glancing back and forth from her notes to her drawings. Without breaking focus, she stretched out one long leg, pointed her toes, circled her foot and then repeated it with the other. Mari was amazed at Gia's ability to concentrate, to shut the world out so completely.

I'd be sitting here watching all the bees and butterflies, listening to the fountain, anything but concentrating on schoolwork, thought Mari.

She laughed. "I hope I've given you enough time and I can tempt you to share this wine with me." She moved Gia's notepad a little and set a bottle on the table.

Gia jumped in surprise, and her sketchbook fell to the ground. "I didn't even hear you come up." She shoved her sunglasses back up on her nose, stretched her hands high over her head and shook out the kinks and then rubbed her eyes. "I've been working for hours already. I could really use a break. A glass—or two," she grinned, "sounds wonderful." She bent over to pick up her sketchbook and stacked it and the notebook to one side.

Gia squinted up at Mari, one hand over her eyes. "You look marvelous. Did you do something to your hair? It's amazing! When you stand in the sunshine like that, the red is so fiery. I love it!"

"Thanks. I didn't do anything though. You know how I feel about coloring my hair. It's probably just the sunshine. By the way, my dad's been spying on you," Mari chuckled. "He said you looked a bit sunburned from your excursion this morning and sitting out here in the sun for so long, so I grabbed this for you." She held out the hat and then laughed again. "Wait, let me take those." She removed the fruit and held it in her hand.

"He's always looking out for me." Gia set the hat on her head at a jaunty angle, twisted her long hair up into a knot at the base of her neck, secured it by sticking her pencil through the center and smiled up at Mari.

"Let me take these satsumas inside, and I'll get some wine glasses and an opener." Mari disappeared into the casita's living room.

She cleaned the fruit and set it on the windowsill, washed her hands and then went off into the bedroom in search of a hat for herself. With her hat in one hand, she carefully picked up the corkscrew and a couple of glasses and glanced again at the fruit, tempted to take one back out to share with Gia. And then she smiled, recalling how, when she was just a teenager, she had taken a sip of her father's wine after eating a piece of a satsuma. *Ugh, what a mistake! It completely spoiled the flavor of the wine. I'm not doin' that again,* she chuckled. *They'll be far better tomorrow morning with our coffee.*

Gia jumped up and took the corkscrew and glasses from Mari and put them safely on the table. "This is from your parents' vineyard?" She picked up the bottle and turned it in her hands.

"You bet. Dad's really proud of this one. He sent it out for us to try."

"Your family's vineyard produces some of the most wonderful white wines. I always miss their Airén when I'm in Madrid."

Mari pulled out a chair and dropped onto it to relax while Gia pulled the cork from the bottle and poured two glasses. "¡*Salud*!"

"¡*Salud*! I haven't seen you all morning. Tell me about your day and what you've gotten done."

"I'm glad we decided to skip going to the festival today. It was a perfect day to go touring downtown. There weren't a lot of people out and about when I was there." Gia paused to draw a deep breath and then plunged on again. "It gave me a chance to do some research for my Revitalization of Cities class. What an amazingly creative way the Metropol Parasol is to revitalize the plaza!"

"Someday, you're going to design something equally exciting."

"If I ever get this degree in architecture done," groaned Gia.

"You will. One class at a time, my friend."

Gia looked sideways at Mari. "Ha, ha! I'm doing two classes at a time. It's a real struggle, but I do love it. All the fabulous buildings, the evolving spaces. That's why I'm specializing in urban planning and revitalization."

"Really?"

"I just love it. It's amazing what can be done to change inner-city areas and make them more attractive and habitable."

Mari smiled happily at her friend's enthusiasm. "That's exciting, knowing what you want to do next. And you're halfway done with your program."

"Yeah, it's all downhill from here!" Gia replied with a sarcastic chuckle.

They sipped their wine for a few minutes and watched the birds bathing themselves in the fountain in the courtyard. Gia tilted her head back, closed her eyes and sighed in contentment.

"So—you've had a productive day then?" asked Mari finally.

"I'm so excited. I actually completed the research for my paper. This Parasol site is so interesting." Gia jumped up from her chair, wine glass in hand and began to pace back and forth as though she were lecturing in front of one of her classes.

Mari leaned back with her glass in her hand and watched Gia.

"When the Parasol is finished, in the basement, they'll have ruins from a Roman district they found there—I'm glad they didn't destroy it." She turned to look at Mari, as though to assure herself she was paying attention.

Mari nodded her head, and Gia continued.

"And there'll be a market with shops and a stage for concerts and events on the main level. And *then*, on the roof, they've planned to build a restaurant, a viewing gallery and this undulating walkway—" she made a wave-like motion with her hand.

Mari smiled.

"From up there, you're supposed to be able to see the skyline of the city." Gia gestured widely with her free hand, palm up, as though pointing out the cityscape.

"Wow, that's more information than I ever knew. It's hard to keep up on things being out of town—well heck, out of the country—with Spectrum."

Gia sat back down and tipped some more wine into her glass, then held the bottle out toward Mari with a raised eyebrow. Mari nodded, and Gia filled her glass again.

"I was happy when my professor gave us this project. I love this class. Exploring different ways architects have renewed and reused urban spaces has become so fascinating to me."

Gia set her glass down and leaned forward, speaking intensely. "You know, when Chicago's Millennium Park opened in 2004, Frank Gehry was considered to be on the cutting edge of the next century of architecture. It's completely different from the Parasol, but this is the future of architecture."

"I must say, you definitely have a passion for this stuff," said Mari admiringly.

"Oh, my goodness, I'm such a geek! This is probably way more than you wanted to hear when you asked about my day!"

"Well, I did ask," Mari replied, and they laughed. Gia leaned back and took a quick gulp of wine.

She pointed up. "Look." Mari's eyes followed the direction of her finger to a majestic imperial eagle flying overhead.

"Beautiful! Hey, before I forget—my dad said we need to have dinner with him tonight before we get too busy this week. We'll go to the inn, and my brother will prepare something special for us."

"Oh, good. Dinner with your dad and seeing Leonardo and getting to try out his latest culinary creations—it all sounds wonderfully relaxing to me."

Mari picked up the almost empty bottle of wine and tipped the last few drops into her glass. "What would be even more relaxing is another bottle of wine."

Gia giggled, "Absolutely. Festival week is always hectic, and we need all the relaxation we can get now."

Mari jumped up and leaned toward Gia, "Ssssh, don't tell Papá. I have my own private wine stash," and disappeared into the casita. She came back with a fresh bottle in hand. "I'm glad that Joseph arrives in the morning because we *so* need to practice every day for the flamenco competition. And—my new dress arrived just in time."

Gia teased, "Of course. You probably don't have a single flamenco dress in your closet to wear."

"Yeah, not a single one," Mari laughed and poured more wine into their glasses. "I have tons of them, too many to count! But this is the best one yet. It's truly a piece of art! Ever since I found Lydia in Paris, it's been so easy for me to get a dress made that matches my ideas exactly."

"She is definitely an artist."

"I'm so glad I found her. Our collaboration is really special. I just meet up with her to discuss my sketch, I bring her some fabric that I find somewhere in the world, and *voilà*, my vision comes to life!" Mari turned to Gia in excitement, "For next year, I want to take a couple of my old dresses and reuse them to make a new dress. I'm already mulling over what I can do. I think having an old dress become a new dress would be so much fun and a challenge to design."

"Talk about a passion," teased Gia. Both women laughed together. "You look forward to this every year, don't you?"

"I do, I do. I've been dancing the flamenco since I was six years old. You know, my mom made me my first little dress, and I'd twirl around the house, mimicking the dancers and performing for my family."

Mari jumped up and began dancing, "Like this." She laughed

as she performed some of the easy steps she'd learned as a child.

Gia hopped up and tried to follow along. Mari glanced over and began to laugh at Gia's attempts to dance the flamenco. They spun around and around, smiling and laughing, and finally, dizzy and completely out of breath, they collapsed onto their chairs.

"I used to brag to all my little friends that my mom called me her '*Flaminquette*'," gasped Mari.

"That is so adorable. I bet you loved that name."

Mari caught her breath. "Oh, I did, and I still do."

"You're going to win that competition this year, just like you have in the past."

"Between you and me, I hope so. This year is the first time Joseph and I will be performing together and the first time that he's been in a competition like this. Sometimes, I feel like we've nailed it, and then there are the times I wonder if we've practiced enough."

"At least focusing on this competition has been a good way to help him get through the worst of his break-up with Anusha."

"Speaking of Anusha, she and my mom won't be back from Madrid until after dark tonight, so let's go in and make up the second bedroom for her before dinner. Then I'll show you my new dress."

Gia turned her head abruptly in surprise. She glared at Mari. "What? Anusha's coming?"

"Uh-oh. Didn't Anusha tell you?"

"I haven't spoken to her in a year. Since the big fight."

Mari looked down and gulped and then said in an even voice, "Anusha called me to talk about Joseph because she wants to get back together with him. I told her we'd be competing here this week."

Gia's voice rose in exasperation. "Why would she call you and not me?"

"I don't know. I can't read Anusha's mind. Maybe she feels awkward about the whole 'you slept with Joseph' thing."

"But why didn't you tell me?" said Gia, clenching her teeth in annoyance.

"I thought you knew."

They paused in awkward silence and stared at the fountain and sipped their wine.

Finally, Gia responded with a snippy edge to her voice, "So, what else are you hiding from me? What else is there you think I know that I don't? I thought we were like sisters, like best friends, that we shared everything."

Really? I love her dearly, but sometimes she doesn't get it that her insistence that we share everything suffocates me. It makes me so frustrated, I just want to scream. Friends don't tell each other everything. No one does.

Mari looked at her as she shook her head. "Do you really want to know that Sal hit on me every time I was in the bar before he met you? Or that I slept with Joseph before you met him?"

Gia's face turned white. She leapt up from her chair and leaned in toward Mari, her fists clenched, her voice quivering in anger. "Really? More secrets? You slept with Joseph, too? But Anusha called *you*? Wow, this is unbelievable!"

"What's unbelievable is your anger. This happened a long time ago. We weren't even dating. It just happened two or three times. We were at the bar late when they closed, we'd both had a lot to drink, and we just wanted companionship for the night. No attachment whatsoever. Not even a mention of dating."

"Seriously? Like that is a good excuse not to tell me. You also didn't tell me that you talk to my brother sometimes and that he couldn't have kids!"

"And I suppose you need to know that I slept with your brother on his eighteenth birthday. You guys visited, and we snuck away and made love." She took a deep breath, and her voice became gentle. "And it went on until he met his wife." Her eyes moistened as she remembered.

Gia sat down heavily on her chair and buried her face in her hands, trying to make sense of it all. Finally, she said quietly, "If that's true, why didn't you tell me?"

"When I was with your brother, you were only, what, fourteen years old? I would never tell a kid about my love life. I wouldn't do that in a million years."

"But you could have told me when I got to Madrid."

"By then it was all in the past. Your brother was happily

married. Why bring up old things? Not to mention, I didn't and don't ever want to hurt you."

"But I should have known."

"It wouldn't have changed anything."

"But you should tell me these things."

"Okay—maybe I should have shared some of those things. If so, I'm sorry I didn't."

Gia sniffled, trying not to cry. She sat, her body stiff, completely silent for several moments. Mari stood up, walked over and knelt next to her. She wrapped her arms around Gia's waist and hugged her. But Gia turned her head away.

"I'm sorry, Gia. That was wrong of me. That was my temper speaking. I'm so sorry," Mari said.

Gia sat for several long minutes without speaking. Then, finally, she relented and hugged Mari back.

"Apology accepted—but did you really sleep with my brother?"

Mari went back to her seat and looked at the fountain. "Yes. And I still love him to this day. He was so special. Although I was older, what we had was a little like what you had with Pierre. Even though I'd slept with other people before, he hadn't, so he was like a first love. Something like that, you never really forget. Some part of you always compares every love to the first one you properly fall in love with. And then he found your sister-in-law, and they were crazy for each other."

"But he's single now. Don't you stay in touch? Don't you want to get together and see if the spark is still there? Don't you want a second chance with him?"

"He calls occasionally, but now that I'm with Spectrum, I'm hard to get hold of, and I don't call him back."

"Why not?"

Mari thought about that for a moment. "I don't want to go back there. It was so innocent, so perfect. I want to keep that memory. And now I—travel for work. I have—other interests." She gave a little shrug and shook her head.

"I want you to find love, Mari, maybe even get married and have kids."

"We'll see what life brings." Mari looked at Gia intently. "Are we okay?"

Gia gave an uncertain little nod. "I guess so."

"Anusha's on the way, so let's go in and make up the bed. We'll share and let her stay in the second room so she can have a bit of privacy. And I'll show you my new dress." As Mari stood up, she added, "By the way, when Anusha arrives, please just give her a hug, and let's not make all this a scene."

Gia smiled stiffly and stood up. "Okay. I'll be a good girl. Honestly, Mari, I just want to put all this behind us."

♦

In the morning, the three women were having coffee on the veranda outside the house and discussing the week ahead when Mari's mom, Gabriella, brought out a plate of *melindros*.

"Ahhh, my favorites. They smell wonderful. Did you just make these?" asked Gia.

"I made them last week because you were coming, and I took them out of the freezer before I went to bed last night. I just popped them in the oven this morning to heat. I know how much you love them."

Simultaneously, Gia said, "Awww, that's sweet," and Mari said, "Gia, you know you're the favorite daughter." The three women laughed. Anusha looked on, enjoying their light exchange.

"I spoke to your mom this morning."

"Mmmm-hmmm." Gia bit into a *melindro* that she'd dipped in her coffee.

"I can't wait for her to be here again this year, Gia. I see her so rarely these days. Now that you're in Madrid, I think she feels like she can't leave the farm as often to visit."

"I can hardly wait to see her, too. When we're all together here, I feel bad. The men are so outnumbered," said Gia, and they all chuckled.

"Gia, you really should go see your dad," said Gabriella. "You know, he's not getting any younger, he hasn't been well, and you haven't seen him since your sister-in-law's funeral. And you really should see your brothers, too."

"Yeah, I should go," said Gia reluctantly. "Maybe Mari can come along with me to see my dad—and my brother."

Mari kicked Gia's shin under the table, and Gia looked over her coffee cup and smirked at her. She turned to Gabriella. "My dad is so difficult to be around. He won't let it go that I'm not married, that I'm not being taken care of by someone. He just doesn't get it. I can take care of myself."

"I know about difficult fathers," Anusha smiled at Gia.

"It's just because he loves you, and he wants you to be cared for," said Gabriella.

They sat and chatted a while longer, enjoying the pleasant weather. As the back door of the house opened, they all looked up, and Mari's dad emerged with Joseph behind him. "Here's your young gentleman." He looked at Joseph and said, "Too many women out here for me. You're on your own, young man. I'm going back inside."

"Nice to meet you, sir," replied Joseph and shook his hand.

Mari saw Anusha watching the exchange and how she shifted in her seat and looked nervous. Joseph walked over to the table and said, "Good morning, ladies." He stopped dead in his tracks when he saw Anusha.

"What are *you* doing here?"

Gia, Mari and her mom got up and went into the house without saying a word.

Joseph set down his guitar and sat across the table from Anusha.

"What are you doing here?" he repeated.

"I love you, and I want us back together."

"So, you decided to surprise me? You could have called."

"I thought you would be happy to see me."

Joseph's mind was in a whirl. It was unbelievable to see her, and part of him just wanted to scoop her up in his arms, but the other part was angry at her assumption that he would simply take her back right there and then. "You told me very clearly not to come after you. Not to call. Not to get in touch." He shook his head, sadness reflected in his eyes. "You wanted me out of your life."

"Even after a whole year, I still can't stop thinking about you and how much I love you."

"What if I've moved on and don't love you anymore?" he said.

Anusha's eyes opened wide, and she began to cry. Through her tears, she said, "I really hope that's not true. If it is, I made a terrible mistake not coming to you sooner."

Anusha continued crying, and Joseph just stared at her, thinking.

"I fell for you the first time I saw you, when you dropped those books on the table in the library and disrupted my studies, disrupted my life," she said. "You were so attractive and kind and funny. It was such a struggle to be together. But you were patient with the restrictions my family imposed. You're such a good man, and I love you more than I can say. I was jealous that you'd been intimate with Gia. I thought you loved her."

"I never loved Gia, except as a friend. We were just two unattached young people having a good time."

Anusha continued crying. "I've spent a year asking myself, should I do what's right for me, or do I stay mad at you and go find a good Muslim man to marry and make my family happy? What should I do?"

Joseph continued staring at her silently as she went on, "It was a lot to think about, and the pressure from my family's been strong. But I finally decided I had to follow my heart, and you hold my heart in your hands. I had to come back to you and beg you to be part of my life again. I no longer care what you did before we met or what's happened in this past year while we've been apart. That's history and has nothing to do with us today."

Joseph finally broke his silence. "Are you absolutely certain? You were so angry at me and at Gia."

"I said a lot of things I wish I hadn't. I apologized to Gia last night, and she forgave me. We're okay now. I told her I'm still not comfortable with what you did, or with that creepy contract, and she understands my point of view. I know that now you only have her accompany you to events to protect me. I've accepted that. And so, I'm here to tell you I'm sorry. Will you accept my apology?"

"I was attracted to you from that first day in the library, too. And I think I fell in love with you when we started spending time together and getting to know one another," he said.

"I did, too, but I was too afraid to tell you. I love you. Will you please come back to me?"

Joseph continued to stare at her, and she shifted in her seat uncomfortably. He looked down at his hands for a moment and took an uneven breath. "I haven't been with anyone since we fought. I've never loved anyone but you."

Anusha's stomach clenched nervously as he stood up and walked around the table and took her hands in his. Pulling her up, he gathered her into a long hug.

"You'll have me back?" he asked. "Truly?"

"On one condition." Anusha leaned back in his arms and looked at Joseph. "That you promise to love me forever."

Anusha smiled as he answered, "Yes, yes, yes, yes." She snuggled into his arms again and gave him a sweet kiss.

He put his cheek against hers and closed his eyes, whispering in her ear, "You are my favorite, my only. You always will be. I love you, Anusha."

Mari and Gia had been peeking out the kitchen window. When they saw Joseph and Anusha kiss, they came tiptoeing back out and asked, "Is it safe? Have you made up?"

Anusha blushed, and Joseph gave them a huge grin of thanks. "Mmmm-hmmm," he replied. Leaning his cheek against Anusha's forehead, he asked Mari, as though nothing had happened at all, "Where do you want me to put my guitar? I didn't know if we were going to practice today."

Mari smiled at them both. "Not today, we have other plans. Set it over there, just inside the casita door, and you can leave it here unless you need it tonight."

As Joseph returned, Mari continued, "I thought we could practice in the morning before the festivities begin."

"That sounds perfect."

Joseph picked up the empty chair and placed it close to Anusha and sat down. He took her hand in his and reached over with his free hand to take a *melindro* from the plate. "I've already checked into the hotel, so what's on the schedule for today?" He bit the cookie in half.

Mari teased, "Sorry we can't give you two lovebirds any more time alone," and she grinned, "but we need to leave in a few minutes to get to the fairground and secure our table in the *caseta* before the midday parade starts. I always get excited about the parades during the Spring Festival. They're so colorful."

"Me, too," Gia added. "I think it's my favorite festival in Spain."

Mari smiled at her. "Then, after the parade, we can do what we want."

"You know there is a bullfight on most days of the festival," Gia said to Joseph playfully, "and I figured you would want to go to that. But you can still count me out."

Anusha laughed. "I'll go. I've never been to one, and I want to see what it's all about."

Joseph smiled at Anusha and squeezed her hand lightly. "That's my girl."

◆

When they arrived, the *caseta* was still nearly empty but had already been decorated by the families and friends who shared it. As they walked through the tent, Mari showed off the decorations provided by her family. Anusha looked around. "This is so festive."

Mari led them to their table, chattering along the way. "Gia and I always have this table. It's right here, next to the street, so we'll have an excellent view of the parade."

Because they were so early, there were still no servers. Mari and Gia brought beer and wine and plates loaded with tapas from the kitchen at the back of the tent. Meanwhile, Joseph and Anusha looked around, taking everything in—the women in their fancy dresses, the men dressed to the hilt, the hustle and bustle that precedes a long-awaited event. Anusha gave a contented sigh and leaned against Joseph while she watched all the goings-on.

On the way back to the table, Mari looked at them and

whispered to Gia, "Look at the lovebirds. It's amazing how those two have fallen right back into the routine they had before they separated. In fact, they seem to be even closer after just these few hours." She sighed, "It must be true love."

Gia giggled, "Maybe they are split souls who have been looking for one another for centuries and have finally been united." She nudged Mari, and they both giggled.

They ate while it was still fairly quiet, and Mari explained to Joseph and Anusha, "I wanted to get here early and make sure you two were settled and got the lay of the land. It will get a little crazy in a bit when the tent fills up and today's parade starts."

"Mmmm, this tastes great." Joseph broke off a piece of his tapa and fed it to Anusha.

"Oh, delicious," groaned Anusha, her mouth full of chicken liver pâté and toast.

Mari continued, "The parade of carts and horses is quite majestic. You'll both love it. The riders will all be dressed in the typical *traje corto*, an Andalusian country worker's suit."

Gia pointed to the street behind her. "Because we're so close, we'll be able to see every detail."

Mari said, "Be warned, we will be lured away by friends we only see once a year at this festival. So, you two may end up on your own here." She paused and smiled at Anusha. "But that shouldn't be a problem."

Gia chimed in, "Many of these people are friends who we've known since the beginning of time."

"I'm sure Anusha and I can keep ourselves entertained." Joseph reached over to stroke Anusha's arm and asked Mari, "When does the bullfight start?"

"I don't know, but you should wander over there," Mari pointed down the street, "once the parade is over. As I recall, even before the bullfight starts, there are all kinds of activities in the arena that you also might want to see."

The four of them chatted some more about the festival and made plans to meet back at the *caseta* after the bullfight, about ten or so that evening.

When Mari and Gia were pulled away by their friends, Joseph

slid his chair over, so it was right next to Anusha, and when he sat down, his leg touched hers. Even though the two of them were in the crowded caseta, they were so focused on each other that they didn't notice anyone else. They spent the next hour catching up on the previous year.

Anusha became quiet. She turned slightly to face Joseph and put her hand on his thigh. He was surprised by a gesture this intimate from her and placed his hand over hers.

She said softly, "I've decided I want to stay with you this week."

"Of course, we are going to spend the entire week together."

"No, at your hotel, at night, together." He looked at her in astonishment when she continued, "I want to make love with you, every night."

Joseph smiled at her tenderly. "Are you sure? That would make me the happiest man at this festival, but are you sure?"

"We've been together for a long time, except for this past year. Even then, we stayed faithful to each other. We love each other. I think it's time for us to consummate our relationship," she said.

Joseph leaned forward and kissed Anusha, a long, sweet kiss, his tongue just lightly sweeping over her lips. It was the first time they'd ever kissed like that. And then, he immediately kissed her again. She sighed with happiness.

When Joseph finally pulled away, he looked at Anusha. "Are you sure?" he repeated.

She gave him a huge smile and nodded vigorously. "Oh yes!"

"I've loved you for so long. I'm looking forward to tonight. How will I get through the rest of the day now?"

Anusha giggled. "The sweet pain of anticipation."

Joseph smiled and nuzzled his face into her neck. "I'm so happy," he said.

When the four of them met back up that evening, Joseph told Mari and Gia that Anusha was going to spend the night at his hotel.

Gia grinned. "I knew it! Finally!"

"I'm so happy for both of you. But how are we going to get

your clothes to you?" Mari asked.

"We'll share a cab back to the house, get her suitcase and then go on to the hotel," said Joseph, thinking, *That'll give Anusha a chance to back out if she has second thoughts.*

"That's perfect."

Anusha blushed, embarrassed that she had made this big decision to sleep with Joseph for the first time, and everyone else was talking about the practicalities, as though it were just a normal everyday occurrence.

Oh, my goodness. I'd already packed all my clothes back up, hoping for this. Why didn't we just sneak off to the hotel. Why did we tell them? Anusha thought.

Gia raised her glass, "To Joseph and Anusha. Have fun! Enjoy each other!"

Mari kicked Gia under the table.

Anusha blushed and then Joseph blushed and then all four of them laughed and clinked glasses.

◆

Anusha's black eyes sparkled and danced with excitement, her heart beat faster, her breath came more quickly. It felt like it was taking Joseph forever to unlock the hotel room door. But—at last—he swung it open, turned to her and pulled her into his arms. After kissing her soundly, he put his arms around her waist and twirled her, laughing, dancing, across the threshold and into the middle of the room. They clung together in a long, intimate kiss before he pulled himself away to bring her suitcase inside.

Joseph looked at Anusha as he crossed back to her and said in a hoarse voice, "You are the most beautiful woman in the world. I can't believe you want me."

"I love you, Joseph—I want you so much."

"I love you, too."

She reached out to touch his face and brushed away a tear. "You never put any pressure on me. You were so patient. Thank you for your kindness."

Joseph kissed her again, more tenderly this time. Then, he carefully removed her hijab and pulled the pins from her hair. It streamed, long and dark down her back. "I've never seen your hair before. It's even more beautiful than I thought it would be." He lifted it to his face and let it slide through his fingers. "It's like silk. And so soft, so fragrant."

She leaned close and, with her lips brushing his, she murmured, "I've imagined this night so many times." She wrapped her arms around his neck and whispered, "This is my first time. Teach me, Joseph."

"I love you so much. We'll teach each other, together." He took her hand and pulled her toward the bed.

Anusha chuckled. "I do know how to start." She reached up and began to unbutton his shirt. Joseph drew an uneven breath and took her hand in his to slow her down. Using her other hand, she continued to the next button—and the next. She looked up and gave him a saucy smile, and he wiggled his eyebrows as he grinned back at her and released her hand.

With all the buttons unfastened, Anusha tugged his shirttail out of his pants and slid his shirt off his shoulders and let it fall to the floor. She ran her fingers lightly over his bare chest. Her breath came quickly as she moved in close again to explore his chest with her fingertips, gently nipped along his collarbone and continued downward to suckle his nipples and kiss his belly.

He gasped, his heart pounding, "And I need to teach you what?"

Anusha smiled up at him. "I'm just loving you."

Joseph pulled her back up to him and took her face between his hands, drawing her into a sensual kiss. Gently—then more insistently—his tongue parted her lips, and he explored. She moaned into his mouth, and tentatively—then more boldly—she began to explore in return.

Finally, "May I remove your clothes?" he asked.

Anusha could only nod, her breath coming faster, panting. She was consumed by the feelings pulsing through her. Joseph lifted her dress gently over her head and let it drop to the floor—somewhere behind him.

He looked at Anusha standing there in her lacy bra and panties.

"Ooooh—you're exquisite—so beautiful—" he said, his voice a rough whisper. His fingers shook with excitement—he caressed her neck—her breasts—stroked his hands up and down her torso—shivers of anticipation—his fingers on her back—her full breasts released from the lacy bra—his hands catching them—featherlight kisses drifting across the tops—thumbs on nipples—hardening—a deep shuddering breath—a moan—a cry of pleasure.

He stepped back when he felt Anusha's hands at his waist, unfastening his trousers and letting them fall to the ground. She looked down, and her eyes widened.

"I go commando, and you can tell I like you." They both laughed, the tension broken temporarily. They continued to laugh as Joseph pulled Anusha down onto the bed.

She leaned over him for another long kiss. Her hand drifted down his chest, pausing to tease his taut nipples, and then continued downward. Her fingers closed around him—and stroked.

With a quick breath and a smile, he interrupted the kiss to say, "A teaching moment—this will be over in a hurry if you keep doing that because I love it—so very much."

He raised her hands above her head and held them with one of his. His fingers stroked her breasts—his mouth on her nipples—gently sucking, biting—teasing—tongue—teeth. Her chest rose, her back arched, she gave a soft moan. He released her hands and feathered kisses across her ribs, and down the soft skin of her stomach, paused and then laid his head on her belly and stroked her hip with his hand. "My God, you're so beautiful. I love you so very much."

Anusha purred deep in her throat. She had never imagined it would feel this way. The heaviness, the heat, the wetness between her thighs, her body overflowing with love, her desire for him.

Joseph skimmed his hand down her thigh and from the inside of her knee, up her leg. He paused, his fingers just touching the hollow at the top of her thigh. "May I?"

Anusha responded, with a quivering breath, "Oh yes—please—please—yes—" Her hips moved in anticipation.

She gasped as Joseph's fingers moved into her, and her hips jerked as he slowly—expertly—tormented her.

He watched her with a smile. Her head was thrown back, her eyes were closed and her mouth half-open as she moaned with pleasure. Her fingers gripped the quilted cover of the bed. He felt her tighten around his fingers. He withdrew and gently, reverently parted her legs.

"Why did you stop?" she gasped.

"There's more."

He kissed his way up each leg from knee to apex and then lowered his head, and he kissed her—gently—skillfully.

"More—please—please," she begged.

Through her moans, he heard her say to herself, "This—isn't anything—like—what my girlfriends—described."

Joseph chuckled, his mouth against her, tickling, and she squirmed as he continued his exquisite teasing.

She moaned in pleasure—tingles—shivers rippling across her body—she gasped—she cried out. She'd never felt anything like it before—the quivering—tightening—tightening. She wanted it to go on forever.

At last Joseph moaned gently against her, and Anusha shuddered and cried out.

She lay panting, slowly unwinding, an occasional quake still shaking her insides. He moved up beside her and rested his hand on her lower belly and kissed her shoulder and caressed her hair from her face.

"Wow," she whispered.

"'Wow' is right."

As she lay there, unable to move, she felt his hardness against her. Touching him, she asked, "What are we going to do about this?"

"Ah, he wants to be inside you. But it may hurt a bit."

"I know, but I'm ready."

"Let me get a condom."

"No need. I was hoping for this, and I've been on the pill for a while."

Joseph lay back and laughed, and she joined in. He leaned

over and gave her a long, probing kiss. Anusha felt him straining against her. And then he was kneeling between her legs.

Afterwards, they lay side by side, fingers intertwined, as their heartbeats slowed, and their breathing returned to normal.

"Wow."

"'Wow' is right," replied Anusha.

They both laughed out loud. She leaned over to drop a light kiss on his mouth.

Joseph propped himself up on one elbow and gave her a quizzical look. "Your girlfriends told you what?"

Anusha laughed. "They are all married women, and they talk about this stuff. I just listen."

"You're a good listener." He tickled Anusha. She giggled and tickled him back.

"I need your advice," she said. "Before I left, my dad had just started talking about arranging my marriage after graduation. Right now, he's just talking about it, but time will fly past. Should I tell him about us?"

Joseph touched her face affectionately and pushed her hair back, "Let's talk to your brothers and see if we can come up with a game plan—But let's not talk about that now.

Later, they ran their hands gently over each other's bodies, touching—guiding—exploring, learning and teaching, and finally, they fell asleep in one another's arms.

Chapter Eleven

August 2007

On the Terrace

Madrid, Spain

A pair of hands reached around from behind and covered Gia's eyes. She shrieked loudly, her book went flying, and she scrabbled to remove the fingers from her face. Then she smelled his cologne, and with her heart still racing, she said, "Sal! How could you do that? You scared the crap out of me. It'll take me hours to get over this trauma." He slowly removed his hands from her eyes and walked around to sit next to her. She giggled and continued to pepper him with questions. "What were you thinking? How could you pull that on a woman alone in her apartment? I was so engrossed in my book, I didn't even hear the door! And what are you doing here anyway?"

Sal stroked his hand up the warm skin of her tanned leg. "I was being stealthy, Minx." He smiled and leaned over to kiss her.

"It's nice that you're here so early." Gia's mouth opened under his as she began to respond to his kiss. She tucked her hand into his and stood up. "Shall we go inside?"

"It's one of the best days we've had this month. Let's sit out here and enjoy the sunshine and chat."

"What are you talking about? Just chatting would be novel." Jokingly, she cocked her hip and drawled in her sexiest voice, "No wham, bam, thank you, ma'am today?"

"Ouch. That was harsh."

"Honestly, I'm not trying to be mean, it's just that's what happens on your appointment days. The sex is always great, but then you rush off. I figure it's all you can fit in."

Sal tipped his head. "I see."

"It's like having dessert first," she tilted her head to mirror his and smiled at him, "and the dessert is spectacular."

As Gia sat back down, she murmured sadly, "But it is only a contract."

Sal looked at her thoughtfully, and then with a twinkle in his eye, he said, "Stay here. I've got a surprise for you."

"Really?" She turned in her chair and watched him walk into

the living room.

He came back outside and sat beside her and handed her a small white box fastened with a coral ribbon. "Ooooh, just like my robe but smaller." She beamed at him. Sal nodded and gave her a wink.

Gia carefully untied the ribbon, opened the box and looked inside. Her eyes widened, and she sat speechless.

"Do you like it?" Sal asked.

"It's incredible. I love it." She turned to kiss him, and then she lifted the necklace out of the box and cradled it in the palm of her hand. "Will you help me put it on?"

"Of course." Sal took the ends of the chain, and she lifted her hair out of his way. He fastened the clasp deftly and drew his fingers along the base of her neck and down the side of her chin and then touched her lips gently with the tip of one finger. Gia shivered.

Her fingers smoothed over the surface of the pendant. "Oh, my goodness, I have to see this." She leapt up and ran inside to look in the mirror above the fireplace. Sal came and stood behind her, his hands resting on her shoulders as they peered into the mirror together.

"Sal, this is lovely. But it must have been so expensive!"

"I had it designed for you. A special gift, designed for a special woman, for a special day."

Gia's eyes sparkled as she admired the necklace—and the way they looked together. She leaned back against him as she touched it again. "It's exquisite."

He slipped his arms around her. "The jeweler bought a building from me, and during our negotiations, I found out he designs custom pieces. I immediately thought of you."

"Sapphire, my birthstone. But it's *your* birthday tomorrow, and you brought *me* a gift instead," she said as she touched each stone in turn.

"Umm-hmm. I had it made for your birthday next month, but then I couldn't wait."

"And these three, square stacked stones. They're similar to the art deco designs in some of the fixtures here in this building."

"Precisely. That way you'll always think of The Peacock—and me—wherever you are in the world."

She swallowed hard, wondering what their chat would be about.

"By the way, that white gold is beautiful against your tan."

"You put a lot of thought into this gift." She spun around and wrapped her arms around his neck. "Thank you *so* much! I'll always treasure it." She pressed her lips to his, and then the kiss went on and on, deeper and deeper until finally, Gia pulled away. "Shall I thank you properly now?"

"That can wait, Minx." He kissed her again.

Suddenly, she leaned back in his arms and said, with a sparkle in her eyes, "Well then, grab a bottle of bubbly and a couple of glasses, and I'll meet you on the terrace."

Sal followed her instructions with a smile. With the bottle half open in his hands, he grinned as Gia came through the doors from the dining room, singing, "Happy birthday to you, Happy birthday to you, Happy birthday, dear Be-eeeast, Happy birthday to you." She stopped in front of him and giggled, a plate of cookies in her hands.

He set the bottle on the low table and immediately grabbed a cookie, his favorite—*Polvorones de Canele*—and shoved it in his mouth. "Ah, I love these." With his mouth full, he mumbled, "Ohhh, my god. I look forward to these every year. Mmmm. Why don't you make them more often?" He set the plate next to the bottle and threw his arms around her, lifted her off the ground and spun around and around and around, humming, "Mmmm," into her hair.

Gia giggled. "They're special birthday cookies!"

She was always delighted when the boys raved about her baked gifts. She didn't bake sweets very often, but for their birthdays each year, she always made their favorites—cookies for Sal, biscotti for Raul and brownies for Joseph—as a special treat.

Sal spun again, making her giggle harder.

As he set her down, he put his hand on the small of her back to steady her. "Why don't we relax and just talk. Come." He motioned to the two chaises.

"Okay," said Gia in a small voice, a knot forming in her stomach. *What's going on? Is he breaking the contract?* she thought.

Hesitantly, she walked around to her chaise while Sal twisted the cork from the bottle with a satisfying pop. "You know, Minx, the cinnamon in these cookies will go perfectly with the bubbly." He filled the glasses, the liquid frothing to the tops, handed one to Gia and sat next to her. He clinked his glass against hers.

"Happy birthday to us," she giggled.

After they'd sat sipping their wine for a moment, lost in their own thoughts, Sal pointed to the book lying at the foot of her chaise. "What are you reading?"

What is going on here? Gia wondered. She loved this new interest in her, but it was so unlike him. He rarely asked about what she was doing or how she spent her time away from him.

"It's a biography of an American architect named Frederick Law Olmsted. He designed all kinds of landscapes—New York's Central Park, California's Stanford University campus, Boston's Back Bay Fens, as well as the 1893 Chicago World's Fair. He's considered the father of American landscape architecture. I'm such a geek—it's the third time I've read this book."

He reached over and picked up her book. "When was this guy born?"

"Early eighteen hundreds."

"I didn't know you were interested in landscape architecture. I thought you were only interested in buildings and urban planning and city revitalization."

He remembered? she thought. "Landscape architecture is part of urban planning and revitalization." She continued in a fake prim tone, "I have many interests and like to read everything." She ran her fingers along his thigh absentmindedly.

Sal jumped up suddenly, and without saying anything to Gia, he moved his chaise right next to hers and placed a table beside each of them.

"But the cookies are all the way over there on that table next to you, Sal," she whined.

"I know—because they are mine." He grinned wickedly and sat down.

"Heeey, no fair," and she leaned across him to reach the *Polvorones*. He moved the plate a fraction farther away.

Then, pretending to relent, he took one off the plate and set it on her thigh. "Okay, you can have one." Gia giggled. "Nope, they're mine." He snatched it up and held it out of her reach. She strained to take it back but could only touch it with her fingertips. Sal laughed and finally gave in and slowly fed bits to her, washed down with sips of the bubbling wine.

They sat for a moment longer while Sal held her hand and ate another cookie. "Have you spoken to your mom lately?"

"Have you spoken to your mom lately?" she responded cheekily.

"Ha, ha, no. But seriously, how's your family?"

"They are all doing fine." Not sure where this conversation was going, she paused before responding further to his question. "My brother, Carlos," she glanced at him, "has started dating, and that's all my mom can talk about. It's been over three years since his wife died, and my dad has been hounding him to get remarried."

"Your dad is a tough cookie." He laughed as he lifted another cookie in the air.

"Very funny. He's the reason I'm here. He's the reason I ran away. He's the reason I met you."

"You said it was because he was arranging your marriage. But you never told me the whole story." He took a bite of the cookie.

He's acting so strange, Gia thought and said, "Where do I begin?"

"Just start at the beginning."

Gia took a big swallow of wine. "You know, families have interesting dynamics. So, don't think poorly of my dad. I've finally come to terms that this is just the way he is and the way he was brought up."

"I understand. My dad can be difficult, too. No matter how well I do, he always expects more. I guess that's the reason I work so hard. I think I'm trying to prove to him that I'm as good a realtor as he is. And that's why I'm closer to Mamá because I don't feel any judgment from her—"

Gia was touched that he had shared this with her and thought again, *What's going on here?*

Sal interrupted her thoughts. "Pleeease, tell me the story," he begged.

Gia smiled ruefully as she thought about the events that had led up to her departure. "My father had good intentions when he tried to marry me off, and he certainly was persistent. The first time, I was sixteen, the second, seventeen, and that last time I knew, as I approached my eighteenth birthday, there would be another attempt. Each year, when the harvest was over, my father presented me with a new suitor. Each time, he had promised me to a man and indicated to him that I would accept his proposal. All without consulting me."

"That's presumptuous."

"I know." Gia leaned across Sal and stretched as far as she could. He nudged the plate ever so slightly toward her, and she picked up a cookie with the tips of her fingers. As she straightened up, she kissed him lightly. "Want a bite?" He opened his mouth, and she pulled the cookie away, giggling, "Mine."

She settled back on the cushions of her chaise, and Sal tapped her on the end of her nose with his forefinger. "You're an evil tease, my Minx. That's what I've always loved about you." Gia swallowed, trying to ignore the butterflies in her stomach.

She cleared her throat. "It was the same ceremony every year, right after my birthday. Sunday afternoon after lunch, my mom would bring me back into the dining room. My brothers would be out, and my father would be sitting at the head of the table." Gia stared off at the distant clouds as she recalled, "My father would announce that I would be married in the spring, and he would tell me about the man I was to marry. And they were all so wrong for me.

"The first was a local teacher in his thirties, the second a merchant from a good family and part of the local society but already thirty-six, and the third was an ugly rich farmer with children my age." Gia shuddered, remembering.

Sal reached over and took her hand. "Are you okay?"

"Yes, this is like therapy. It's making me realize just how far

I've come since then. The last time I went home, my dad still nagged me about getting married, but he seemed to respect that I hadn't just bent to his wishes. He obviously loves me, but now he treats me like a woman instead of a child."

"I wish I could get there with my dad—but please—go on."

"I know my father was looking out for my well-being. The first suitor should have been a good match since we had many common interests. Even with the merchant, I would have been well cared for and a respected member of the town. So, I agreed to go on one date with each of them, but there were just no sparks."

"The sparks are critical, aren't they?" He glanced at her and smiled. She nodded and smiled back.

"After the dates, I would hike into the hills and meet my boyfriend, Pierre, under our tree, and we would laugh together at the absurdity of it all, and then we'd make love." Gia tipped her head to the right and said, with a sentimental smile, "Pierre was my first love."

Gia sighed, "As the third fall approached, when I was about to turn eighteen, I asked my mom, 'Why does he keep doing this? This isn't working for me. What does he not understand?'

"Mamá said, 'It's a tradition in his family that the father arranges the marriages to make sure the daughters are cared for. It's expected, and he won't do it any other way.'"

"Traditions are very strong in my family. My grandfather was a realtor, then my dad, and now me. It was expected that I would follow in their footsteps. But that's a story for another time, so please, go on."

"When my father called me in to offer me the ugly farmer, I told him flat-out, 'No, I'm not doing it.'

"My father said, 'You won't marry a teacher, you won't marry a merchant, and agriculture is what this community is about. He's a farmer, he has more land than we do, you'll be well taken care of.'"

Gia's voice started to shake a little, she became animated and gestured with her hands as she recalled, "Without saying anything, I ran out of the house into the hills to my favorite place on the big rocks that protrude from the hillside."

She sighed again. "I sat there brooding for about an hour, and then my mom showed up. She knew where I was because it was where she brought me as a child and where we frequently would go for chats."

With a small smile on her lips, Gia remembered their conversation. She picked up Sal's hand, studying it absently, tracing the lines on his palm. "I was so frustrated. I started to cry on her shoulder, and my mom held me tightly. She said, 'It's his way of showing he loves you.'

"I told her, 'I can't do this. I do want to get married and have a family, but I want to live first, travel and have adventures before I choose a life partner and settle down. So, I can't do it his way. I have to leave.' I saw my mom's eyes tear up, but she agreed, even though she didn't want me to leave. That's how we became co-conspirators."

"Wow, your mom sounds like a wonderful woman."

"She is. She even tucked a note into the lunch she packed for me to eat on the train on my way here to Madrid. I still remember every word of it. *My lovely Gia, I'm excited for you on your new adventure. You're going to do great! Travel safely, and make wise choices, but most importantly, follow your heart. Love you forever, Mamá.*"

Gia wiped a tear off her cheek, and Sal squeezed her hand. "I'm glad your dad chased you away, so I could meet you."

"I'm glad he drove me to you, too."

Gia turned toward Sal and said, "I have to ask you, what's going on today? I absolutely love just sitting here and chatting, but since we started more than three years ago, you have always come for your appointment, we've had fabulous, amazing sex—and then you've left. So, what's up? Why is today different?"

"This past weekend, I had a colleague who almost died. I've been driving myself really hard the past couple of years to get that coveted 'Madrid Realtor of the Year' award—for me—for my dad." He shrugged.

"I know you have, and you deserve that award for all your hard work. You'll get it this year, I know you will. But who almost died?"

"It was a guy in another office who you haven't met. He's been on the other side of the table from me in many negotiations. I respect him tremendously." He paused. "He overdosed on cocaine and is still in the hospital under observation. But we think he'll pull through."

"Holy moley. That's serious."

"It is, and it made me stop and think about what's important. I've been using cocaine occasionally to boost my performance, but is it that important? I really want that award. But I also realized we've had this contract for three years, we've grown so close sexually, we've spent so many hours together for business events, but I don't really know you at all. We're just two people in a contract. I don't spend real time with you, and that's why I stopped working early and came over."

Gia climbed over and straddled Sal's lap. She gave him a sweet kiss. He rubbed his hands up and down her back and ran his fingers through her hair, ending with a gentle tug. She hugged him and whispered in his ear, "Thank you."

She slid back onto her chaise and teased, "So with all this time on our hands, what will we do?"

"How about we mix things up? We get another bottle of cava, in a little while we have some food delivered, we eat out here on the terrace, and we just hang out."

"That sounds lovely."

Later, in the dark, Gia tipped her chaise back, so she could see the sky, all full of stars. "Great idea," said Sal and tipped his back as well.

The two lay there, admiring the stars that twinkled in the evening sky, and talked about how nice it would be to sit on a hill outside the city so they could have an even better view of the night sky. Their conversation slowly wound down, and they fell asleep, hand in hand.

At about three a.m., Sal woke to a siren below and looked over at Gia. She was still sleeping, despite all the noise. He smiled at how beautiful and peaceful she looked. One arm was thrown back over her head. Her necklace had slipped to the side and was resting on the top of one breast. His gaze lingered. Then he smiled again and got up.

He went to her desk and wrote her a note that said, "*Wham, bam, thank you, ma'am?*" and drew a little heart with a smiley face inside it and left it under the empty bottle. He took a throw from the couch in the living room and tucked it around her. She stirred and turned, her hand tucked under her cheek.

Sal brushed Gia's hair off her forehead and kissed her gently and whispered, "I love you, Minx."

Chapter Twelve

December 2007

Christmastime in Paris

Paris, France

"Has he said it again?" Mari asked Gia.

Light snow had begun to fall gently as they walked arm in arm through the Marais to a small neighborhood bistro, not far from their hotel.

"I don't even know if it really happened the first time. I was barely awake, but he put a little heart on the note he left me. So, it makes me want to believe he told me he loves me. But no, he's never said it again."

"I know I told you to watch out for him. But I must say, you two certainly have chemistry."

"Mari, I love him, and I'm very worried about him. He's been working so hard—so many hours. He's canceled our appointments a lot lately so he can work even more. And I'm not sure, but I think he's using more cocaine than before—a lot."

"Oh, Gia. That worries me, too. He seems to make you so happy, but then when he arrives high, you must be so disappointed and sad."

"Thankfully, he doesn't come high very often, and it's not like he's stoned out of his mind or anything like that."

"Have you told him you love him?"

"You know I can't—because of the contract." Gia grimaced. "So, I have to pretend I didn't hear what I think I heard."

"You're in a tough position, my friend." She gave Gia's arm a little squeeze. "But I know you two will figure this out eventually."

Mari looked around at the streetlights haloed in the falling snow. "This district is one of my favorite parts of the city. I always stay here when I'm in Paris."

Gia turned and walked backwards as she looked toward the river, chattering away. "It's charming. I can understand why you would stay here. And the view of Notre Dame is absolutely breathtaking. Maybe we can take a tour. I was only here overnight with Raul before that first cruise, so we really didn't get to see very much at all. I want to see everything."

"Let's see how much we can squeeze in—around our shopping." Mari grinned at Gia. "Don't forget, we're having dinner with Lee tomorrow night. Fong's out of town, so we can have a real girls' night. Now, do you have a list of what you want to see most? We'll see how much we can cram into this visit."

"It's right here in my pocket. Oh, I'm so excited that you have another life here in Paris, Mari." Gia smiled at her. "I can hardly wait to meet Lydia. And it'll be such fun to catch up with Lee."

Once they were settled in the bistro, Mari ordered a carafe of house red for them, and Gia looked around. "The woodwork here reminds me a little of Jaime's."

"I know. I think that's why I like to come here in the afternoons when I've been out and about. It's like a little bit of Madrid."

"So, tell me about Lydia."

"Lydia—where do I begin—Lydia's the woman I bought my Schiaparelli brooch from, remember? She and I have become good friends since then." Mari glanced at Gia, who nodded, and she continued, "We're meeting here to finalize the design for my new flamenco dress for the April festival next year. She's so talented. I want you to meet her. I think you'll really like her."

"I must say, the dresses she's done for you are fantastic."

"Our meeting was serendipitous," Mari smiled. "She's actually your age and a feisty little thing. Whenever I happen to be in Paris, we get together for a drink or a quick meal—or something. Who would have known we would become so close?"

"I can't wait to meet her."

Shortly after their wine arrived, Mari's face broke out in a huge smile, she waved her hand wildly in the air, and a petite, blue-eyed, red-headed woman, her face covered with freckles, smiled and walked toward them. They stood up to greet her. She took Mari's face in her hands and gave her a warm kiss on the cheek. "*Coucou*," she said. Then, as she turned toward Gia, Mari said, "Lydia, this is Gia." Lydia shook Gia's hand and said, "*Enchantée*, any friend of Mari's is a friend of mine. And she's told me so much about you."

Gia replied, "Nice to meet you, too. I hope it was all good."

Lydia caught the waitress's attention and chatted with her briefly in fluent French before she ordered a Dubonnet rouge.

"How very French of you," laughed Mari, and Lydia laughed back, looking into Mari's eyes with a smile, sharing a private joke.

"Well you know, it's been three years since I came here from Dublin."

The two women dove into conversation while Gia sat back and watched them.

Mari asked, "How's it going with Shane these days?"

"Oh, he is still a total jerk. And I'm really the one who keeps his business going. But at least I can put aside some of the money I earn for my dress design business. I still think it'll be a few more years, though, until I can go out on my own."

Gia was starting to feel a little left out, and there was something about Lydia that made her uneasy. In an effort to be friendly, she asked, "What do you do for him?"

"I'm his office manager." She added with a sly smile, "and I help ensure he has products to sell."

Mari said, "The funny thing is, now she works in the shop where she and I met, where the pawnbroker tried to cheat her over the price of my brooch."

"Shane still tells that story, but he always insists that you stiffed him on the price." Lydia and Mari exchanged another look and laughed.

Still chuckling, Lydia continued, "He's still trying to take anyone he can for as much as he can get away with."

And that's something to laugh about? thought Gia.

The waiter set Lydia's drink in front of her, and after a clink of their glasses, Mari went on, "I know I've told you this before. The dress you made for this year's competition was a huge hit. The number of compliments I got for your work was off the charts. You know, you really should consider moving to Seville and designing flamenco dresses full time."

"No thanks! I want to be a designer here in Paris. If you can make it here where the competition is so fierce, in my book, that's real success." She scooted her chair closer to Mari and picked up her drawing pad. "That last dress was special. But I've got some great ideas for this one and ways we can reuse the fabric from your old dresses. Did you bring them with you?"

"Oh, yes." Mari picked up the bag she set by her feet and opened it wide.

Lydia reached in and pulled out the dresses. They spilled across her lap as she examined the material. "This fabric is fabulous, exactly like you described." She had a pencil in her hand and made adjustments to her sketch as they talked back and forth about the fabrics, lines, movement, drape and colors.

Idly, Gia watched the two women bent over the sketchbook as she thought about all the sights she wanted to visit. She took the list out of her pocket and added, *"I.M. Pei's pyramid entrance to the Louvre. And Leonardo da Vinci's chateau at Clos Luce,"* but she knew the chateau was two hours outside Paris and that they might not have time. Engrossed in her own plans, Gia wasn't paying attention to their conversation until she heard Lydia ask, "How's your mom doing?"

"She had the biopsy a couple of weeks ago, and we were on pins and needles waiting for the results."

"I think that's the worst part—not knowing. But she's okay?"

"The results were benign, thank goodness. When they called with the news, I'd never heard my dad sound so relieved. I think he was more worried than any of us realized."

"Men—they try to keep it all in and not share their feelings."

Gia was taken aback by their conversation, since Mari had said nothing to her about it. While Mari and Lydia went back to their sketches, Gia drank another glass of wine and alternately looked around the bar, flipped through her guidebook and watched people come and go past the window.

◆

"That was a perfect day for shopping," Gia said the next evening as they returned from a marathon shopping spree. "Look at all of that." She motioned to the bags they had piled on the spare chairs by their table in the bar of the hotel lobby. "I think we bought out the entire city." They looked at the mountain of bags and burst out laughing.

"I think we must have."

"At least I got the perfect dress for the awards banquet next month and perfect little Christmas gifts for each of the boys."

"Too bad you couldn't have Lydia make a dress for you."

"How hard is it to make a long black dress that plunges almost to my waist in the front and scoops nearly to my tailbone in the back?"

"But Lydia is so talented."

"No, thank you." She shifted in her chair, uncomfortable with the direction the conversation was headed. *Oh no, not Lydia again?* she thought.

"I know, there wasn't enough time. Having to shoehorn her dressmaking and design work in around her work for Shane means it usually takes her a couple of months to produce one of her masterpieces."

"Even if there were enough time, I don't think it would have worked for me."

"What do you mean? She is so gifted. Everyone would be envious if you wore one of her dresses."

"Uh—I just don't think so." Gia gave a heavy sigh of exasperation.

"What's wrong?"

"Do you really want to know?" said Gia with an edge to her voice. "Really?"

"Of course, we've known each other forever and have been through so much. You know you can tell me anything."

"Well—it's just that my opinion of Lydia is very different from yours."

"What do you mean?" Mari stiffened her back slightly as Gia continued.

"I love you, Mari. And I know that you and Lydia are friends. It's just—oh, I don't want to hurt your feelings."

"Just spit it out, will you?"

"Well—" Gia paused, "—okay. There was just something about her that didn't seem right."

"What?"

"She wouldn't look me in the eye, she didn't really answer my questions, and that made me uncomfortable. She seems a bit shady to me."

Mari thought about this for a moment before responding. She looked over and shivered in a sudden draft as the street door to the bar opened, and a well-dressed couple came in, holding hands and chatting about their afternoon. They leaned against the bar, obviously regular customers since the bartender quickly set drinks in front of them without a word.

Turning back to Gia, she said defensively, "Lydia's had a tough life. She's completely on her own. Her mom died three years ago. Her dad is an alcoholic and was abusive to her. The night of her mom's funeral, her dad came home drunk and beat her. That's why she ran away. She had to sell her mother's jewelry to live. Yeah, she works in a pawnshop, but she's the office manager. It's a good job, given the cards she has been dealt."

"I know you're her friend, and I'm sorry she's had a rough life, but I have to be honest with you, I have a completely different opinion of her."

"What do you mean?"

"To be blunt, I don't think she was honest about what she does for Shane. What the heck does she mean by 'I help ensure he has products to sell?'"

"What does it matter?"

"I think she's being evasive about what she does, and that, maybe you're so amazed by her dresses—and your friendship— oh, I can see how close you are—so close, you can't see that there is something that's not right about what she does at that pawnshop. What if she gets into trouble with the police? I don't know her, I don't care about her, I only care about you, and I don't want her to hurt you in any way."

"That's crazy and just a bunch of speculation, Gia."

"And when did you get so close with Lydia that you share personal family medical information that you don't even tell me?"

"Tell you what?"

"About your mom's biopsy?"

"Oh, that—it was just a little lump in her breast."

"But everyone was worried, and you didn't think to share that with me? We talked about this in Seville. You said you were going to share everything with me, Mari."

"I never said that, and nobody shares everything with anyone. This 'sharing everything' obsession you've got is not realistic."

"Sure, it is. My mom says that she and your mom share everything."

"Really?" Exasperated at having the same conversation over and over, Mari said in a terse voice, "It's just not possible or practical, Gia. Grow up. It's just a saying. When you say you tell someone everything, it's just another way to say you're super close to someone and you share a lot of personal information. Did your brother tell you everything? No. Do you really tell me every little detail of your life? No. You haven't mentioned a peep about what happens at work, but I've heard from friends there that all kinds of drama has been going on lately. Seriously, Gia, no one tells anyone everything. It's impossible."

Gia looked away and sat for a few minutes without saying anything. They each took a sip from their cocktails, and Mari sighed. The hotel bar was slowly filling with customers, there for a quick drink before they went out for the evening or relaxing at the end of a cold day out and about in Paris. The conversation was uncomfortable, but Mari knew they needed to resolve this for once and for all. She and Gia both stared into space, thinking about what she'd said.

After a lengthy silence, Gia finally replied, "Okay. So, you're saying you think I'm taking the 'tell everything' saying too literally?"

"Yep."

Gia sat quietly for a few more minutes, "I hear you." She paused again, "You know, I guess I don't tell you everything."

"What do you mean?"

"About two years ago, I thought I was pregnant with Sal's baby."

"What? Really? And you didn't tell me? That's a big thing."

"I was pretty scared and upset for a week or so, but it really didn't matter—if I was, I was. Only time would tell. I guess it was like your mom's biopsy. It's the not knowing that gets to you."

"Wow, that must have been really scary," Mari said softly. She reached out to take Gia's hand.

"Yeah, Raul helped me through it. He's been such a good friend."

Mari squeezed her hand. "I'm not the type of person to share everything—with you, or with anyone."

"I get it now. Well, I have one request then."

"What's that?"

"While we don't literally 'share everything' with each other, let's agree to always be honest with each other."

"I can agree with that. It's part of any healthy relationship— or friendship." She smiled kindly at Gia.

Comfortable that they finally had resolved the issue, Mari nudged Gia and commented, "Do you suppose they are having an affair?" She gestured to the couple at the bar who couldn't seem to keep their hands off one another. Gia giggled. They continued to watch people come and go as the bar filled up. "Oh, look at her lovely dress—what a contrast between those two—he's so gorgeous, and she's so—ordinary—"

Finally, Mari said, "Back to our conversation from yesterday—what are you going to do about Sal? You can't go on yearning for him forever. Now that Joseph and Anusha are back together and Raul has David, maybe you should think about ending the contract and move on with your life. You're more than halfway done with your degree. Your whole life is ahead of you."

"I didn't take your advice about Sal before. Instead, I've fallen in love with him. And I don't even know if he loves me, too. So, shame on me for not paying more attention to you. Maybe it is time to move on."

"I'm glad you've finally realized it."

Gia scrunched her nose at Mari, as if to say, "Okay, okay, you told me so." Mari smiled. Gia had made that same face since she was a small child.

"I need to be straightforward with you about something, Mari."

"Okay."

"Lydia isn't being honest with you."

"Seriously, you're going there again?" said Mari sharply. "This is ridiculous. You have no idea what you're talking about."

"I can tell that you don't see it. But—"

Mari got up abruptly and walked away without a word. Gia watched her walk toward the toilet. After a few minutes, she came back out but didn't return to her seat. She walked over to the big window in the lobby and stood there for several minutes, her back stiff, rubbing her arms as if she were cold, all the while watching people on the street pass by, watching the snow as it began to fall again.

Mari took a deep breath. *Oh my God! I can't believe we went there. We had so much fun this afternoon. But then she started with the 'friends tell each other everything' again. When she's needy like that, it tries my patience. It suffocates me. She calls me her best friend. We might be family friends, but she's not my best friend. We got through it today—just like we did in Seville. Now she's going on about Lydia—again. That pushes me to the limit. Breathe. Just breathe.*

Gia waited patiently, watching Mari.

Mari returned to her seat. "I've finally realized that we are both grown women, and it's not only me looking out for you anymore. Now you watch out for me as much as I watch out for you."

Gia smiled at Mari and said, "That's what best friends do."

"I suppose. You're an adventurous young woman. You took a huge chance moving to Madrid on your own, and you continue to take chances in life. The boys and that contract, working toward your architecture degree—I'm usually more practical and cautious."

Gia raised her eyebrows, "Usually?"

Maybe I should tell her, Mari thought. "I don't usually jump into relationships. But you need to know—Lydia and I are more than friends." Gia looked at Mari, not believing what she was hearing. "Since the first time we met to discuss the design of my dress, there was this thing, an immediate spark between us. It happened so quickly." Mari blushed. "Now, if I'm not working, I'm here, in

Paris—with Lydia. I don't go to Seville very often anymore."

"You're a lesbian?" Gia said in an astonished voice. "I never knew."

"Actually, I'm bisexual. I like women—and men. I always have. I'm attracted to the person's soul, not their gender—I love Lydia, Gia."

"Really? I've never heard you say you love someone—except me or your family. I never knew you were bisexual or ever saw you with a woman. In fact, I've never seen you with a partner at all. I've heard you mention being with someone off and on, but never for long."

"Gia, I'm a very private person, but I know you won't share this. It's just with Lydia—things are different. We've been together for years. There's a feeling of—permanence, I guess. You're the first one to know. I haven't even told my family."

"I'm happy for you, Mari, that you've finally found someone. But beyond that, I honestly don't know what to say—because I don't like her, and I don't trust her. I'm so sorry."

"So—you're saying you think Lydia is dishonest based on what—your gut instinct? You just met her yesterday—I've been with her for a long time, and I think I know her far better than you can after just one short meeting."

"No, not just gut instinct. Oh, I didn't want to tell you this. But now I feel like I should."

Gia looked off into the distance and gathered her thoughts. "On the way out of the bistro, I saw Lydia take something out of a woman's bag sitting on a chair beside one of the tables. You didn't notice because she had stopped next to the table, and she touched your face and that distracted you. But she was very skillful, like she's done it a lot before. She slipped it into her pocket as she walked by. Oh, Mari, I know it sounds crazy, I know you love her, but you really need to be careful."

Mari thought, *Lydia is reckless and daring. That's what attracted me, that's part of what I love.*

Chapter Thirteen

January 2008

Realtor of the Year

Madrid, Spain

"And now, the moment you've all been waiting for. Let's wrap up our ceremony with the Annual Madrid Realtor of the Year award. I'm pleased to recognize Salvador Medina for his outstanding sales, which exceeded every other realtor's by fifty percent." The crowd gave him a standing ovation.

As Sal stood up, Gia jumped excitedly to her feet and gave him a kiss and a hug and whispered in his ear, "This is so exciting. Congratulations, Beast." Sal grinned and winked at her.

"Sal, please come up to accept your award."

He slowly made his way to the front of the room, shaking hands with friends and colleagues as they reached out to congratulate him. He shook the Master of Ceremonies' hand and stood next to him, smiling broadly.

"Sal is a third-generation realtor. His motto is 'Continuing the Legacy', and his commitment always shows. He's dedicated, enthusiastic and a team player as well. Also, Sal is a killer golfer and loves closing the deal at the nineteenth hole." Everyone laughed, and he continued, "Congratulations! You worked hard, and you definitely deserve this award."

Sal went over to stand behind the microphone. "Thank you so much for this recognition. I am humbled to receive this award." He held it up over his head. "However, I couldn't have done this without the untiring support of my team, so a big thanks to each of them. Please stand up, all of you. It really is our award and not only mine." Sal paused, smiled again and said, "And if any of you want to play a round of golf, let me know."

The crowd laughed and stood again, clapping loudly.

As he returned to the table, he shook more hands along the way. A realtor pulled Sal in close as he shook his hand. "You've been bringing Gia to these banquets for years now. She looks stunning tonight. Are you ever going to make an honest woman of her?"

"All things in good time. All things in good time," and they both chuckled.

When he got back to the table, he pulled Gia up into his arms and gave her a big hug. *Would I want to commit to something like marriage?* he thought.

"Let's go celebrate and get a drink somewhere. Just the two of us," she whispered.

"Oh, we *will* celebrate," Sal winked at her.

Gia giggled, "Obviously, but let's stop for a drink first."

"Okay, but just a quickie."

"You're all about quickies, Sal," she gibed gently. They both laughed.

Gia took his hand. "Follow me. I know a shortcut. One of the bennies of having worked at this hotel for years is that I know all the best ways out."

Once they were on the street, they walked slowly, holding hands in the cold evening air. "Let's stop here," said Sal, pointing to a small bar. They found an intimate table in the corner, and he ordered their drinks.

When he excused himself to go to the toilet, Gia gazed at the small candle in the center of the table and smiled wistfully and thought, *I wish we could have more times like tonight, relaxed and pleasant, knowing that we will go home together.*

When Sal returned, he was sniffing and rubbing his nose. "Are you getting a cold?"

"I hope not. No time for a cold. I've got too much work to do."

Sal chattered on about the evening, the award, all his accomplishments, how hard he had worked in the past year.

Gia smiled, happy to see him so excited and upbeat.

As they finished their drinks, Sal winked at Gia. "Let's go celebrate properly now, Minx." Even after all the years they'd spent together, Gia felt a familiar tug to her heart and that ever-ready thrill of anticipation in her stomach, and she took a quick, little breath. Just the thought of him—

As they entered the apartment, Gia turned on the lights while Sal went to the bar to pour them each a glass of champagne. Suddenly, he walked back to her, turned her toward him and pulled her hard against his body in a long, sensual kiss. Gia felt her body quicken and moaned her desire for him.

After a long while, he broke off the kiss and handed her a glass of champagne. Gia raised her glass and, still breathing hard, toasted, "To my realtor of the year." Sal smiled, and they both took a sip, and Gia looked passionately into his eyes. She noticed how dilated his pupils were and recalled his sniffing, his talkativeness earlier in the bar. It suddenly clicked.

Her oldest brother had struggled with cocaine addiction for years. Gia remembered how he looked and behaved those times when he was using and how her mother would cry about it. And now Sal—

Gia's face became serious, "You're using."

Sal was surprised that she could see it, now, an hour later. *It really wasn't very much,* he thought. He set down his drink and pulled her into his arms to distract her and quickly changed the subject. "You look amazing tonight. Your Parisian dress is beautiful." He stroked his hands down her sides, his thumbs caressing her bare skin along the open back to her dress. "Let's see what you're hiding underneath. I can't wait to be inside you." She felt his hardness pressing against her.

Gia hugged him back and paused for a moment. *Should I continue or just let it go and not let it spoil our evening?*

She decided and backed away a few inches. "We need to talk about this."

"There is nothing to talk about. You're just imagining things."

"I saw what cocaine did to my brother and to my family, and I won't let that happen to us."

Sal became defensive and raised his voice. "I'm not an addict. I'm just trying to celebrate, for God's sake. Tonight, I received the biggest award of my career. I've been chasing it for years. Cut me some slack."

"Getting high is a selfish way to celebrate when this was our evening."

"*Our* evening? *I'm* the one who worked so hard. Anyway, why don't you join me?"

Gia said in an icy voice, "That's the stupidest thing you've ever said to me. Are you crazy?"

"Why are you being so mean? How do you think I was able to work all those hours, sell so much real estate and get this award? I had to be ON—ON—ON—all the time! I've been doing this for a lot longer than I've known you."

"I know."

Gia turned her back and walked away into the bedroom. "I worry about you, Sal. I just want you to be happy and healthy," she said through her tears.

He followed her and sat on the bed next to her and held her hand gently. "I'm sorry, Minx. I've got things under control. It won't happen again. It was just to celebrate tonight." He ran his thumb across the underside of her wrist. And Gia finally let him take her in his arms.

Afterward, they lay there quietly, Gia's head nestled on his shoulder. *I'm glad he decided to stay a little longer tonight,* she thought. *Make-up sex is really fantastic. Maybe we can make this all work out.*

Sal lay there, thinking about her, what it would be like to be with her every night. He stroked Gia's hair until she fell asleep, and then he slipped out quietly.

In the elevator, he thought, *She's so special. I can't fuck this up. I can control the drugs.*

Chapter Fourteen

September 2008

A Serial Killer

His boss walked over to him and propped a hip on the corner of Edgar Spring's desk. "Tell me why you've been hovering around my office all day and make it quick. You know how short-staffed we are, and you know we're all crazy busy with Hurricane Hanna barreling in on us—that's the eighth major storm this season, and we could get hammered by this one. On top of that, we need to keep up with the presidential election. I don't have enough hours in the day. You're the *Raleigh Weekly News'* society reporter. You know your job. What is so important that you need to interrupt me?"

Edgar set down his notepad and stuck his well-gnawed pencil behind his ear. "It's not about a wedding. It's not about any social event. It's about a murder."

"What do you mean, a murder?"

"Um, actually, a series of murders." Edgar looked around and noticed that his colleagues were watching them. "Uh, can we talk in your office?"

His boss huffed loudly and gestured toward his office with his thumb and strode off briskly. "Come on, then."

Edgar grabbed his notebook and a stack of files from his desk and followed quickly. He gently closed the door and walked over to sit on the scarred wooden chair in front of his boss's desk. He cleared his throat and began to speak. "Back in June, I got an anonymous tip about some murders."

"Edgar, you're a college intern covering social events. What the hell are you talking about?"

Edgar cleared his throat again and sat up tall to hide his nervousness. "In June, I got a call from this woman. She sounded older—intelligent. It wasn't a long conversation, but it was obvious she had information to share, and for some reason, she called me. Maybe she met me at one of the events I covered. A wedding, the annual Lauch gala, a community concert. I dunno."

"Get on with this, would you. I've got stuff to do, you

know?" His boss waved his hand toward the credenza under the window, piled high with stacks of paper.

Edgar pushed his glasses up on the bridge of his nose and tapped his notepad with his finger. "She said, 'There are some killings in Raleigh you should check out. Do you have something to write with?'

"I always have my notepad and pencil, so I just said, 'Yes. Go ahead.'"

"And?"

"She gave me a list of four unsolved murders that happened between 1998 and 2007 and said, 'Look into them.'" He paused.

"Go on," his boss said, finally interested in Edgar's story.

"And she hung up. I didn't have a chance to ask any questions."

"What about caller ID? You could have called her back."

"Nope, unlisted number."

"She called you directly? And you've been sitting on this since June?"

"I didn't want to give you a half-baked story, sir. I didn't even know if the call was legit. I had to check my sources and do my research like you taught me. And we had so many weddings over the summer. Then I started school again this month."

"You didn't think you should share this with me?"

"It could have been a hoax or a prank call. I wanted to check it out first. You're too busy to waste your time if it was a dead end," he said, trying to placate his boss.

"And?"

Edgar stared for a moment at his notepad lying on top of the stack of folders in his lap while he gathered his thoughts. He took his pencil out from behind his ear and fiddled with it as he said cautiously, "I think we have a serial killer in Raleigh. That woman probably thought so, too."

"Yeah, right." His boss leaned his head against his high-backed office chair and laughed loudly. Then suddenly he stopped, "What the hell are you talking about, Edgar?"

Slightly frustrated, Edgar scooted to the front of his chair and put his hands on his boss's big wooden desk. "You know I don't want to be a society reporter forever. This could be my big break, sir. Seriously, I did my homework, and we have a serial killer. For some reason, he targets red-headed women and kills them in parking lots."

His boss stood up, rubbed his chin and walked over to gaze out the window. He turned to look at Edgar. "Hmmm, what do you have to back this up?"

Edgar watched his boss pace back and forth between his desk and the window. "I did a lot of research. I went and got the few newspaper articles I could find on the four murders. I studied all of them carefully." Edgar pushed up his glasses again and added nervously, "And my roommate works at the PD. He got me copies of the police files." He tapped the stack of files with his forefinger.

"Why hasn't anyone put this together? There are lots of good journalists in this town. What did they miss?"

"I know. Based on my research, sir, I have a theory about that—reporters were just focused on other more important things, the bigger issues—on politics and the economy, increasing numbers of hurricanes, exposing historical abuse cases, celebrity scandals, that drive-by shooting and the rising murder rate between 2003 and 2008 in Raleigh. All four women were insignificant. I don't think anybody really paid any attention to what appear to be four random murders spread across ten years."

Finally intrigued, his boss walked over to his conference table, motioned to a chair and said, "Show me what you've got."

♦

"Did you see the *Raleigh Weekly News* article about the Parking Lot Strangler," Cal asked his three friends as they sat smoking in the Cigar Bar at their golf club. Cal took a deep puff of his cigar.

I can't believe Cal is so fascinated by all that gossip, Tracey thought.

"Do you actually read that rag?" asked Jim in a disparaging tone as he stretched his feet out toward the fireplace, grateful for the warmth after being out in the unusually raw, wet September afternoon.

"It was at the barbershop, and all the guys there were talking about it. I had to see what it was about."

Tracey said scornfully, "That paper is full of garbage. In fact, that's what Marie uses it for, to line the compost bucket." He leaned back in his comfortable leather chair and reached over to pick up his scotch from the small table beside him. He took a long, satisfying swallow. "Mmmm."

Cal continued, "What's funnier than the article is what happened after I left there. I was driving along, on my way here, and I saw this young kid, fifteen years old or so, standing alongside the road with his thumb out. The rain was coming down in buckets. So, I picked him up and asked him where he was going."

Jim asked, "Why would you pick up a total stranger?"

"He was just a kid, and he looked miserable. I felt sorry for him. He was scrawny, he just had a thin jacket, and he looked cold." Cal took another puff. "Anyway, we're driving along, and on the radio, the announcer is talking about this Parking Lot Strangler. And the kid looks at me and says, 'Hey man, I'm really surprised you picked me up because I could be that serial killer.'

"I look at him and wait a moment, and then I say, 'It's highly unlikely there are two serial killers in this town.' And the kid thinks about it for a minute, and then he puts his hand on the door handle like he's real nervous, and he asks me to let him out at the next corner."

Cal and Jim roared with laughter, and Jim said, "That's *classic.*"

Sam looked across the coffee table and shook his head gently. "Why would you say that to the poor kid?"

Cal just shrugged his shoulders. "It was too good not to." Jim and Cal did a fist bump and laughed again.

After a moment, Sam asked, "Now that you've piqued our interest, what was in that newspaper article."

Tracey listened idly as he smoked his pipe and sipped his scotch. He glanced over at Sam and raised his eyebrows.

Cal went on, "The newspaper claims there's some serial killer out there who strangles red-headed babes in parking lots and takes an earring. Supposedly he's been doing this since 1998."

Tracey choked on his scotch and began to cough.

Sam reached over and pounded him on the back. "You okay there?"

Tracey nodded. His face turned red, and his eyes watered as he continued to cough. He waved his hand for the bartender to bring him a glass of water. He took a deep breath and a sip of water, and then he choked and coughed again as Sam said, "Those poor women. I wonder if the police really think it's the same killer?"

♦

Tracey's car skidded to a stop in the driveway beside the kitchen door. He leapt out and dashed up the steps. He'd hardly paid attention on his drive home from the golf club as he replayed Cal's comments over and over again in his head. *I need to see that paper. I have to know what they wrote.*

His fingers shook so hard he could barely fit the key into the lock—but finally—he managed to get the door open, and he rushed inside.

His breath coming in short gasps, he stood at the counter and shuffled frantically through the stack of newspapers that Marie had placed there.

Where is the damn thing? Marie always gets a copy. It has to be here. It just arrived this morning. Did she take it home with her? She can't have used it already. I wonder if she read the article. I wonder if there is anything that can identify me.

At last, paper in hand, Tracey sat down heavily on a stool in front of the large island and laid it flat in front of him. And immediately, his Siamese cat, Mrs. Whiskers, jumped up onto the paper and laid down, stretching languorously in the sunshine, begging for a belly rub. He picked her up and scratched her between her ears. "Not now, Mrs. Whiskers," he said with rare impatience and put her down on the floor.

He walked over to the sink, turned on the water and splashed it on his face and wiped his face on the towel spread over the edge to dry.

Back at the island, Tracey sat down again on the bar stool and scanned the paper. His face whitened as he read the short article. It was just as Cal had told them—all the women's names, where they died, the missing earrings.

RALEIGH WEEKLY NEWS   SATURDAY, SEPTEMBER 6, 2008

A Serial Killer in Raleigh

by EDGAR SPRING

Four women died in Raleigh, North Carolina between 1998 and 2007, seemingly at the hands of a single killer. All four women were strangled. All four women had red hair. All four women were missing an earring. As far as the police could determine, except for the missing earrings, none of the victims had been robbed. Yes, many women were murdered in Raleigh during those ten years, but these four have similarities that cannot be overlooked.

On April 2, 1998, Maggie Wilson was the first victim of the Parking Lot Strangler. She was murdered in the parking lot across from her art gallery, MJW Expressions, and was found lying across the seat of her car with her keys in the footwell. Maggie had red hair. One earring was missing. No suspects were identified.

On January 17, 2002, Ruth Sampson was strangled in a downtown parking lot. She was found lying on the ground next to her sedan with her house and car keys under the vehicle. Ruth had red hair. One earring was missing. No suspects were identified.

On January 1, 2005, Zoe Abrams was found strangled near her car in a parking garage not far from the Lauch Art Museum, where she had been serving as a bartender at their New Year's Eve Gala fundraiser. Her keys were found beneath her body. Zoe had red hair. One earring was missing. No suspects were identified.

On December 20, 2007, Sheila Kovacs was strangled in a dark corner of a downtown parking lot. She had gone to the popular club, A Passion for Jazz, for drinks with a group of colleagues to celebrate the upcoming holiday. They all departed the club together at about 9 p.m. and went their separate ways. Sheila was found just before midnight lying between her car and a building at the edge of the lot with her keys in her hand. Sheila had red hair. One earring was missing. No suspects were identified.

Four redheads, all strangled in parking lots, all missing one earring, none the victim of a robbery. These murders have not been solved. They have all become cold cases. But the *Raleigh Weekly News* will continue to follow this story about the Parking Lot Strangler.

Who is this Edgar Spring? Where did he get this information? How did he tie it all together? Why now? What happened? What am I going to do? I come from a good family. I'm a judge. I'm well-respected by my friends and colleagues. What made me do this?

Chapter Fifteen

December 2008

Gia's New Job

Madrid, Spain

"Mamá, I got the job! I got the job! I got the job!"

"I'm so proud of you, my dear," said her mother calmly, knowing how hard Gia had been studying and how far she had progressed with her course, "for continuing with your studies as well as starting a new job. When do you start?"

"I'm not sure when I officially start. That all still needs to be figured out. I'm so excited. I'll be traveling with Spectrum and seeing so many new places. And maybe I'll get to work with Mari again."

"Okay, just don't neglect your classes. I'm sure the change in scenery and seeing all that different architecture and those new places will give you lots of inspiration."

"It does inspire me. Every time I cruise with David and Raul, I come back more motivated. So, I promise to finish my architecture degree. That's my top priority."

Mari walked in the door and waved at Gia who was wandering around the living room as she talked to her mother. "Mamá, Mari just arrived. She's spending the next few days with me before she heads to Paris."

"Say hello to her, dear, and I'll let you go."

"Mamá says hi, Mari."

"Say hi back," Mari said as she walked into the bedroom to drop off her suitcase.

"Mari says hi."

"I'm so proud of you, dear. Congratulations again on your new job. When you get a start date, let me know."

"Thanks, Mamá. I will. I love you. Tell everyone hi for me."

As soon as Gia hung up, she ran into the bedroom and tackled Mari in a giant, running hug. "I got the Spectrum job! I got the job. Can you believe it? I got the job."

Mari peeled Gia off her and laughed, "That's fantastic. When do you start?"

"I just got the offer letter, so I don't know. I have to send them my acceptance. I have to quit at the hotel. I have to figure out what to do about my classes. There's so much to do. And then I have to tell the boys. Oh my, how will I tell them?"

Mari said, "You know, it's sunny outside, and it's so warm for December. Let's open some cava to celebrate and talk out there."

They walked back to the living room bar and opened a bottle of their favorite sparkling wine. As Mari poured it into the glasses, she said, "As usual, Sal has stocked the bar with the best. Thanks, Sal!" Gia giggled.

Gia picked up her glass and two wraps off the couch. Mari took her glass, looked at the bottle and smiled. "Why not!" She grabbed the bottle by the neck, and they headed out the French doors to the terrace.

They snuggled down under their warm throws in the sun, and Mari raised her glass. "To your new job." They clinked glasses and sipped.

Gia tilted her face up to the sunshine and said wistfully, "I'm certainly going to miss The Peacock." She sighed deeply. "This is not going to be easy."

"It's easy to give notice. You just go in and say, 'I'm quitting,' and tell them the date. People do it all the time, so I wouldn't worry about that."

"That's not what I'm talking about. It's about the boys. It's about Sal."

"Ohhh, yeah." Mari gave a single, slow nod of her head, her face serious as she thought about Gia and Sal.

Gia sipped her wine and tried to focus. "I never imagined almost five years ago, when I was just eighteen and I stumbled into this arrangement, that I would have found such a great group of friends. We've had fabulous experiences. The travel, the love, the laughter, the friendships, the highs, the lows. My life is so rich and full." She swept her arm in a wide gesture at the terrace and the apartment. "And how am I ever going to leave this?"

Mari looked around. "Well, your living quarters will certainly be different."

"Yeah, that's for sure. I'll definitely miss this apartment."

"You know, you can stay in Seville on your time off if you want. My parents would love to have you there. Life at the casita is so easy, it's private, you have the pool, you have company if you want it with my family or not if you want to be alone."

"I hadn't thought about all that. Even though we've gotten over the whole marriage thing, I definitely don't want to spend weeks at a time with my dad. We aren't that comfortable together."

"Then it's settled. The casita will be your home away from Spectrum. I'll let my mom know."

"Awesome! I'm so excited about this new job. I want to see more architecture. What better way is there to do it than traveling on riverboats around the world? No matter how much I want to stay in Madrid with all my friends, it's time for me to move on and try new things."

"That's right. And you'll love it."

"I never thought I would be the one breaking the contract with the boys." Mari sipped her wine as Gia talked. "I have the Christmas cruise with Raul from the nineteenth to the twenty-ninth. I'll tell him when we are together with David.

"I'll tell Joseph at our Monday appointment. Anusha's coming with him for our annual Christmas celebration, and it'll be perfect to let them both know at the same time."

Mari poured more cava into their glasses. "Okay, two down. Now—what about Sal?"

Gia took a deep breath, "Ahhh, Sal. My Sal—I love him so much—how will I ever be able to leave, especially him?"

She paused to think about it for a few minutes. "I know. I have final exams before I leave for the cruise. I'll focus on those, and Sal will understand when I cancel our appointment. Anyway, he's working hard to get Realtor of the Year again, so he doesn't have a lot of free time himself."

"Is he leaning on cocaine again?"

Gia hesitated. "I don't know—well—maybe—yes." She sighed deeply.

"I'm sorry, Gia. He's like two different people. One when he's using and one when he's not."

Gia nodded, "I know. Earlier this year, it was better, but

every time he arrives these days, I'm walking on eggshells. I never know which Sal will walk through that door, if he is going to be abusive or the sweetest man on earth."

"Abusive? Has he hurt you?"

"Oh no! Just verbally abusive. Sometimes, he says the cruelest things. He's only hurt my feelings—and my heart. I know I'm not what he accuses me of being. But it still hurts so much."

"Oh Gia, verbal abuse is still abuse. I'm glad you're breaking the contract. I'm glad you're getting away from that. You can't change him. Only he can, and he has to want to and arrive at that decision by himself." Mari reached over and patted her knee. "I'm so sorry you've been dealing with this alone."

"It is especially hard to see someone I love, who, underneath everything, is a wonderful man, be so mean. Anyway, he has a lot of holiday parties with colleagues and clients, so it's always a busy time of year for him and me, and that makes him even more stressed and more likely to dip into the cocaine."

"How are you going to handle that?"

"It's part of the contract. So, I'll attend all the parties I can before I leave for the cruise, but I'll wait to tell him when we meet for the New Year's Eve party."

"So, you'll keep this a secret from him, and then 'Happy New Year, Sal. I'm leaving'? I guess he deserves that for the way he's been treating you."

"Oh, come on, that's not nice."

"You wanted me to be honest with you, right?" Mari said, with a knowing twinkle in her eye.

"Argh. Be careful what I ask for, huh?" She laughed at herself.

"I was just teasing you, Gia. I know this will be tough, no matter what you do. But I'm here for you. You know that."

"I know. I guess I'll have to negotiate my start date to be after the New Year."

"I think that should be easy to do."

Gia jumped up from her chaise. "Okay, this is making me sad. I need to be distracted from thinking about Sal." She ran inside.

From the terrace, Mari heard a Frank Sinatra recording blaring out through the open doors. Gia came out dancing, the wrap sliding from her shoulders and another bottle of cava in hand. She set the bottle down, closed her eyes and began moving slowly to the music.

Mari stood up and grabbed Gia's hand, and they began to dance together. "Old Blue Eyes. He's my favorite, I love his vintage sound, all that heavy jazz influence, I love his lyrics, I love his sexy voice, and I can't resist dancing to his music. Good distraction!"

Gia leaned back, looking up into the sky. "Let's dance and celebrate all night long!"

Ending the Contract

Madrid, Spain

On Monday evening, Anusha arrived before Joseph so she and Gia could spend some time together. After she'd hung her coat by the door, Anusha reached into her bag and handed Gia a beautifully wrapped gift. "Merry Christmas, Gia."

Gia said, "You shouldn't have. But I'm not complaining about you embracing Western traditions! And I guess, through knowing you, I've learned a thing or two about your culture, too." Gia giggled and turned around to hand Anusha a gift.

Anusha parroted back, "But you shouldn't have!" and they both laughed. "It's fun to get to celebrate twice as many holidays, between Joseph's faith and mine." She looked across the apartment. "As always, you've outdone yourself, Gia. Every year, your decorations get better and better. I love these sweet little nutcrackers you've added to your collection this year." She touched the delicate ornaments clustered on the table near the couch.

"It's been so much fun to decorate this beautiful apartment with beautiful holiday things."

Gia handed Anusha her traditional warm spiced sangria. Anusha sipped the drink and said, "Mmmm—I always look forward to this. You know, both Joseph and I have become red wine and champagne drinkers lately. We must have picked that up from you." She grinned. "But there's something so special about your Christmas sangria."

"Uh-huh, it's my secret recipe."

The women wandered around, arm in arm, looking at the decorations and chatting away, admiring the icy crystal balls nestled in the garland draped over the mantel and the tree—that stood in front of the French doors to the terrace—with its subtle gradation of colored glass ornaments from dark green around the bottom to smaller ornaments in the palest of greens as they reached the top.

When Joseph let himself into the apartment, Anusha ran over

into his arms, and they kissed affectionately.

Gia went into the kitchen to check the food and to give them a moment to themselves. She called over her shoulder, "The warm spiced sangria is in the thermos on the bar, Joseph. Help yourself. Or have a beer, if you prefer." Gia snickered, recalling Joseph's reaction to her very first offer of sangria.

Over dinner, Gia suddenly paused, tapped her knife gently on her wine glass and lifted it, "I'd like to make a toast to you two—and to new horizons." They touched glasses with a light clink, and after taking a sip, Anusha leaned over to kiss Joseph. He laid his hand on her cheek and smiled lovingly.

As Gia watched them, a smile played across her lips. *Look how comfortable they have become, showing their affection for one another,* she thought, and said, "I have wonderful news—for me." She paused.

"What do you mean—'for me'?"

"Well—I didn't think I would hear so soon—"

"You're killing me, spit it out."

"While I was in Seville last year, I finally sent in a job application to Spectrum. I've wanted to work there ever since the first cruise Raul and I took with Mari."

Anusha gave a little scream, jumped up, ran around the table and hugged Gia. "You got the job!!! I'm so happy for you. This is so exciting. I've been telling you that you need to spread your wings. When you return from your cruise vacations, the look on your face when you talk about what you've seen is priceless. Now you get to do that full time!"

With a sad look on his face, Joseph said, "I'm so happy for you. But I'll really miss you. You've become such a dear friend." He hesitated before he walked around the table and wrapped Gia in a long hug. Then he moved away and took Anusha's hand and asked, "But how will Anusha and I see each other without you here to cover for us?"

Gia looked at them, her eyes filled with concern, and said to Anusha, "I really think it's time to get your brothers to help you convince your parents to accept your relationship with Joseph."

Anusha glanced at Joseph. "We talked about that when we were in Seville in 2007, and here we are at the end of 2008, and we haven't asked them yet. We just keep putting it off."

"Maybe I should just go to your dad and ask for his blessing."

"Oh no! He won't listen to you, and he'll directly forbid me from seeing you. Who knows what kind of restrictions he'd put on me?"

"Why don't you start with Anusha's brothers?" said Gia. "There's more strength in numbers. You know that Haidar and Ahmed already like you and support your relationship, so you need to get them to help you win over Yani and then your parents."

"Precisely." Joseph looked at Anusha, "Are you okay with this?"

"I think it's our only option. My mom always sides with my dad, and he is continuing to pressure me about an arranged marriage as soon as I finish my PhD. So, we have a lot to overcome and not too much time before my dad actually arranges something for me."

"Believe me, I completely understand that. Remember, my dad kept trying to arrange marriages for me, too—until I ran away."

Joseph nodded. "What if we don't get a blessing from your mom and dad?"

"Then I choose you. We'll go on without a blessing from them. It's as simple as that." She took Joseph's hand in both of hers and held it reassuringly. She smiled. "We could always follow Gia's example and run away."

♦

Spectrum Cruise, *The Vermillion*

"I love Christmas! It's so festive. Look at all the decorations and the twinkling lights, all those holiday ornaments. And that tree is absolutely stunning." David gestured in his exuberant fashion as they entered the lounge of *The Vermillion* after dinner on the first night of their cruise.

Gia glanced at Raul and David. "You two get us a table, and I'll get the drinks. That way I can chat with Sasha. I haven't seen him in a while."

David grabbed Raul's hand, kissed it and said, "Ahhh I get you to myself again." Raul grinned and gave David a quick kiss, and they wandered off with their arms around each other's waists.

Gia watched them approvingly. She walked up to the bar and waited for Sasha to finish with some other guests. Then he came around the bar to give her a hug. "Welcome back, Gia. I'm so happy to see you."

"I've missed you, Sasha. The last couple of cruises I've been on with the love birds over there haven't aligned with your schedule. So now I need to catch up with you and my wine education."

"Would you like to begin tomorrow afternoon when things slow down a bit?"

"Of course. May I please have a red wine? Your choice. And make something special and a little fantastic for the boys. We mustn't disappoint David."

Sasha chuckled and went to work on their drinks. Gia leaned forward and whispered, "I have big news."

He paused and looked up. "What's that?"

"Raul and David don't know yet. I'm telling them in a bit. I got a job with Spectrum. Can you believe it? I start early next month."

Sasha reached across the bar and squeezed Gia's shoulder. "That's fabulous news. Spectrum only hires the best, and you are one of the best I know. I can't wait to be your colleague."

"As well as my friend. It will be so new and exciting."

"You'll do great. Any idea where you'll be working?"

"Not yet. We'll see."

He placed the three drinks on a tray and said, "I'll bring these over. Walk with me. Mari is running around helping guests. The usual first-night madness. I doubt you'll see her tonight."

"No surprise. Hey, how are the renovations coming along on your place in Slovenia?"

As they approached the two love seats, set at right angles in front of a low table, Raul and David were holding hands, still deep in conversation, catching up on the month since they had last seen each other. Sasha didn't interrupt but quietly set their drinks in front of them.

He turned to Gia. "The farmhouse is coming along well. It should be finished by April or May next year."

"That is so exciting!"

"Let's catch up tomorrow. I see a few guests at the bar, and both my bartenders are new. Let me go give them a hand."

"Off you go, then. And thanks, Sasha." Gia smiled and nodded at him.

She sat quietly and sipped her drink, listening to David and Raul with half an ear. Her mind wandered to her new job. She began to imagine what it would be like to work and live on a river cruise boat just like this one, and she smiled to herself.

"Gia, what are you thinking about? You look like you're a million miles away."

She was so lost in thought that Raul had to ask her again.

"Oh, actually, I wasn't far away. I was right here."

David reached over and pinched her gently on the arm. "Yep, she's right here."

"Hey!" She laughed and pinched him back.

Gia took a sip of wine and caught Raul's eye. She set her glass on the table and looked at him intently. "Next month, I start working for Spectrum."

Raul choked on his drink and coughed.

Gia smiled with excitement. "Can you believe it! I got the job! I got the job!"

David raised his glass in a toast to Gia, "To your next adventure. I'm so happy for you."

"What about school?"

"I've already handled that," she smiled. "I was able to withdraw from my classes for next semester and get a full refund. I've enrolled in their on-line program with no loss of credits, so I'll be able to graduate on schedule."

Raul's face lit up. He grinned and looked at Gia, his eyes glowing. "Wow—well done—it would have been so easy to let all that hard work fall by the wayside. I'm proud of you, Gia."

"Are you crazy? I've come too far to quit now. I'm not giving up my dream to be an architect." The three of them clinked their glasses again.

Raul and David looked at each other, and Raul said, "I'm going to tell her." David nodded his agreement.

"Tell me what?"

"You've just made our news a lot easier to tell."

"And? You're pregnant?"

They all laughed. With a solemn look on his face, David said, "I wish."

"In all seriousness, I'm moving to Rotterdam in the new year," said Raul.

"But what about your dream to become head of pediatrics in Madrid?"

"Dreams evolve. We are opening our own clinic in February. We'll be doing what we love, and we'll be able to work together."

"Wow, that's huge!" Gia jumped up from the love seat and gathered them both into her arms for a hug. "Besides my new job, this is the happiest news this month!!!"

She returned to her seat. "Well, I guess this means the contract is officially broken."

Raul nodded. "I guess so." He and Gia smiled at each other, and they all lifted their glasses.

"To the end of the contract."

She looked at Raul, her eyes dancing with mischief. "Has David convinced you to move into his yellow cube house? I know you love it so much."

Raul rolled his eyes at her. "It's only temporary. We'll look for a real house soon, one that's near our clinic."

The boat floated by a quaint village on the riverbank, all lit up for the holidays. They talked about how charming it was until it had passed out of sight and then about how lovely Rotterdam always looked during the holidays—the Christmas market, the indoor ice rink all decked out for the season, the outdoor tree.

Sasha brought another round of drinks, and as he set them on the table, David said, "The master bartender is certainly the master! He knows exactly what we like and when to bring us more."

Sasha shook his head, smiled at David and patted him on the shoulder as he turned back to the bar.

Raul asked Gia, "Have you told the other guys about your new job yet?"

"Joseph, yes. Sal—no." She shook her head a little sadly.

"Why did you hesitate?"

Raul always picked up on the nuances of what she said—and left unsaid, so she wasn't surprised when he continued, "The contract is finished, right?"

"Yes, of course."

"So, we can share with David, too?"

With an impish tone in his voice, David said, "Ohhh, give us the details, darling."

Raul said, "Don't worry, Gia. Whatever we share will stay among the three of us."

"I told Joseph on Monday. He and Anusha came over for our annual Christmas celebration."

David blurted out, "They're a couple, aren't they?"

"Shush, let Gia talk." Raul nudged him with his elbow.

"Yes, they are. They have been for a few years. Anusha and I go out all the time, just two girls out on the town, so she can meet up with Joseph because her family still doesn't know they are dating."

"So, you're covering for Raul and me, and you're covering for Joseph and Anusha, too?" David looked at Raul. "Wow. Secrets."

Raul mouthed to David, "The contract."

"Now, with me about to be out of the picture, their challenge will be to get her whole family on board and to accept Joseph as a suitor. Her dad will be the tough one to convince. He insists his daughter marry a Muslim, and her mother and Yani always follow his lead."

Raul said in a somber voice, "They're going to need a lot of luck"

"They are. It's a huge cultural gap to bridge. They've been putting off the conversation, but now that I'll be gone, they have to find a way to convince her family."

Gia started to take a sip of her wine, and then she paused. "Hmmm." She put her glass back on the table and abruptly changed the subject, "Sal will be my challenge."

Raul looked at her hard. "What's going on between the two of you? It seems like things have changed."

Gia gazed out the window, collecting her thoughts, thinking back, trying to decide how much to share.

Her eyes welled up, and she said in an unsteady voice, "Things changed last January." She paused.

Raul and David waited. Normally Gia rattled on, but it was obvious that she was serious and would share her thoughts in her own time. She picked up her glass and looked down into it, watching the wine swirl as she turned the stem between her fingers.

"Were you aware he was doing drugs, recreationally, for as long as I've been around you guys?"

"Oh yes, he's dabbled in them from time to time since university. But it's never been a big deal."

"Well, in January, it became a big deal."

Raul looked aghast, "I'm sorry. I should have kept an eye out after our last conversation. Between my work schedule and my relationship with David, I've been too focused on myself. So, tell us, Gia, what happened?"

"The past two years, Sal has been working even longer hours. In hindsight, I think the drugs have become his coping mechanism. We had our first big fight after the annual Madrid Realtors' Award dinner in January. He decided to celebrate and went into the bathroom to use at a little bar where we stopped for a quick drink. I confronted him. He blew up, and I was so angry. Then he apologized and said it would never happen again. Things were good for a while, but then he began to fly off the handle more and more easily. He's into cocaine pretty heavily now. I've been walking on eggshells, so I don't set him off. But that doesn't always work. And he says very hurtful things for no apparent reason."

"That's verbal abuse, and verbal abuse is abuse."

"I know, David. Mari said exactly the same thing."

"You shouldn't put up with that. You should have left

already. I'm sorry you've had to deal with it on your own," said Raul.

Gia sniffled. "To top this all off, I've fallen in love with the idiot." She smiled at the irony of it. "At least Sal doesn't know how I feel about him."

Raul went over and sat next to Gia, put his arm around her shoulders and gave her a hug.

She began to cry and buried her head on his shoulder. She went on in a muffled voice, "I don't even know if I should tell him I love him. I don't know how to tell him I love him. I don't know how to tell him I'm leaving. I don't know what to do about the drugs. In the contract, I wasn't supposed to fall in love, but I did. I just don't know what to do about it."

Raul kept his arm around Gia for a few minutes more and stroked her hair with his other hand. Then he held her away from him and looked into her teary eyes. "Sal is doing drugs and has an unpredictable temper. You need to move out of the apartment first before you tell him anything."

"What do you mean?"

David said, "It's Sal's apartment. You're breaking the contract. That means you won't have any rights. So, pack up all your clothes and personal belongings and get them out of there before you tell him. If he loses his temper, you need to be able to just walk out the door. If he thinks that he's not in control, he may lose his temper. He could become more than just verbally abusive."

"Isn't that jumping to conclusions? What makes you think it could go that far?"

He went on, "For a while, I thought about specializing in treating addiction, especially to drugs. So, I spent a pretty heavy year working with addicts and victims of addicts. What I learned is that in these situations, you have to plan for the worst-case scenario and be prepared. Sal, unfortunately, may be under the influence when you talk to him, and you don't know what his state of mind will be or what could happen when you tell him you are breaking the contract."

"Gia," Raul waited until she turned her head and looked at

him. He stroked her cheek tenderly, "We love you, Gia, and we want you to be safe."

♦

Madrid, Spain

Gia paced the floor—back and forth—back and forth—in front of the fireplace, an untouched glass of their best French champagne in her hand. She glanced around. The apartment looked stunning, still decorated for the holidays. She adjusted a small ornament on the mantel. There. Everything was perfect.

She ran a hand down her long, form-fitting silver dress, slit to the middle of her thigh, showing off one tanned leg, and put a foot out to admire her new, strappy, silver heels. She nodded, pleased at the effect. And then she looked in the mirror to check her hair. She adjusted the loose knot at the nape of her neck— there, it was exactly right. Satisfied, she turned her head from side to side to admire the way the loose tendrils brushed her face and neck. She knew Sal would be pleased when he saw her.

She went back to her pacing, dreading the conversation ahead, playing variations in her mind—back and forth—back and forth.

When his key finally turned in the lock, she froze for a second and then moved to the bar to pour Sal a glass of champagne.

"Minx, you look good enough to eat. Shall I?" he said. His low sexy voice and the pet name always made her heart beat faster—even now.

But that night, Gia ignored his remark and her body's response to him, trying not to focus on the difficult conversation they would have later, and handed him a glass of champagne. "Merry Christmas and Happy New Year." She paused a heartbeat before adding, "Beast."

"Oh yeah, same to you."

He took a gulp of champagne, set his glass on a side table and pulled her against him. He gave her a hard kiss, his hands groping her roughly, pinching and pulling.

Gia yanked away from him, careful not to spill her champagne and turned her back on him.

"I've got to drain the beast." He walked a little unsteadily into the bedroom, shutting the door behind him.

Gia's heart pounded. So, that was how it would be. She set her glass on the mantel and sat in a chair beside the fireplace and tucked her hands under her thighs in a futile attempt to control their shaking.

She looked up and realized the door to the powder room was open and the bedroom door closed. *Why isn't he using the powder room? Why is he in there?*

Gia waited another moment, listening to hear the toilet flush. Silence. Her heart began to pound. She stood up and walked slowly to the bedroom door, afraid of what she would see. "Sal, is everything all right?" she called out tentatively as she turned the knob and cautiously peered in.

Sal was leaned over the dresser and looked up, startled to see Gia.

She took a few hesitant steps into the room, saddened and angered by the scene in front of her—a neat row of powder on the dresser's glass top, Sal leaning over, a rolled-up twenty-euro note in his hand.

He smiled widely. "Join me?" She shook her head, on the verge of tears, unable to speak. "Come on, it's New Year's Eve, and we're celebrating!" he said and waved the euro note toward her in invitation.

She looked at him, her eyes hard and cold. "You're using in *my* apartment, in *my* bedroom. You promised you had it under control."

"Technically, it's my apartment—I'm celebrating. What's your problem, and why are you so uptight, anyway?"

"I thought you would want to make tonight special."

"Tonight is special because I'm taking you to dinner at one of the finest restaurants in Madrid, and then we're going to my boss's party, which is part of what you signed up for when you signed the contract. And then we're going to come back here, baby, and—" He grasped his crotch crudely.

Gia gasped and burst into tears of anger and disappointment. Instead of waiting to have one last, lovely evening with Sal, she spat out, "Oh, the contract? The contract is over. It's over right now!" and stormed out of the room.

Sal followed. "Don't be melodramatic, Minx. It was just one little line."

He grabbed her shoulders, forced her around to face him and pulled her toward him for another kiss. She turned her head to the side. "Minx, don't be difficult, this is what you signed up for." He grabbed her hair, turning her face back to him and kissed her hard, forcing her mouth open. She struggled to pull away, and Sal tightened his grip on her shoulder and head. Her hair tumbled out of its pins.

"No! No! No! Enough! Stop! You're hurting me." Gia tried to yell out as his mouth smothered hers.

Sal didn't stop—kissing—manhandling her—his hands grabbing—his pelvis thrusting against her.

Her heart pounded in fright. Gia worked her hands between their bodies and shoved him as hard as she could.

He gripped her wrists behind her and tangled a hand in her hair and forced more rough kisses on her. She wrenched one arm free and slapped him in the face with all her strength. "Enough! Stop! Let me go! Get off me!" she yelled.

Caught by surprise, Sal let go. She sobbed and slapped him again, hard. "When I say stop, I mean STOP!" She stumbled back.

They both breathed heavily and looked at each other in shock.

What just happened? she thought. *What did I just do? I've never hit anyone before.*

I've got to get control of this situation, thought Sal.

"I'm so sorry, Minx. Let's sit down and cool off before we go out." Sal grabbed his champagne, took a deep gulp and began to refill his glass. He held the bottle out toward her.

Gia walked toward the door and then spun around. "Go out? Are you *crazy*? After that, do you really think I want to be around you?"

"Oh, come on, Minx, I was just trying to have a bit of fun."

Gia picked up the keys from the table next to the door and said to him in a sad, dull tone, "Don't you know? I love you. I cannot do this. I cannot watch someone I love so much destroy himself and hurt those around him."

Sal looked annoyed. "None of this was about love, it was just a contract."

"The fucking contract is done!" she said in a low, angry voice and pointed at him. Her jaw tightened. "And you—" her finger stabbed the air, "you need to get help."

"I need help? You're the whore! You're the one who has been kept by three guys! You're the one fucking three guys!"

"But it has only ever been you that I loved!"

"Yeah, right, I'm sure you tell us all that," he sneered.

"For years, I've only slept with you. I'm not a whore." She rubbed the back of her hands across her cheeks, smearing the mascara running down her face.

"You're splitting hairs. You were paid, well paid and given a great place to live. In return for that, we fucked, just fucked. I could have paid a whore. At least I wouldn't have had all this drama. At least she wouldn't have complained about my drugs. At least she would have been okay with me just leaving after sex. You're always asking for more. 'More. More'." he whined.

"You are a nasty bastard. Raul and David told me this would happen."

"You talked about *us* to Raul? And who's David? Someone else you fucked?" Sal's voice became louder. "You're nothing to me, nothing! All you were was someone to fuck."

Gia's arm swung back in anger, and she threw her keys across the room at him. They hit Sal's face hard, slicing his cheek. He reached up to touch his face and looked in astonishment at the blood on his fingers.

Her own violence shocked Gia. "I've become like him," she murmured as she looked at the blood running down his face.

Chapter Sixteen

July 2009

Sasha's Birthday Party

Slovenia

"SURPRISE!"

"Happy birthday!"

"Happy fiftieth!"

"Surprise!"

Sasha's mouth fell open as he walked into the farmhouse late in the afternoon, his arms full of bags and packages. He and Fong had spent most of the day in town, working through Kisho's exhaustive shopping list.

Friends popped out from doorways, from behind curtains, from his kitchen and it took a moment to register that his closest friends were really there, in his house, calling out birthday wishes.

Sasha looked at Kisho, standing in the middle of the great room with his arms spread wide in welcome. "How did you ever pull this off?"

Fong came from behind Sasha and took the bags from his hands. "Surprised, huh?" he chuckled in delight.

"You knew?" Sasha accused him.

"It was my job to keep you away from the house until everyone arrived, until Gia had dinner well in hand, and not to allow you to come home early under any circumstances."

"So, that's why you kept adding stops along the way?"

"And lunch. All those phone calls? Those were all Kisho, giving me updates."

Both men laughed as Fong carried the bags into the kitchen. Along the way, he paused to lean over and give Lee a smile and a kiss.

"Kisho is a sly dog. He has been working with us on this party for months." Mari wrapped her arms around Sasha and kissed his cheek. "Happy birthday, my dear friend."

Gia, in bare feet with her hair twisted up on top of her head, held in a careless knot by the chopstick she'd shoved through it, pushed in to give him an exuberant hug. Sasha hugged her back. He looked over her shoulder.

"How did Raul and David get here?"

Gia giggled. "On the train?" Everyone laughed.

Raul hugged Sasha next. "We've been conspiring with Kisho for months to make this happen. David and I wouldn't have missed it for the world."

"But I saw you in April on your annual cruise. Were you already planning this?"

David enveloped Sasha in a huge hug. "Oh, months before that, darling. You couldn't decide if you were going to be here in Slovenia or in Tokyo for your fiftieth, so *you* weren't very helpful with our planning."

Sasha saw Lee approach. "You knew and kept it quiet? I thought you at least would have given me a warning." He kissed her on the forehead and then remembered she and Gia had stayed home with Kisho that day to bake his birthday cake. "Well, I just hope that a huge chocolate cake will make an appearance later this evening."

Lee hugged Sasha. "Never in your life would I have ruined this surprise. As for chocolate cake—I don't know what you're talking about," she said with a wicked smile as she glanced over at the sideboard where an elaborately decorated cake stood.

Sasha followed her eyes and moaned appreciatively, "Now *that* is a chocolate cake to celebrate with!"

Kisho finally took Sasha in his arms and gave him a tender kiss. "Why do you think I was insistent on coming here? I wanted there to be plenty of space, and I needed everyone to be close enough so we could all get together and celebrate you. All these wonderful friends insisted on being here."

A single tear escaped Sasha's eye and ran into a crease on his cheek. "What dear friends you all are. I'm so glad to welcome you here to our little piece of paradise."

Gia looped her arm through Sasha's and herded the group into the kitchen where the air was redolent with the rich smell of her cooking. She wanted to continue with dinner preparations but not miss all the fun. "Sasha, it took your fiftieth birthday party to finally get a chance to come visit your vineyard. I love cooking in farmhouse kitchens, just like I did with my mom back home.

You've done a splendid job renovating it. You've given it so much character. Your house is more lovely than all your descriptions."

"It was completely a labor of love. It took longer than we first anticipated because there were certain parts, like this kitchen, that I wanted to either do or personally oversee myself."

Gia rattled on, "This reminds me of my apartment in Madrid combined with the farmhouse I grew up in. I'm glad you were able to keep all the old floors and beams—but still have it function as a twenty-first century home."

Kisho said, "It was so dilapidated when we bought it, but it had good bones. In fact, all we had were bones at first. We were lucky the original hardwood floors somehow survived, and we were able to restore them. But the beams are actually not original to this house—we rescued them from one of the outbuildings that we had to demolish. I am glad we fooled you into believing they were part of the original structure."

"Past and present—it's all so seamless," said Gia. "Oh no," she laughed, "I'm geeking out again."

Mari said, "The outside is still so traditional and looks centuries old."

"It is," grinned Kisho.

Mari turned to Gia. "It looks kind of like your parents' farmhouse or so many other ones in southern Spain."

"That's exactly what our goal was!" beamed Sasha. He paused and looked around the kitchen island. He felt so blessed to be surrounded by these special friends and his partner. He clasped Kisho around the shoulders and gave him a kiss. "Friends should be together to celebrate each other's landmark life events," he said. "This is perfect." He pulled his apron from a hook and stepped around to the other side of the island to help Gia with dinner.

David immediately said, "Hey, birthday boy, why are you in the kitchen, cooking on your special day?"

"Where else would he be?" asked Kisho. "He cannot watch someone else cook, especially in his kitchen."

Sasha said, "I've found a kindred spirit in Gia." He squeezed her hand and went on, "I love talking with her about food and, finally, to have the chance to cook with her—I wouldn't pass it up for the world!"

Mari said, "I'm so happy to see two of my dearest friends have become so close."

"Well, your friends are my friends. And our midnight soirees showed me just how special Gia is. I'm glad to call her my friend."

"Midnight soirees?" Lee asked Mari.

"On board the boat, we meet once or twice a week late at night, after we've officially finished our work, to 'compare notes' on the guests' needs. We bring wine, fruit and cheese and, of course, chocolate—Gia's contribution. I'm not sure who has more of a sweet tooth for chocolate, Gia or Sasha."

"Cannot miss the chocolate," Sasha laughed. "We do have serious conversations, but then it ends up being time to relax and let our hair down and get to know one another."

"Those midnight soirees were how I adjusted to riverboat work and life so quickly. Mari and Sasha took me under their wings. And we do have a good time," grinned Gia.

She nudged Sasha's shoulder with hers and said, "But enough about work—we need to prepare food."

Raul walked over and unwrapped the foil from a couple of bottles of champagne. "Shall we make a toast?"

Everyone replied with an enthusiastic, "Yes!"

He popped the corks, poured eight glasses of champagne and handed them around.

Kisho raised his glass and said, "Happy fiftieth birthday to the most wonderful man in the world."

Everyone held up their glasses in a toast, "To Sasha!" and took a sip.

Raul said, "Mmmm. This is wonderful champagne."

"But of course, nothing but the best on this day," said Mari.

Sasha looked around to his circle of friends, "To friendship."

David added at the end, "Hear, hear."

Everyone repeated, "To friendship."

They raised their glasses again and sipped.

After a moment of silence, Fong lifted his glass, "Sasha, you have enriched my life. To our wonderful friendship, and to your fiftieth birthday."

"We couldn't imagine our lives without you. You've become a dear, dear friend to both of us over the past ten years," Lee continued.

"I'm so happy you're both here." Sasha ducked his head, embarrassed at all the accolades.

Caught up in the moment, Fong pulled Lee toward him, bent her over in a dramatic dip and gave her a passionate kiss.

"You two will need to go to your room if you keep that up," David pretended to scold.

Lee touched her mouth with a satisfied smile as she regained her balance. "Where did that come from, Daniel?"

"Yes Daniel, I told you not to drink that fourth beer," teased Sasha.

Fong threw his head back and roared in laughter. This was in such contrast to his usual formality that everyone stared at him in astonishment and then broke out laughing. Lee joined in, "So that's what this is all about. Four beers, hmmm?"

Gia pointed at him with the knife and gestured at the island filled with food, "There're munchies here to soak up some of that alcohol."

They all gathered around, eating tiny hors d'oeuvres, olives, almonds, stuffed mushrooms, and fresh bruschetta, laughing and chatting away, interrupting one another, finishing sentences as only old friends can do.

Raul opened more champagne. It reminded Gia briefly of Sal. Raul noticed as a sad look crossed Gia's face. Then she recovered and said, "Kisho, since you're standing there doing nothing—" and everyone laughed, "—would you please bring up a few bottles of wine and open them so they can breathe before we sit down for dinner?"

"Come on, Fong. I need help with this." They obediently went off to the wine cellar to forage. "And—I have a great bottle you need to try," whispered Kisho.

Sasha began to help Gia cook. "Another thing that attracted us to this property was that the owner included his wine cellar with several hundred bottles of wonderful Cabernet Franc from his— no, that would be *our*—vineyard."

"Well, while we are here, we'll take a stab at reducing your holdings!" David said to more laughter.

"I need a volunteer to set the table—David and Raul." Gia giggled and pointed at them. "You can find everything you need over there." She vaguely waved her champagne glass in the direction of the huge butler's pantry and then took another sip.

"Yes, darling!" David headed off to follow her instructions. He disappeared into the pantry and said over his shoulder, "Look at this *amazing* collection!"

Sasha and Gia continued to work together in the kitchen. "I designed that butler's pantry specifically so everything you need for the table is in one place, each set of dishes, cutlery, table linens, serving pieces, etcetera, all stored together."

David overheard him and poked his head out. "You're not kidding. There are different place settings, glasses and linens for different seasons and holidays. All shelved together. Shall I use these beautiful yellow plates with the white roses on them?"

"You choose, David," Sasha said.

"Or I could use the Christmas china. It's absolutely stunning."

"Christmas is my favorite holiday, so I will be perfectly happy if you choose it. Whatever floats your boat, David."

David spent a few more minutes in the pantry, thoroughly examining the entire inventory. Since he'd been told to choose, he decided he would use the opportunity to have a good look around first. Sasha grinned as he heard David talking to himself as he mulled over his choices.

Raul went around the island and whispered to Gia, "Are you okay? I noticed you went to your sad place for a moment there."

"It's just all the champagne and a momentary flashback to Sal. There are some lovers you never forget. Sal was all about champagne and great sex. It always brings him back. In a fond way—mostly."

Raul chuckled, "Speaking of lovers you never forget—how about Pierre? If Sal was champagne and great sex, what was Pierre all about?"

"Outdoors and romance."

"Did you call him like you said you were going to?"

"Yes, as a matter of fact. And my timing was bad. He's living in Paris with a girlfriend, and he's *mad* about her."

Before Raul went off to the pantry to help David, he gave her a quick peck on the cheek.

"If you need to talk—" he said near her ear.

"No, honestly, I've moved on," Gia replied as she began to chop the vegetables.

Raul gave her a quizzical look.

She smirked and raised her voice, "Who's ready to party?"

"I am," Lee and Mari answered in unison.

Smiling, Raul shook his head and called out to David, "Did you get lost in there?"

David laughed. "Come on in here and take a look. There's so much cool stuff. We could set fourteen complete tables and have lots to spare." Raul stepped in and looked around. David grabbed him and said, "While we're alone—" and wrapped his arms around him and gave him a long kiss and a furtive squeeze to his behind.

"Trust you to find a way to be alone in the middle of a crowd," Raul laughed.

David said, "Now that I have you captive here, darling, you can help me carry some of this stuff out."

"Ah, I see right through you. You seduce me to get help. Just your average kitchen wench." They exchanged a lingering kiss.

Lee turned to Mari. "I saw a flower basket and scissors on the terrace. Would you mind helping me cut some flowers for the table? Maybe we can make low arrangements in those crystal bowls from the sideboard, so we don't have them blocking our line of sight.

"And we can catch up with each other, too. I want all the news from Paris and the latest about Lydia," Lee went on.

Mari snagged an open bottle of champagne from the sideboard and headed off to the terrace. As they walked out, she said, "And I want to hear about your new place in Ostia. Do you love being back in Italy—hey, I saw some beautiful rose bushes over there. Let's go see if any of those would work."

Lee picked up the scissors and basket and dragged Mari by

the hand into the garden.

With great care, David and Raul set the long refectory table on the terrace, just off the kitchen, with a navy linen tablecloth and the yellow plates with white roses. They returned to the pantry to take out the crystal tea light holders and placed them on the table in a random arrangement. They put candles in them, ready to light just before they would all sit down to dinner.

As they stood admiring the table, Raul looked up to see Lee and Mari laughing and passing the bottle back and forth as they wandered toward the terrace. *This will be an entertaining evening,* he thought. He nudged David and they laughed as they stood and watched the two women giggling as they tried to walk and drink from the bottle, froth running over onto the flowers in their basket.

Mari and Lee arrived with their basket full of champagne-soaked white and yellow roses and trailing vines from the garden. They chattered non-stop as they very slowly and precisely trimmed the stems and tucked the roses into the crystal bowls that David and Raul had arranged among the tea lights. They giggled as they tried to dry the roses and then trailed the vines around them and along the table between the small candles.

Amused, David watched them. "How did you match the roses with the plates? You were already outside when we decided we'd use them. They're absolutely perfect."

"Kismet." Lee and Mari laughed at their own wittiness and leaned against each other, giggling helplessly.

In the kitchen, Sasha and Gia discussed their latest cooking techniques while he helped at the stove. Finally, he left her to finish the last details, turned around and walked out to the terrace. He gave a small gasp. "You guys!" he said fondly. "The table looks so festive and romantic!" He put his hands over his heart. "What a spectacular birthday setting—overlooking our vineyard!" Sasha went over to them and gave David and Raul a kiss on the cheek. "Thank you both."

David and Raul looked at one another, and David said, "Are we good or what?"

Mari pretended to whine. "Well, we helped, too." Then she

and Lee giggled again.

Sasha laughed. "Of course," he said before giving her and Lee a kiss on the cheek as well.

Once Kisho and Fong had opened the wine on the rustic sideboard on the terrace and had gotten the glasses ready, Fong turned to Kisho, "You were right. That bottle was remarkable!"

Kisho nodded in agreement, only slightly less tipsy than Fong after the glasses of wine they'd consumed in the cellar. He poured the wine and then poked his head into the kitchen and said to Gia, "Is that food ready yet? It smells divine, and I am starving."

Gia had just finished piling the platters with bread, meats and vegetables. "Everyone come here and grab a serving dish to take outside."

Once the table was full and the candles lit, the group stood back to admire the scene, the beautiful table filled with flowers, candles and food, and the vineyard on the rolling hills a gorgeous backdrop.

The breeze blew gently across the terrace.

"What's that incredible smell?" Gia asked.

Sasha smiled. "It's the vineyard."

"At this time of year, when the sun is hot all day and the grapes are ripening, they have that flat, dry, dusty scent. It is one of the most wonderful smells in the world to me," Kisho said.

"It's like nothing else I've ever smelled before." Gia breathed in deeply and turned to Mari. "I've never been to your family's vineyard at this time of year. Does it smell like this as well?"

Mari giggled, "I suppose it does. I hadn't ever thought about it. I only drink the wine."

"To me, that's the smell of life, of growth. It returns every year—I couldn't ask for a better place to celebrate my birthday," Sasha said. "And for my fiftieth, to be here surrounded by my dearest friends as well, it couldn't be more perfect."

Kisho teased, "As you keep saying—" and they all laughed.

"But it's true! It's absolutely wonderful!" protested Sasha.

They stood on the shaded terrace in the warm, late afternoon, looking out over the vineyard, breathing in the country air, the smell of the grapes, the scent of the jasmine winding over the top of the terrace.

Kisho turned to the sideboard and handed each person a glass of wine before they sat down. He placed more open bottles at each end of the table and remained standing. He lifted his glass and in a sentimental tone said, "Sasha, I know I already said this, but because I have had a lot of wine, I get to say it again."

Mari and Lee giggled, and Kisho continued, "You are the love of my life. You are a devoted, kind and gentle soul, who has made my life full and wonderful. Thank you for giving your life to me. Your love has touched not only me, but the lives of all the people at this table."

Raul turned toward Kisho and Sasha, "You know, we've always admired the love you two have for one another. You're such an inspiration to us. And you've made us feel like part of your family, too."

"A crazy family, but a family nevertheless," David looked around.

Gia stood up.

Mari looked at Lee, sitting across the table from her, and said in a loud whisper, "This must be serious."

"Sasha, we've all become like family. When friends choose to become a family, it's a strong bond, and we know we'll all be there to take care of one another. Happy birthday. I love you all."

Everyone held up their glasses in silence and took a drink of wine.

Mari leaned across the table and whispered loudly again to Lee, "Gia needs more to drink."

Sasha looked at his glass and said, "Kisho, I think we *all* need more wine."

The group burst out laughing.

Everyone filled their plates and began talking across and down the table. *What wonderful chaos,* thought Gia and looked across at Raul. She caught his eye and said, "Family chaos."

He grinned. "I'm loving every moment of it."

Kisho was sitting across from Sasha, with David to his right. He turned and covered David's hand with his. "I heard you and Raul moved in together. That's wonderful."

Raul interrupted from the other side of the table, "Much to the disappointment of my family. They've completely disowned me. Their loss because I came out ahead." He opened his arms as if to embrace the group around the table, "All of you, and David, are my family now."

David replied in an unusual moment of solemnity, "Yes, it was a big sacrifice for Raul. He has given up a lot for me." He kissed the tips of his fingers and blew a kiss across the table to Raul as he went on, "And now—now we are planning to buy a house together."

Kisho said, "That is wonderful. Do you think you will get married? I do not know why Sasha and I keep picking countries that are not as accepting of our lifestyle. But we are committed to each other, and that is all that matters." He looked across the table and smiled into Sasha's eyes.

"I would marry Raul tomorrow. I have no family but him." David said.

Mari said back, "What about us? Are we just stray kittens?"

"Just champagne kitties out in the garden," said Lee, and she and Mari began to giggle again.

Fong turned to Sasha and asked quietly, "So when are you going to finally retire and live here at this beautiful estate full time with that wonderful wine cellar?"

"I'm trying to convince Kisho to sell his consulting business. I'd like to retire when he does. And I hope that happens sooner rather than later."

"I love my business, and I have a few good years left in me, so do not put me out to pasture yet," Kisho said lightly.

"Yeah, but with or without Kisho, you can live here and write," Fong said to Sasha.

"I'm not a writer."

"But you are a storyteller," Gia said.

The group lingered over their meal, drank, chatted, laughed and reminisced. Kisho stood up to open yet another bottle of wine and filled each glass.

And finally, as the sunlight began to wane, Mari and Lee began taking dishes into the kitchen a few at a time and giggled every time they caught one another's eye. The group continued their conversations as they slowly stood up and finished clearing the table.

In the kitchen, they worked together to tidy up. And when they were done, Raul proclaimed in a deep, solemn voice, "The kitchen is closed."

Gia teased, "You always say that," and they all laughed.

Kisho and Fong slipped away to place comfortable, cushioned chairs around the fire pit at the edge of the lawn. As they walked back into the kitchen, Kisho said, "We have prepared wood for a fire this evening."

David patted him on the shoulder. "Let's go and enjoy this beautiful evening."

On the terrace, Kisho refilled their wine glasses and they wandered over to the chairs. He followed with a carrier of opened bottles that he set on a low table behind one of the chairs. They chose seats and sat down, and he picked up a long match and lit the kindling.

Mari remained standing, balancing carefully. "I haven't given my toast yet."

David said, "Couldn't stay quiet, huh?" and Mari joined in the group's laughter.

She gave David a sideways grin and said, "Seriously?" before continuing, "Happy birthday, my dear Sasha." She placed one hand over her heart, and a blank look crossed her face. "Oh shit, I forgot my toast," she said. Lee doubled over and giggled quietly trying not to spill her wine.

Raul grinned at Mari, "To Sasha, and to all of us."

They raised their glasses one last time as the sun dropped lower in the sky and repeated, "To all of us."

The sky had filled with high, wispy clouds, and the sun reflected off them in brilliant oranges, reds and yellows, as though reflecting the flames from the fire in front of them.

Sasha said, "Look at that amazing birthday sunset tonight."

"I arranged it just for you," quipped Kisho.

After it had grown dark, Kisho put more wood on the fire and without a word, Gia stood up and went into the house, a smile on her lips.

Suddenly, the sound of Frank Sinatra's voice wafted across the lawn. Kisho stood in front of Sasha, a hand outstretched. "May I have this dance?" and Sasha took his hand as the music began to play *The Best is Yet to Come.*

Moments later Gia reappeared carrying a tray filled with shot glasses and a bottle of *rakia.* "Look what I found." Raul jumped up and took the tray from Gia's hands and set it carefully on the small table next to David's chair.

"Good find, Gia." David stood up and pushed Raul aside with his elbow, "Leave this to me." He opened the bottle and poured large shots into all eight glasses.

Mari grabbed a glass. "¡*Salud*!" she shouted out before downing the shot.

"¡*Salud*!" the others called out, following her lead.

Lee looked at Fong, "You know, I think I'm drunk."

"I think you probably are," he said with an affectionate smile and patted her on the bottom.

"You're a lightweight." Mari leaned close to Lee as she spoke.

"Let's dance." Lee tipped her head back and flung her arms wide as she turned in a slow circle and then began to tip dangerously to one side. Fong caught her and drew her close, "Let's dance in the moonlight, Daniel."

Gia poured another shot for herself, David, and Raul, "We need to catch up with them."

Mari grabbed David's hand, "Come on, Davey, I need to get on the dance floor."

And they all danced and laughed into the early hours of the morning.

♦

The next afternoon, carefully nursing their hangovers, Sasha, Kisho, Fong and Lee stood in front of the farmhouse with their arms around each other's waists and waved goodbye as the rest of their friends departed.

"Goodbye!"

"What a great time!"

"Happy birthday!"

"See you soon!"

They piled into the car and drove down the dirt road away from the farmhouse.

Sasha's News

Slovenia

"Mari—" came a heartbroken cry through her phone. She instinctively looked at her clock. It was five a.m.

"Mari—"

"Sasha? What's wrong? Tell me. What is it?"

"It's Kisho—Kisho had a stroke, a massive stroke."

Her stomach tightened in dread at what she knew would come next. "Oh, Sasha!"

Before she could say anything more, he went on, "He died in my arms before the ambulance arrived." Sasha started to sob uncontrollably.

Mari began to cry. "Oh, Sasha. Oh, no—what can I do for you?" Her voice choked.

"He's gone—Mari, I'm in such pain—it hurts—it hurts so much. We were so happy this past week. We were supposed to grow old together—here at our farmhouse. Why? Why did this happen? Kishooo!" he howled, and his anguish poured through the phone.

Tears ran down Mari's face as she tried to comfort her friend. "Oh, my dear, dear friend. I wish I were there to hold you." Sasha broke down completely. Mari heard the phone drop to the ground.

A moment later, Fong's strained voice came on. "Mari, are you there?"

"I am—this is so dreadful—I'm in complete shock," Mari said through her tears. She got out of bed and walked out to the casita patio, one arm wrapped around her torso, cradling her grief.

"We're all in shock. Sasha called me at around one this morning—they'd already taken Kisho's body away. Lee and I stayed on with them for a few days after the party and then went to Lake Bled before we were to drive back home to Ostia. Thank goodness we were still close by. We came back here immediately. We got here about half an hour ago."

"I'm so glad you're there for him," Mari said in a soft voice.

"When we arrived, we found Sasha sitting out on the terrace

in the moonlight, staring at the vineyard. I think some part of him is waiting for Kisho to come home."

"Oh, my heart is breaking." Mari's voice choked with a sob.

"Lee has been with him since we arrived. He won't accept anything to eat or drink. He's just sitting and staring."

"Oh, poor, poor Sasha—" She inhaled, her voice shaking as she fought to gain control. "Shall I inform Spectrum for him?"

"Yes, will you, please?"

"Of course. I'm sure they will give him all the time he needs."

"Okay. At least that's one thing I won't have to worry about." Fong's voice broke.

"I'll be there tomorrow."

"That's not necessary. We have to leave in a day or two for Tokyo to settle Kisho's affairs and deal with selling his business. I'll be with Sasha through it all."

"I feel so helpless. Is there anything I can do from here?" Tears poured down her cheeks.

"Not right now. I'll keep in close touch." His voice grew uneven as he held back his own tears. "Oh wait, please tell Gia, David and Raul. Especially Gia. She and Sasha have become so close."

"Absolutely. How are you and Lee doing?" she asked with concern in her voice.

"It hurts to see our dear friend suffering so. He's strong and has been there for all of us." Fong's voice cracked. "I know he'll get through this, but his heart is broken. Kisho was truly his other half, his soulmate." Mari heard him trying to compose himself before he continued, his voice shaking, "The house doesn't seem the same without Kisho here. He was so full of life and joy. Now, it's so empty. It feels like he'll walk back through the door, laughing and—" The sound of a single, heartrending sob echoed through the phone. "At—at this point, we simply need to help Sasha get through these early days. We'll have time to grieve after that."

Mari pressed her fist into her mouth and bit down hard, pain to fight pain.

"I know you and Lee will take care of Sasha. Please, take him in your arms and hold him for me and let him know I love him very much. If you need anything, anything at all, let me know. Oh God, I feel so helpless, like I should be there with him." She bit down again, and her face contorted with pain—pain in her hand but more pain in her heart.

"There's nothing more anyone can do here. Once Kisho's memorial is arranged, I'll call you with the details," Fong said dully.

"I assume that will be at the farmhouse."

"I'm sure it will. I just can't talk to Sasha about those details yet."

After they said goodbye, Mari hung up and sat and put her face in her hands and cried and cried and cried, her body wracked with tears.

Some while later, she sat up, staring blindly at the courtyard fountain as the early morning sun peeked through the trees, bright light that didn't deserve to be there that day. *It should be grey and cloudy,* she thought angrily, *it should be raining. The sky should weep for Kisho.* Tears seeped from behind her eyelids again. Even the sound of trickling water from the fountain failed to soothe her. *Nothing is more devastating than losing someone so suddenly and knowing you will never see them again, never have time to say goodbye. Nothing,* she wept.

Chapter Seventeen

August 2010

Getting Away

Raleigh, North Carolina

The sun cast their long shadows across the tee box in front of them. Tracey and Sam paused quietly for a moment on the last hole. With their drivers in hand, they stood admiring the view of the magnificent Bagley Farm clubhouse with its stone facade and immense chimney, sweeping shingled roof and tall windows, nestled in the hollow at the bottom of the hill. The Neuse River flowed past on its left, the surface gleaming in the sunlight.

"It will be nice to get out of this heat and have a tall, cold gin and tonic," Tracey said.

"It sure is hot, but what a perfect day for a round. Thank goodness the humidity was lower, and we've had that little bit of a breeze. Otherwise, I might have been tempted to throw in the towel early."

"I'm glad we were able to play alone today. I like golfing with Cal and Jim—they are fun guys—but without them we get to talk about more than women or the latest scandal that Cal read about in the local rag. Anyhow, I wanted to let you know, I'm taking a break."

"What do you mean, taking a break? From golf?" Sam asked as Tracey took a tee out of his pocket.

Tracey pressed the sharp end of the tee into the pad of his thumb. He stared across the fairway as he replied, "I'm going away for a while."

A chuckle in his voice, Sam said, "It sounds like you're going to prison."

Tracey laughed nervously. *I hope not*, he thought and leaned over to place his tee and ball in the ground. He checked his direction carefully before hitting his drive with a resounding thwack. After his swing, he looked over at Sam and said, "I'm glad we had the course to ourselves. It's been a relaxing round, just taking our time and catching up."

As they got into the cart, Sam looked at him a little perplexed, "Where are you going? How long will you be gone? Are you okay?"

"I'm fine. I leave next week. I'll be away for about four months. I want to travel in Europe. It's been on my bucket list since I was in college, but it never seemed to be the right time. There was always something else I wanted to do more."

Before he drove the cart off to their balls, Sam paused and turned to Tracey. "You've never mentioned that before."

"I know. It just struck me how much I need a break. It's been a tough two years since my folks died. After I retired last year, I spent far too many hours trying to understand all the details of their foundation, endowments, various philanthropic works, their finances. Their deaths and then my fortieth birthday last month started me thinking about how little time we really have and what I want to do with my life. You know, I got a healthy inheritance from them and from my grandparents. Life is short. I've decided it's time to travel. Yesterday, I was rummaging around on the internet, and I saw an ad for a river cruise in Europe—in Ukraine, actually. It sounds a little exotic and seems like the perfect way to begin my adventure. So, I went to their website and booked it. After that, who knows?"

Sam nodded and turned back to drive the golf cart away from the tee box. "What about your obligations here?"

Tracey thought, *He'll never understand. I need to go somewhere else, to find a change of scenery. Ever since the newspaper published that garbage about the serial killer, I've known I have to get away. It's been more than two years now since I killed that woman. I haven't killed again. I need to continue to keep that impulse under control. I have to.*

"The world can function without me here," he said after the briefest hesitation. "I've been delegating more and more to the museum board members. They're a competent bunch. And the gala is in good hands—it has been for years. The committee knows what to do. I'm sure it will go off without a hitch without me here bothering people about it." He chuckled, "I'll just swoop in at the last moment and make my 'Welcome to the Lauch Art Museum Gala' speech."

Sam parked the cart next to Tracey's ball, and before Tracey got out, he patted him on the shoulder. "You have a good team around you at the museum. But what about the Sarah's House fundraiser?"

As Tracey got out and selected his club, he said, "We've just about finished wrapping that one up. There're a few last details we have to follow up on, and then it's over for this year. In September, the regular group will start to put together what we need for the next one, but as you know, that doesn't get underway seriously until early in the new year."

"I'll miss you and this game of ours. But you're right. It is a perfect time to get away. And you appear to have everything under control."

Murder in Zaporizhzhya

Spectrum Cruise, *The Krasnyy*

Tracey sat in what he considered to be the best corner of the boat's bar for people-watching. His eyes followed passengers as they came and went, alone, in pairs, in groups, some stopping for drinks at the bar, some choosing chairs arranged around small tables and others just passing through.

He held the pen in his left hand and tapped the end lightly against his teeth as he contemplated the remaining squares in that day's sudoku and ran his slender fingers through his greying hair. He looked up as Sasha set down his cognac.

"I can never get my head around sudoku," said Sasha. "And you're living on the edge using a pen!"

Tracey laughed. "You do crossword puzzles in pen."

Sasha looked at him in surprise. Tracey continued, "I saw you this morning."

"You're very observant, Judge Lauch."

Tracey smiled and thought about how similar many of the skills were for their two professions, judge and bartender.

Once everyone had been served their after-dinner drinks, Sasha came back over to chat with Tracey. "How did you like Kyiv, Judge?"

"Interesting. I made it to St. Sophia's Cathedral, and it was stunning, just as all the guidebooks say. I'm glad Mari recommended it. But I'm not much for guided tours—I prefer to find little out-of-the-way shops and restaurants, to ride the streetcars and buses and experience cities like the people who live there. So, I broke away from the tour group to wander around and see the city on my own. That's how I stumbled across a toilet museum."

"The Toilet History Museum?" Sasha laughed out loud, "I haven't made it there yet. What did you think?"

"You haven't been there?"

"Not yet."

"I have to confess, it was actually pretty entertaining," Tracey chuckled. "In fact, it may have been the funniest thing I've visited in a long time. It's not very large. I'd recommend it to anyone who has a skewed sense of humor and an hour or two for something different."

Sasha leaned closer to Tracey and whispered, "It wasn't shitty?"

The two men laughed.

"Well, it will tell you everything you ever wanted to know about toilets and even what you didn't know you wanted to know. It's located in an old fortress with wonderful baroque music playing in the background. Every so often you can hear the sound of a toilet flush as you wander through rooms full of commodes. At first, I wasn't sure I had heard that, but then I heard it again intermittently as I wandered on."

A woman sitting a few seats away had been admiring Tracey's strong jaw and clean profile, the way his hair curled slightly against his neck. *He looks like he should be a politician,* she thought. She leaned over and said in a light British accent, "That sounds brilliant! I'm sorry I stuck with the tour group and missed that one. I confess, I've been eavesdropping on your conversation, Judge. It sounds like you had a much better time than I did."

Tracey looked at the attractive, fortyish woman sitting on her own. "They had hundreds of toilets from all different periods of time. The restrooms were a museum in and of themselves. You could choose what era toilet you wanted to use, though I was relieved—ahem—to discover that they all were quite modern in function.

The woman snickered, "Quite relieved, were you?"

"I'll certainly be able to talk about it at dinner parties for years and years to come."

"Dinner and toilets?" She paused, "I guess one always leads to the other." The three of them chuckled companionably.

She looked at Sasha and raised her empty glass. "I'll have what he's having." She smiled and angled her head toward Tracey.

She's pretty—and witty. And she's flirting with me. This might be fun.

Sasha poured a cognac for her while Tracy continued, "But if I bring up the toilet museum at a dinner party, people may think

I have a potty mouth."

The woman laughed. "I would dare you to bring up toilets at a table filled with your judge colleagues," she retorted.

"In a heartbeat. Very few of us are actually staid old men— or women."

"Thank heavens for that!" She winked at him. "I didn't know judges could be such fun."

Sasha noticed how well they were getting along and interrupted, "Excuse me. A table by the window has opened up. If you'd like to take it, I'll bring your drinks over."

"Would you like to join me," Tracey motioned to the table, "to continue this conversation where so many people won't be privy," he grinned, "to what we say?"

The woman chuckled, and as she stood up, she said to Sasha, "And when we finish these, would you bring us another round, please?"

"Why not! We don't have to drive," said Tracey. For some reason, this amused them both.

Sasha smiled. "My pleasure." He picked up their drinks and carried them to the small table.

They sat down face to face and introduced themselves.

"Tracey Lauch—judge—retired."

She mimicked, "Charlotte—professor—English."

"That's why you're so skilled at repartee."

"Guilty as charged, Judge."

They both laughed. She turned to him. "You're retired? You're far too young. Retired judges definitely are old and grey and weathered looking."

"Thank you. I'm actually forty." He ruefully touched his salt and pepper hair. "I retired after my parents died a couple years ago."

She touched his hand. "My condolences, Tracey."

"Thank you."

They angled their chairs slightly toward the room and continued their lighthearted banter as they watched the activity in the lounge.

Sasha glanced around to see if any of the guests needed

anything. On his way back to the bar, picking up empty glasses along the way, he noticed an attractive, slim black woman sitting there and played his mental game, trying to guess her age and occupation. *Early forties,* I think.

"Hi, I'm Sasha Martinescu, how can I help you?" He reached out to shake her hand and noticed she wasn't wearing a wedding ring and had a firm, assertive handshake. *She's most likely single, and she probably works with a lot of men.*

"I'm Emily Bissett. I'd like a large glass of red wine. If you would choose, please."

He selected a bottle from the wine cooler. "How are you enjoying your cruise on *The Krasnyy*?"

"I think this is just my favorite of all the lines I've cruised with. This is my ninth river cruise and my second on Spectrum."

Sasha pulled the cork from the bottle he'd selected, took a small sip from his tasting glass and carefully poured her a generous serving. "Do you know about our naming convention for boats? They are all named after colors of the spectrum but in different languages."

"That's clever. And what's the translation of *'Krasnyy'*?"

"It's 'red' in Russian," said Sasha. He set her wine in front of her and then poured another round of cognac for Tracey and Charlotte.

Emily continued, "I've tried for years to convince Spectrum to hire my security company. Even though my other clients— other cruise companies—have found our services very helpful, Spectrum seems to think they don't need our help. So, I thought I would take a few cruises to get a feel for them."

"Spectrum takes security very seriously," Sasha replied in a neutral tone.

"They do, and it appears to be pretty solid. But I'm tenacious, so I'll keep trying." Emily smiled and handed Sasha her business card.

Before putting it in his shirt pocket, Sasha looked at it. "Oh, you're from Raleigh, North Carolina? Haypress Security. You're the owner."

"Yes, the buck stops with me," she grinned. "As a matter of

fact, I believe that gentleman sitting over there is also from Raleigh."

Sasha smiled back at her. "Excuse me for a moment while I deliver these drinks to him."

Charlotte turned to Tracey. "So, how do you know Sasha?"

"From here, at the bar. We met yesterday when I came in for an afternoon gin and tonic."

"It seems like you've known each other forever."

"We just hit it off. Something clicked between us. I watched him again last night. I admire what a great bartender he is. He is observant, attentive and very personable. He can converse with anyone about anything."

Charlotte and Tracey sat in comfortable silence, people-watching as they sipped their drinks, a candle flickering on the table in front of them. Suddenly, Charlotte began to chuckle.

Tracey glanced at her. "What's so funny?"

"Those two men over there just gave each other a bro hug."—she barely got the sentence out before her chuckle changed to an outright laugh. "I was wondering"—she laughed again—"is there a safe"—more laughter—"a safe groin perimeter"—gasping—"you guys have to maintain when you bro hug?" By this time, tears were running down her face.

Tracey chuckled as he watched her pick up a napkin from the table to wipe her eyes and said, "Hmmm—toilets and then groins—is there a southward trend here?" He leaned back and laughed, and Charlotte lost it again.

Tracey thought, *I haven't enjoyed spending time with a woman so much since Helen moved. What fun!*

The two were just recovering from their bout of laughter when Emily stopped by the table. "Judge Lauch? Fancy meeting you on this cruise. I'm Emily Bissett. We met about ten years ago—at a museum reception."

Tracey stood up and shook her hand, "I remember. What a small world. It's nice to see you again. This is Charlotte." He looked at Charlotte. "I don't know your last name."

"French. Charlotte French."

He glanced at her, and his lips twitched as he struggled to

control another bout of laughter. He looked back at Emily, "Charlotte and I just met."

"It was very nice to meet you. I don't want to interrupt your evening. I just wanted to say hi on my way back to my room."

"Maybe we'll have a chance to chat later. It was very nice running into you again. Have a good evening." Tracey smiled, nodded and sat back down, his shoulders shaking, and dropped his face into his hands.

As soon as Emily was out of hearing distance, he sat up. "Seriously," he gasped, "seriously—your last name is French? Seriously? You're a Brit, an English professor and your last name is French," and he completely lost it again.

Charlotte and Tracey chatted late into the evening. He confessed that he wanted to travel more and visit more places around the world, but he also liked the comfort and convenience of river cruises, especially high-end ones like Spectrum, that pamper their guests.

"So much world, so little time," she said with a gentle touch of sarcasm, "You know, there are river cruises in the US."

He grinned and put his hands up in mock surrender. "I know, I know. But frankly, I've never looked into it. I've been lured by the prospect of travel farther afield. I always figured I could do those US cruises when I got older and didn't want to travel such great distances."

"One of the first things I did when I moved to Washington State was to take a cruise down the Columbia River, through the Gorge and on down to the Snake River. It's truly one of the most spectacular river cruises I've ever taken."

"That's one I'd like to take someday."

As they talked, Tracey thought, *I do want to spend more time with this woman.* So, before they finally said good night, he asked, "Would you join me for dinner tomorrow night?"

Charlotte beamed at him. "I would love to."

◆

After she finished serving dinner, Gia poked her head into Mari's office. "I can't attend the midnight soiree tonight."

"Do you have a hot date?"

"Yeah, right—with my hair. I'm going to color my hair and then I'm going to call Raul."

"Color your hair? Now this will be interesting. I hope you're not going for blue."

"I'm not sharing anything more." Gia tossed her head, "You'll have to wait and see."

"Ooooh, so mysterious. Scoot now—I have work to do. Have fun and say hi to the boys for me!"

The color applied and the funny plastic cap over her hair, Gia looked in the mirror and grimaced. She knew if she weren't careful, she'd get the dye all over her hands and phone. *What a mess that would be.* She set a timer on her phone and put in her earbuds and called Raul while she waited for the color to take.

David saw Gia's name on Raul's caller ID and picked up the phone. "Hello, darling."

"Oh my gosh, it's so funny you picked up."

"Raul just stepped out of the room, and I saw your name. I knew he wouldn't want to miss your call."

"Before he gets back—remember at the farmhouse when you dared me to dye my hair?"

"You didn't—"

"The dye is doing its thing as we speak."

"Finally! What did you think of the color I picked?" he chortled.

"It *is* bright, and we'll see how it turns out."

They both laughed. "You have to send me a picture when you're done."

Gia heard Raul in the background. "Who's on the phone?"

David said, "It's Gia," and then to her, "I'll hand you over to Raul, and don't forget to send me the picture."

"Hello, darling," said Raul, and she heard the smirk in his voice.

Gia said with a giggle, "You'd think 'darling' was my name, as often as the two of you call me that."

Raul laughed, and they chatted about the first part of the cruise through Ukraine, how he and David were doing and about

Joseph and Anusha.

Before she hung up, Gia hesitated and then asked in a small voice, "Has Sal surfaced yet?"

Raul's voice became serious. "We're all very concerned about him, sweetheart. No one's heard from him in months."

"I'm so worried about him. It seemed like he was using more and more regularly and more heavily."

"I know that even though you're trying to move on, you still love him, Gia. We all do. All we can do is keep looking for him and hope for the best."

"I know. It's scary not knowing where he is—ooops, sorry, but I have to go and get this dye out of my hair."

"Dye?"

She said briskly, "I really have to go, ask David about it, love you both, bye-bye."

♦

Gia hopped from one foot to the other on the dock in Zaporizhzhya, waiting for Mari to join her, waiting for Mari to see her new hair—waiting—waiting. It was early and the first time they'd ever had a morning off together during a cruise. And Mari was wasting the day. Finally—there she came, strolling along, stopping from time to time to chat with passengers and answer their questions, just taking her time, apparently completely unaware of Gia's impatience. Mari walked off the boat and tucked her arm through Gia's. "Come on, let's go."

They strolled along, arm in arm, Mari pointing out sights of interest. Meanwhile, Gia was about to burst, waiting for her to say something about her hair. *I'll give her one more block*—she thought.

"You'll really enjoy Lilla's Coffee & Cream," said Mari, fully aware of Gia's impatience, teasing her. "I discovered it a couple of years ago on my first Ukraine cruise. They serve coffee in the most delightful little pots. And the pastries are out of this world," she chattered on.

Finally, Gia yanked her arm free from Mari's and spun around to stop in front of her. "Well—what do you think?"

"I think you're really going to like this café. It is small and has a nice, intimate atmosphere. The staff is very friendly, and like I said, the pastries are to die for."

"No, no, no, no, no—I know the coffee place will be wonderful." Playing with her hair, she continued, "My hair, Mari—what about my hair?"

Mari laughed out loud and smiled, "It looks great. You've done a good job—but what made you choose *that* color?"

"The dye is all natural, it's vegan, it's semi-permanent, it will wash out. I love how it looks and how fun it is."

Mari shook her head and laughed. "But the color?"

"The box said it's 'Ruby Red'." She flipped her hair back off her shoulders and said, "Don't you just love it?"

"It certainly is, ahem, ruby red. But why *that* color?"

"Don't you love it? It's sooo different, it makes me feel happy and alive. You're a redhead, and you always seem to have fun. Shouldn't life be about having fun and letting loose?" Gia twirled around, the skirt to her sundress billowing out, and the morning sun reflecting off her hair.

They continued walking up the street, side by side. Mari reached over and took a lock of Gia's hair between her fingers. "It is red, it is fun, and I can see it makes you happy. But the *color*?"

Gia tucked her arm through Mari's and smiled merrily. "It is a brighter red than I thought it would be, but that's the surprise in the box!"

◆

The aroma of fresh coffee drifted out to greet them as they climbed the short set of steps to the café. They took seats at a small table in the middle of the room.

"Mmmm, it does smell delicious," said Gia, inhaling deeply. "I smell chocolate. I wonder if they have chocolate croissants." She picked up the menu card and glanced at it, "Oh, good."

They chatted comfortably until the server brought them their orders, complete with a small pot of coffee and a cup, and they busied themselves with cream and sugar and first delicious bites of flaky pastry.

Then Gia began to laugh. "You know, David dared me."

Mari looked at Gia quizzically.

"My hair. At Sasha's farmhouse, as we were saying our goodbyes after his birthday party, David slipped a package into my carry-on bag with a note, *'I dare you! Love, David'*, and I've been carrying it around for a year trying to work up the courage and find the right time to use it. Now that I'm comfortable with working for Spectrum, I finally decided to dive in and do it."

Gia ran her fingers through her hair, enjoying the texture of it and pulling it up to look at its red color. She held it against her cheek, let it slide through her fingers again and lifted it up to catch the light beginning to shine across the room.

Mari laughed and shook her head fondly. "You and David. You're such a pair."

"Oh, I need to take pictures for him." She handed Mari her phone and struck a silly pose. Mari quickly snapped one. They burst out laughing, but finally, they were able to get a couple of good pictures of each other and one of them clowning around together. Gia looked through them and sent a few off to David.

The women leaned back, pastries demolished, enjoying their coffee. They chatted about David and Raul. Then Gia filled Mari in on the latest news about Joseph and Anusha—and Sal.

Gia said, a wry smile twisting her mouth, "You know, Sal would hate this color."

Mari reached over and gently took Gia's hand in hers, "But it makes you happy."

Gia held up a lock of her hair to the light again and laughed a little. "It does."

Then they poured their second cups of coffee and settled down to plan their day.

Mari told Gia she was on a mission to buy fabric for her next flamenco dress. She had to get to the textile shop before they went back to the boat. She'd been waiting for this stop on the cruise to make her purchase because she especially liked the textiles in that particular shop. "I'm off to Paris at the end of this cruise. I can't wait to see Lydia again. It's been over five years since I bought that little brooch from her. And now we plan to celebrate our anniversary in style."

Gia's jaw tightened, and a pang gripped her—*Of jealousy? No,* she assured herself. *Mari is still as dear a friend as ever. Concern?* she asked herself as she thought back to that Christmas trip to Paris. *Yes, concern. I wouldn't want anything to happen to her because of Lydia.*

Gia changed the subject abruptly—she didn't want to hear any more about Lydia. This little visit to the café was *her* time with Mari. "I'd love to go with you but spending a few hours looking at textiles would kill me. I want to go for a real hike in the countryside, but I don't have enough time." She pulled out her guidebook and map. "So, I'm going to have to settle for a walking tour of the old city." She laid the map on the table and began to trace the route she'd planned. Mari pointed out some spots on the map, making suggestions for additional sights.

A shadow fell across Gia's map, and they both looked up. Judge Lauch had stopped beside their table, holding a takeaway coffee.

"Good morning, Mari, Gia," he said.

Mari was used to being approached when she was off the boat. She looked up and recognized him immediately. "Good morning, Judge Lauch."

"Mari, I was wondering if you could recommend a cigar shop to me? I have to buy some Ukrainian cigars for my golf buddies."

"Of course. I bet they've never had them before." Mari pointed out the window of Lilla's, to the left, and described how to get to the shop. Then, grabbing Gia's map, she said, "Here, it's like this," and they leaned over as she traced the route.

Tracey nodded and began to thank her when Mari's phone rang. Startled by the sound, they all jumped. She glanced at the display and said to Tracey and Gia, "Excuse me, this is my mom calling." She tucked her hair back behind her ear and picked up the phone.

Tracey froze, staring at Mari, watching the way the sun played on the red highlights in her hair. Then, suddenly, he said to Gia in a thick voice, "Would you please thank Mari for her time?" and walked out very quickly with his coffee clutched in his hand.

He walked half a block along the street until he came to a bench across from a small park. Sitting down, unmoving he stared into space. His thoughts tormented him. *First I killed Maggie—she made me so angry. But I thought I could stop—after I killed Ruth. I thought I could stop—after I killed Zoe. I thought I could stop—after I killed Sheila. Every time, I thought I could stop.*

Tracey stood up abruptly and walked to a nearby trash can, flung his half-drunk coffee into the bin and agitatedly ran his fingers through his hair, over and over, pulling at it, trying to pull himself back from the darkness that dragged at him.

He sat back down hard on the bench. "Why?"

He looked over and saw Mari and Gia exit the café. Gia put on her sunglasses and hugged and kissed Mari, who said a few words back and pointed up the street. And then they went off in different directions.

He got up and slowly followed Mari. She went into a textile shop. From where he stood, he could see her in the window, touching fabrics and talking to the shop owner. He walked farther down the street to the smoke shop she'd recommended. He went in and spent some time talking to the owner about the various cigars, the origin of the tobacco, the flavor, and eventually, he bought three fat cigars for his buddies.

With his purchase in his hand, neatly wrapped in paper and tied with red string, Tracey left the shop and leaned his back against the wall next to the window. He stood on his left foot and propped the other against the wall behind him. He pulled his map of the old city out of the pocket of his loose linen jacket and studied it, trying to decide where to go, trying to escape his emotions, trying to quell his desire to kill.

Meanwhile, Gia had started out on her walking tour, her thoughts wandering everywhere but on her walk. For some reason, she couldn't focus on her surroundings. *I'd much rather be hiking today than walking around this city.* She paused and gave herself a mental shake. *But there're some buildings I promised myself I'd see and photograph.* She forged on a few minutes longer and then stopped again. *This just isn't working.* She stood, tapping her fingers against her camera, thinking.

Suddenly, she began to laugh out loud. That morning's discussion with Judge Lauch had given her a great idea for a prank to play on David. *I'll buy him a cigar, a big, fat, smelly stogie, and I'll dare him to smoke it. And he and Raul will need to send pictures. Since David's not a smoker, he'll probably cough and turn green, maybe he'll even—yep, that'll be perfect payback for the hair dye. I can hardly wait to see the pictures.* She doubled back, passed Lilla's and headed down the street to the cigar shop.

Tracey had his head down, looking at his map, and Gia didn't notice him as she entered and made her purchase. *Oh yes, this will be good,* she thought as she left the shop, grinning to herself.

"I don't want to go there." She heard a familiar voice. "I don't want to go there."

Gia stopped and saw Tracey looking down at his map. "Judge Lauch, were you speaking to me? Can I help you? Can I help you find something?"

Gia's voice jolted Tracey back to reality. He looked at her blankly for a moment and then shook his head to clear it. "Hi, Gia. I'm trying to decide what to do next. I must have been talking to myself. I do that sometimes. Comes with retirement. I'm—I'm just trying to find the shortest way back to the boat that has some interesting sights along the way. I was eliminating what look like longer routes." Tracey was relieved that she'd come along and distracted him. Maybe he could get through this after all.

Gia said, "I can show you a good short cut, but you'll have to excuse me before we reach the boat, so I can continue my walking tour." Gia pushed her new red hair back from her face.

Tracey watched her. *What is it with these young women? They ruin their hair, dying it these wild, artificial colors. If she'd only dyed it a more natural color, like Mari's, that would be so much more attractive.* The familiar yearning returned at the thought of Mari.

He tucked his map into his pocket as they walked away together and turned into a narrow street. Gia tried to make polite conversation with him.

Tracey's mind turned back to the café, to Mari's graceful neck as she pushed back her luxurious auburn hair, to the red, glinting as it caught the morning sun. He imagined finding a dark spot down some alley and choking her—the sound of her groaning—his excitement—giving in to the urge—he began to breathe harder and broke out in a sweat in anticipation.

Abruptly, he stopped. He took a deep breath and wiped the sweat from his forehead, and he called out to Gia, who by then was several steps ahead of him, "Hey Gia. Thanks for showing me this shortcut. I think I'll wander around for a bit and find a little snack before I go back to the boat. Again, thank you."

Gia stopped and turned around. She pointed down the street and said, "You see that main street down there in the distance? Cross over it and then walk to the right for about four blocks. You'll see a sign for the docks there." She noticed the glazed look in Tracey's eyes, how he was sweating. "Are you okay, Judge Lauch? You don't look so well."

"I'm fine. I just need to have something to eat. I stupidly skipped breakfast."

Gia continued, "Can I call somebody? Are you sure you're going to be okay? Would you like a bottle of water? I've got one in my bag." She rummaged around in her backpack. "You don't look well at all."

Tracey smiled at Gia. He took a deep breath. "No, really, I'm fine. Enjoy your walk." He turned and went off down a side alley.

I'll check on him when I get back on the boat, she thought and headed off to find some interesting buildings to photograph.

Tracey glanced over his shoulder. Gia was out of sight. He slumped against the building, staring at his hands. He stood there in the small alley, breathing in and out, listening to his heart rate slow, composing himself. Finally, he pulled his shoulders back and stepped briskly back out into the narrow street, only to collide hard with a slim, young woman. Everything flew out of their hands.

Startled, he blurted out, "Oh, I'm sorry! Did I hurt you, Mari?"

"Excuse me!" she said at the same time.

He drew a quick, sharp breath. *Excuse me. Why did she have to say that?*

They bent over to pick up their belongings, and their heads bumped together with an audible *thunk.*

"Oooof," they said in unison and stood back up, leaving their things lying on the ground.

"That was quite a bump. Did I hurt your head?" he said.

She touched her forehead gingerly, "I don't think so."

"Do you mind if I take a look?" He leaned toward her.

"Thank you. Actually, it really does hurt." She bent her head toward him. "I'm running late for my shift, so I wasn't paying attention. Excuse me."

Excuse me. He inhaled again, more sharply this time, and paused for a brief second. Holding her auburn hair back with a gentle hand, he ran one finger lightly along her forehead. "There's already a lump forming, and you'll probably have a nice bruise later. I'm so sorry."

She was still dazed by the impact. "No, I should have been watching where I was going. How's your head?"

"I'm fine. I've always had a hard head," he chuckled.

He picked up their belongings and tucked his cigars into his pocket. As he handed her package and purse to her, their fingers touched, and he felt a jolt of excitement.

"I'll walk back with you."

They began to walk, slowly, and she touched her head again with cautious fingers. He looked at her and clenched his hands. A frisson of anticipation ran through him, and he felt the familiar stirring in his groin. He looked around. They were alone, approaching a narrow alley that seemed to angle off to nowhere, dustbins set out randomly. He stepped behind her and wrapped one hand over her mouth and nose to stifle her cries and the other around her throat, forcing her into the alley.

As he tightened his fingers, he whispered angrily, "Why? Why?" Waves of emotion washed through him.

Her struggles lessened and finally stopped. He laid her carefully on the ground behind one of the bins. Like a lover, he leaned over and tenderly brushed her hair off her face one last time, took her earring and put it into his pocket.

He looked at the carefully tied package of fabric and her handbag. Reaching into his pocket, he took out a handkerchief and wiped his fingerprints from them.

Tracey continued along the narrow street toward the boat and put the handkerchief in his back pocket. His breath still ragged, he looked at the long street stretching ahead of him. He was so aroused—so angry—so ashamed—so sad—his desire to kill now satiated. He forced himself to keep his eyes straight ahead, to not look back. He fingered the earring in his pocket and willed his anger and his arousal to diminish.

Finally—it felt like hours later—he arrived back at the boat. He immediately sat down in the lounge. He ordered a tall gin and tonic and continued to struggle to regain his composure.

Sasha asked, "How was your morning, Judge? You look a little warm. Did you go ashore? Did Charlotte go with you?"

He took a deep breath. "Yes, for a little while, and then I split off to run some errands while Charlotte was on a tour." Tracey cleared his throat, pulled out the cigars and said, "But I got some cigars for my golf buddies. That will make them laugh. Cigars from Ukraine. Imagine."

When Sasha walked away, Tracey pulled the lime off the swizzle stick and squeezed it into his gin and tonic As he sipped his drink, he stared out the window and thought about his morning, about how he loathed that part of himself that lost control, that killed women but how he loved the arousal that accompanied their moans and struggles and how his need to feel that arousal drove him to kill again and again.

He sipped his gin and tonic. *Why? Is it just the sexual arousal and gratification?*

When he set down his glass, he absentmindedly picked up the swizzle stick and rubbed it between his fingers.

He sat back and replayed all five murders in his mind, his fingers and thumb continuing to rub the sharp plastic stick, harder and harder, his heart pounding faster and faster. *I felt that arousal with each one, even with Maggie. She was the beginning. She abandoned me, and I had to kill her. Am I killing her—over and over?* he wondered.

He felt the pain as the stick rubbed his finger raw. He dropped it on a napkin on the table beside him and put his finger in his mouth, tasting the salt of his blood. He took a deep breath, calming himself.

Charlotte's voice in the distance caught his attention. He watched her cross the lounge toward him. He pushed the dark thoughts away as he crumpled the stick and napkin and shoved it into his empty glass. He looked at the abrasion on his finger and stood up to greet her with a kiss on her cheek.

Chapter Eighteen

October 2010

How Do You Go On?

Spectrum Cruise, The Scarlet

Deaths

MARILYN (MARI) TERESA OLIVER

Died on 11 August 2010 in Zaporizhzhya, Ukraine. She was born in Seville, Spain on 10 June 1975 to Mateo and Gabriella Oliver. She is survived by both parents and her brother, Leonardo.

Following in the footsteps of her parents and brother, Mari served in the hospitality industry after graduating magna cum laude in international hotel management from the European College of Hospitality Services. She joined the concierge staff at the prestigious Hotel Reina Catherine in Madrid and went on to fulfill a personal dream to work and travel aboard a river boat. She served as a concierge with the Spectrum River Cruise Line for four years until her death at the age of thirty-four.

Mari was an accomplished flamenco dancer who competed from the time she was a small child and won many prizes at competitions and festivals throughout Spain. She worked with Lydia McKay of Paris to design her unique dance costumes based on vintage designs that she loved.

A memorial service will be held in Seville for family and close friends followed by a private burial in the cemetery at St. Martín's Catholic Church.

All the passengers were gone for the evening. Sasha finished his closing routine, made one final swipe across the counter with his bar cloth and hung it away carefully. He looked around with a little smile of satisfaction. There, everything is ready for tomorrow, he thought. He reached up, took two large glasses from the rack overhead and poured healthy servings of Gia's favorite Bordeaux into each. He walked quietly over to the corner of the lounge where she sat, curled at the end of a loveseat, one long leg tucked up under her. Her face was sad, and there were dark shadows under her eyes. He handed her a glass silently and sat down next to her.

The two friends took a few sips of wine and then they chatted briefly about the day's events and the more unusual passengers on the cruise.

Gia sat up straight with a panicked look on her face. "Did Mari ever tell you about Lydia?"

"Yes. Have you told her yet?"

"I can't even face that right now." Gia's face crumpled without warning. "This doesn't feel right without Mari here." She held her glass between her hands and cried, harder and harder. It had only been two months since Mari's murder, and Gia found that sadness and desolation would sweep through her without warning—while she was cleaning rooms, standing in the shower at the end of her shift and frequently when she was with their mutual friends. And then the tears would come.

Sasha reached over and took the glass from her hands. He set it softly on the table alongside his and put his arms around her, holding her gently against his chest, rocking her slowly while his big hands stroked her long, dark hair, and he whispered, "Shhh, shhh, shhh," as though she were a small child.

When her tears finally stopped, Sasha took his handkerchief and tenderly dried her eyes and her face. She looked up and gave him a tearful smile. She noticed how the lines on his face had deepened since Kisho's death a little over a year ago and even more since Mari's death. His crisp black hair had far more grey than she remembered, and the tenderness in his eyes scarcely masked his own pain and sadness.

"How did you get through this past year without Kisho?" Gia asked. "I can't imagine life without Mari. She was my best friend." Her lips trembled again, and she drew a deep breath, willing the tears away.

"Sometimes, I wasn't sure I would make it. It hurt so badly, I wanted to die, too. I was so angry at him for leaving me, abandoning me. Our future was over before it had really begun. He's gone—forever." Sasha's eyes moistened, and he blinked hard to hold back his own tears. He cleared his throat and continued.

"All those feelings are still there. Sometimes they're sharp, like knives cutting into me. But they've grown less frequent. I smile more. I focus on the good things in life. And I go to our vineyard every chance I get. I walk among the vines. I scream and yell at the gods for taking him from me. I weep. I drink our wine. He's not there, but somehow, in our house and on our land, I feel his presence. And then I cry again."

"I know just what you mean about sharp pains, they are horrible, sometimes they feel unbearable. I just want it to go away. I don't find comfort in the Seville casita. When I stayed there for Mari's funeral, it was just a building. Without her, it's nothing to me. I don't have anywhere to go. I'm so lost, Sasha. Our break begins next week, and I have nowhere to go. What do I do? I'm so lost."

Sasha reached out and took her hands and smiled kindly at her. "We all grieve differently. You'll have to find your own way to deal with this. Let's just take one step at a time. Come home to the vineyard with me for our break. We have good memories of Mari and Kisho from last year. We can talk and remember them together. And if you don't want to talk, you can just relax and read, or walk in the hills, or cook with me. Time doesn't ever heal those wounds. But it makes them easier to live with. Lean on me, on Raul and David. We'll get through this together."

Chapter Nineteen

August 2011

The Wedding

Rotterdam, The Netherlands

Raul and Piet walked arm in arm around the garden behind the restaurant, checking everything one last time. Raul looked up approvingly as he and the restaurant owner paused under the large tree that shaded the entire patio. "Piet, this is perfect. Exactly as I imagined." Raul smiled happily at the speckles of sunshine on the flagstone surface, where the sun just barely peeked through the leaves and reflected off the fairy lights which were strung generously through the lower branches. Silver cranes danced above the dinner table on gossamer tethers, and he reached out to touch one carefully and smiled. "These are here in memory of our friend, so he can be part of our happiness, too. This is magical."

"Nothing but the best for you and David. When he first brought you here, I knew he had found the love of his life. And so, it makes me and Johanna very happy to give you this night in our garden and dinner from our kitchen as our wedding gift."

Raul replied, his voice choked with emotion, "David and I are so grateful. We can't thank you enough. This is truly a special place for us. And you've made it so beautiful."

"You know, this place has history for David. I bought it about fourteen years ago. I got it for what we could make of it, not for what it was then. This garden was horrible, with trash everywhere, and the inside was a disaster. But—it had potential, and as soon as I saw the garden, I knew one day it would look just like this.

"David was one of our earliest customers. Over the first couple of years, while we were renovating, it had a permanent layer of plaster dust and areas that were blocked off. So, we sold inexpensive food and drink to make some money to help pay for the work. David and his fellow medical students would come and spend hours studying together in the corner. I feel like Johanna's good food is what saw them through all those years of school. And David became a member of our family."

"Wait a minute. You've known David since he was a young

medical student? That's a detail he missed sharing," Raul smiled.

"I know, I know. I keep finding out things about Johanna, even though we've been married thirty years. That's the fun about marriages—"

"What I have to look forward to," Raul groaned in mock dismay.

"We are happy to be part of this. You know, this catalpa was here, in this very spot, when we bought the land. I've been pruning it and cultivating it since then," Piet placed his hand fondly on its trunk and smiled. "It's now thirty feet tall, and that canopy spans twenty feet."

"It's truly majestic," said Raul. "I love its shade."

"And I've been babying the flowering shrubs in that corner. I designed this garden so that something is always in bloom. But it's really at its best at this time of year."

Piet chuckled to himself as he continued, "I bet David didn't tell you that he would come help with the garden in those early days just so he could hang out with our kids when they were small."

"He does love kids."

"It was fun to watch him play pranks on them while they were cleaning up, hauling away trash and planting. You see that herb garden?" Piet leaned back against the trunk of the tree and pointed to the plot alongside the restaurant. "That was David's idea—he and the children built the first part of it for Johanna one Mother's Day. It's much larger now, and we grow all our own herbs. They're a part of our secret ingredients."

"That's my David."

Raul could feel Piet's passion for the garden and smiled. "Honestly, the landscape back here is what made me want this venue for our wedding." He spread his hands and waxed poetic for a moment. "The tree, like an enormous umbrella, will protect us while we are sitting beneath it for dinner. The sound of the breeze through the leaves will be music for us all. And the flowers behind the arch will provide a romantic backdrop for the ceremony." Raul smiled, his eyes twinkling as he listened to himself.

He cleared his throat. "I'm responsible for arranging the location, the food and the drinks. Your help—your gift—has made this infinitely easier for me. Again, thank you both."

"And the fairy lights and the cranes in the tree—is that also as you wished?"

"It's better than I had dreamed. It's so romantic. We and our friends can sit around the table for hours, with the fairy lights and candles, and look up to see that Kisho is with us in spirit—and, you may not know this, but those pomegranate flowers also have special meaning to all of us."

"I knew that the cranes did, but not the flowers. I thought you just liked them."

"Our dear friend, Mari, died last year. They were her favorite flowers, and we wanted her here in spirit as well. Oh Piet, the flowers, the place settings, all the crystal and silver and candles, they are exactly as I imagined." Raul turned to Piet. "But I think you've set places for one too many."

"We'll take care of that. The attention you've given to every tiny detail and your thoughtfulness about all the arrangements is amazing, Raul."

He chuckled. "That's why I'm in charge of the setting—do you mind walking through what we need before the ceremony begins?"

"Not at all."

Raul walked over to stand in front of the doors that led from the restaurant to the patio and gestured to the right. "The musicians will be here in the corner. They will play before and during the ceremony and then during dinner. After dinner, once they have left, the DJ will work his magic from here as well."

Piet smiled and nodded in agreement. "That works. When people enter, they will hear the music, but their eyes will be drawn to the arch there at the back of the garden."

"Exactly. When our guests arrive, your waiters will hand them a glass of champagne and gently direct them toward the arch where they will stand on either side to welcome us when we walk down the 'aisle'."

"We will make that happen."

Raul turned to Piet. "Will you and Johanna be attending? You have to. I assumed you would be, but I never actually asked you."

"Of course, we'll be here for the ceremony. And we'll personally bring out the cake and celebrate with you then. In between—we have to take care of the restaurant."

"Great—oh, one last thing—could the waiters come through to remove the champagne glasses just before the ceremony?" With a shy laugh, he continued, "David and I certainly don't want our guests paying attention to anything but us."

"But of course—well," Piet replied, looking around, "I think we have everything covered. Take a close look and let me know if there are any last-minute changes that need to be made. I want it to be flawless for you and David."

◆

It was time, early evening, the daylight just beginning to wane, and the musicians began playing the joyous notes of Pachelbel's Canon in D. The guests' chatter stopped as they all turned toward the doors at the entrance to the patio.

Two waiters, dressed for the occasion in black tuxedos, opened the double doors and held them wide as the couple stepped out onto the patio, hand in hand, huge smiles on their faces. They paused for a slight moment, a contrast in light and dark. David, his blond hair shining, wore a white evening coat with tails, and Raul, slim and dark, wore the same in black. They had small coral pomegranate blossoms tucked through their buttonholes.

Their guests broke out in applause as the elegant couple began their walk toward the arch. Raul tipped his head in solemn acknowledgement, and David beamed happily.

Piet and Johanna slipped out the door and stood against the building to watch. They smiled at the beautiful scene, Johanna sniffled, and Piet took hold of her hand and held it tightly. Johanna loved any wedding but especially this one. She leaned on Piet's shoulder and sighed, "Such a beautiful, happy occasion."

Anusha murmured to Gia, "They are both so handsome."

"Oh—aren't they," whispered Gia.

Raul looked up as they approached the delicate arch. His eyes widened in surprise as he saw Joseph standing, smiling, beneath it, his hands stretched out, palms up, in welcome, and Sal—Sal, smiling, standing to the left.

Raul stopped, and his face broke out into a huge smile. He put both hands over his heart and turned to David. In a voice full of emotion, he said, "He made it!" David shrugged in mock innocence, and the guests all laughed with happiness.

"I had to be here for you, my brother," said Sal.

Raul wrapped Sal in a big bear hug, lifting his feet off the ground, pounding his back, and they both grinned at each other. "You've made my day."

Raul stepped back beside David, still smiling. "Did you know?"

"Of course, someone had to know."

"And you didn't tell me?"

David chuckled, "Can we talk about this later? We've waited so long—let's get married!"

Raul looked around, confused. "But where's the minister?" Everybody laughed again, while Raul tried to figure it out.

Finally, Joseph took pity on him. "I'm ordained. I did it online. Will that do?"

David said to Raul quietly, "I thought we should be married by someone who cares about us."

Raul's eyes welled up. "Don't make me cry. My eyes will be all red." David squeezed his hand.

They approached the arch, and David's groomsman, Lars, said, "Enough with entertaining us. Let's get you two married."

♦

The grooms, hands holding each other's faces gently, kissed at the end of the ceremony. The guests applauded and cheered. In the far corner of the garden, Piet set off firecrackers with a bang, and Raul jumped in astonishment.

"Surprised you, huh?" said David with an impish grin on his face.

Raul nudged his shoulder against David and gave him

another kiss. "You continually surprise me. You make me so happy," he murmured.

David nodded his head, pressed his cheek to Raul's and whispered back, "You make me happier."

The tuxedo-clad waiters came around with more champagne. David's best man, Lars cleared his throat and raised his glass, "To the charming couple." He pointed his glass toward Raul. "It's about time you made David an honest man."

"And finally, with no doubt, the happiest man on earth," said David, and he leaned over and kissed Raul yet again.

Everyone sighed, "Awww—" before taking a sip of their champagne.

Gia walked up to them with a handkerchief clutched in one hand. She tipped her head to admire the striking couple. But before she could say a word, David tugged the handkerchief out of her hand and put it away in his pocket. "Hey, no crying at the happiest event of the year." She smiled and gathered both of them in her arms and hugged them, swaying back and forth.

"This is indeed the happiest event of the year," she agreed. "Congratulations." Gia pulled away and touched the flower on Raul's lapel and said, with a catch in her voice, "I'm glad Mari could be here with us." Raul pulled her back to him in a comforting hug.

Sasha hugged David. "Congratulations. I could never marry the love of my life, but I'm so glad you and Raul were able to."

Raul put his arms around Sasha and held him tightly and said in a muffled voice, "Thank you. We are so lucky."

Sasha turned away, and Gia gave him a long hug. "I'm so happy you're here to celebrate with us."

"I wouldn't have missed this for the world," he said, a smile creasing his face.

Everyone continued to mill about, hugging everyone else and chatting for a while. They'd all kept in touch, but most of them hadn't seen one another since Mari's funeral.

Sal approached Gia hesitantly. She watched his sexy swagger, and a smile almost touched her lips. But her eyes remained wary. She looked at the scar on his face without a word. Sal reached up to touch it and said, "Some bruiser gave me that."

"They must have been mighty mad at you."

"With good reason. I was being very, very ill behaved and said some very, very hurtful things."

Gia dropped her head for a moment, breathing in deeply as she recalled that horrible last night. She looked up, her face sad. Uncertain, Sal waited. "Yes, you did," said Gia. She felt the old attraction to Sal tug at her heart, but in her head, she heard Mari say, *"Watch out for that one."*

Sal admired her tall heels and slim-fitting dress with the old heat in his eyes. "You look more beautiful than ever. You're wearing our color."

"Coral was my favorite color long before I met you. It was purely coincidental that you used it in the apartment," she said, her voice deliberately emotionless. "You just assumed it was 'our color'."

She drew another deep breath, "You look very well, Sal."

"That's eighteen months of clean living for you."

Gia's eyes opened wide in surprise. She simply said, "Good for you."

Sal felt Gia's coolness, but he continued, "After you left, I was completely lost without you around. I didn't realize it then, but you were what kept me centered. Things spun out of control. Then I stopped working, and the drugs and alcohol took over my life. It may sound trite, but one day I just got up and looked in the mirror, and I knew I couldn't go on like that, and I needed to pick myself up and get better. I wanted to be able to face you again. I decided if I was going to do it, I was going to do it right. I checked myself into a twelve-month residential program, and I've been out and clean for six months. I wanted to know I could stay clean before I saw any of you. I reached out to Joseph last month, and it was his idea to surprise Raul today."

"Why are you telling me this?" she asked flatly.

"I'm sorry, Gia, for what I said and what I did, and I'm sorry you took the brunt of it. You deserved more. You deserved better."

"Are you saying that because that's what you've been told to do? One of the steps in the program?" she said with a bitter edge to her voice.

"Yes, I am, but even more, because I mean it with all my heart. I really do. Through my therapy, I realized I had turned to drugs to try to meet what I believed were my father's expectations of me. I stayed on the drugs so I could quiet his voice in my head telling me, '*Work harder, son.*' I was in a vicious cycle, and you were caught in the middle. I'm so sorry."

"I'm sure you are," she said, the edge still in her voice. And then, with a raised eyebrow, Gia pointed to his champagne glass.

"Sparkling cider, Minx."

♦

The waiters came out announcing that dinner was ready, and the group drifted toward the table.

Sal absentmindedly placed his hand on the small of Gia's back to guide her. Her heart gave a little hiccup, but she desperately tried to ignore it. As they approached the large round table, Sal pulled out a chair for her.

I was finally getting over you. And now, here you are. Why? she thought bitterly. *Why? I wanted to enjoy tonight, to celebrate Raul and David. And now, here you are. Why?*

Gia looked across the table, watching David and Raul sit down. They looked so happy under the tree sparkling with fairy lights. She scowled as Sal sat down next to her and thought, *I wish you weren't here. You're taking me back to the day my heart broke, my world shattered. How dare you!*

Surprised at the anger she still felt, Gia looked away and closed her eyes for a moment. She tilted her head back and drew a deep breath to calm herself. And when she opened her eyes, she noticed the silver cranes hanging from the tree. She stood back up to touch one.

Sasha pulled out the chair on the other side of her. "May I?"

"Of course. Nothing would make me happier." Gia touched his shoulder and guided his eyes to the cranes. He smiled reflectively as Gia plucked one from the tree and handed it to him.

A single tear ran down Sasha's weathered cheek. "Kisho," he

whispered. "Thank you, Gia."

Raul noticed their exchange and walked around the table. He leaned between them and said, "Fong and Lee couldn't be here today, but they sent these, one thousand silver cranes, to make sure Kisho was here with us, to bring health and happiness to us all." Gia put her hand on Sasha's knee and gave it a gentle squeeze. He smiled, still looking at the crane he held between his fingers and rested his other hand on top of hers.

Sasha looked across the table and saw the bowl of pomegranate blossoms in the center. He whispered, "Mari."

Gia placed her hands together against her mouth, looked up at Raul and said, "I knew about the boutonnieres but not the centerpiece—how thoughtful of you." Her eyes glistened.

Sasha turned to face Raul and Gia. "This is your day, Raul. Enough with our tears. Let's celebrate. It's a happy day, and you found a way to bring both Kisho and Mari into it. Thank you," and he and Gia smiled at each other.

Raul straightened up, narrowly missing a waiter placing dishes on the table. As he returned to his seat, he passed by Sal, patted his shoulder, leaned over and whispered in his ear, "Thanks again for being here, my brother."

Waiters filled the large table with appetizers.

Before sitting, Raul leaned over to pick up his glass for a toast. "Thank you, David, for making me the happiest man in the world and for waiting for me to realize how much I needed you." They clinked their glasses and took a drink before he continued, "We are being served family-style tonight because we are a family. So, without further ado, dig in!"

Joseph reached across the table for a plate of appetizers. David saw a gleam on his finger, squinted at his hand and pointed. "Hey—what's up?" The comment caught Raul's attention, and he looked at David. Joseph stopped and put the plate down. David lifted his own hand and pointed at his wedding band. "That," he said.

Raul turned to see Joseph smiling shyly. He raised his eyebrows, and Joseph nodded.

"Does Anusha know you're married?" asked David in mock

severity. "We really love her, you know."

Joseph responded, "Ha, ha, ha."

Before Raul could say anything, David tapped his knife against the side of his glass and said loudly, so everyone could hear, "I think Joseph and Anusha have an announcement to make."

"Actually, we have two."

The group went silent and looked at Joseph and Anusha.

"Yes, we ran off and got married a couple of weeks ago, and we were going to tell you sometime this evening."

"And—we have a little Joseph on the way. He'll arrive in about five months," Anusha chimed in as she laid her hand gently on her belly.

"A shotgun marriage, huh?" David laughed.

"When Mari died last year, we decided that life is too short to wait any longer. We knew we wanted kids right away. And then after we found out Anusha was pregnant, we eloped. I know, a bit backward, but it doesn't matter to us."

Anusha continued, "My parents are not happy about this at all. They hadn't even accepted the fact that we were dating. But with a grandson on the way, I'm hoping they will soften up toward Joseph a bit."

Gia raised her hands in the air, shaking them in excitement, and jumped up. She wrapped her arms around Anusha tightly. "We're going to have an awesome baby shower for you!" She pulled back and grabbed Anusha's hand to admire her ring. "How did I not notice this?"

Anusha laughed and replied, "I haven't seen you since our wedding two weeks ago, so how would you have noticed it?"

Gia laughed and gave Joseph a hug. "I'm so happy for you, 'Daddy'!"

During dinner, Sal tried to engage Gia in conversation, and each time, she answered curtly and turned back to an affectionate conversation with Sasha, or to talk to the others around the table, chit-chatting, while taking food from the plates in the center of the table.

Just one big happy family. Obviously, they've done this many times before, he thought with envy and sadness. Finally, he began to chat with Lars and his wife, Anna, who were sitting quietly to his right. "A bit overwhelming, aren't they?"

The two of them nodded their heads in agreement, and Sal asked, "Have you met everyone?"

Lars replied, "We did when we arrived. We've also heard about everyone from Raul over the years he's been with David."

"It has been nice, finally, to put faces to names," Anna said. "But I would like to hear from you about them and how you all fit together."

Sal sat back and laughed before beginning with his, Raul's and Joseph's antics as kids back in the old neighborhood.

When he moved on to Anusha, he explained, "I just met Anusha a month or so ago when I reached out to Joseph. That's when I learned about Raul's wedding and that Raul was with David. I'm sure that sounds weird, but you have to understand, I dropped out of sight for a few years while I dealt with my addiction problem. I'm just now catching up with everyone. Anusha is a wonderful person. She and Joseph have gone through a lot together."

Lars said, "It's good to get back on track. And good to have friends who support you."

Sal glanced at Gia and then smiled as he continued around the table, "That's Sasha. I only met him today, so you'll have to get his story from someone else. Finally, that's Gia." Sal cleared his throat and paused for a moment before continuing, "We— dated for a while."

Gia heard her name and glanced over and smiled, surprised at herself. *That's my old Sal. Always trying to make people feel comfortable.*

As dinner wound down, David nodded to Joseph.

Joseph stood up, reached into his pocket, removed a small piece of paper and unfolded it ceremoniously. "I have a toast from Jaime. *'I'm so glad you've found someone who treasures you. Come back and visit when you're in Madrid. I look forward to meeting your David.'*"

They all lifted their glasses and toasted.

He took Anusha's hand in his and held it as he continued, "I know what it's like to find the love of your life. I found mine, and I'm glad you two have found each other. To you both."

♦

Joseph whispered into Anusha's ear, "It's time," and smiled at her.

She watched him wait next to the restaurant door for the musicians to finish their song and then walk over to them. Anusha couldn't get enough of watching her husband, the way he moved, the way he leaned in to talk to people so earnestly, his hands—she watched him and smiled in contentment. He chatted with the musicians for a few minutes before they stood up and shook his hand. Then they quickly packed up their instruments and slipped out through the restaurant.

Joseph set up two microphones and turned to Anusha and held out his hand. When she came close, he slid his arms around her, hugging her to him, and gave her a long kiss. Anusha leaned back, supported by his arms, and looked around. "It's so romantic tonight. I feel like this is for us, too, since we never had a reception."

"I'm sorry about that."

"Don't be. I loved our wedding, and now, I get to feel like I'm having a reception. Raul and David won't mind if we borrow just a little of theirs." She smiled at Joseph with a wicked little gleam in her eyes.

Then, removing his hands from her hips, she said, "Let's get this party started."

"That's my girl."

Anusha smiled and moved around to stand in front of a microphone while Joseph picked up his guitar and sat on the stool in front of the other. Her dress was a slim column of green, a matching hijab covering her hair. "Will the grooms please come to the dance floor for your first dance?" Anusha announced.

Raul looked at David in surprise. Then, grinning, David stood and offered his hand to Raul, and they took their places on the dance floor, holding hands, facing Joseph and Anusha.

Joseph began to play their song, *Endless Love.*

Raul turned to David, dumbstruck, unaware that, weeks before, David had arranged for Joseph to play the first dance.

David pulled him into his arms, brushing his lips lightly against Raul's. Raul rested his forehead against David's, and they danced their first dance.

When Anusha started singing the lyrics, she and Joseph heard Gia say, "Wow, they're fantastic," and they looked at the table and then at each other and smiled.

"Did you know she could sing?" Raul asked David.

"I had no idea. It's a surprise for me, too. Truly, a night of surprises."

Joseph joined in for the duet. Sasha lifted his hand to his cheek, and Gia heard him murmur, "Oh, they are doing the duet just like Lionel Richie and Diana Ross. My favorite."

"Look, Anusha and Joseph are singing to each other," Gia said, and tears glistened in her eyes. "And David and Raul, too. This is the most romantic thing I've ever seen." Sal reached over and touched Gia's shoulder. Gia shrugged his hand away.

The two men looked at one another, and Raul kissed David as they danced slowly. His eyes shone with love. Then he rested his cheek against David's and whispered in his ear, "My husband."

David whispered back, "My husband," and smiled into Raul's eyes and kissed him gently. And they danced.

After the first dance, Anusha invited all the guests to the dance floor. Sasha stood with his hand out. "May I?"

Gia said, "Of course."

Joseph began to play, and Anusha sang *Can't Help Falling in Love*.

Lars and Anna also stood up, and they kissed before heading to the dance floor.

Gia looped both her arms around Sasha's neck, and he held her close around her waist. She whispered, "Those two keep surprising me! I've known her all this time, and I didn't know she sang."

"Isn't life amazing—always something for us to learn about each other—" he replied quietly. Sasha looked over Gia's shoulder and saw Sal look away, forlorn and a little jealous. As the song ended, Sasha said, "Now, you need to go spend some time with Sal. He's been reaching out to you all evening, and you've turned your back on him every time."

"What?"

"You know perfectly well what I'm talking about. Mari mentioned the two of you had broken up before you started working for Spectrum, that it was bad, that it was painful. But it's obvious to me it's not really over, at least, not for him."

"Oh?"

As he stepped away toward the restaurant, he said, "Go—now," and gave her a little push.

Gia looked back at Sasha and nodded. She paused. She turned to go to Sal, and the butterflies in her stomach fluttered frantically, trying to escape. She took a deep breath and walked back to the table and sat sideways on her chair to face Sal.

"So, are you and Sasha a thing?" he blurted out.

"What are you talking about? We're friends."

"You looked like more than friends to me," Sal replied in a sad whisper, looking down.

"You're jealous! Aren't you? After all this time. I cannot believe it. What are you asking? Do you think I'm dating or even sleeping with Sasha? You heard about Kisho, so what are you talking about?"

"Kisho was his girlfriend, or his wife, right?"

"No. *He* was Sasha's life partner. And *he* died—suddenly," Gia answered abruptly. "I came over here to try to talk. If you're going to behave like this—just like you did about David that last night—" She started to rise.

Sal asked, "So are you with anyone, Gia?" The devastation in his voice made her sit back down.

"We're really going to have this conversation here?" Gia waved her hands around the garden.

"I've been thinking of you non-stop since our fight."

"That was almost three years ago."

"For me, it's still like it was just yesterday." When Sal said this, Gia looked at him, but she said nothing.

Cautiously, Sal reached over and touched Gia's hand resting on the back of her chair.

"What do you want from me, Sal? I've spent all this time

forcing myself not to think about you. Getting out and dating other people—and now this?"

"I love you, Gia," Sal said, with a catch in his voice. He couldn't meet her eyes for fear of the rejection he might see there. "I've loved you from the beginning. I was so jealous when I believed you were sleeping with Joseph—and Raul—and David. I was hurting, and so I lashed out and I hurt you. Joseph told me that you only slept with him that first year, before Anusha, and that you never slept with Raul or David because—" Sal gestured toward the grooms with his head.

Gia took a deep breath, held it for a long moment and released it very slowly.

"I loved you back then, Sal. I loved you hopelessly. But I couldn't tell you. And I never saw your pain. You never gave me any indication of that or of your love."

Together they said, "The contract," and they both gave a little laugh at the irony.

At last, he forced himself to look her in the eye. "The contract was fantastic because I met you, but I know that I also used it as a crutch. I've never told women that I loved them because I was always afraid of the commitment and how it made me more vulnerable. And I told myself I couldn't tell you—because of the contract. But really, I was afraid you didn't love me," Sal confessed. "Gia, can we try again—like two normal people—in a normal relationship?"

"You said some very hurtful things. You broke my heart, Sal—I'm afraid you will do it again."

"I know. I'm sorry for what I said and for how I behaved. Please give me another chance, Gia."

"Sal, I'd need to learn to trust you again. I don't know—I just don't know."

His eyes pleaded with her.

"I'm traveling for work. I'm not even in Madrid anymore—I just don't know." She slowly stood and held out her hand to him with a small smile. "Let's just start with a dance."

As they walked to the dance floor, Gia saw Sasha go into the restaurant.

◆

Sasha walked back through the bar from the restroom and paused when he heard, "Sasha. Is that you?" He looked over to see Judge Lauch and Charlotte French sitting at the bar. With a smile of surprise on his face, he walked over and shook their hands.

"Nice to see you both. What brings you to Rotterdam?"

Charlotte replied, "We're on a Spectrum cruise from Basel to Amsterdam and have taken the Rotterdam add-on."

"As a matter of fact, Mari recommended it to Charlotte before she went missing," Tracey added. He hadn't heard anything about her death and was curious to find out what Sasha knew. "Did they ever find her?"

"You don't know what happened to Mari?"

Charlotte shook her head slightly, her brow furrowed. "Only that she went missing."

"Mari didn't go missing. She was murdered in Zaporizhzhya that day." Sasha's jaw tightened, and he looked away sadly.

Charlotte gasped, her hand at her throat. "How dreadful. The poor woman."

"Have they found out who did it?"

Sasha's voice broke. "Not yet, but I'm still hoping they'll get them in the end."

Tracey shifted in his seat slightly as Charlotte said, "To think we were on the same cruise with her. That could have been any of us." As she saw the sorrow on Sasha's face, she changed the subject. "So, what brings you to Rotterdam?"

"A wedding, back there," he pointed.

"Oh, the one in the garden? I peeked out back and saw the romantic setting. How wonderful." She smiled at Tracey.

"It is wonderful. It's a small gathering of dear friends, using this opportunity to celebrate life."

"That's lovely. Too often we forget to celebrate life and only get together for the bad times."

"Yes," he said simply, the single word heavy with sadness. After a moment, he went on, "Your new hair color is very flattering."

Charlotte, relieved by the lighter tone, sat up tall and touched her hair. "Oh yes, isn't it great? I was getting too much grey, and I've always wanted to be a redhead. I just did this today, in the salon in our hotel."

Tracey abruptly ended the conversation. "We don't want to hold you up, Sasha. It was good seeing you. Maybe we'll bump into you on a cruise in the future."

"I hope we do," Sasha said as he reached out to shake the judge's and then Charlotte's hand.

◆

Sasha stepped through the restaurant door with a fresh drink in his hand and stood watching the wedding group, tapping his finger gently against his lips. He smiled as he listened to *The Way You Look Tonight* being sung by Anusha. Gia was still dancing with Sal.

A moment later, he saw Gia say something to Sal and bury her head on his shoulder. Her shoulders shook, and he drew her in closer and kissed her temple to soothe her. After a few more moments, he led Gia over to a bench in a dim corner of the garden. Gia dropped down, leaned over, pressed her elbows tight against her torso, with her face in her hands and kept crying. Sal stroked her back to comfort her.

Gia said, "This was Mari's favorite song. She was like my sister. I miss her so much every day."

"Minx, Minx, it'll be okay. Go ahead and cry. I'm here for you."

Through her sobs, she went on, "We would drink wine and listen to Old Blue Eyes and dance with each other. I haven't been able to listen to even one of his songs since she died—she loved the music from that era, and Sinatra was her favorite—we used to dance all night in my apartment in Madrid—oh, *your* apartment, I mean." Sal flinched at her correction. "—just playing his records over and over again. Now, she's gone. God, I miss her so much."

"Ah—yes—I remember."

Gia continued crying, "Mari's family was devastated. And Mari—my Mari—I finished my architecture degree, she encouraged me throughout the whole process and then she didn't even get to see me graduate. She wasn't there with me. I—miss—her—so—much," she hiccuped.

As Sal sat holding Gia, he looked up and saw Sasha watching them. Sal beckoned him over to the bench to help him comfort her. Sasha sat down on the other side of her. Sal was still rubbing her back, stroking her hair, and he said, "While we were dancing, Gia told me about how you would get together in the late evenings after work and how close you three had become."

"I still miss Mari. Our midnight soirees have never been the same without her," Sasha said sadly. "But Gia and I have grown even closer." He slipped his handkerchief into Gia's hand, and Sal smiled at the sweet gesture.

Gia looked up at Sasha with red eyes. "When Mari was murdered, I finally understood how truly devastated you must have been when Kisho died so suddenly."

Sasha looked at both of them. "I'd lost my other half. But pain is part of living, along with all the joy and happiness. Sometimes, we don't value those we're closest to until all we have left are memories. We think there'll be more time. I did with Kisho."

"And I did with Mari," she said.

He reached out to take Gia's hand between his and saw Sal tighten his arm around Gia's shoulders. Sal glanced over at him, took a deep breath and gave him a little smile and then relaxed his arm again.

"Gia, I saw how you were hurting from your break-up with Sal. I watched the two of you together tonight. I can see your love for one another. Please, don't make that mistake."

Gia said, "Oh Sasha, you're so wise. But the bottom line is, it still just sucks."

Sasha laughed ruefully. "That's true."

Sal looked up at the dance floor and watched David and Raul laughing. "And tonight, we're here to celebrate the joy and happiness of love."

Gia finished wiping her eyes and looked at Sal and said, "You've become wise, too."

◆

Sasha looked across the garden. He watched Piet and Johanna carrying in the wedding cake and a waiter carrying a fresh tray of champagne. He nudged Gia and pointed, "Oh, I hope it's chocolate." Gia gave him a watery grin as she blew her nose.

"Let's find out," Sal said.

As they walked to the table, hand in hand, all three of them, they heard Raul say, "I cannot believe we got married with no decision on a last name."

"We just can't agree on one. I know we have to figure this out for the wedding certificate. Otherwise, we'll need Lars to change it later," David added.

"I know it's easy to change it later. But we shouldn't get married and then change our name later. It's not the same. I really want to leave here tonight with our married name."

Gia looked at them and interrupted, "You guys haven't figured that out yet?"

Raul said emphatically, "Nope, it's been a sticking point for months."

"I don't know why it's so hard. I figured it out months ago."

"What? Why didn't you tell us?"

"Hey, I know better than to get in the middle of this type of discussion. This is between the two of you."

David pleaded, "Come on, Gia, help us. Please, please."

"Well—"

"Please, sweetheart, do it for me," Raul begged.

"I'll do it for Raul, but not for you, David," Gia said and smirked at David.

"He's your favorite," David teased back at her.

"Yeah, right." Gia rolled her eyes, and pointing at each of them, she said matter-of-factly, "You're Raul Miguel Hernandez. You're David Michel Meijer. You should be Raul and David Michael. That is a new name, but not really because both of your middle names mean Michael anyway. How hard was that!"

Everyone stopped. David smiled. "You know, that's brilliant."

Raul agreed. "Yes, and why didn't we think of it. Why did you think of it?"

Sal said, "Because you're too close and because Gia is very wise." He winked at her.

Raul caught the wink and smiled happily to himself. *They'll be okay.*

Sasha said, "We've taken care of the names. Now, let's get to the cake. And I do hope it's chocolate."

"What is it with chocolate cake? Have you always had a thing for chocolate cake?" David asked in jest.

Gia smiled at Sasha, knowing what his response would be.

"While some people celebrate with champagne," he nodded toward Gia and Sal and smiled, "I celebrate with chocolate. 'Chocolate is for special occasions,' my mom used to say."

"That makes sense," David laughed. "Let's cut it then."

All the guests sat down except Lars. "Now, I have a toast."

He raised his glass, and the others followed suit.

"Here's to my lifelong friend, David Michael, and his husband, Raul Michael. To love, to new names, and to a new life. May you and your baby girl live happily ever after."

Anusha said excitedly, "What? You're having a baby, too?"

David leaned over and kissed Raul vigorously, and as he sat back up, he did a double-arm pump. "Yesss!"

Raul looked at Lars in excitement. "So, all the paperwork is done?"

"That's what you hired me for. I got the news yesterday, but I wanted to give it to you today, as a kind of wedding gift. Congratulations!"

Commotion broke out around the table as everyone jumped up and ran over to hug the new dads.

Gia heard Sasha say under his breath, "This is the joy and happiness," and she looked at him and nodded in agreement.

As the guests finally settled back down at the table, Joseph asked, "So when does she arrive? Will you be able to honeymoon in Crete first?"

Raul and David said simultaneously, "She's not born yet."

Raul continued, "The due date is in October."

David said, "I planned this very carefully. I wouldn't let anything stop our honeymoon."

Anusha grabbed Raul's hand in excitement. "If we are one family, then our babies will be cousins!" she said.

"Let's cut the cake," Sasha said, and everyone howled with laughter.

"He wants to know if it's chocolate," Sal smiled at Sasha.

"But, of course it is," giggled Gia. "I was the one who ordered it."

"Mr. Michael, are you ready to do the honors?"

"Oh yes, Mr. Michael."

And they both held the knife together, grinning giddily at each other.

After devouring the cake, the group sat back in their chairs and quietly gazed at the tiny lights in the tree and the cranes swaying gently in the breeze.

Raul said, "This has been the best day ever."

"It was—and that's because the cake was chocolate." Sasha laughed at himself, and they all joined in.

"The best day ever." Gia repeated the words silently. She smiled at Sal, and he reached over and gently took her hand in his.

After a moment, Gia lifted her glass and said to the group, "To friends who are family."

Drinks with Tracey

Rotterdam, The Netherlands

"What cake?" asked Tracey.

"How could you miss the cake? It looked fabulous. It just passed by, right there." Charlotte pointed. "The cream frosting, the roses, the layers, it was beautiful."

"Hmmm, maybe I missed it since I am facing you, not gawking at everything going by," Tracey said lightly and scooted a little closer to Charlotte.

She laughed and turned to face him. "That's the beauty of the seat I chose. I can admire you—and watch everything else, too." She smiled seductively.

He reached over and tapped the edge of her empty glass. "Shall we have another?"

"It's late, and I would prefer to go spend some alone time with you."

"Alone time with you is always nice," he replied as he looked down at her leg and ran his fingers suggestively along her silky thigh and under the edge of her skirt.

"Let's get the check, Judge," she breathed in his ear.

Tracey helped Charlotte off the bar stool, watching, appreciating how her skirt slid even higher along her bare thigh.

They walked toward the exit, and Tracey reached around her to open the door. Unexpectedly, she stopped, and they ran into each other. Charlotte turned around, said, "Excuse me, my love," tucked her hair behind her ear, pressed herself hard against him and kissed him greedily on the lips.

Excuse me. Tracey froze as he felt the familiar tightening in his groin. Charlotte looked down, grinned and beckoned to him as she turned to leave. And then she was already waiting for him outside, and he stepped out onto the dimly lit sidewalk and took her hand.

We hope you enjoyed this first book in the Spectrum Series.

Just so you know, while Gia is the main character, Raul is hands down our favorite. He is the kind of person you want to have as your best friend. He's calm, reliable, and you can ask him anything about anything. And The Peacock – if we were the type of people to say OMG, we would say OMG!! We adored it! For us, it's not just a location, it's a character as well. And here's a secret – Tracey's relationship with Charlotte wasn't planned at first – but once she made an appearance, with her carefree attitude and quirky humor, we wanted her as a friend too.

We realize we ended this book with unanswered questions. Will Tracey kill his lover? Does Gia get back together with Sal? How did Lydia respond to Mari's death? Well, the good news is, the story continues in book two!

We value thoughtful comments – they help us fine tune the books and the series. So, tell us what you liked, what you loved, even what you hated. Please do us a favor and post a review of *The Killings Begin*. We'd like to hear your feedback. Reviews can be tough to come by, and you have the power to make or break a book - **https://amzn.to/3tRa0yx**

Thank you for reading our book,

Rohn & Jody

Death in a Dark Alley

Available on Amazon, August 29, 2022

For Frank Tomas, life's too short for hard work and monogamy, it's all about instant gratification, even if that means breaking a few rules here and there.

Isabelle Ronaldo thinks otherwise and has worked hard all her life to achieve success.

But despite their differences, the pair are the best of friends.

That is, until they learn of each other's secrets.

As they navigate through their own complex lives, Frank and Isabelle are unwittingly drawn closer to a deadly threat. The Parking Lot Strangler, Tracey Lauch, is still on the loose, despite the efforts of ex-cop, Emily Bissett, and has decided to take another European trip on the Spectrum River Cruise Line…

This is the second exciting novel in The Spectrum Series of psychological thrillers set against a backdrop of contemporary romance. Although it can be read as a standalone, readers of the first novel, *The Killings Begin*, will enjoy becoming reacquainted with familiar faces as well as meeting new characters.

Acknowledgments

A heartfelt thanks to our families and friends who have supported us throughout this adventure and provided invaluable advice and comments.

Steve Ruegnitz, thank you for introducing us. That's why this series exists.

We are especially grateful to all our pre-publication readers for their insights and suggestions that vastly improved the telling of this story. In particular, we'd like to thank our beta and developmental readers, Mallory Paxton, Gavin Pay, Rae Ann Dilks, Jan Erkes, Jessica McCaleb, and Marianne Ward.

Here's a special thanks to you, Erik Walton, for your crucial advice about the importance of thinking about our stories in the context of the series, as well as for the use of your motto, "Continuing the Legacy". To Cailey Ehgoetz, a shout-out for your insights about Tracey's motivations. For your technical assistance with Photoshop, Luis Morales, your help was critical. Kathryn Goldman, thank you for your ongoing legal advice. To Mykola and Maryna Bogdanenko, who own the Toilet History Museum in Kyiv, Ukraine, thank you for allowing us to use your museum as a vehicle to introduce Tracey and Charlotte. And finally, to Miranda Summers-Pritchard, a huge thank-you for your skilled editing.

We couldn't have done this without all of you.

About the Authors

Robin Bradley grew up in a home where they had no TV, and so everyone read voraciously and played with words. She is often known to say things like "Speaking is one-way; talking is two-way, a conversation," or "Passive voice? Really?" She loves a good story, whether it's reading, hearing or telling it. She inherited her love of writing from her family - her mother was an English teacher and published poet, and her uncle was a reporter for the San Jose Mercury. Robin also writes poetry, although she hasn't published any yet. Besides writing, Robin keeps very busy as the president of her condo board and loves wine, cooking, and reading.

Jody Leber-Pay loves writing because she gets to be a collaborator, an inventor, a researcher, a storyteller, a problem solver, a writer, an editor, and a techie. She finds the process of going from an idea to a published book fascinating, and that's what keeps her motivated. Before writing fiction, Jody authored technical documents for work and published a technical book. When she's not writing, Jody enjoys the great outdoors - walking, hiking and golfing.

Robin and Jody met in 2016 on a European riverboat cruise from Budapest to Nuremberg. As a way to pass the time while they traveled through the series of locks from the Danube to the Main River, Robin, Jody and a handful of friends sat around in the afternoon, drinking Chianti, laughing and making up silly romantic stories.

The development of those stories into the Spectrum Series began with an email from Jody to Robin: "By the way – You still interested in the Lock Series? … it will be fun."

And so began their unusual, long-distance friendship and their collaboration on the Spectrum Series.

Working as Bradley Pay, they found that their unique interests and skills were complementary, but it was their enjoyment that kept the process going. Creating the first book and outlining the remainder of the series was hard work but far more fun than they had imagined at the outset.

Some of the original characters remain, albeit much evolved, and many new characters have appeared. These stories are no longer the bosom-heaving romances of our river-cruise days. Instead, although the love interests remain, they are now haunted by an international serial killer who changes the course of the characters' lives.

Made in the USA
Middletown, DE
11 November 2022

14630016R00183